Chin Up, Honey

**Center Point
Large Print**

**This Large Print Book carries the
Seal of Approval of N.A.V.H.**

Chin Up, Honey

Curtiss Ann Matlock

CENTER POINT PUBLISHING
THORNDIKE, MAINE

This Center Point Large Print edition
is published in the year 2009 by arrangement with
Harlequin Books S.A.

ISBN: 978-1-60285-596-0

Library of Congress Cataloging-in-Publication Data

Matlock, Curtiss Ann.
  Chin up, honey / Curtiss Ann Matlock.
    p. cm. -- (Valentine series ; 7)
  ISBN 978-1-60285-596-0 (library binding : alk. paper)
  1. Weddings--Fiction. 2. Oklahoma--Fiction. 3. Large type books. I. Title.

PS3613.A834C47 2009
813'.6--dc22

2009025564

For my two mothers
Anna Marie Henderson and
Frances Kinsey Matlock

and for
Timothy James Matlock

Home Folks

1

He put his mouth close to the microphone. "Goood mornnnin', Valentine-ites! It's ten-O-five once again in southwest Oklahoma, and time to take a break with Brother Winston and the home folks. That was the legendary *Mis*-ter Bill Monroe singin' us in with 'Bluegrass Stomp.'

"I played that tune for my neighbor Everett Northrupt. His wife, Doris, told me last night that she wants him to get some juice flowin'. So that one's for you, Everett. If you can keep your feet still to that, you're dead."

In his tenth decade—his *final* decade, as he saw it—Winston Valentine found himself smack in a new career as a radio personality. He was happy as a dog with two tails.

"School's finally out for the summer, and my little buddy is here with me again. Say hi to the folks, Mr. Willie Lee." He swung the microphone lower for Willie Lee, who was a little short for his twelve years of age.

"Hel-lo, ev-er-y-bod-y. This is Wil-lie Lee and Mun-ro," he said in his careful speech that did not come easy.

Munro, paws up on the desk, barked once, then

9

hopped down and followed after the boy, who returned to sit in a nearby chair. Munro laid his chin on the boy's untied tennis shoe.

Winston continued. "We are brought to you by . . . uh, Tinsley's, your hometown IGA grocer, where they're offerin' a spectacular special of $3.95 a pound on top-choice Kansas City strip steaks. Great price, but seems a long ways to go just to get a steak.

"Oh, the boy here didn't appreciate that one. He's shakin' his head."

The boy was twenty-five-year-old Jim Rainwater, who worked the electronics across the room.

"Just so you out there can get the picture, this young man is as full-blood Chickasaw as they come nowadays, with long hair in a ponytail. Girls, he's handsome and single. But he has a tongue ring, and I don't know how that works out with kissin'."

Winston grinned at the blush stealing over the young man's high cheekbones.

"Let's see . . . the weather . . . well, we got some. Sunny skies and headin' for a high of ninety-five. Whoo-eee, that's pretty hot for the end of May. There's a chance of storms on Friday to cool things off.

"Now, our topic of discussion today is 'Signs Around Town.' I'm startin' off with the sign at the railroad crossing on the north highway. Hasn't anyone but me ever wondered about it? It says: No Stoppin' on Tracks Due to Trains."

He paused a moment. "I ask you—due to what *else* on a train track?"

Jim Rainwater cast him a grin. Winston was off and running.

"Who would think you are not supposed to stop on the tracks because a dog or a chicken or anything other than a train might come along? In fact, why would anyone stop on the track, if he could help it? Just to hang out while dead lice fall off 'im?

"The phone line is open to take your comments. And don't forget, this is birthday celebration day. We'll take calls while we listen to some music— big John Cash with the answer for the blues: 'Get Rhythm!' "

The music started as Winston pushed aside the microphone and mopped his face with a handkerchief. Jim Rainwater gave him a worried eye.

"I'm not expirin' yet, so relax," Winston said and winked.

Willie Lee, who had disappeared around the corner, returned with a cold bottle of water and handed it to him.

"Thank you, Little Buddy." He unscrewed the bottle cap with gnarled hands that he often felt surprised to see as being so aged and upturned the bottle in his mouth. His eye noted a missing tile in the old ceiling.

11

The low-wattage AM station was located in a small block building at the end of the dirt road behind the car wash. It had long sat abandoned until Tate Holloway, publisher of the *Valentine Voice*, had bought it last winter and put it back on the air from 6:00 a.m. to 6:00 p.m. This endeavor had been financed by Holloway, hitting big bucks when his semi-autobiographical novel about a poor boy growing up in East Texas stayed in the top ten of the *New York Times* best-seller list for eight weeks. At one point the book reached number two, topped only by the ever-popular author Nora Roberts. The station was run by Jim Rainwater, the only paid employee, who oversaw a staff of volunteer disc jockeys putting forth an eclectic format, everything from classic jazz to automotive discussion to French lessons on Fridays.

Each mid-morning, all over town and within a twenty-five-mile radius, radios in kitchens and barns, shops and vehicles were tuned to *Brother Winston's Home Folks Show* at 1550 AM on the radio dial. People loved Winston Valentine, and he loved them back.

Over at Blaine's Drugstore, Vella Blaine was working behind the soda-fountain counter. She called to her niece's boy, Arlo, who was entertaining three teenage-girl admirers by flexing his immense muscles as he served up ice-cream cones.

"Break loose from those girls and turn up the radio," Vella told him.

She wanted to hear the birthday announcements. Specifically, she wanted to see if Winston remembered that today was her birthday. He was her best friend, mostly by being her oldest friend. They had what could be called tenure, which she felt gave her every right to certain expectations.

It was silly at her age to want to hear a happy birthday on the radio. Sillier still not to tell anyone it was her birthday if she wanted birthday wishes. She thought of all this as she halved lemons for the fresh lemonade—the Wednesday summer special—and kept an ear tuned to the radio, unconsciously swaying her hips to the good old country-western music.

Her sultry hip movements were noticed by Jaydee Mayhall, who sat at the counter and happened to look up from his cup of latte. He blinked in surprise at the sight, and also at feeling a stirring of manly response. As he sipped from his cup, he did some calculating. He had to be younger than Vella by what . . . ? Ten or twelve years, at least.

This thought brought Jaydee's eyes to his image reflected in the mirrored wall behind the sundae dishes. Jaydee was fifty-six, but he didn't look it. Everyone said so. He had used that Just For Men on his hair until the past few months, when he couldn't seem to keep up with it. He wondered if he might be letting himself go.

He removed his glasses and dropped them inside his coat pocket.

Vella looked into the mirror, too. It was right in front of her face, as it had been for the better part of her life. Mature? Old. She closed her eyes. Her husband of nearly forty-eight years had finally died, and her boyfriend, who had seemed so promising, had gone off with another, *younger,* woman, something she was sad or glad about, depending on the moment. Right then, she experienced a slice of fury at the desertion and sent the knife in a swift chop through a lemon.

The next instant she had the clear imagination of Winston's voice, announcing her true age out over the air waves.

She grabbed a towel and, wiping her hands, found the telephone number for the radio station on the card beneath the phone. *It's my birthday, Winston . . . just say happy birthday. I will never speak to you again if you say my age.*

Buzz, buzz, buzz, came the busy signal.

Over the radio, Winston started in with the birthday announcements. Vella tried the phone number again.

Buzz, buzz, buzz.

Plunking down the phone, she returned to making the lemonade. With each of Winston's celebratory announcements, she threw a half a lemon into the manual juicer and brought the handle down, hard.

14

At the very last, when she had thought Winston was finished and without mentioning her, and she was both disappointed and relieved, here he came out with, "There's one more birthday that wasn't called in, but I happen to know it. Ever'body go by and wish my good friend and neighbor Miss Vella Blaine a happy birthday."

Vella paused with her hand on the thick handle of the juicer.

"I have known Miss Vella all of her life, and I happen to know that she is sixty-five today. Happy birthday, Miss Vella!"

Oh, Winston, you dear old friend!

Vella, heart full and eyes misty, smiled while happy birthday wishes rang out all around the soda fountain. Vella found herself near tears. Jaydee Mayhall even lifted his cup and said gallantly that she was a fine-looking woman, *for her age.* He was a pompous ass, but she appreciated the backhanded compliment.

"I didn't know today was your birthday, Aunt Vella," Arlo said. "I woulda' baked you a cake."

"Oh, sugar, that's sweet, but I don't need any cake." Vella was again rapidly punching numbers for the radio station into the phone. This time the call went right through, and when she got Winston on the line, she said in her most sultry voice, "Thank you for my birthday present."

"You're more than welcome, darlin'."

When she hung up, she turned to see little old

Minnie Oakes approaching from over at the pharmacy, her purse swinging on one arm, while her opposite hand swung a bottle of Milk of Magnesia. Minnie was a childhood girlfriend who was actually two years younger than Vella but had always seemed twenty years older.

Minnie came up to Vella and shook the blue bottle at her. "You are not no sixty-five years old!"

And Vella replied, "I know it's hard to believe, sugar, but I am. You heard it on the radio."

"That was Randy Travis, singin' 'Satisfied Mind' right here at 1550." Winston pressed the left earphone tight against his ear. His hearing, like other parts of his body, let him down on occasion. "We got Wynona Yardell on the line, to tell us about a right absurd sign. Go ahead, Miss Wynona."

"Hi, ever'body . . . I'm callin' about the sign on the highway goin' east. It says . . ." She started giggling. ". . . well, you may not think it is funny, but it seems funny to me. It says . . . Caution, Wet Pavement When It Rains."

She went into gales of laughter, and everyone listening to the radio laughed as much at her laughter as at what she'd said.

Out on the highway heading into town, Belinda Blaine turned up the volume of the radio in her champagne-colored Cadillac, saying, "My word, one thing about Winston's show—it is a never-ending source of entertainment."

Receiving no comment from her passenger, Belinda glanced over at the woman. Emma had seemed distracted all morning. A little pale, actually, when usually Emma Berry was one of the most bright and shining women in town.

Then Winston drew Belinda's attention again, with an advertisement for the Merry Male Maid Service, which was offering a special all month.

Belinda's thoughts went from musing about hiring the Merry Males to the fact of her mother having six years shaved off her life right on the radio, which put Belinda back in her early thirties, and because it was on the radio, everyone was going to believe it.

"We can get you interviewed on Winston's show," Belinda said, the idea coming suddenly. "He loves to do that, and then we'll be gettin' advertising for free."

Belinda and Emma Berry were on their way back from a gift shop up in Lawton, where Belinda had placed Emma's greeting cards and framed calligraphy on consignment. Emma's cards had sold so well at the drugstore that Belinda had decided to branch out. She was having energetic fantasies of a line of cards, calendars and framed prints, then on to tea towels and teacups and T-shirts. Marketing was the key, and *that*, Belinda knew, was her own specific and golden talent.

Her rapid thoughts caused her foot to press on the accelerator. She whipped around vehicles as she came to them. Basically, Belinda drove with the attitude that no one would dare challenge her.

"And there's the Fire Department Auxiliary's summer craft fair comin' up. I'll check the dates on that. We'll have to stock up for it."

Realizing Emma had still not said a word, Belinda glanced over to see her looking out the side window.

"Sugar, did you hear me?"

Emma's head nodded. "I . . ."

Belinda glanced over again and saw that her friend had pressed a tissue to her face.

Crying? Was Emma crying?

As if in answer to the unasked question, the woman burst into sobs.

The next instant a siren sounded from behind.

"Oh, for heaven's sake!" Belinda knew even as she glanced in the rearview mirror that it was her husband, Deputy Lyle Midgett, flashing his patrol car's lights.

She might have ignored him, but he tended to get into such a sulk when she did that. He drove up right up beside her, indicating she needed to pull over. She shot him a warning look. He knew that she did not like to take her Cadillac off the pavement and expose it to more dust and dirt than absolutely necessary. She went on another quarter mile and turned onto a small paved road.

"Now, honey, how do you think it looks for you to always be speedin', and me the first-deputy?" Lyle said right off, bending down to her window. He was tall. "I really, *really* wish you wouldn't speed, darlin'. Oh, hello, Emma. How are you today?"

"Fine."

"I don't speed on purpose, Lyle. I don't think, *I'm gonna speed and make Lyle look bad.* And no one thinks a thing when I speed, 'cause I have been drivin' this way my whole life—every bit of those years we lived together—and you never felt it reflected on you. Now I'm stopped, and in fact, Emma and I are gonna sit here a minute and discuss some things, so you can go on. I want to put the window up. This wind is messin' up my hair."

"Okay, darlin'," he said in his gentle tone. "But please don't speed anymore. At least not anywhere near town."

"I won't, sugar," she said, blowing him a kiss as the window slid up. "Until next time," she whispered. Belinda knew herself well and without apology.

In her side-view mirror, she watched Lyle as he walked back to his patrol car, running her eyes from his broad shoulders downward over his lean hips. She had not married Lyle Midgett for his brains. It was for everything below his neck, all of which was quite large and strong, and that included his heart.

Then she turned her attention to Emma. In Belinda's estimation, blue-eyed pale blondes were generally really highstrung, even if they were not natural blondes, which Belinda knew that Emma was not. Every six weeks, Emma came into the drugstore and bought L'Oreal No. 9.

"I'm all right. It's nothin' . . . I was just . . ." Emma gave her a wan smile, then broke off, her gaze going to the radio. Her eyes widened, and then her face crumpled.

Belinda looked at the radio, which seemed innocent. Don William's voice was singing out, ". . . *another place, another time . . .*"

She reached over and punched the Off button, then pulled tissues from a box in the backseat and shoved them at Emma, who was bent over and just boo-hooing her heart out.

A practical woman, Belinda checked her watch and waited. After a minute and a half, Emma was coming back to herself.

"You have mascara smears, sugar," Belinda said. "Here's some lotion. There's a mirror over the sun visor."

Emma repaired herself. "I'm sorry . . . it was hearin' Don Williams. You see . . . John Cole . . . and I . . . went to see him in concert once for our . . . anniversary."

Oh, dear, she might go again. Belinda handed over more tissues, and Emma took them but managed self-control, which Belinda both admired and

20

appreciated. Displays of emotion wore on her nerves.

"John Cole and I have separated," Emma said. "We're gettin' divorced."

Belinda, who was rarely surprised about anything, was stunned. "Oh, *honey* . . . I'm so sorry to hear that."

She shut up, not wanting to say anything to get Emma started again, and to calm her own emotions. Good Lord, if this could happen to Emma and John Cole, two simply lovely people who seemed like the perfect couple, what did that say about her own chances as a fairly new and somewhat reluctant married woman?

"Thirty-two years. We've been married thirty-two years."

Emma's voice was a hoarse whisper filled with so much sadness that Belinda felt struck to the core.

"Well, these things happen," Belinda said at last, swallowing down a lump. "What is it? Another woman? Men just lose their minds when they get middle-aged." She had seen it time and again, although she was quite certain her Lyle never would. It was the really intelligent ones who did. Women were so stupid about intelligent men.

"Oh, no! At least I don't think so. John Cole isn't like that."

Belinda thought the wives were always the last to know.

Emma said, "It might be easier if it *was* another woman, because maybe I could fight that. It's just that we don't have anything in common anymore. We don't talk. We don't . . . relate." She broke off and flipped down the visor again to look in the mirror. "John Cole has decided to be married to his job, and I've decided I've had enough of being his cook and maid at home."

Despite her good sense, Belinda felt depressed. The situation was exactly why she had resisted marrying Lyle for so long. She had feared that once they married, complacency and boredom would settle in. She had set herself not to let that happen, but maybe there was nothing she could do. Reality of life on earth was just too big.

Just then, Emma's purse began ringing, startling them both. Emma dug for her cell phone. Immediately upon answering, her face brightened. "Hi, sweetie!"

A boyfriend? Belinda flipped down the driver's visor to check her own appearance and repair her lipstick, while keeping an ear tuned to the conversation. It wasn't like she could help hearing. Everyone said she was nosy, but she wasn't. All she did was pay attention to people.

She heard Emma tell whoever it was that she was heading home and would be there to meet "Honey," whoever that was. She would make lunch for "us." Belinda imagined a very handsome man, but then, as she flipped her sun visor back up,

22

her gaze went out the windshield to the main entry of the Valentine cemetery directly up ahead.

"That was Johnny," Emma said. "He's on his way. I have to get right home."

Johnny was Emma's son. Belinda was both relieved and let down at that mundane fact, but her attention was mainly on a sign to the right of the wrought-iron arched entry to the cemetery.

"Do you see that sign? I have never seen that before. I don't think it was there when Daddy was buried."

Emma looked in the direction Belinda pointed. "Well . . . my goodness."

The two women looked at each other, and Emma laughed, her face just lighting up.

Belinda pulled out her own cell phone and called Winston.

"I have a sign for you, Winston. Out at the entrance to the Valentine cemetery, at the front. Yeah . . . it says . . . now, it's right beside the entrance, and it says . . . All Donations Welcome."

When Belinda let Emma off at her house, Emma said, "Belinda, please don't tell anyone about me and John Cole."

"I won't, sugar."

"I mean really. I don't want a lot of talk to get back to Johnny until I have a chance to tell him myself."

"Well, of course you don't, and there's no reason for me to say a thing to anyone."

Belinda felt a little hurt that Emma would think even for a second that she would go and blab.

Many people considered Belinda a gossip, but she was not the one who blurted out anyone's intimate secrets. Just as Emma had done, people were all the time telling her stuff. She didn't know why. And she didn't know why *she* would be called the gossip, when it was *others* who were the ones telling her everything.

Why, if she told even a fourth of what she knew, before nightfall there would be two marriages that would be broken up and several people losing their jobs and uncountable people fighting mad with each other.

Gracie rode in the passenger side of Johnny's new Mustang convertible. Her left hand was captured in his, and she held her hair with the other. They came over a hill, and there was Johnny's hometown. She looked ahead to read the town sign as they flew past: Valentine, OK, Small Town in a Great Big World.

Johnny pointed out the school he had attended—all grades in one group of connected buildings. Quite strange to Gracie, who had gone to enormous schools in Baltimore. And there, down a gravel lane, was the source of the program coming from the car radio. Gracie had never heard anything like it: jokes and people's birthdays and really old-timey country music.

And Johnny knew the lyrics to most of the songs.

He drove down Main Street and pointed out his family's convenience store, reminding her that there were three stores, and that he and his father were planning to open a fourth next year.

Then right in the middle of Main Street, he stopped, jumped out and ran over to grab a bouquet from the bins of flowers outside the florist shop. He did nothing more than call through the door to have it put on his bill, then returned to plunk the flowers in Gracie's hand. Traffic backed up behind the car, but no one honked. In fact, the guy driving a pickup truck that had to stop when Johnny ran in front of him waved and called hello.

Johnny drove on through town to the other side and down a road to show her an acreage they might consider buying to build a house. She liked it, and then she reminded him that his mother was waiting.

"Okay, just one more place," he said, and drove her down a short road to see a sign.

"We got Mr. Johnny Berry of the Quick Shop on Main on the phone. I did a bit of a plug for you, young man. You have a sign you'd like to point out to us, Johnny?"

"Thank you . . . and yes, sir. There's a sign that says Dead End, Thirty-five Miles an Hour."

The man on the radio laughed and asked the location of the sign, which Johnny gave and went on to tell how Dead End was on the top, with the speed limit right below, both on the same post. As he spoke into the phone, he cast Gracie a grin, his teeth all even and white. Gracie loved his pretty teeth. She loved everything about Johnny Berry.

He snapped his cell phone closed and leaned over to kiss her. When they broke away, she saw his eyes searching hers.

She took his face in both hands. The ring he had placed on her left hand just that morning sparkled in the sunlight.

"I am the luckiest girl in the whole world to be marrying you, Johnny Ray Berry," she said, looking deep into his blue eyes. "Now, let's go tell your mother."

"O-kay." Shifting into gear, he pressed the accelerator and headed the flashy convertible back out on the open road and toward his family's home, which was a sprawling ranch-style house in the middle of acres of grass and tall trees. Gracie's heartbeat picked up tempo when she saw it. She wondered what his mother would think. She knew Johnny was certain of his mother's reception but worried about his father's. He hadn't said this, but Gracie had learned to listen to things Johnny did not say. He had chosen a day when his father was out of town to tell his mother of their engagement and to show her the new car, of which his father had disapproved.

They had no sooner stopped at the end of the

drive when a woman came flying out the back door to throw herself at Johnny. Standing there, Gracie watched him lift the woman clean off the ground and whirl her around. Gracie could hardly breathe. She actually felt a little jealous.

Then Johnny looked at Gracie. "Mom . . . I've brought Gracie."

He had not told his mother about bringing her, Gracie realized hard and fast. But smooth as anything, Mrs. Berry said, "I see that," and the next thing Gracie knew, she was being hugged.

Then, after releasing Gracie, his mother went all around the car and all but hugged it, too, saying over and over again how red it was, how sporty it was, how perfect it was for him.

Gracie saw Johnny get this really silly grin on his face, and on the way into the house he asked for a peanut butter and banana sandwich, which apparently was a lot more important than setting up an opportunity to tell his mother about being engaged.

As it turned out, Mrs. Berry already had her son's favorite sandwich made, along with a plate of grapes and cold sweet tea. Then Mrs. Berry queried Gracie as to *her* favorites and was able to produce them—a turkey sandwich with romaine lettuce, and Keebler Pecan Sandies and a cup of hot Ceylon tea with lemon and sugar. It was as if the woman had some sort of magical pantry. And she seemed thrilled to please Gracie, who had the impression that if she had asked for a steak, Mrs. Berry would have produced one and cooked it right up for her. It was amazing.

Winston leaned close to the microphone.

"To close out the show, we have been notified of another rather curious sign. Our young caller, who did not give a name, brings our attention to the sign out near the juvenile detention center on the north highway. It says: Be Aware—Hitchhikers May Be Escaping Inmates. Nothin' unusual about that, but, folks, this sign is shot up with so many bullet holes that you can hardly read it."

He paused.

"On that note, we'll close out today's show with this favorite by Ray Stevens, 'Everything is Beautiful,' going out from Willie Lee to Gabby. Remember Isaiah 41:10, and God bless and keep you until tomorrow . . . and don't go pickin' up any of those hitchhikers out on the north highway, 'cause they're obviously armed."

2

Emma

Just as soon as she waved Johnny and Gracie off, Emma raced back inside to the kitchen wall phone and called John Cole on his cell phone number.

While listening to the rings, she tucked the

receiver into her neck and began to clean the dishes. It rang five times, and then voice mail picked up. It wasn't even John Cole's voice, because he had never put a message on it.

She jammed the receiver back onto the base and finished cleaning up in a vigorous manner. As she considered her options for reaching her husband, she all but wiped a hole in the counter.

John Cole had mentioned plans to drive to Oklahoma City. This did not mean he had gone, because he rarely made hard-and-fast plans. But he was a man of a few habits, and one of those was to stop into his office at the end of each day. She could call him there, but John Cole never did answer the office phone. It would be answered by Shelley Dilks, his secretary. *Office manager,* as the woman had made a point of saying.

It was annoying as all get-out to have to go through the woman to reach her own husband, Emma thought, again reaching for the telephone. She paused with the receiver in hand. The possibility that John Cole might have told the woman about their . . . situation caused a sort of short circuit in Emma's brain. Then she remembered guiltily that she had told Belinda Blaine.

Taking a deep breath, Emma dialed the office number. It rang twice before the woman answered.

"Berry Enterprises offices, Shelley Dilks speakin'."

"Hello, Shelley. This is Emma. Is John Cole in?"

"Well . . . yes. Just a minute and I'll see if he can get the phone."

And why would he not get the phone for his wife? Emma squeezed her eyes closed. *If Shelley Dilks knows and spreads the word about me and John Cole, I will snatch her baldheaded.*

"Hey. Emma?"

At John Cole's voice, her eyes flew open.

"Yes . . . hello." She thought his tone actually seemed welcoming, as if happy to have her call him. Although maybe she imagined it. She had not felt at all certain about anything with him for a long time.

"Are you in your office?"

"Well, yeah. Why?"

Just then the receiver was about jerked out of her hand, as she had become so agitated that she was walking right out of the kitchen and had reached the end of the phone cord.

"John? Are you there?"

"Yeah."

She lowered herself on the kitchen stool to prevent further accidents. "Are you in your office alone?"

"Yes, I am."

"Well, I have somethin' important to tell you. I don't want you distracted by Shelley or somebody and stuff goin' on. Why don't you close your office door?"

"It is closed, Emma Lou. What is it?"

She opened her mouth, then closed it. Suddenly the fact of Johnny's engagement was too big and tender for words. She pressed a knotted hand to her chest, as her memory flashed back through the years and she recalled telling John Cole of having gotten pregnant at last, after their years of desperate trying. She had done this same thing, gotten him on the phone and not been able to say a word.

"Emma?" he said with a bit of alarm.

"It's good." She reached for a tissue.

"O-kay."

She imagined that familiar patient expression he got when he settled in to out-wait anything and everything. John Cole could have the patience of Job. It was annoying.

She swallowed, took a deep breath and got it out. "Our John Ray is gettin' married."

"He is?" His tone was more confused than surprised. It generally took John Cole some time to absorb news of such magnitude.

"Yes, he is." She doubled over and stared through blurred eyes at her red-painted toenails.

"I just saw him yesterday mornin'." He still sounded confused. "I took over some cases of oil for the Lawton store. We're runnin' a special this week, and I let him have a case that I got from the supplier as complimentary. He didn't say anything about gettin' married."

"He talks to you about money and business. He talks to me about life and love. Besides, I don't think he had asked her then. I kinda' got the idea it all happened last night . . . that he got the ring just yesterday."

"He just bought a car."

"I don't think there's a limit on these things."

The line hummed with disapproving silence.

She said more gently, "Our son is a man, grown and fully capable of makin' good decisions for his own life."

"Yeah, I guess so." Then, "Who is he marryin'? Is it the one with the long, dark hair—Gracie? Is that her name?"

"Yes," Emma said, with some impatience at his question. Who else could it have been? John Cole just didn't pay attention to anything besides business.

"She is the only girl he has been datin' for the past six months, at least . . . but I think he's known her since way last fall, when she moved to Lawton and came into the store up there. They met when he helped her get her keys out of her locked car. She's the really pretty one that you said looks a little foreign and has all that hair. She wears clothes like something out of a fashion magazine. Lots of black, like they wear up north. They haven't broken up once in all these months. He's brought her out here twice this spring to Sunday dinner . . . oh, but the second time, you were gone to the NASCAR races down in Dallas."

That her son had only brought Gracie twice, now three times, in those months seemed a telling commentary. Gracie was special.

"I've seen them together a number of times," John Cole said in a defensive tone. "I dropped by his place and took them to lunch at Wendy's once. She seems a nice girl."

"All of his girlfriends have seemed nice. Well, except for that one that had the line of earrings not only in her ears but in her nose and eyebrows, too, and it wasn't that she wasn't nice, she just seemed a bit obsessed with poking holes in her body.

"But Gracie is a woman, John Cole, not a girl. She's a lovely, intelligent and solid young woman. I knew from the first time I saw her that Johnny was ready to settle down. I told you that, remember? Johnny never had a girl like her before. We talked about that. She's young, but she is an assistant manager for the M. Connor store—her mother is an executive of some sort for the entire M. Connor chain," she supplied, refreshing his memory with important facts.

He said, "I don't know what those stores are."

"It's a chain of very upscale women's clothing stores in malls from coast to coast. The one where Gracie works just opened last fall."

John Cole avoided the mall like the plague. He bought most of his clothes at Tractor Supply or Wal-Mart stores. Emma didn't necessarily see anything wrong with this; they had once seen a famous country-western star wearing the same shirt as John Cole down at the Dallas airport. The man had even laughed and pointed at John Cole. The shirt was a real nice Panhandle Slim, no-iron and all. Still, refusing to go into a mall did limit one's clothing choices.

"You will probably have to go to the mall to get a good suit for the wedding." Her thoughts raced on. "It may be that you will need a tux. I think Gracie comes from a right well-to-do family. The wedding may end up being real fancy. We might have to go down to Dallas to get you a suit."

This was met with silence that she only barely noticed, because her mind was running along with possible contingencies. She went on to tell him that the kids wanted the wedding sometime in the middle of September, but were in consultation with Gracie's mother and all their friends about the exact date and location.

Gracie's mother might want to hold the ceremony in Baltimore, although the kids seemed to favor a wedding right there in Valentine, which would be the most practical thing. Johnny's friends and family were all within driving distance, and most of Gracie's friends were in Dallas. There wasn't but Gracie's mother up in Baltimore. Apparently Gracie's mother had been divorced since Gracie was a baby, and her father was not in the picture. From what Emma had gathered, the only other family was Gracie's mother's parents, who spent a lot of time in Paris.

"I can understand if her mother would want to have her only daughter's wedding up there where she is, but it will sure be a mess tryin' to haul everyone up there. Your daddy won't go, because he is never gonna step on a plane." John Cole's daddy said that if a plane broke a fan belt, there was no place up there for it to pull over.

"We could all drive up," said John Cole.

The image popped into her mind, all of them in a long caravan, like a bunch of gypsies. She thought of the luggage her mother would require. Her mother practically took her entire home when traveling.

"Mama said somethin' about a writers' conference in September. I hope it won't be on the wedding day . . . or if it is, that she hasn't already paid for it."

"We've got the big Convenience Store Expo up at Oklahoma City in September," said John Cole. "The second week in September."

To which Emma instantly replied, "I don't think that is near as important as John Ray's wedding. You can miss it one year."

"I was just mentionin' it, Emma Lou."

She bit her bottom lip.

Then she said, "We'll know more about everything on Sunday. The kids are comin' for dinner—we're gonna have a little family engagement celebration and talk over the wedding plans. I think it would be good for you to be here on Sunday, if you can."

"I'll be there," he said instantly.

"Well, good." Then, "John?" When heart-stopping serious, she used his first name.

"Yeah?"

"I think it would be a good idea for you to come on home. We just can't do the divorce now. It would tear Johnny's world apart at a time that is supposed to be filled with joy—his and Gracie's special time. We need to just drop the idea and make everything seem normal, at least until after the wedding. Don't you think so?"

She squeezed her eyes closed.

"Yeah, I think you're right."

Everything just melted inside of her. She had always been able to count on John Cole's excellence as a father.

It was a lot to take in. First she was getting divorced from her husband of thirty-two years, then her son was getting married, now her husband was coming home.

What about sleeping arrangements?

She entered their bedroom and gazed at the bed—king-size, solid cherrywood. She had bought it back when they got their first home. John Cole never had paid much attention to the interior of the house. Every time she bought something, he would grouch about her spending money on it, but then, when the piece was in the house, he always really liked it.

There was no way John Cole could manage sleeping in the guest room. He would end up making the family room his bedroom and his recliner his bed.

She entered the walk-in closet, where one side still contained most of his clothes, with a line of boots and shoes below. She gathered up her night-gown and robe and slippers, carried them down to the guest room, then threw them over the end of the bed. She wasn't going to move her clothes, because she could not have anyone know she wasn't still in her own room. Then she returned with two large wicker baskets to the bathroom, where she swept her things off the counter and out of the drawers, carrying them down to the guest bath and tucking them in the cabinet.

Subterfuge was going to be a lot of work.

3

Emma and John Cole

She kept watch and saw his truck coming up the drive. She hurried to the back door to meet him, but stopped in the kitchen doorway.

"Hi."

"Hi." He carried his duffel bag and shirts in a bag

from the cleaners. "I'll put these away—I'll be right back," he added, as if she might think he was never returning.

Emma watched him go off down the hall, then turned and flew around the kitchen, pulling the bowls of chicken salad she had already prepared from the refrigerator, closing it with her foot as she ripped the plastic wrap from the dishes. She arranged the salad—made John Cole's favorite way—with sunflower seeds and halved grapes on a bed of lettuce, with celery sticks and cherry tomatoes on the side. The effect was something as pretty as a magazine cover.

Maybe John Cole would see what he had been missing.

Realizing her train of thought, she yanked out the celery sticks, as if to tone down the inviting food. He likely wouldn't eat them, or even notice, anyway.

Studying the prepared plate of food, she thought that she was in a most frazzled state. But then again, what other state was natural for a woman in her situation?

Hearing the sound of the television, she went to the entry of the family room. John Cole was standing there in the middle of the room, remote control in hand, staring at the television. *Headline News* was on—a report on a disaster somewhere.

Emma was not certain what she expected of him, but she did think he could have thought of something better than to turn on the television at that particularly significant moment.

She said, "I have your supper ready. Do you want to eat in here?"

"Yes . . . that'd be nice."

She didn't know why she had bothered to ask.

They sat in their respective chairs, a large table in between them, facing the big-screen television, where NASCAR highlights flickered on the screen.

Emma had for so long wanted to buy a regular couch, so that they could sit side by side. She thought if they could have sat close together, held hands and touched more intimately, they might have revived their passion for each other. But John Cole had refused to give up his chair.

She wondered what he might have done if one day, when he arrived home, she was burning his chair out in the yard. She imagined the scene. The hardest part would be getting the chair outside. John Cole had a heavy-duty dolly in his garage, though. She probably could use that. Or else smash the chair apart with a hammer and take it out piece by piece, about like one did a cooked chicken.

Then she began to imagine shooting out the television with a shotgun. They did not have a shotgun. She would have to borrow one. Vella Blaine had a shotgun; that woman's prowess with a gun had been written up in the newspaper.

Perhaps Vella would lend Emma the shotgun—or maybe Vella hired out as a crack shot. The television would be an easy target.

Just then, she realized that John Cole had begun talking, telling her how good the chicken salad was.

"Thanks for makin' it," he said. "I was more hungry than I imagined."

"You're welcome."

Their eyes met and skittered away from each other.

Emma tried to think of something else to make conversation. Her conscience pricked, and she said, "I told Johnny that we would give him and Gracie money toward a nice honeymoon—I didn't say how much, just that we would."

John Cole nodded. "Okay."

More NASCAR watching.

"Do you want to call your daddy and ever'body tonight and tell them about Johnny and Gracie?"

He raised an eyebrow at her. "I guess . . . if you want to."

"It's up to you. He's your daddy. I thought of callin' Mama, but she's up in Oklahoma City at one of her writer things, and I imagine she's really busy up there and won't hardly hear a word I say. You know how she is. Unless she calls here, I'll just wait until she gets home on Saturday."

John Cole, looking really tired all of a sudden, said he didn't feel like calling. "We might as well wait until we have a date and details to tell 'em, anyway."

She said okay. They finished their meal without further conversation, while NASCAR continued on the television.

Later, Emma sat at the kitchen table with a yellow legal pad, and a wedding etiquette book and wedding planning magazines that she had bought over the past few years, knowing that this day was bound to come. Dreaming about it. Actually trying to prepare herself for the change to being the mother of a man married to a woman.

John Cole came in and said what he so often did, "Oh, there you are. I wondered where you'd gone."

"I'm right here. I'm workin' on a preliminary list of people on our side for the invitation list. There's more than I had imagined. If the wedding is here in Valentine, I imagine that most all of your side will come over. Well, maybe not Violet—I think she's still got the agoraphobia. But I know Charlie J. and Joella will come and bring your daddy, and most everyone else will come, too.

"Then there's quite a few Berry employees and some other business people it would be nice to invite. With just my first thoughts, I've come up with over seventy people, and that is not including the church congregation. It's customary to invite the entire church where the ceremony is held, and

I think we would do best to prepare for about a third of them to actually show up, especially the ones that have known Johnny from childhood."

"It might be enough to cause them to decide to have the weddin' up north," John Cole commented, bending into the refrigerator.

Emma gazed at the list. "Well, we can easily keep it to just family. That isn't so many . . . and I think Johnny will want his family there."

The idea of having the wedding far away from home about made her sick. But then she reminded herself to be glad that Johnny had not run off and eloped, as he had often said he would do.

She looked up and saw John Cole, a Coke in hand, leaning against the kitchen counter, gazing at the floor.

He was here—home—she thought, running her eyes from his head to his boots.

His eyes met her own. She felt a little silly, getting caught looking at him, but she couldn't just look away now that he had seen her.

He said, "You know, I just keep thinkin' about how small he was when he was born and yet he had those really big feet."

"Oh, my gosh . . ." She remembered, too, and smiled. ". . . They didn't fit any of the booties that came in the newborn sets."

John Cole gave a small grin, then tipped up his Coke and drank deeply.

Emma looked back at the list of names in front of

her. She could not believe that John Cole remembered any of that, much less spoke of it. Tears welled in her eyes. And for some odd reason she was afraid for him to see.

"I guess I'm goin' on to bed," he said.

"Good night." She saw him pause uncertainly. "I'll come later," she said. "I'm sleepin' in the guest room. I . . . thought it might be best."

There, it was said. She checked his face for his reaction. There was nothing.

He nodded and said, "Good night."

Her chest felt crushed. But then, "John Cole?"

"Yeah?"

"Thanks for comin' home."

"He's my son, too, Emma."

His words struck hard. She opened her mouth to reply, to say that she well knew that. But he was already out of the room, and for some reason, she couldn't figure out exactly what to say to stop him.

Lying against the pillows in the darkened guest room, Emma gazed out into the hallway and saw the dim silvery light shining from the television down in the master bedroom. She could faintly hear voices. It was funny how so small a light and soft a sound could go such a distance in a silent and dark house.

She fluffed her pillows, lay back again and breathed deeply. Over the past few days, she had often felt that she just could not get enough air. She

43

felt that way now, tried inhaling deeply again, then repositioned the pillows and herself. Accepting that she was as comfortable as she was going to get, she lay staring up at the ceiling and recalled the conversation in the kitchen.

It was rare for John Cole to reveal any deep emotional thoughts as he had in speaking about Johnny as a baby. Sometimes she didn't think John Cole even *had* any deep emotional thoughts, nothing beyond a fondness for television, car racing, making money and Coca-Cola.

He's my son, too. As if she did not know that, as if to say that she tended to act like Johnny was all hers.

She supposed she did, a little. After all, she had so desperately wanted a child.

And John Cole had done his very best to give her one, too.

4

1968—1971
It's a Boy!

After two years of marriage, they decided to have a baby.

Actually, Emma decided. John Cole did not seem to care one way or the other, although he did get a little anxious to accomplish having any children they wanted while he was in the Navy so they could let Uncle Sam pay the medical expenses.

So Emma went off the birth-control pills, which so many women of her generation had believed to be *the way* of life, totally disregarding the popular margarine commercial of the time: *It's not nice to fool Mother Nature.*

Things did not quite go as planned.

When she did not get pregnant that very first month, she was quite surprised. A few more months, and she still did not get pregnant. It seemed like more women than she had ever seen were pregnant all around her, but she was not.

She began to read books about getting pregnant, started to take her temperature and try various sexual positions conducive to conception. Once, she threw her back out and therefore missed two perfectly ripe chances to conceive.

Finally, after a year, she sought medical help. Time was wasting, and she needed to take advantage of what the Navy medical services could do for her, free of charge. After checking her over, putting her through all manner of tests and having her try a number of the things she had already tried, to no avail, the doctor said that John Cole needed to be examined.

John Cole, who rarely said no straight out, looked at her like he would rather eat live frogs.

Emma was ready for her persuasion, which was that she didn't think an examination or any test was too much to ask. After all, she got a Pap smear every year. That wasn't any fun. And she herself was willing to go to great lengths to cure their childless state, so she expected John Cole to do his part.

This reasoning, along with Emma crying a lot about wanting a baby, compelled John Cole along.

The day of John Cole's appointment, Emma waited outside the clinic in the car with all the windows down. It was summer at the naval station in Florida and hot as blue blazes. After a little while, John Cole came out, but he didn't get in the car. He stood by her open window and told her that he had to undergo a sperm-count test. He looked disgusted and as if he might refuse to do the test, or as if he might ask Emma to go in with him to help. She hoped he didn't do either and just sat there, not saying anything.

Finally, he went back inside for what seemed a long time, while she waited, sweating in the car and feeling guilty about making him do something he didn't want to do. She promised herself to make it up to him, and that night and in the following weeks, she cooked his favorite foods, waited on him hand and foot, even left the air conditioner on high all night and never complained.

The test results arrived. John Cole's count of live and volatile sperm was in the extremely low category. It said right on the results that his ability to impregnate her was in the bottom percentile.

It was hard news. John Cole got more quiet than usual, and Emma went in search of finding out what could help a man's sperm count. She ran up a bill of twenty-five dollars just on long-distance phone calls to her mother, who excelled in research and who could also ask the other women in the family. She scoured the library and read long into the night, then started feeding John Cole protein drinks, vitamins E and C, and putting wheat germ in every recipe that she cooked—hamburgers, meat loaves, oatmeal, even salads.

When it came to chocolate cake, John Cole balked. "Good God, Emma. You're gonna wheat me to death."

She begged him to go without underwear, so that his little sperm wouldn't be overheated and would be able to swim correctly. She followed her ovulation carefully and figured out how to prop her legs up on the headboard for ten minutes after sex, although John Cole really got afraid she might have a stroke from such antics. His fear over this, coupled with Emma's demands on him, caused him to lose a lot of sleep and risk getting into great trouble during the day at his duty post, because he tended to nod off if he sat anywhere too long.

A little over three years later, after she had finally given up trying and reluctantly decided to seek an education for some sort of career, she turned up pregnant. By then, John Cole was out of

47

the Navy and they had returned to his hometown in Eastern Oklahoma, where he worked at the Berry Hardware Store and Emma spent her days keeping their tiny apartment over the elder Berrys' garage spotless and making cute crafts. John Cole had set his sights on buying one of the big fancy vans so popular at the time. He had to change that idea and accept a baby instead, along with paying a lot of the medical bills out of his own pocket, as their medical insurance was poor.

The evening Emma went into labor, John Cole had fallen asleep in front of the television. She had been engrossed in reading a magazine article about tie-dyeing when she began to feel odd. Her back hurt, and she thought she felt contractions. She checked the instructions from the doctor and wondered if she was truly in labor.

She woke John Cole and told him what was happening, then asked, "What do you think?"

"Well, *I* don't know," he replied to her question, gazing helplessly at her. He lay back again in the recliner and dozed off, until fifteen minutes later, when Emma shook him again and said that she was fairly certain she needed to get to the hospital—and quick.

Going into something of a panic, John Cole called his parents, who came running over from their house. They all got into Papa and Mother Berrys' big Plymouth and headed through pouring rain to the hospital. Every couple of minutes throughout the drive John Cole would ask her, "Are you all right?"

How did one answer, when one's body was seized with a wave of constricting pain at about the same time as the question was asked?

Just before they got there, Emma began to feel that she was about to deliver. She hiked up her dress and began to remove her panties.

John Cole grabbed her hands. "We're not at the hospital!"

"I don't care!" she cried. "And neither does this baby!"

John Cole moved to the far side of the seat, plastering himself against the door, while Emma removed her panties and tried to remember her Lamaze breathing.

Then her father-in-law called out, "Hold on, Emma, we're here!" He hardly ever said anything, and his voice startled her. She was swung to the side as he turned into the emergency drive. Before the car had even stopped, Mother Berry was out and running inside. John Cole helped Emma work her way out of the backseat, leaving her panties stark white against the dark velour.

In front of them, the emergency room doors parted, and here came Mother Berry pushing a gurney, with a nurse and orderly following and trying to catch up. There ensued a great deal of fumbling and arguing in the effort to get Emma up on the gurney. This ended when she stalked off—

as best as she *could* stalk while bending over in a contraction—leaving the others to follow her into the emergency room.

After all the rush, Emma was in labor for thirty-six hours, in which they told her that her contractions were just not strong enough, and she told them they weren't the ones having them.

For most of those hours, John Cole stood by her bed, holding her hand. A point came when the doctor gave her something to make her drowsy so that she could rest. John Cole was led away to an adjacent room—to let him lie down. To this day, Emma was quite certain the reason for the delay was that the surgeon had not wanted to be disturbed on a weekend. He arrived on Monday morning.

John Cole was once again beside Emma, holding her hand. "You have to let go now," the nurse said firmly, prying Emma's grip loose. "He cannot go into surgery."

"Blow, honey . . . blow. . . ." John Cole called in a tired voice, as they rolled her away to surgery.

"Oh, God, my blow's done gone. Would y'all just hurry the hell up and give me somethinnnn . . ."

The next thing she knew, someone was patting her cheek and calling her name. "Mrs. Berry . . . Mrs. Berry, can you hear me? Do you know what you had?"

She thought someone must be speaking to her mother-in-law, and she wished they would shut up.

A little while later, "Mrs. Berry . . . wake up. You had a baby boy."

"I know," she managed to get out.

"She's awake . . . she knows she had a boy."

Oh, you idiot, I knew all along I was going to have a boy, she thought, and went back to sleep again.

When she next came awake, she heard voices, someone telling John Cole to call her name. He said it softly, "Emma . . . Emma . . ."

She got her eyes open, and there was John Cole's face, only inches away. He was smiling at her like he'd lost his mind. "We had a boy," he said, and he kissed her gently and took her hand again.

"Oh, God, Emma, I was scared you were gonna die."

The idea was a little shocking. She had not even thought of it, and she had not realized John Cole's anguish.

Her heart flooding, she reached up and placed her palm to his warm cheek, saying, "Honey, it's okay. I'm just fine . . . it's okay."

The next instant, her sweet baby was placed into her arms. She looked down at him and fell totally, indescribably in love in a way she had never before known.

5

Together Again

The next morning, when Emma peeked out into the hallway, the television was silent and John Cole was snoring softly.

She hurried into the bathroom, where she washed and moisturized her face, gazed at her image for a few seconds, then applied more moisturizer under her eyes and a bit of blush to her cheeks. She gave thanks to her mother and grandmother for high cheekbones and good skin.

In the kitchen, the coffeemaker with its timer set last night already held a full pot. Emma got her mug from the cabinet.

John Cole's mug was there, pushed a little to the back. Pulling it out, she held it in both hands for several long seconds. Then she sat it next to the coffeepot.

Smiling and humming a bit, she took her coffee through the shadowy living room to her workroom at the far end of the house, where she rolled open the Florida windows to the sweet morning air and watched the sun come up at the end of the long driveway. As she gazed at the sight, her mind traveled back over the years.

"Oh, John Cole, I love it!" she had said of the house the first time they had driven up the drive.

"Don't get carried away until we see the inside."

She knew that so many times her high emotion had embarrassed him. She would try to hold herself down. She had not succeeded too well on that particular day, as she went from room to room. "Look at this . . . oh, look at this." Poor John Cole had stood helplessly, knowing that he did not have a chance of saying no.

Turning from the bittersweet memory, she switched on the lamp over the worktable and sat on the tall swivel stool. Neatly arranged at the right were various calligraphy pens, pencils, color and glitter markers and glue, and stacks of papers in a myriad of hues and textures.

After several minutes of sipping coffee and thinking, she chose crisp, white card stock, on which she drew a racing-red sports car. She added two stick figures holding hands, round faces with smiles, sunny-brown hair for the boy and long dark hair for the girl. Inside the card, she wrote in a fine script: *Congratulations, sweetheart. I'm so happy for you. — Mom, who loves you.* She added a decorative flourish, her bit of trademark.

She carefully set the card aside to let the ink dry before inserting it into an envelope.

Next she chose ivory linen paper. Gracie's card would need a touch of elegance. First sketching in pencil, then filling in with colored pen, she drew a door decorated with a plaque that said *Welcome,*

Gracie. She added a tiny, shiny, red-checked ribbon from her box of trims. Inside the card, at the top, she drew another plaque that said The Berrys. After staring at it for a long minute, she quickly drew berries on the plaque. And then bigger berries beneath, turning them into people. She was a blueberry, John Cole a strawberry, clusters of cranberries behind them. Did cranberries grow in clusters? Her mother, who technically wasn't a Berry, was off to the side—a raspberry with bright purple hair.

Possibly Gracie would find Emma's cards a rather poor effort at art. Perhaps she was one who preferred something elegant and store-bought.

"Good mornin'."

"Oh!" She jumped and almost flung aside the pen. "I didn't hear you." She felt silly.

"I'm sorry. I tried not to scare you. I knocked."

"Oh . . . I was . . . you know."

She swallowed as she watched him come fully into the room, in careful steps, as if still trying to ease in. Golden sunlight streaming through the windows made patterns over his face and body, causing her to realize that she had been lost in her work for some time. Her heart tumbled over itself with gladness at seeing him in their home once again.

And then she thought that, still, he was handsome. His eyes in the warm morning light were very blue, which never ceased to affect her. *He seemed happy to be home.* She averted her eyes to the paper in front of her.

"I see you got a fancy new coffeemaker."

"Yes. It was on a great sale."

John Cole was scanning the stacks of cards along the edge of the table, flipping through them. "You've been busy," he said.

"Yes." There had been so much time when she couldn't sleep.

Reading the inside of one, he chuckled and held it up in an appreciative manner.

It was a card with a drawing on the front of a frazzled woman and a quote that read: *Thanks for loving me just as I am.* Inside it read: *It took a whole lot of time and difficulty to get this way.*

"It's one of the most popular ones," she said, feeling foolishly pleased. "I also draw it with a man, or a boy or a girl. Belinda's sold all that she had for the drugstore, and now she's putting them into a gift shop that she owns with another woman."

Did he even recall that Belinda had taken some to sell at the drugstore? A thrill sliced through her with the telling—and satisfaction when his eyebrows rose in surprise.

"It's not all that much money, really, but it's nice to have people want them." She suddenly felt very shy.

"I'm glad you're doin' so well with them. I told

you when Belinda took some, that I'd be glad to put them in the Stops. You seemed like you didn't want to do that. You said it would be too much work."

"I guess I didn't think they would sell. And I didn't realize how easy it was to get them printed. It's nice, too, that Belinda handles the business part. All I have to do is the creating then. I'm not so good at business things."

He gazed at her, then sipped his coffee. "You were when you worked at Berry Corp.—good at business."

She was surprised by his compliment and didn't know what to say to it.

"You can tell Belinda to count the Stops as another outlet. It's silly not to. You own the Stops, too, you know."

"That's true," she said. "I just didn't think of it, and I guess Belinda didn't, either. She'll be excited when I tell her. She has all these plans." She was a little embarrassed by Belinda's elaborate plans, to tell the truth.

John Cole told her the best location would be at the larger Berry Truck Stop and suggested places for display. He said he would alert the clerks. She simply nodded to everything, while drawing a birthday cake.

Quite suddenly, she was gazing straight into his blue eyes.

They broke the gaze at the same time.

John Cole said, "Well . . . I guess I'd better let you get to it . . . and I'd better get on to work. I'm already late."

He went out the door, and she reached for her mug of coffee, finding it empty. She felt self-conscious about going into the kitchen. He might think she was finding an excuse to follow after him.

She felt like crying . . . *silly, silly.*

And then, suddenly, there he was in the doorway.

He said, "Would you have a minute to talk . . . about us?"

Emma managed to get out, "Well . . . yes. Of course," and had to clear her voice in the middle of it.

Did he want to talk about a divorce?

Panic swept her. She didn't think she could talk about divorce. She would just say she had to focus on the wedding. *Dear God, keep me sensible.*

John Cole came back into the room and straddled the chair, then sat there gazing downward. The little-boy-lost expression came over his face and shoulders. It was an expression with which Emma was thoroughly familiar, and not so impressed anymore.

In fact, he did this so long that she began to get annoyed. She wanted to say, *Will you get to it, already? I have things to do, and I am not takin' over your emotions on this thing.*

Just when she was at her last nerve, he said, "I've had a lot of time to think the past few days."

He paused, and something seemed required on her part. "I have, too," she got out.

Another moment's pause, and he said, "I've missed it here. . . .I've missed you, Emma."

She was surprised by his direct and intense gaze. "I've missed you, too." Her voice cracked.

"I know we've had some difficulty for a few years. I know I've been busy . . . and that you haven't been happy."

He paused yet again, but she had nothing to say.

He continued then, going on to say that he knew he kept getting too busy with his work, and that he just wasn't too good at talking. As he went on in this manner, she began to get impatient again. It was all of a similar vein to what he had said in the past, whenever she had tried to motivate him to see they had problems in their marriage that needed to be addressed—namely that he needed to *take part* in the marriage.

The idea struck her, though, that his speaking voluntarily just now *was* taking part.

"I've really missed *us*, Emma."

"I have, too."

Silence stretched again, while they each sat there as if waiting to see what the other was going to say or do.

"I was thinking . . ."

"I'm glad you . . ."

They both stopped.

John Cole said, "You go ahead."

"No, you go ahead."

He shifted and gazed at her, and she had about decided he wasn't going to say anything when he came out with, "I was thinking that . . . if you are willin' . . . maybe we could go see a marriage counselor."

"What?"

"I thought we could go to a marriage counselor. I got this card from the bulletin board at the Stop." He pulled a business card out of his shirt pocket and passed it over to her.

She looked from the card to John Cole, and then back to the card again. "You want to go to a marriage counselor?"

"Well, you said once that you wanted to do that. I think it would be good to try."

She gazed at him.

"Okay, you said it a lot of times." He got to his feet. "I wasn't ready to do it before. I apologize for that. But . . . look, I'm ready to give it a chance, Emma. Are you?"

Well, of course, she had to say yes. Heaven help her, though, because she also had to stop herself from rolling her eyes.

And somehow, during the course of it all, she ended up agreeing to be the one to make the appointment.

"New Hope Counseling. Catherine Owens speaking. May I help you?"

Owens? Emma checked the business card. *New Hope Counseling Center, Theodore M. Owens, Ph.D. and Catherine Owens, Ph.D., LMFC. Individual, Marital and Family Counseling.*

The therapist was answering the telephone?

"I would like to make an appointment, please," Emma said. "But first, can you tell me something about the therapists?"

"Certainly. There are two of us—myself and my husband, Ted Owens. I am a licensed clinical psychologist, and licensed marriage and family counselor. I've been practicing for twenty-five years. Ted is a licensed clinical psychologist and has been practicing for thirty-four years."

Emma felt at once reassured by their ages and a little put off. They might be worn out.

"We both counsel all manner of issues, but I generally handle women's issues, and Ted handles anger management and all addictions. What sort of difficulty are you having?"

Emma said, "Uh–we would like marriage counseling. My husband and I." She had the idle thought that maybe they needed anger management, too.

"All right. I would be glad to help you with that," the woman said in a positive manner that Emma instantly appreciated.

The woman gave Emma several choices for appointments, and Emma chose Thursday afternoon the following week.

Later, when she told John Cole the time of the

appointment and the name of the therapist, he said with a note of alarm, "Therapist? I thought we were seein' a counselor."

"We are. That's what marriage counseling is. Therapy."

"Oh. And it's a woman?"

"Yes," Emma answered.

After several seconds, he said, "Oh," again and let it go at that, demonstrating that he was learning when to shut up.

6

1550 AM on the Radio Dial
The Sunday Morning Gospel Hour

The music faded, and Winston came on. "That was Barbara Mandrell's rendition of 'Amazing Grace.' Glad to have you here with us this bright mornin', where our generous sponsors this week are the *Valentine Voice*, the area's award-winning newspaper, and the good folks of the First United Methodist Church."

He paused for a thoughtful moment. "We have a First Baptist Church, too. As far as I know, those are the *only* Methodist and Baptist churches in town, so I don't know why they don't just call themselves the Onlys—the Only United Methodist or the Only Baptist.

"Anyway, the folks at the First Methodist invite

61

you all to join them this mornin' for services. Sunday school is about to commence over there, I think . . . ah, I can't find my listing . . ."

He felt odd. A little swimmy-headed. He saw Jim Rainwater shoot him one of his worried looks.

Averting his eyes to the tune list, Winston looked through his reading glasses and read, "And now here's Ricky Skaggs, givin' us some bluegrass gospel."

His chest felt a little tight. But a man did not get to his nineties and not have a lot of odd-feeling moments. Not wanting the kid getting his shorts in a knot with worry, he pushed up from his chair, saying, "I'm goin' to the john. Don't get worried."

He tried not to shuffle his steps as he left the room. He had a sudden and odd longing for Willie Lee. Sunday mornings were the one time since school had gotten out that his little buddy did not accompany him. Willie Lee's mother insisted on a quiet family gathering around the breakfast table on Sundays.

But in that moment, Winston wished so much for the companionship of the boy that he had the disconcerting sense of being close to tears. It rather rattled him. It was said that when a body went into a heart attack, emotions got all mixed up. He had experienced a heart attack a number of years previously, but mostly what he recalled was waking up and people annoying the hell out of him.

In the bathroom, he splashed water on his face

and dried it with a paper towel. He purposely avoided looking in the mirror. These days the image in the mirror was some strange old man, not himself at all.

He threw the paper towel in the trash and stood bracing himself on the windowsill, trying to summon the memory of the man he had been in his prime, tall and straight, with steel-gray hair and a chiseled jaw. It wasn't so much what a person looked like. It was more how a person envisioned himself—that was what a person projected.

Just then a movement beyond the window caught his attention.

A figure was walking along the side of the road in the distance. A young man, wiry and with a bare torso, what must have been his shirt hanging down from the waist of his jeans. He was moving at a fast pace and kept looking back over his shoulder, then up and down the road, in a curious manner.

All of a sudden, in one swift motion, the fellow jumped over the barbed-wire fence around the pasture across the road and disappeared.

Winston jutted his face closer to the window. His vision was not what it once had been, of course, which was why he couldn't drive any longer. Yet he knew he had seen someone, and now he was gone. Just disappeared right before his eyes.

He was about to check his own pulse when he saw a head pop up from the tall grass along the fence line. Yes, it was a head. It turned from side to side, looking up and down the road. The growing sound of a siren reached Winston's ears.

The head disappeared into the weeds. A few seconds later, a sheriff's car came speeding past, lights blinking and tires throwing up dust. The siren faded.

Thrilled that he had not gone round the bend and started imagining things, Winston thought of telephoning the sheriff's office, but he wanted to see if the head popped up again, so he kept staring at the spot.

No head showed. He looked as far as he could up and down the road. He wondered if the figure had moved on in the cover of the sand-plum bushes to the cedar trees.

There came a rap. "Winston . . . you okay?"

He jerked open the door. "I'm fine. Things get slower when you get older. You'll find that out. Everything you got is gonna drop south and get slow as molasses in January."

Jim Rainwater shook his head and turned, heading back to his controls.

Winston followed, thinking again about telephoning the sheriff's office, when the door to the building opened and Willie Lee came through it.

"I am here," he announced and came straight over to Winston.

"And so you are." Winston gazed in surprise at the boy and his dog. The boy's eyes were very blue behind his thick glasses.

"Willie Lee insisted on comin' down here early and waiting for you," said Tate Holloway, the young boy's stepfather, who followed the boy and the dog through the door.

"Well, that's fine . . . I appreciate you, buddy."

"Winston—you ready?" called Jim Rainwater.

"I'm comin' straight away."

Willie Lee slipped his hand into Winston's larger one, and together they went into the studio, where Winston sat back down, put on the headphones and pulled the microphone close.

Willie Lee and his dog took their accustomed places, while Tate pulled up a stool and opened the Sunday paper.

Winston drew himself up. "Gather 'round, children. We're ready for the anniversaries."

Finding his voice, in fact all of him, returning to full strength, he read clearly from the listing in front of him, sending congratulations to Mr. and Mrs. Ryan Showalter, who were to celebrate their third anniversary on Monday, and to Frank and Lisa Ruiz, celebrating a whopping six months, and to Herbert and LaVerne Riddick, who the past week had celebrated *fifty-four* years of marriage.

"I've known little LaVernie since Herbert brought her up from down in Hennrietta, Texas," said Winston. "I asked her the other day what was her secret for her lengthy marriage. She said it was because Herbert never forgot their anniversary. Herbert told me that LaVernie never let him forget it. Now that's what I call two sensible people—a woman who says what she wants, and a man smart enough to listen."

Vella was in charge of the altar flowers that month at the First Methodist. She had bought pots of blooming bromeliads on special from the Home Depot and saved the Ladies Circle some twenty-five dollars. Actually, she saved herself some twenty-five dollars, as she bought them through the Blaine's Drugstore account and donated the flowers, thereby transferring the expense in part to Uncle Sam. So she was doing her part and keeping the economy going. Things just passed along in life.

"Let me help you."

She was a little surprised to see Jaydee Mayhall coming forward. He took one of the pots right out of her hand. "Well, thank you, Jaydee. Please set that one over by the piano." She wondered what he wanted; Jaydee was not a man to do something for nothing.

The church was filling up. Inez Cooper came flittering past and stopped to point out that the pot in front of the pulpit was off-kilter. Vella didn't think so.

"Well, it is," said Inez as she bent to shift it a micro-inch.

Vella opened her mouth, then closed it and pivoted, going to take her normal place in the third pew. As she adjusted her skirt, she looked up to see Jaydee approaching.

"Hope you don't mind if I sit beside you today," he said, giving her his winning smile. He *was* a handsome man. He had always put her in mind of Douglas Fairbanks Jr., not that she ever wanted to tell anyone that. Not only would she be showing her age, but most of the time Jaydee was too annoying to compliment.

"Well . . . no," Vella answered, in something of a confused state, but for some reason stopping herself from saying that the spot was saved for the Peele sisters, Peggy and Alma, who sat there every week. There were no nameplates on the pews, after all.

Out of the corner of her eye, she saw Jaydee settle himself and smooth his sharply creased trousers. She wondered what in the world was going on with him. His behavior was hardly customary. The memory clicked in of him being somewhat disgruntled two months previously, when she had purchased the old oil-field building and lot west of town, getting to the property ahead of him. He might now know of someone who wanted to buy it and was hoping to get it from her cheap, then resell it. She had been in financial dealings with Jaydee before. He never could go at anything directly.

The Peele sisters showed up and were affronted at having their space taken. They could have squeezed between Jaydee and Bingo Yardell, who held down the other end of the pew, but instead Peggy Peele said, "We'll just move back," and hauled Alma after her, while Alma whined that she was too short to see from the back.

It *was* rather nice to have a man sitting beside her at church, Vella thought, taking note that Jaydee was a good-smelling man. One thing that she had always appreciated about her now-departed husband was that he had always smelled good.

Then here came Belinda and Lyle.

"Lyle and I thought we'd like to sit with you today, Mama," Belinda said. She looked right at Jaydee and all but told him to move.

He did—closer to Vella—saying, "Good mornin'. Nice to see you, Miss Belinda."

"Yes, you, too," Belinda replied after staring at him a moment.

Lyle said he didn't think they would all fit in the pew, but Belinda went right ahead, working her way in and pulling Lyle behind her. Vella moved her feet out of the way of her daughter's little crystal spike heels that could possibly take out a toe.

Vella knew well that it was Jaydee sitting there that had brought her daughter. She felt in a very odd place, with people who rarely had much to do with her suddenly coming at her like magnets.

Belinda leaned around Jaydee and said, "Mama,

do you know why the First Methodist Church is called the 'First'?"

"No . . . no, I really don't."

"Jaydee, do you know?"

"No, can't say as I do."

Vella thought her daughter was about to give the punch line to a joke, but instead Belinda said, "Well, I don't, either, but I'll bet Daddy would have known. Don't you think so, Mama? Daddy knew all sorts of details like that," she told Jaydee. "He came to church here with Mama for over forty years."

"I remember that," Jaydee said.

Then Belinda added, "How many times have you been married now, Jaydee?"

"Three," he replied. "I've been lookin' for just the right one."

Emma saw the clock as she pitched the ham into the oven. Grabbing her purse, she raced out the back door.

John Cole was at her car, slamming the hood. "Got your oil changed." He wiped his hands on a rag as he stepped back.

"Oh. Thank you."

He nodded. "Do you need me to check on anything in the kitchen?"

"No. The ham will be fine, and I'll throw everything else together when I get back."

"Have a good time."

"I will." She thought they sounded like she was going on vacation, rather than to church services.

They were being exceedingly polite, tiptoeing around each other. Two strangers under the same roof. But still in separate beds.

John Cole wasn't even in the bed. He had taken to sleeping in his recliner.

She fought with herself about that all the way to church. She really should make the first move and suggest that they both move back to their bed. After all, if they were working on their marriage, it wasn't a good idea to sleep separately. Another voice countered that John Cole was perfectly capable of making the first move. But she thought that she really should at least bring up the subject.

By the time she pulled into the church parking lot, all of the voices inside of her admitted that both she and John Cole were being childish.

The opening music had started. She went up the steps along with the stragglers who had been catching last-minute cigarettes out on the front lawn. Stepping through the door, she paused, running a speculative eye over the sanctuary, seeing it with her new status as mother-of-the-groom. If the wedding took place in the morning, it would be beautiful like this—graceful and joyous. In late September it would be warm, but not too hot. The fans would stir softly, and the light would fall in an ethereal glow through the stained-glass window over the altar, much as it was at that moment.

Then she saw her mother leaning out into the aisle with a hurry-up expression. Emma did, and her mother smiled in welcome and passed her a hymnal with all the service's songs efficiently marked by bits of paper.

A moment later her mother leaned over and whispered, "Why do you think they call it the First Methodist Church?"

"I don't know," answered Emma, who was still preoccupied with visions of the wedding. Then, noting her mother's questioning expression, she offered, "I guess because it's on First Street."

"I don't think that answers why there are First United Methodists Churches all over the country. They can't all be on a First Street . . . can they?"

Pastor Smith stood on the altar steps and offered up the ending prayer to send the congregation out into the world with love and peace in their hearts. At the piano, Lila Hicks played "Pass It On."

Emma bowed her head and thought about hurrying home to make the dinner. She thought of all the food she would put on the table and her family gathered around it, and how she was welcoming a new woman into the family. She raised her head and there was light streaming in through the high windows behind the pulpit, and it was as if the light streamed right at her, filling and overflowing her heart with gratitude. She was suddenly starkly aware of what she and John Cole had been about to throw away.

When she got home, she hurried to the guest room and bath, and gathered up all her things and took them back to the master bedroom. A lot of the warm emotion that she had experienced at the church had already begun to wear off, but she sure did not want Johnny or Gracie to see her things in the guest room. What sort of example would that set for them?

7

Mother of the Bride

Sylvia Kinney was a beautiful woman of forty-five who could, and often did, easily pass for ten years younger, even though this would have had her giving birth to her one and only daughter at fourteen. She would rather have people think she had gotten caught up in youthful foolishness than know the truth of her having made a big mistake at twenty-two, when she should have known better. She was desperately trying to save Gracie from making the same mistake.

Gripping the telephone receiver, Sylvia Kinney paced the white carpet of her bedroom in a fashionable apartment in Baltimore and tried talking sense to her daughter. She tried cajoling, threatening and, uncharacteristically, pleading—everything she could think of to convince her daughter two thousand miles away not to marry that bubba with whom she thought she was in love.

Finally, thoroughly frustrated, Sylvia came out with, "My God, Gracie, he's nothing but a redneck boy with no future beyond the possible ability to acquire a lot of junk cars up on blocks in the yard."

She knew instantly that she had made a serious error.

"Yes, Mother, I know," came Gracie's cool reply. "I'll always know where he is at night, right out in the backyard playing with our children."

"Oh, Gracie . . . I didn't really mean it like that. I didn't. I just don't want you to do something that . . ."

"I'm going to marry Johnny, Mother. I wish you could be happy for me. Goodbye."

There came a loud click and the line hummed.

Sylvia slowly set the phone aside. Her gaze went to a gilded frame holding the smiling face of her daughter. She picked it up and gazed for a long moment at the image. She swallowed back tears and breathed deeply. As far as she had ever seen, crying did nothing but cause wrinkles. She could not afford wrinkles. Not in the modern business world. Looking into the mirror, she finger-combed her dark hair that still did not need dyeing.

On closer inspection, there was a white hair. She plucked it out.

Then, hopping up, she tossed off her slippers,

quietly opened the door and tiptoed down the hall to peer into the living room at her lover, Wadley Johnson, who was asleep on the couch where he had retreated last night, because she would not let him sleep in the bed with her. She had not let another man sleep in her bed since her idiotic blunder with Gracie's father, which she still blamed on the fantasy of Paris. These days, when she went to Paris, she always wore dark glasses and never drank wine.

The sun was coming in the wide windows, and Wadley had pulled a pillow over his face. He was still in his dress slacks and shirt, his coat and tie thrown on the floor.

She and Wadley had been to a club to listen to Wadley's jazz-playing friends and had not gotten in until nearly three in the morning. Wadley very often slept until noon, anyway. As he would say, his career as a rich playboy required certain habits.

Wadley R. Johnson was forty-eight, handsome, charming and rich. He had three ex-wives to attest to this. He wanted to make Sylvia number four and last, so he said. Sylvia, however, believed that his record was against him and that her own was not promising, either.

For a brief moment she considered waking Wadley and asking him to make breakfast—he could cook, and she did not—or to go down to the breakfast shop and get them something.

But he was always so chipper and loving in the

morning. He would probably get all amorous and ask her again to marry him, and she was feeling especially vulnerable.

She went back to her room and threw herself into bed.

The conversation with Gracie played back over her mind . . . *right out in the backyard playing with our children.*

Oh, good Lord. She would be a *grandmother.*

She pulled the covers over her head and tried to figure out how she was going to face the mess she was in.

Just over twenty-two summers ago, right after graduating college, Sylvia had flown to Paris and gone a little crazy. Intellectually, she understood it well. She had spent the better part of her life being super-responsible. Her parents, Albert and Margie Kinney, had been of an irresponsible and distant nature. Their entire world had been each other. They had hardly noticed they had given birth to a child. At an early age, Sylvia had learned to take care of herself, as well as the difficulties of her parents.

When Sylvia was thirteen, her mother died. Her father went on to run even more quickly through his large family inheritance. What money was left now was thanks to Sylvia's shrewdness. Her father and his new wife, Giselle, were living comfortably, even enjoying yearly trips to Europe and Florida.

Whenever anything came up, such as a glitch in air-flights or a gallbladder operation, Sylvia was called to handle the matter.

But that summer after her college graduation, where she had graduated with the highest grade-point average of any student for the five previous years, Sylvia escaped this pattern for a short period and went off with fast friends all over Europe. She finally had time to fall in love, for the first time in her life, with Paul Mercier, an American who was in Paris studying art. She became pregnant and married him.

Sylvia had explained all about her rashness in marrying Gracie's father and how impossibly different they had been from the beginning. She had not painted Paul as an ogre, just very irresponsible, and far more in love with art and the free-and-easy life than he had been with Sylvia or with Gracie. Artists were like that, Sylvia had explained. Paul had eventually faded from their lives, and they did not need him. End of story.

In fleeting honest moments, Sylvia admitted to herself that she wanted to bury that part of her life so deeply as to make it seem that it never happened. The problem was that in doing so, she also buried Gracie's history. This fact had not seemed too important at the time, nor for years afterward. As Gracie grew older, Sylvia convinced herself that nothing about Paul mattered and those memories were better left alone. So, for a million reasons that she was at a loss to explain, Sylvia had never mentioned to Gracie the small fact that Paul Mercier was a black Creole.

8

Gracie

She was glad to have a few minutes after the phone call with her mother to put herself back together before Johnny arrived to take her to Sunday dinner with his parents.

Her gaze fell on the card Emma Berry had sent her. Gracie had cried when she had received it, and now, looking at it, she had a fantasy of her mother calling back and saying something like, "Oh, Gracie, I've just been so silly. You've made a good choice, and you are going to be so happy. I'm proud of you, and I support you all the way." She imagined it so thoroughly as to even listen for the phone to ring. It did not.

Gracie told herself that she should not be surprised at her mother's attitude. She and her mother had been at odds for all of Gracie's life. Gracie could still recall being six years old and wanting to wear a certain pair of pants that her mother did not want her to wear.

"You won that fight, Mother, and you have won just about all of them since—but you are *not* going to win this one," she said aloud to herself in the mirror as she got herself ready to go to the home of her future in-laws.

They were very different, she and her mother. Her mother was keenly intelligent and exacting. Gracie was of average intelligence and easygoing. Gracie's teenage years had been spent in hard attempts to please her mother. She had even pressed herself through constant study and tutoring to get into Bryn Mawr, where her mother insisted she go. She had gotten into the prestigious college by the skin of her teeth and had made it through two years, when, thankfully, illness had given her an excuse to drop out before being kicked out. She spent six months in bed, suffering an indefinable form of chronic fatigue. After she recovered, she refused to return to school. She had gotten away with that by allowing her mother to get her a job as a clerk with the local M. Connor store. This was intended to last only until Gracie was stronger physically, but as it turned out, Gracie had loved it and excelled.

She found her talent in clothing sales. She enjoyed helping people be happy. She succeeded so well that she was awarded an impressive number of promotions and cash bonuses. Finally she had pleased her mother.

In fact, her mother had been so pleased and encouraged that she had wanted Gracie to move on up into a buyer position at the corporate offices, or perhaps even into design—both more respectable, as she saw it. That would require Gracie finishing college, of course.

Gracie had refused. Adamantly. She was saved from a further fight when she was promoted to a management position that handled store openings, and by an executive quite high up in the company. Her mother recognized that it would be poor policy to try to change another executive's directive. She acquiesced, but was clearly disappointed.

That was when Gracie perceived that her mother was a perpetually disappointed woman, and that she, Gracie, was more or less a contented one. She did not desire the same things as her mother, and she also possessed a certain assurance that what she did desire would come without a lot of striving.

She looked for an excuse to move as far away from her mother as she could manage at the time, which turned out to be the opening of one of the company stores in Dallas. There, she gave in to following her own natural inclinations, which resulted in an amazing happiness. When she moved to open the new store in Oklahoma—even farther from her mother in terms of travel—and met Johnny Berry, she recognized in him someone who was also quite happy and whose desire was the same as her own: namely to be happy, and to be so with her. She knew she had found the man of her dreams.

• • •

As a gift for Mrs. Berry, Gracie bought a pot of daisy mums in a basket. She held it on her lap on the drive down to the Berry home.

"I don't want to get into my mother's objections to our marriage with your mom and dad," she informed Johnny. "My mother will eventually come around, and there's no need to mention anything about it now and get feelings hurt." She was not at all certain that her mother would come around, but she was a lot happier to hope so.

Johnny said, "Okay."

"We'll just say that my mother is really busy at this time, and that you and I want to do the wedding ourselves—that's the truth, anyway." She saw a wilted daisy bloom and pinched it off.

"Okay."

"And we'll ask your mother to help. She'll like that, don't you think?"

"Uh-huh," Johnny said, with a nod.

She rather wished he would speak in more than one-word sentences. Then she took his hand, very grateful for his smile in return and for his pleasing nature.

Spying another small broken bloom, she pinched it off and thoroughly examined the entire plant, pinching off any flowers that were not perfect. Maybe she was a lot more like her mother than she'd realized.

Gracie volunteered to set the table. The silverware was real silver, handed down through five generations of Emma's family. The china and crystal were silver-rimmed and handed down through three generations.

There was an arrangement of flowers as a table centerpiece, the napkins were linen, and a silver coffee and tea set sat ready on the polished sideboard, where Gracie's gift of daisies also sat. Emma had raved over them. They really did look pretty there, especially with the window blinds that were arranged so that light filtered through.

The entire effect was like something off the cover of a *Better Homes and Gardens* magazine, and Gracie almost sent Johnny off to locate a camera in order to take a picture to send to her mother.

Although her mother was likely to say, "Good grief, have you ever seen so much old clutter?"

As she carefully placed the table settings and filled the crystal water glasses from an iced pitcher, she could hear the drone of the television in the adjacent family room, where Johnny and his father sat with eyes glued on the television set and the broadcast of a car race. Once or twice a shout went up.

Gracie loved the sound. She felt delighted that her man liked to be at home and to enjoy something with his father. That he *had* a father, a real *family*.

She kept an ear tuned toward the kitchen, as

well, listening to Emma and *her* mother, Mrs. Jennings. The two women were physically so different as to not look at all related. Mrs. Jennings' voice was deep, from at least fifty years of the cigarettes that she stepped outside to enjoy every so often, and her accent was a very long Southern drawl. Emma sounded Southern, too, but her voice was lighter and often laughing. Mrs. Jennings was a good head taller and thicker all around than her daughter, with dark eyes and steel-gray hair, while Emma was blue-eyed, fair and petite. Both women had really nice complexions, although Emma wore a lot of makeup. In Gracie's opinion, Emma could have done without.

Mrs. Jennings was apparently not as inclined to domesticity as was her daughter. The entire time Emma was preparing the meal, her mother sat on a stool in the kitchen, drinking coffee and talking about an incident at a writers' conference that she had attended the previous week. Her upset appeared to be with a woman who had told Mrs. Jennings that she could not be from the South because she lived in Oklahoma.

"And it wasn't so much what she said, it was her attitude, standin' there with her hand on her hip, sayin', 'Oklahoma? That's not in the South.' Like she was the last *word*."

She was now in about the third full telling of the tale. The first time, Emma had said, "Did you tell her you were from North Carolina?" and that was when Gracie learned that both Emma and her mother were from way over on the East Coast. The information aroused the somewhat unsettling realization that there was so much she did not know about this man with whom she intended to join her life.

This time Emma said, "What did she say when you told her you were from North Carolina?"

"Not really anything. Perhaps she didn't believe me . . . or has no concept of the fact that people move around. Bless her heart, she apparently has no idea that the Five Civilized Tribes that made up Oklahoma in the beginnin' were all from the South. She's from Georgia. She ought to know how her bunch pushed the Cherokees out here and stole their land, then Sherman sent half the inhabitants of three states runnin' out this way."

She spoke with the correcting tone of a history teacher, which she had been. Now retired, Mrs. Jennings wrote essays on social and historical perspectives that were carried in several small-town newspapers.

"I always thought Oklahoma was in the South." This was Mr. Berry's mild voice. Gracie looked through the entry to see him standing in front of the open refrigerator. "Maybe she has us confused with Nebraska on the map. Where's the Coke I put in here a while ago?"

"Well, I don't think many people know exactly where Oklahoma is," said Mrs. Jennings. "The weathermen all stand in front of it when givin' the national weather. And with the sorry state of education in this day and age, no one seems to know that Oklahoma was Confederate during the Civil War. They just rewrite history all the time."

"That was a long time ago, Mamaw. Western's the style now," came Johnny's playful voice. He called his grandmother Mamaw.

Observing the two through the doorway, Gracie tried to imagine one of their future children calling *her* mother "Mamaw." That would happen *once*.

There was so much food. Sliced ham, potato salad, a vegetable gelatin salad arranged on the salad plates, lima beans—Mrs. Jennings called them butter beans—and corn, candied yams, a cold plate of sliced tomatoes and broccoli and celery sticks, a basket of rolls and rich cornbread of a sort Gracie had not before seen, and several saucers of soft butter and something called chow-chow. Johnny leaned near her ear and whispered that she wouldn't like it.

"Good mercy, Emma, you cooked like it's Christmas," said Mrs. Jennings.

"Well, it is a celebration," said Emma, with a smile at Gracie and Johnny. Then, to Gracie, "Now, honey, anything you don't like, you just don't eat."

Emma was up twice to get things from the kitchen for Mr. Berry and Johnny. Whenever

Johnny ate over at Gracie's apartment, he got up and got his own salt and pepper and whatever else he might need. She made a mental note to speak to him about doing the same at his mother's home. She would need to teach him before he got to his father's age.

Then Mrs. Jennings was addressing her, saying something about knowing a family of Kinneys when she was a child and lived in Washington, D.C. during the war. She meant World War II, Gracie realized.

"Myrna Kinney . . . I haven't thought of her in years. I don't remember her daddy's name, but they were from somewhere up near Baltimore. I wonder if they could be some of your kin. Stranger things have happened."

"I don't recall a Myrna. My mother is an only child—she's Sylvia Colleen. Her father was also an only child, and so was my great-grandfather. I don't know about before them."

"Oh, I was speakin' about your father's family. I must be confused. I thought your last name was Kinney."

Gracie looked at the woman. "Yes, it is. Kinney is my mother's name. My father's name was Mercier. Paul Mercier. He and my mother divorced when I was a baby, and my mother returned to her own name. I never knew him."

She prepared to answer questions as she watched Mrs. Jennings take this in, but then Emma was returning to the table with a basket of fresh hot rolls and saying, "Mama, lots of women started keepin' their own names back when Gracie was born . . . or to do like Julia Jenkins-Tinsley down at the post office and use both names."

"Well, I know that . . . but it plays havoc with genealogy."

"Are you goin' to keep your last name, Gracie?" Emma asked. "I know in business it is sometimes easier."

Gracie saw Johnny's eyes widen slightly. She replied that they hadn't talked about it, but she thought just for the first months she might go by Kinney-Berry and then change all the way over to Berry. "What do you think, Emma?" Johnny's mother had told Gracie to call her Emma or Mom, but Gracie wasn't ready yet for Mom. She did want to start by building a bridge with the woman, though.

"That sounds very sensible," said Emma. "And we are very excited about you two gettin' married . . . aren't we, John Cole?"

"Yes, we are." Mr. Berry always seemed a little shy but really nice.

Gracie found Johnny's hand under the table, and he smiled at her.

"I look forward to meetin' your mother," said Emma, smiling at Gracie in a way that required a reply.

"And she looks forward to meeting everyone

here, too." Gracie folded her napkin in her lap. "In fact, she wanted to come today, was going to fly down for the weekend. But at the last minute an emergency came up at headquarters—something about the French division. She's going to have to fly over there in the morning. To Paris. She goes a lot. She's the only one in their office who can speak French. My grandparents were always taking her over there when she was a child."

She could hardly believe she had come out with all of that. She looked to see Johnny's reaction, fearful that he would betray her lying, but he was scooping up chow-chow with a roll, as if it was going to be gone in a minute. And all of what Gracie said *could* have been true. Her mother did speak fluent French and for that reason handled much of M. Connor's business in Europe.

"Perhaps I could call her," Emma said. "I'd like to introduce myself."

"Oh, she's hard to catch when these emergencies come up like this. Her hours get erratic. And she might already be gone. She wanted to get the first flight that she could. She said that for the next few weeks she'll be out of pocket but would be calling me to touch base."

"Well . . . I can send her a note. Before you leave, I'd like to get her address. And when you speak to her, please let her know that I look forward to gettin' to know her."

"Oh, she wants to meet you, too. She'll be

coming out soon . . . right after she gets back from France." She averted her gaze, and her eyes fell on her glass. "This iced tea is delicious. Might I have some more?"

As Emma rose to reach for the pitcher on the sideboard, Mrs. Jennings said, "That's *ice* tea, honey. Iced might be grammatically correct, but it isn't said that way down here. If you want to be grammatical, you could say *cold* tea."

"Oh," Gracie said.

Emma refreshed everyone's tea, and when she was once more seated, she brought up the subject of the date for the wedding.

"We were thinking the third Saturday in September, if that would work for you." Gracie watched Emma's face.

Mrs. Jennings put in that perhaps the church should be consulted to make certain it was available.

But Emma replied that she had asked Pastor Smith that morning, and he had said it was available the entire month of September. "He also said that he is going to check, but he believes the Catholic Church will recognize your marriage in a Methodist Church. Just in case this is important for the future."

"There's the Episcopal Church here," put in Mrs. Jennings. "It's really pretty . . . dates from the twenties and has stained-glass windows on either side."

"Episcopal isn't the same as Catholic, Mama. Gracie is Catholic."

"Well, it isn't so different. They have priests and wear a collar and robe and all that hoo-rah."

"Some Methodist ministers wear collars and robes and all that stuff, too. It doesn't make them Catholic." Emma looked at Gracie with some excitement. "The church is small. It holds about two hundred and fifty, maximum. Do you think that will be okay?"

"I don't think Methodist ministers wear collars," Mrs. Jennings interjected. "I've never seen one wear a collar."

Gracie waited to see if Emma would respond to this comment, but she didn't. Feeling a little uncertain as to which thread of conversation to follow, she said, "We are not planning a very big wedding. We just want family and a few friends. We are going to pay for it ourselves, aren't we, Johnny?"

"Uh-huh." Johnny nodded as he finished off a roll.

"Well, we are plannin' on helpin' you with the wedding," said Emma. "We want to . . . and anyway, it is tradition for the parents of the groom to pay for the weddin' ring, the groomsmen's gifts, the bouquet, the mothers' corsages, things like that."

Gracie took this in and felt a little apprehensive.

"Okay," Johnny said, reaching for the last roll in

the basket. Gracie had never seen him eat so much. He loved his mother's cooking. She had been trying to pay attention to the dishes and was going to look everything up in a cookbook.

Emma began talking of the various relatives who were likely to come into town for the wedding and making plans for booking a block of rooms at the Goodnight Motel.

"My mother will stay up at my apartment," Gracie said quickly, thinking that her mother would come unglued at the idea of staying at the aging motel on the edge of town. Her mother was particular about amenities.

Gracie explained that one of her friends was going to give her a wedding shower. Emma proposed giving them a couple's bridal shower to introduce Gracie to the family and a few neighbors in Valentine.

"That way you can get to meet the family before the weddin' in a relaxed atmosphere," she said. "I read all about it in one of the weddin' magazines."

Gracie was touched by the idea and getting more nervous by the minute about the woman's enthusiasm. She felt it likely that things could get out of control.

They did. Somehow the event ended up turning into a backyard barbeque, with Johnny's father cooking steak and pork ribs in his secret sauce, a soda-fountain machine from one of the Berry stores, and possibly tap beer. Mrs. Jennings put in the suggestion of where to get plastic cups and paper plates at discount.

Gracie didn't think it was going to look much like the lawn-party bridal shower she had attended once in Philadelphia.

9

Mother of the Groom

Emma remembered her camera before the kids left. "We have to get a picture for the engagement announcement!"

The late golden sunlight was perfect. She positioned them at the front fender of the Mustang. "Yes, yes, I want you in front of the car."

When she got through taking Johnny and Gracie's picture, she had John Cole get in with them. He was always reluctant to have his picture taken. He liked to be cajoled, and Emma did so. After this, she had her mother join in. Her mother then took a picture of Emma and John Cole with Johnny and Gracie. It was all so much like old times, when Johnny had lived at home.

Finally Johnny called a halt. He hugged and kissed Emma, and hugged his father and grandmother, and Gracie was hugged by everyone, too. Then the two young people roared away in the Mustang, down the lane, and it was as if they took a lot of the air with them when they went.

Emma's mother followed, driving away much more slowly in her aging and faded Impala, going to her garden apartment over at MacCoy Senior Living Center.

Watching her mother's car until it was out of sight, Emma was struck with a wave of melancholy. Her mother had moved out to live near them in Oklahoma two years ago, because most all of her immediate family—the Macombs—had died. The exceptions were a couple of aunts who were mentally out of this world and one sister with whom Emma's mother had never gotten along. Even most of the Macomb cousins had died or gone off out of sight. Somehow the Macombs tended to lose members of the family. They seemed to go off to the grocery store or away on vacation and never return. They had not been especially close people, yet they had been Emma's people. She barely knew her father's family and didn't count them at all.

Now, here were Emma and her mother, the end of that branch of the Macomb family tree. Emma thought about how someday her mother would be gone, and she, Emma, would move up into her place as the last matriarch. It appeared Gracie would be the one to move into Emma's place. She felt sad and grateful at the same time. She had prayed for years for a daughter. It appeared that Gracie was the answer to that prayer. *Thank You, God.*

With high emotion filling her heart for the second time that day, she walked back into the house, which seemed starkly empty and silent, as it always did when Johnny left. Except, of course, for the television that John Cole was once more watching.

She finished tidying the kitchen, then sat at the kitchen table with a yellow tablet to compose the engagement announcement for the newspaper. She went through five pages before she got it exactly how she wanted it. She ended with the line: *A September wedding is planned in Valentine, where the two plan to make their home.*

She imagined it. The voices and laughter of grandchildren would fill the house. She would have children around her again, to cook for and kiss boo-boos, sing lullabyes, read books. They would need to get another calm riding horse to join Old Bob, and the children would ride in the afternoons. They would have to get a permanent dog, and not just the stray hound who passed by on occasion to be fed out the back door. And build a tree house. She could still do something like build a tree house. On rainy days she would bake cookies and make blanket forts in the living room.

She was in the midst of imagining all of these wonderful things when John Cole came in to get a Coke and bag of corn chips, and asked her what she was doing.

"Writing the engagement announcement," she told him happily, and then read it to him.

His response when she finished was, "Have they said they are makin' their home in Valentine?"

"Well . . . not straight out. But a house down here in Valentine will be much less expensive than one up there in Lawton. Where do you think they will live?" She did not know why John Cole always had to make comments that just threw cold water all around.

"I don't know. I just asked."

"I'm lookin' forward to them livin' nearby and to havin' grandchildren to enjoy. Aren't you?"

"I haven't thought about it. I guess so."

She found that answer unsatisfactory. "Don't you want grandchildren?"

"That isn't what I said, Emma. I haven't even thought about it. We only found out a few days ago that Johnny was gettin' married."

"Well, it certainly isn't like a big surprise. He's a grown man . . . lots older than you and I when we married. It has been a fair assumption since he was a baby that one day he would be grown and havin' babies of his own. That is what people do. I've imagined it."

"That is not somethin' I have done, okay? I'm not like you, Emma. I don't go imaginin' all sorts of things."

"What do you mean by that?"

"I don't sit around and think like you do, that's all."

"What is wrong with thinkin'?" She did not appreciate him criticizing her, which she knew he was doing, no matter how innocent he tried to make it out to be. He had always accused her of imagining things.

"Nothing. I just am not like you, Emma. I don't spend a lot of time thinkin' everything six ways from Sunday."

"I don't see anything wrong with thinkin' about the future and plannin' for it. You can't have anything if you don't plan for it. Everything that is here was planned first." She gestured, indicating the surrounding kitchen.

"I didn't say there was anything wrong with it, and I didn't say I don't plan. I just don't think about the same things that you do." He was edging out the door.

"Obviously," she said, annoyed and a little embarrassed, because the entire argument was stupid. She couldn't even figure out how they'd gotten into it.

Later that night, she got all excited about an idea that came to her. She went to the family room to tell John Cole, which likely was a mistake, since he was watching the replay of a NASCAR race.

"Why don't we have a pool put in for the barbeque? The younger people would really like that, and then we'll already have it for when we get grandchildren."

John Cole looked startled. "That's a big project. I don't know if you could get a pool and the yard all finished in time for the barbeque."

"Oh, sure we can," Emma said, delighted to have a rebuttal for that excuse. "Charlene MacCoy got one put in last summer. She said it was amazing how quickly it all got done. I think she said it only took about a month."

John Cole's response was to throw around a lot more cold water by pointing out the expense of a pool in addition to the expenses of the wedding and the gift of the honeymoon, and all sorts of things that *could* come up, such as having to go to Baltimore for the wedding.

Emma, who had also been thinking all day about having the inside of the house painted, said, "Well, a pool will be an investment. We've talked about one before, and I want one for when we have grandkids. I'll just look into it. It won't hurt to see."

She really wished John Cole would have confidence in her good sense. She had not once in all their married years gone overboard with spending. She had pinched pennies as much as he had for many years, and as a result he now enjoyed a comfortable home. He just could not seem to see that they did not have to pinch pennies anymore. Of course, when he wanted something, he darn well got it. It all just made her so mad that she had to go clean the kitchen sink, then move on to scrubbing the floor.

As she was getting ready for bed, she went to the window and looked out into the dark expanse of the yard, imagining a pool sparkling beneath the moon.

The thought came: she and John Cole might like to sit out beside the pool at night, or even go skinny-dipping. Maybe *that* would get him away from the television.

Then she suddenly realized that in the background of all her fantasies of their growing family was John Cole. He was there in her images—supervising the building of the pool—and a new patio, of course—the purchase of a horse for the grandchildren, sawing the wood for the tree house, dragging blankets from high shelves and putting together tricycles.

Sitting with her and talking, holding her hand, kissing her . . . making love.

She tried imagining life without John Cole. Family suppers, grandchildren, the living room with his recliner and him not in it. She could not do it. In fact, she felt a little panic about it.

It suddenly occurred to her that she was doing exactly what John Cole had said she did: thinking everything six ways from Sunday.

And a very good thing that one of them did some

97

thinking, she thought, going into the closet and putting on her slinky silk nightgown that she liked to wear to remind herself—and hopefully John Cole—that she was a woman.

She fluffed the large bed pillows and settled herself against them in an artful, womanly manner. She wanted to present an attractive picture when John Cole came through the door and found her there. She imagined a number of compelling things to say to him.

It turned out not to matter, though, because John Cole did not even come to bed. He fell asleep in his recliner and slept there all night. Probably not thinking at all.

10

Winston and Willie Lee

Earlier in the spring, when elderly Winston Valentine came upon an old electric wheelchair at a yard sale, he bought it and began using it to help him get around town. The wheelchair's electric motor shortly proved unreliable, however, so Willie Lee often ended up pushing. Quite quickly the pair became a familiar sight on the streets of Valentine—the old man wearing a straw cowboy hat and riding in a wheelchair pushed by a boy with a Dallas Cowboys ball cap, invariably on crooked, and followed by a spotted dog.

Most days after their morning radio program, Winston took Willie Lee to the Main Street Café for lunch, because Willie Lee's mother hounded them both about eating vegetables. Afterward they would go across the street to Blaine's Soda Fountain to get ice cream.

Winston insisted that Willie Lee abandon the idea of the extra distance required to use the cross-walk and cut across in the middle of the block, often holding up traffic. Winston often quite boldly used his advanced age and Willie Lee's position as an eternally sweet mentally challenged person to do just what he wanted to do.

No one minded except First Deputy Lyle Midgett, and he had given up trying to get them to quit the illegal and hazardous practice. Deputy Midgett would much rather face any criminal than Mr. Winston's sharp tongue. Half the time he was not even certain what Mr. Winston was saying. Whenever he saw the two crossing illegally, he would turn around and go in the opposite direction, so that he did not have to feel he was derelict in his duty. It was a comfort to know that the sheriff had admitted to the same thing, saying, "There's no one who can tell Winston what to do."

The boy would push Winston in the wheelchair through the door of the drugstore, and the old man would rise and call greetings to everyone as he walked across the room to the soda fountain. There he would spend half an hour or so holding court and pretty much pretending that he was at least twenty years younger. He would hand out cold sweet tea and latte and barbeque and banana splits, along with advice and opinions. On good days, Claire Ford would come in, slip up on a stool, smile at him and ask for a strawberry milkshake, her favorite. He would make it extra thick and watch her rosy tongue savor the sweet pink cream off the long-handled spoon. On really good days she would be without her husband, and Winston would imagine himself at least thirty years younger, and sometimes he almost got some excitement in his pants.

During this time when Winston was occupied, Willie Lee, with Munro quietly at his heels, would occupy himself in the magical world of the magazine section. The plate-glass windows of the drugstore had wide wooden windowsills just right for sitting and reading, which was why Belinda Blaine kept insisting the magazine section needed to be moved, but she could not figure out where else to put it. Willie Lee would sit on the windowsill, and look at magazines about bicycling and skating and skiing and car racing. He could not read the words, had even quit longing to read the words, but he looked at the pictures and dreamed of doing these things himself, just like a normal boy.

"Where's your mama?" Winston asked Belinda on that afternoon's visit to the drugstore soda fountain.

"She's gone off with Jaydee."

"With Jay*dee*?" This was a surprise. Startling, even. "Gone off to where?"

"I don't know, just off." While he was dealing with this, she added, "And Claire was already in earlier. You missed her. She and Larkin were goin' off this afternoon to Dallas."

Everyone was off, and here he was. His Claire had not even informed him about a trip to Dallas. There had been a time when she told him just about everything. Now, more and more, she was slipping away from him.

That day's visit to the soda fountain proved a total disappointment. Not one person he even faintly wanted to see appeared. Lillian Jennings, who was always going on about something in history, came in and wanted to know what Winston knew about the War Between the States. He told her, "Nothin'. I'm not *that* damn old." And then Deputy Lyle Midgett came in and said that they had not yet nabbed the thief who had made off with two wrenches and a cash box containing fifty-five dollars from Sybil Lund's perpetual garage sale.

Winston had not told anyone about seeing the young man that the deputy had been chasing jumping over the pasture fence and hiding, and he didn't want to speak of it now, because he didn't want to appear old and forgetful. That he *was* becoming old and forgetful was too much to bear.

He realized that he wasn't only forgetful, but that he was being for*gotten*. His two best friends were Vella and Claire, and they were at that moment occupied with other men. Younger, livelier men. And it was not too hard to be younger and livelier than him, who was in the very twilight of his life.

Over on the windowsill, Willie Lee felt Munro get to his feet and press against his leg. He looked at the dog, who looked back with dark eyes.

In his familiar manner of knowing things without hearing words, Willie Lee immediately put the magazine back in its correct place on the shelf, then went straight to the wheelchair and rolled it to the end of the soda fountain counter, where Mr. Winston was leaning on the freezer.

"Ah . . . buddy," Winston said, taking note of him. "Let's get our ice cream and blow this joint."

He started to make their ice-cream cones, but Belinda said that she would do it and told him to sit down.

Vaguely aware that Belinda had ordered him and that he didn't have the gumption to go back at her, and that she had never before offered to make him anything, he allowed her to do so and settled himself heavily into the wheelchair.

Willie Lee could not recall ever seeing Belinda make ice-cream cones. He stood nearby and watched. She was skimpy on the ice cream, but he didn't think it a wise thing to say so to her.

With Winston carrying the desserts in a cardboard container on his lap, Willie Lee rolled him out onto the sidewalk and over to a bench beneath the shelter of a redbud tree, where they sat side by side and ate their cones, Munro licked his treat from a dish, and vehicles and people passed by. Most everyone cast a wave or called a greeting.

One of these was pretty little Gabby Smith, who waved enthusiastically out the passenger window of her mother's minivan as the vehicle slowed in a line for the stoplight. "Hi, Willie Lee! Hi, Mr. Winston!"

There was in this feminine enthusiasm enough energy to cause Winston to smile and wave in return.

Willie Lee reacted by scrambling to his feet as fast as he could. Winston saw the boy's ice cream tilting precariously on the cone.

"I heard you on the radio this mornin'," called Gabby, pushing her curls out of her face as the minivan began to roll forward.

"I . . . I . . . hel-ped." Willie Lee was on tiptoe at the edge of sidewalk.

"I listen every day. Come see me, Willie Lee!" Gabby called, leaning out the window as the minivan rounded the corner of Church Street and disappeared.

Winston reached out just in time to catch Willie Lee's ice cream. It plopped into his hand. Willie Lee, blinking behind his thick glasses, looked from the now-empty cone to the mound of ice cream in Winston's palm.

"Here ya' go," Winston said, and dropped the melting ice cream back on the cone.

"Thank you." Willie Lee positioned himself back on the bench.

"You're welcome." Winston slung the excess ice cream from his palm, then held his hand out away from his clothes while he finished his own ice-cream cone. A man with his years behind him no longer worried about small inconveniences.

"Miss Gabby is still right sweet on you, I see."

Willie Lee shrugged. Winston detected some gloom.

"Is there a problem?" Having a sense of great disappointment in his own life at the moment, he felt irritated at life for bothering the boy.

Willie Lee shrugged again. "I am not . . . grow-ing."

"Well, yes, you are. Your mother had to buy you new jeans just last month, said you'd grown a foot."

"She was ex-ag . . . ex-ag . . ."

"Exaggerating."

Willie Lee nodded, then said in his practical manner, "People do not grow a foot in a month. Pa-pa Tate said."

"But you have grown into larger pants," Winston pointed out. "And you're not done growin' yet. Not by a long shot. Besides, even if Gabby grows taller, that doesn't matter. Lots of tall gals go with shorter boys."

He tried to think of an example and came up short, which seemed a funny pun. He hoped to remember it for his radio show. He liked to write down his thoughts, but his hands were busy at that moment.

Willie Lee said, "I mean . . . in-side." He looked solemn. "I am re-tar-ded. I can-not have a girl-friend." He hung his head, holding out his melting ice-cream cone.

"Eat your ice cream," Winston said. Then, "Who told you that you cannot have a girlfriend because you are retarded?"

"Just some-one." Willie Lee focused on licking his ice cream. It had been Mrs. Pruitt, the librarian at the Valentine library, who scared a lot of the children. Mrs. Pruitt had the idea that all the books in the library were her very own, and she would just as soon that children not be allowed to handle them.

"Yeah, well," said Winston, "that someone is all wrong. Of course you can have a girlfriend."

Winston considered pressing the boy to get the name of this someone and go set the person straight. Such a person was the type who liked to make other people feel small, mostly because they themselves were shriveled up.

Willie Lee interrupted Winston's thoughts by saying, "I know I am slow, aannd I will ne-ver be fast-ter. At scho-ol I go to the class for spe-cial ed, but it means *slow*. Men-tal retar-da-tion. There is no cure."

Winston couldn't recall ever seeing Willie Lee so sad. He found himself upset at the boy's pain and unable to form an instant comeback, something that did not often happen. Thinking on it, he finished his ice-cream cone, took napkins from his shirt pocket and cleaned himself up.

"Yes, my little buddy," he said finally, "I'll admit that you do not think just like everyone else, and the term slow is used and quite accurate by many standards. Nevertheless, as in all things, it is a matter of perspective. Maybe the world and people in it go too fast. Did you ever think of that?"

Willie Lee looked up, frowning in thought. In Winston's opinion, and that of a number of observant people, the boy had pockets of rare understanding inside of him that had nothing to do with intellect.

"Being slow is not such a bad thing and has nothing whatsoever to do with havin' a girlfriend. Girls prefer boys who are not so fast."

He reached over and began to wipe up Willie Lee. Suddenly becoming aware of his actions, he handed the napkin to the boy, saying, "The female human is somethin' *I* know a bit about. I've had a bunch of girlfriends from the time I was younger than you, and two wives, and the first of those was a doozie. I've learned from experience that as long as you speak to a female's heart, she isn't gonna care how well you think or how tall you are."

"I can-not re-ad. I will not be a-ble to take the test and get a dri-ver li-cen-se and take my girl-friend on a date. That is what a boyfriend does."

"Aw, you got somethin' better than readin', Little Buddy. You have that trust fund, son. You can buy a car and hire someone to drive you on a date. You won't ever need a driver's license. You could go on a date right now, if you wanted."

"I co-uld?"

"Yes, sir, you could." Winston was proud to solve that problem. He was counting up Willie Lee's assets and became happier by the moment.

"I can absolutely assure you, son, that you are more than qualified to have a girlfriend." He rested a hand on the boy's small shoulder. "You have everything going for you. You're a healthy and even handsome young man with a secure future, and there are pitiful few people who can say that at any age.

"But most importantly, Little Buddy, your heart overrules your intellect, and that is the main neces-sity for gettin' along with girls." Then, after a moment, he added, "Really, for successful living, I'd say."

11

Mothers and Daughters

From the *Valentine Voice*:
  June 3, 1998
  Kinney—Berry
Mr. And Mrs. John Cole Berry of Valentine are pleased to announce the engagement of their son, Johnny Ray Berry, to Miss Gracie Louise Kinney, daughter of Mrs. Sylvia Kinney of Baltimore, Maryland.

The prospective groom serves as a manager and vice president of the Berry Quick Stop Enterprises.

The bride-elect is a regional manager for the M. Connor chain of women's apparel.

A September wedding is planned in Valentine, where the two plan to make their home.

When young Paris Miller, who was clerking at their Quick Stop No. 1, called to let Emma know that the Wednesday afternoon edition of the *Valentine Voice* had arrived, Emma went right down to get four copies. John Cole had wanted to know why she didn't just make copies from one clipping, but she said it wouldn't be the same. Men simply did not understand these things.

Just as she entered the store, a boy running out about knocked her down, followed by Paris yelling after him. Emma stood there watching the dark boy in a baggy T-shirt, with a girl with splotchy-crimson spiked hair hot on his heels, disappear around the corner of the building.

Emma went into the store, which was totally vacant, and realized that Paris had abandoned the cash register. She forgot about the register, though, as her gaze lit on a newspaper lying on the counter, folded back to the engagement announcement. Paris was a kind girl.

As Emma started to read, Paris came huffing back through the door. "Oh, Miz Berry—I'm sorry I forgot about the store! I didn't really . . . I just wanted to catch that little creep. He shoplifted a handful of candy bars. I gotta call the sheriff."

"Oh, no, honey. Let him go. He's only a little boy, and it was just candy bars. All children want candy." Emma generally did not believe in pursuing children, and in any case, her attention was totally on the picture of Johnny and Gracie. "Didn't their picture come out great?"

Paris agreed about the picture, and then protested that it wouldn't be right to let the boy go. "He is old enough to steal, and we might be the ones to save him from prison when he's older."

Taking full note of the girl's upset, Emma looked up to see Paris's frowning furrowed brows—each one pierced through with a gold ring. She was such a lovely girl. It was a shame that she felt the need to poke so many holes in her body.

Emma said, "Perhaps he'll return, and you can catch him in the act and instruct him. That would be the best thing. I doubt if the ...ff could find him now."

"Yeah . . . I guess."

Emma's attention returned to the announcement. Reading it aloud, she winced. "Oh, dear. I used the word plan twice."

Paris peered at the paper. "No one'll notice."

"My mother will," said Emma. "But maybe no one else. Their picture just captures attention." She grinned at the teenage girl. "Johnny is just so *cute*."

"Yeah, he is," said Paris, grinning back.

Emma took up four copies of the paper and headed out the door, then came back and got two more.

Paris waved as the woman left. She wished that she had a mother who thought as much of her as Mrs. Berry thought of Johnny. For an instant, in which she blinked hard and looked downward, she wondered what having such a mother would be like.

Paris's mother had left her years before, just gone off and left Paris, who had not yet turned ten at the time. Not even knowing who her father was, Paris lived with her grandfather, a Vietnam vet who was in a wheelchair. Because she was only fifteen now, she'd had to talk Johnny Berry into giving her the job at the Quick Stop, and it was only part-time for the summer. But Johnny had already given her a raise and said she did a real good job. It was a start on her goal to pull herself and her grandfather up out of poverty of the sort where that little thief probably came from, by the look of him.

That boy might have gotten away this time, but Paris would keep a sharp eye and catch him the next. With the zeal that only a reformed shoplifter herself could feel, she determined to set the boy straight.

As it turned out, Emma did not need to worry about getting extra copies of the paper, because she ended up receiving them all over town.

When she got gas at the Texaco, old Mr. Stidham, who was always sitting out front in a frayed lawn chair and talking to all the customers, gave her his copy of the newspaper, and she picked up another at the bank, from two young tellers who told her that they thought Gracie was sure a lucky girl.

"Probably can't have too many of these," said Julia Jenkins-Tinsley at the post office, passing over a paper.

On her way out of the post office, Emma encountered Charlotte Nation, manager of the *Voice*, coming in, who passed her a manila envelope, saying, "I was just goin' to mail this to you. It's a couple of clippings of the engagement announcement. Congratulations."

"Oh! Thank you." She had not realized the newspaper attended to such personable details, or even that Charlotte Nation, a bare acquaintance, would recall who Emma was.

As she headed down the sidewalk, she was further congratulated on Johnny's future by Bonita Embree, who was washing the windows of her bakery, and two women, who were power walking and slowed only a fraction as one called, "Congratulations on Johnny's engagement!"

"Thank you," Emma said, being a little embarrassed that she did not know who the two smiling women were, although they obviously knew her.

Continuing along the sidewalk, she became faintly aware of being really happy. It seemed that the sun on the old brick buildings was brighter than normal, and the late spring air sweeter. The early days when they had first moved to the small town came in quick, fuzzy snapshots across her mind, and mixed in with fantasies of the wedding and the future with her son's family all around her. She picked up her pace as she headed for Blaine's Drugstore.

The bell over the door rang out as she entered the store. The musky scents came to her—those of old building mixed with that of Evening in Paris sold at the small perfume counter. Belinda called a greeting from the soda fountain. Delighted to find the woman in, Emma cast her a hello and a wave. "I'll be right over. I'm goin' to get pantyhose first."

She selected two packages of hose from the rack. She felt a little guilty, because the Quick Stop No. 1 carried hose, too, but of a cheaper variety than Emma liked. She had told John Cole this and recommended the brand she preferred, and he had told her no one would pay that price at the Quick Stops.

The only people at the soda fountain were Belinda, leaning against the freezer, and her mother, Vella, who sat on her tall stool, smoking one of her thin cigaroos.

"Our slow time—business will pick up around five, when people head home from work," Belinda explained, dropping a copy of the newspaper atop the stack Emma had laid on the counter. "Saved the announcement for you."

"Those pantyhose are on sale—half price," Vella instructed Belinda. Then, to Emma, "What else can I get for you, sugar?"

Emma ordered a glass of cold tea, with lemon. No place in town had better cold tea, which Vella herself made several times a day. The idea occurred—perhaps Vella would not mind sharing the recipe for Emma to serve at the bridal-shower barbeque. Emma was about to pose the question, when Vella turned the subject back to pantyhose.

"I remember when those came out. You know what I like best about pantyhose? You don't have to wear panties with them."

"You don't wear panties with your pantyhose?"

Belinda said. Her eyebrows rose, and she blinked.

"Well, nooo. *Why* would I do that?" replied her mother.

Belinda shrugged, saying, "Well, I do."

Emma watched the two women, Vella wearing a frown and Belinda a bland expression.

"I don't know why you would do that," said Vella, speaking with some vehemence. "The panty is made into them. That's why they are called *panty*hose. That is the purpose of them, so you don't have to wear panties."

"I don't think that is their sole purpose," was Belinda's calm response. "They are hose that come all the way to the waist is all, so you don't need garters . . . but you do need panties."

Vella took that in for about three seconds, then turned to Emma. "Let me just ask you. Do you wear panties under your pantyhose?"

"Well . . . no." She really didn't, but in the face of the woman's sharp expression, she thought she might have said no even if she did.

Vella smiled in satisfaction, and Belinda's eyebrows went up, then came down in a skeptical frown.

"I told you. The reason they are called *panty*hose is because the panty is made in," Vella stated. "I don't know *why* anyone would wear panties with 'em. Not havin' to wear panties is the point."

"Okay, Mama. It's your choice."

"It is also common sense. I don't know *why*

anyone would want to wear drawers all bunched up under pantyhose. Do you?" she demanded of Emma.

"I imagine some would."

"Well, the panty is right there—there is even a cotton crotch. I don't know why anyone would want to wear two panties, because that is what you have with panties under 'em."

"Not all pantyhose have the cotton crotch," Belinda said.

"They don't?"

"No, Mama."

Emma was a little surprised. She had not known this, either, which seemed telling, somehow.

Vella said, "Well, I don't know why anyone would wear those, and I don't know why anyone would wear panties with *panty*hose. Lord, before we had pantyhose, we had to wear panties, and garter belts or girdles. They were just for the birds."

Belinda crossed her arms and addressed her mother and Emma. "All right . . . what if you two get in a wreck and have to go to the hospital, and you do not have any panties on?"

"So?" was Vella's reply. "Then they don't have so much to take off in an emergency. Just rip the pantyhose off and it's done."

Emma said she had never considered it.

"My pantyhose are clean," added Vella. "I put on clean pantyhose when I wear them."

Belinda, who moved back and looked down at Vella's legs, said, "You aren't wearin' pantyhose now . . . are you wearin' panties?" There was ripe curiosity in her voice.

"Yes, dear. I almost always wear panties."

"*Almost?*"

"Since when did you get so straight-laced?" Vella asked. "And I just do not believe most women wear panties under pantyhose. It is redundant. I don't know why you would do that . . . I just don't."

Having apparently reached an impasse, the two women shut up long enough for Emma to change the subject to finding a theme for her bridal-shower barbeque. The three of them batted around a number of ideas—country and western, floral, items reflecting family. Belinda was very good at such ideas. She watched an inordinate amount of television shopping channels and the Home and Garden channel. Emma got the times from her of several programs that could be of help with her plans.

Then Charlene MacCoy, who was Emma's hair-dresser, came in. As she slipped up on the stool beside Emma, Vella got right to the question about panties under pantyhose.

"Oh, yes, I do," Charlene replied, blinking with a bit of surprise.

"You do?"

"Uh-huh . . . when I wear pantyhose. I don't wear

them much in the summer, just if I get really dressed up." She went on to explain that she had just always worn panties under pantyhose, just like she always wore panties. Except for a time when she tried going without, at her sister's suggestion, as a way to loosen up.

"All it did was make me tighten up," she said. "I got so nervous about my skirt blowing up in the wind, or gettin' in a wreck and havin' to go to the emergency room, you know."

Belinda said, "These two don't wear panties."

"You don't?" Charlene cast a surprised look from Vella to Emma.

"Just not under pantyhose," Emma said quickly. "I wear panties as a rule."

"There's just no need to wear panties with panty-hose," Vella said emphatically. The phone rang, and as she reached to answer, she added, "I just don't know *why* anyone would wear panties under pantyhose."

With Vella taking an order on the phone, Charlene looked at Emma and asked, "What if a wind came and blew your skirt up?"

Emma admitted that she had never thought of that. "But it hasn't ever happened. And I wear the shapers. They are dark at the top and down the thigh. See." She held up one of the packages of pantyhose to display the picture, as if to present documented evidence.

Then, as Belinda and Charlene talked over the

matter, she more thoroughly examined the picture and print on the package. She had always believed, as Vella did, that they were panty and hose combined. The picture did not show panties underneath. She wondered if there were instructions that she had missed all these years.

Suddenly Vella hissed and waved at them, drawing their attention. Then she said into the phone, "Listen, Lori . . ." and Emma got a mental picture of Lori Wright, the receptionist from the sheriff's office, thirtyish, bleached hair and fancy fingernails ". . . I want to ask you somethin'. Do you wear panties under your pantyhose?"

Vella's expectant smile slowly fell. "Oh, you do . . . thin no-line . . . well, okay . . . it was just somethin' we've been discussin'. . . ."

When she hung up, Belinda said, "That is three to two, Mama."

Vella said, "You get two vanilla and one chocolate shake ready to go over to the sheriff's office. I'm gonna call Marilee," and she reached again for the phone.

Marilee was Tate Holloway's wife, and the conversation was short. Vella's disappointed face reflected the answer. "Marilee says that she wears panties under her hose, unless she's out with Tate . . . and then she doesn't."

They cast each other mystified grins, and then Vella added, "I suppose I'll ask her about that later."

"I'm puttin' her down as a *with*," said Belinda, who had pulled out a note tablet.

Twenty minutes later, Emma left the drugstore, carrying with her friendly goodbyes and well-wishes for all the upcoming bridal affairs, a piece of paper with Vella's instructions for making her delicious cold tea in quantity, the phone number for the construction company that put in Charlene's pool, and the knowledge that she and Vella were in the definite minority concerning wearing pantyhose without panties.

A few women had volunteered reasons. Fayrene Gardner, whom Belinda had encountered on the sidewalk while taking the milkshakes over to the sheriff's office, had said, "I *sweat,* honey."

And elderly Minnie Oakes whispered, "Oh, yes . . . in case I pee."

Vella had even telephoned her other daughter, Margaret, who lived all the way over in Atlanta, and who reported in as a "with." Margaret had her mother's voice, and they could all hear her through the phone as she said, "You made me wear 'em, Mama. I learned it from you."

Mother and daughter had an argument about this, and when she hung up, Vella swore, "I did not teach her that. She says I did, but I didn't."

And she repeated her refrain, "*Why* would anyone wear panties with pantyhose? That is *why*

119

they call them *panty*hose—the panty is built right in."

When Claire Ford and Sherrilyn Earles came in to get strawberry milkshakes to go and both said they wore thongs underneath their pantyhose, not only did Vella say, "*Why* would anyone do that?" but so did Emma and Belinda.

There was a small discussion as to whether a thong qualified as with panty or without, and *with* won out, bringing the total count of panty wearers to eight, while the withouts remained at two: Emma and Vella.

"Well, I'm flabbergasted," Vella said.

As Emma got into her car to drive home, she wondered if she might have been, all these years, a little bit free and loose without ever having known it. Not to have known seemed a very large shame.

Belinda watched Emma disappear out the door, and beside her, her mother said, "You know, I think that is the first real conversation I've ever had with Emma Berry. And after knowin' her all this time."

"She's sort of a reserved person," Belinda replied.

She made herself a mental note not to speak about the intimate information she had learned the previous week. Sometimes things you swore not to talk about just popped out—as the news had from Emma herself when she had gotten wrought up and blurted out the situation with her marriage.

Her mother was saying, "I used to see Emma around a lot more, when Johnny was young. Seemed like she was in here a couple of times a week, doin' things with his school class. We never had a conversation, though. All that time, and never a conversation with her. Huh."

Belinda kept silent. Her mother no doubt would have more to say, because she always did.

"These days people simply don't take time to really talk to each other. We talk *at* each other, but not *to*," her mother said, rising to clean the counter. "You want another glass of tea, sugar?"

Belinda checked her watch as she pushed her glass forward. "Do you want to go wake up Oran for the evenin' rush, or should I?"

Oran Lackey was their latest new pharmacist. Most afternoons he fell asleep in the back of the pharmacy in her father's old recliner. It was the oddest thing. Each pharmacist they hired started out pert as could be and ended up sluggish, just like her father had been. She really wanted to get the pharmacy area remodeled. She felt this would end that problem.

"Let's see if he wakes up by himself," her mother said, then continued, "You know, that was mine and your daddy's biggest problem. We could never really talk to each other. Oh, I talked, but it was like talkin' to a wall. Your daddy just never said anything back. You can't have a conversation like that. But I think I've finally figured it out—no one in your father's family talked to each other. Every one of them had worked hard all their lives, and when you're workin' all the time, you don't have time to talk. You just never really learn how. Maybe if I would have figured that out sooner, we could have learned how to talk . . . or maybe not."

Belinda reflected to herself that she and Lyle didn't talk much and were very happy. She never had been drawn to Lyle because he was a great conversationalist.

"And you know who really knows how to have a conversation?" her mother said.

"Who?" Belinda supplied somewhat automatically, thinking suddenly that her mother really did look young for her age. So many people had asked Belinda in the past few days how old her mother really was. Belinda had kept saying sixty-five, as Winston had reported, because she had already mentally moved her own age back a few years. It seemed smart to start early, and truth about age was something that she remained very relaxed about. She was nearly eight years older than Lyle, but she never had let that bother her.

"Jay*dee*."

"Oh, Mama." Belinda had to turn away from the delight on her mother's face.

"I know he can be way too big for his britches, but let me just say that now I know how he managed to have so many women all these years." She paused, then added thoughtfully, "He is an attorney. What does an attorney do? They talk for a livin', so they really do know how to have a conversation. Jaydee even talks between kisses," she added with a smile of happiness.

"Mama, I do not want to hear about any of your sordid affairs, and least of all with Jaydee Mayhall." Belinda moved to the cash register to count money, which was what she did in any uncertain moment. Then, with an awful thought, "I hope you are bein' careful. Jaydee has had a lot of women."

"My . . . I am not havin' an affair with him!"

Her mother looked shocked and hurt, but Belinda thought that her assessment was reasonable.

"And why would you call any of my affairs sordid?" her mother said, now putting a hand to her hip. "Why would any of them be any more sordid than you livin' with Lyle for five years before you married him?"

Belinda had the thought: *Because you are a mother in her seventies.* However, she said, "I'm sorry," to end the discussion. Arguing with anyone was a waste of time, and certainly got her nowhere with her mother. She efficiently counted the money and placed it in the bank bag.

Vella watched her daughter, who kept her attention focused on filling out the bank deposit slip. Vella almost stretched out her hand to touch her daughter's arm, stopped, then swallowed. But time was fleeting.

"Sugar . . ." She waited for Belinda to look at her. "Your father is gone now. Nothin' I do or don't do will bring him back . . . and I'm alive."

"I know that, Mom." Belinda said.

"I loved him the best I could."

Belinda's eyes came up to hers. "Mama . . . you have no idea what it was like watchin' you and Daddy all my life. That's why I lived with Lyle for all those years before I married him. For one thing, I wanted to make sure that he wasn't like Daddy, because I know I'm a whole lot like you, and I did not want to end up like you and Daddy."

Vella swallowed and gazed at her daughter, refusing to flinch from whatever Belinda needed to say to her. It was the most bare-bones honest moment she had ever shared with her daughter.

Unfortunately, the bell over the door rang out and cut off the moment.

Vella looked over to see Miss Lillian Jennings, who was Emma Berry's mother, come across the store to the soda fountain at a good clip in her solid shoes, and with a magazine waving back and forth in one hand.

"I ran into Minnie Oakes down the street, and she said Emma was here. But I see that I've missed her." She glanced around, as if not to overlook her daughter.

Belinda explained that Emma had left just about

124

five minutes earlier. "I think she went directly home."

"Oh, well, I'm here now. I'll have a latte, please, Vella."

The woman settled her ample body onto a counter stool. One thing that Vella admired about Lillian Jennings was that, while large, she never appeared apologetic about it. She wore print dresses and pantsuits of bright colors.

As she got the latte, Vella wondered about the state of the woman's pantyhose. Vella really wanted to find someone else on her side.

Belinda asked about the magazine the woman had laid on the counter.

"It is proof," Lillian said. Holding up the magazine, she thumped the page. "Right here in *Southern Living*."

"Proof of what?"

"That Oklahoma is indeed in and of the South." She brandished the magazine in such a way that Vella drew back with the latte.

"Who said it wasn't?" asked Vella, as she decided that the woman had settled down enough for her to set the big steaming cup in front of her.

"Oh, a poor woman who lacks education, bless her heart. But I have the truth right here on the map."

Lillian Jennings held the magazine forth, and Belinda and Vella peered at it.

"Do you see that? Isn't that Oklahoma?"

"Yes," they both said.

"Now, *who* can argue with *Southern Living Magazine*?"

They all agreed that the magazine was something of a last word.

Satisfied, Mrs. Jennings lifted the wide latte cup in both hands and sipped delicately.

Vella took advantage of the lull to say, "Miz Jennings, do you wear pantyhose?"

She saw Belinda roll her eyes.

"Why, yes, I do. Ever'day," Mrs. Jennings answered. "I put them on first thing in the mornin'. Support hose. Every woman ought to wear them. Helps the veins."

"Do you wear panties under your pantyhose?"

"Well, of course," said the woman without missing a beat. "I wear panties under them, and in the winter I wear panties *over* them, too."

"Oh," Vella said.

After Lillian Jennings had left, Belinda followed close behind, tossing over her shoulder as she reached the door, "Why don't you write *Southern Living Magazine* and ask what is the last word in pantyhose wearin'?"

That evening, Charlene MacCoy was folding clothes out of the dryer when her daughter, Jojo, came to her and shared the big news of a first real date to the dance that was held each Friday night of the summer in the Episcopal Church Fellowship

Hall. Mother and daughter discussed what Jojo, who had just graduated out of eighth grade, might want to wear. Pulling a pair of Jojo's panties out of the dryer and suddenly seeing that they were no bigger than a minute, Charlene decided that Jojo would be wearing both panties *and* pantyhose with any dresses from there on out.

Vella entertained Jaydee for supper and later they sat in her glider out on her patio as the cooling dark came. Vella told Jaydee all about the pantyhose discussion. She could hardly believe she felt comfortable doing that, and also that Jaydee took part in the discussion. He never acted bored, and he had a comment for everything.

He agreed with her that the name "pantyhose" did imply that the panties were built in, and who could think differently? He even offered that he'd had one girlfriend who had not worn panties underneath. He also admitted to having worn pantyhose himself.

"You did?" Vella said, naturally highly surprised.

Jaydee explained that he had worn them a few times when riding cutting horses in competition in the freezing cold. "I put them on over my Fruit o' the Looms, though. They work great under jeans to keep heat in and not be bulky for ridin'. You got to feel that horse under you for performance-horse ridin', you know. My little brother and a few of the guys do this."

"They do?"

"Oh, yeah."

Right after that, Jaydee kissed her, and Vella thought she was in gloryland, with a man who could both talk and kiss.

When Belinda, all showered, perfumed and wearing a lacy red negligee, came out of the bathroom, she found Lyle already in bed, as expected, but unexpectedly, he was hanging up the telephone.

"That was your mother," he said, without looking at Belinda, because he was occupied with straightening the phone cord. "She said to tell you to put down another with."

"Oh, for heaven's sake." Nevertheless, she made a note on a tablet.

"What does she mean by that—'with'?" Lyle asked, finally settled with the cord.

"Oh, nothin'."

Belinda climbed into bed, clicked off the television with the remote and put her attention back where she put it each night at nine o'clock—on enjoying passion with Lyle.

"Why do you always tell me that?" Lyle said.

"What?" Her lips were inches from his, his smooth chest firm under her hands. Lyle worked out every day of his life.

" 'Nothin'.' I ask you about somethin', and you say, 'nothin'.' "

"Because it is nothin' that will interest you," she said, mildly annoyed at the petulant tone slipping into his voice. But then she kissed him and enjoyed the languid rise of sweet desire, and the glorious sensation of being a woman with a man. One thing about Lyle, he was all man. And Belinda was all woman.

"Well, how do you know it won't interest me until you tell me?"

She pulled back and looked at him. "What?"

He said, "Well, honey, I'd just like us to talk a little more. We don't ever talk. Married people need to be able to discuss things in order to have a good relationship."

She took in his use of the word "relationship." "You've been watchin' *Oprah* again, haven't you?" Aggravated, she flopped back on the stack of pillows.

"No . . ." Then, "It was this psychologist guy on the radio while Giff and I was on patrol. He was talkin' about couples who have successful marriages. Bein' able to talk to each other is important for a long and happy marriage."

She could not believe it. All the years they had lived together, he had never paid attention to such things. She had *known* marriage would change the situation. She had just known it.

"Lyle, honey, I am happy. Aren't you happy?" She gave him a cajoling bat of her eyes.

"Well, yeah. Yeah, I am." He smiled.

"There you are." She headed for him to kiss him.

"Yeah, but I want us to talk, *hun-nee*."

Belinda looked at him. "*I* am not gonna be happy if we talk right now, o-kay?"

Lyle sort of pouted, but she whispered in his ear, "We can talk tomorrow, sugar." Then she nibbled his earlobe.

"I just want us to have a happy marriage, honey," he whispered back, getting in one more last word before thankfully paying attention to the relating at hand.

Belinda could not believe what marriage had done to Lyle. What really had her shaken up, though—so much so that she found *she* had difficulty paying full attention—was that Lyle was beginning to seem not like her father but like her *mother.*

Emma clicked on the bedroom television. The old movie *Cat on a Hot Tin Roof* showed on the screen in the armoire. Paul Newman and Elizabeth Taylor. Elizabeth sure had been beautiful. Emma had for years wished to have black hair like Elizabeth Taylor.

Liz went to taking off her clothes down to her slip, and then reached under and removed her hose. The regular kind, although they didn't show garters or panties. She might not even have worn them. They hadn't had pantyhose back then, Emma didn't think, but if they had, she would bet

Liz didn't wear panties with them. Liz went around the room in her slip. And then she was coming on to Paul, who refused to take up with her.

Eyes on the screen, Emma sank down on the bed. She had forgotten this part of the movie. There were Elizabeth and Paul sniping at each other, then Elizabeth just begging Paul to make love to her, and him refusing, coldly, angrily, but no matter—just from them talking to each other, there was passion jumping off the screen.

The whole thing went clear through Emma. She clicked off the television, went to her dressing table, sat and gazed at herself in the mirror.

John Cole's footsteps sounded, coming down the hall. He appeared in the room behind her. She saw him look at her—quickly, then away—and begin to remove his shirt, which he tossed onto his dressing chair.

Taking up the Estée Lauder body lotion, Emma slowly smoothed it on her neck and down over her bare shoulders, where the wide-necked flimsy gown drooped in a sensual manner. Her skin was creamy white. "Good skin," it was called, a gift from her ancestors.

"I'm goin' to take a shower," John Cole said, as if she might have thought he left home when he went into the bathroom and closed the door.

She gazed at her image in the mirror again, thinking that she was having no more luck than

Elizabeth had when she paraded around in her slip, although by the end of the movie, Elizabeth *had* won over Paul. Emma couldn't seem to make headway. She just didn't know how.

At least John Cole had finally begun coming to the bed at night. The first night he did this and found her there, he looked like he might just turn around and leave. He did not, thankfully, and they were as pleasant as either could be, saying, "Good night, sleep well," and then turning out the lights, after which they each lay there breathing in the dark and pretending to go to sleep. Shortly after that, John Cole actually did fall into that little wuffling snore of true sleep. Emma then turned on her side to go to sleep, too, but each successive night that the scenario played out, sleep came harder and harder.

She would lie there on her back and think that if the hole in her chest got any wider, she would surely die. She would see her life stretching before her, years and years of a dry desert without passion and conversation. It was like all of her oomph had gotten up and left, and she could not seem to get it back.

This prospect was so painful that she would cast around in her mind, trying to find out where everything had gone wrong. She would bounce back and forth between herself and John Cole as to who carried the most blame for the situation, and if she lay there long enough, she at last would need to get up to go to the bathroom, at which time she would pass by his side of the bed and wonder what he would do if she whopped him with the pillow.

Would he even be moved to ask her what was wrong, or would they go on pretending and sort of holding their breaths and trying not to upset anything before the session with the marriage counselor?

As she sat there, gazing in the mirror, it occurred to Emma that they were pinning a lot of expectation on a woman neither of them had ever seen.

Just then the telephone rang.

It was her mother, who had called to tell her of the surefire proof of Oklahoma's inclusion in the southern states and to vaguely reprimand Emma for not wearing panties under her pantyhose, and further, to say that the fact was known all over town. It seemed that her mother had run into Minnie Oakes, who had given her the news.

"I thought I had taught you better than that," her mother said.

"I do not recall, Mama, that you ever taught me anything about it," Emma said so sharply as to surprise herself.

"Well, I thought I did."

Unable to think of a positive response, Emma said nothing, and the line hummed for long seconds before her mother returned to the subject of Oklahoma being on the map of the South in *Southern Living Magazine.* She urged Emma to go look at her copy. Emma managed to refrain from saying that she could not live until she hopped right up and did it.

As she bade her mother goodbye, John Cole came out of the bathroom. Emma saw him in the mirror. He wore only pajama pants. Her eyes lit on his bare chest, which was smooth and thick-muscled.

But then he asked, "Who was that?" and she jarred her eyes away.

He had formed the awful habit of always asking her who she was talking to on the phone.

"Mama."

She saw him give her a curious look. Her tone had still been sharp.

Well, what she wanted to say to him was: *Who else in this world do you think I would be talkin' to at ten o'clock at night?*

They got into bed and lay, as on the nights before, looking up at the ceiling.

"Do you mind if I turn on the television?" John Cole asked, already picking up the remote before she answered.

"Yes, I do."

He put down the remote.

She rolled over and did her best to feign sleep, while words seemed to jam up in her throat and threaten to choke her. It seemed quite odd that she could have been so happy and talkative that after-noon at the drugstore.

12

Time Lines

Emma dedicated the morning hours to getting ready for the counseling session. Heaven knew she did not want to appear to be a woman who had let herself go and given her husband just cause to lose interest.

She took thirty minutes to pray and meditate, hoping to get her mind on solid ground. The peace she found from this was pretty well undone, however, by all that came after. She painted her fingernails and toenails to match, showered and washed and fixed her hair, and did a full make-up job. She tried on four outfits before choosing one that she felt sufficed. After several long minutes of debate, she chose to wear pantyhose, and wondered if she ever again would be at peace not wearing panties under them.

By the time she reached the Stop offices where she was to meet John Cole, she was on her last nerve.

"He's in a meetin' just now," said Shelley Dilks. She got up and came around the desk. "You're a little early, you know."

Emma, feeling reprimanded, checked her watch. She was not even ten minutes ahead of time, and she didn't think that counted as early. She always thought that fifteen minutes either way was acceptable.

"You got your hair cut. It looks really cute," Shelley said in a friendly manner, coming close and giving Emma a good inspection.

Emma touched her hair. "Oh . . . yes. Back last winter." She realized she had not seen the woman for the better part of a year. She also noted that Shelley, who was several years younger than Emma, had started dyeing her hair. Emma kept from mentioning this; most women didn't care to have it pointed out.

They chatted for several minutes, during which Shelley was very talkative and complimentary. She seemed so friendly, even anxious for Emma to like her, that Emma felt she should make an effort to visit the offices more. She really had not taken an interest in things going on with the business in years. Shelley went on about this supplier and that employee, as if Emma knew all about them. John Cole rarely spoke about the goings-on at work. That she didn't know a single incident was a little embarrassing, so she didn't say that she didn't know. It all went to show how far apart her life and John Cole's had become.

When John Cole came out of his office with another man, he looked a little surprised and said he hadn't known she was there, as if they had not set a time to meet. She didn't say anything about this, though. It was not a time to get nitpicky. They were both just so nervous.

On the way out to her car, John Cole reached over and took her hand, and rubbed his thumb against hers as he often did when nervous. The more nervous he was, the faster he would rub his thumb, and just then he was rubbing quite quickly. The main problem with this was that his thumb tended to be really calloused. It hurt right that minute, but she was glad to be holding his hand and didn't want to hurt his feelings by telling him to stop.

The New Hope Counseling Center turned out to be in a sixties' ranch-style house in a string of others, all made over into offices. The office on one side handled vacuum and sewing machine sales, and on the other were attorneys. Probably, in one way or another the counseling center fit in with the other two, but still, Emma felt a little apprehensive about the therapists' qualifications.

The waiting room still looked like the living room of the house. She wasn't too impressed with the decor. She didn't mention any of her apprehension to John Cole, though. It wouldn't do any good to add to their general nervousness, which was already rising due to the only other occupant of the waiting room—a woman who, Emma gradually realized, was just crying and crying. She wasn't making any sobbing noise, just holding a tissue over her mouth. She shook and shortly began to sniff.

Covertly watching, Emma became concerned as she saw the woman shake harder.

Emma thought maybe she should go comfort the woman, or maybe tell the receptionist, who she felt really should be watching but didn't seem to be. But she did not want to butt in to someone else's business, and she knew John Cole would give her that annoyed frown if she did.

Hesitating, she began to get a little anxious about the matter. What if the woman got hysterical? What if she had a gun in her purse, and pulled it out and shot them? Such a happening did not seem too far-fetched at a therapist's office.

Finally, without a glance to John Cole, so as not to see him frown, Emma got up and went to the reception counter, leaned far over and whispered, "You might need to know that the woman over there is really upset."

The receptionist nodded with a reassuring expression and whispered back, "She's okay . . . it will only be a few more minutes."

Emma was relieved to know the receptionist knew about the woman, although she didn't think she was handling the matter very well.

Just as she sat down again beside John Cole and saw him frowning, a door down the hall to what had been the bedrooms opened, and a woman came out. She was crying into a tissue, too. John Cole looked as if his skin was crawling. Emma thought that she did not intend to cry. She simply did not cry in front of people.

Another minute, and a vigorous sort of woman

came striding out of the hall and over to them. She stuck out her hand, saying, "Hi, I'm Catherine Owens."

Hope flickered within Emma. This woman was firm, competent, and would understand *important* matters. Emma knew this last thing instantly, as she took in the woman's cut-to-flatter pantsuit and stylish appearance.

Furthermore, the color and style of the woman's office was a lot better than the waiting room. There was a whole wall of shelves with books, and nice pieces of artwork were hung around the rest of the room. There was a basket of magazines. Emma saw the top one was *Modern Decor*. There wasn't a reclining couch, like in therapists' offices in the movies, only a small leather loveseat and a couple of chairs, and comfortable needlepoint pillows.

Emma and John Cole sat on the couch, and the therapist, who said to call her Catherine, sat facing them in her swivel desk chair.

"Okay, so what's going on?" Catherine asked. "What problem brings you in here for counseling?"

Emma, who appreciated the direct approach, looked at John Cole, and he looked back at her. She shifted in her seat, crossing her legs. It had been *his* suggestion to come, after all. He should answer and not leave it to her.

The silence stretched. Emma recognized the intentionally patient expression on the therapist's face. Emma had used silence herself a time or two. Catherine would wait them out.

Thinking someone needed to get started, and since she and John Cole were paying, she said, "Well . . . we had decided to separate, but then Johnny—that's our son—decided to get married, so we couldn't ruin his weddin' by maybe gettin' divorced. And now we think we want to try again." She felt silly as all get-out as soon as the words left her mouth.

"How long have you been married?"

"Thirty-two years," said Emma.

Catherine's eyebrows went up. "You both must have been fairly young when you married."

Emma was familiar with the expression; she could practically see the woman's mind turning. Whenever people heard how young she and John Cole had been when they married, they generally looked at her as if expecting her to be toting a herd of barefoot children and possibly living in a beat-up travel trailer.

Emma explained that she had been seventeen and John Cole nineteen when they married. "But I wasn't pregnant," she added. "We didn't *have* to get married. In fact, our son didn't come along for six years. He's our only child. He isn't a child any-more, of course. He's twenty-six."

"Ah-huh." Catherine, who had slipped on reading glasses, was jotting on a tablet. "That would make him born in . . . 'seventy-two?"

140

Emma said yes, then added, "I call him my miracle. We never did have any more. We wanted to, but it didn't happen."

She wondered if she had been totally accurate. What might have been more truthful was that she had wanted more children but John Cole had not. She considered bringing up this point, as she watched Catherine scribbling on the tablet.

Then she saw Catherine peering curiously over the top of her glasses at her, and realized that she had been leaning forward slightly.

Catherine said, "I'm doing a quick time line to help me get to know you a bit. Let's take a look at your backgrounds. Emma, why don't you go first and tell me about your family? Do you have brothers and sisters? Parents still living?"

"I'm an only child," Emma said, then went on to explain that she was originally from North Carolina, where all of her relatives were from, and that her father was dead, but her mother was in very good health and lived at MacCoy's retirement village.

"When and from what did your father die?" Catherine asked.

"Well, in seventy-five, I think. Maybe seventy-six. I forget, but not too many years after I married. I don't know from what."

She saw Catherine pause in writing and look up at her.

"Daddy just went off one day with this woman in

town. He had gone off for as long as I remember—
he was a travelin' salesman. Sold feed. He went
down to South Carolina, and a few years later
Mama got a phone call tellin' her that he had died.
I was out here by then. I don't really know anything else about it."

"Uh-*huh*."

Watching Catherine scribbling with the pen,
Emma felt her face grow warm. Her father was not
a comfortable subject. Her mother never talked
about him.

Then Catherine asked John Cole about his
family. She called him John, despite the fact that
Emma had given his name as John Cole when she
made the appointment.

John Cole had not offered a word the whole time
and had to clear his throat. "I have two older
brothers and one sister. My father is livin', but my
mother is dead."

Catherine asked him where he was from, and the
ages of his siblings and stuff of that sort. All of
these answers required only one or two words, and
each time he waited for Catherine to ask him
before giving any further information. When she
asked him about the date and circumstances of his
mother's death, he was able to supply, "Cancer . . .
five years ago, maybe." He cast Emma a questioning look.

"Mother Berry died seven years ago in August.
She had been sick off and on for quite a few years,

then one day she died. It wasn't long and drawn out. She just passed right at home, watching *The Young and the Restless*. It was her favorite show." Emma crossed her legs again but then found herself bouncing her foot, so she uncrossed them. The sofa was not meant for someone as short as she was. Her feet barely touched the floor.

"All right. I have an overview now," Catherine said after a minute. She pulled off her glasses. "Let's get back to my original question. What specifically is the problem in your relationship?"

Emma waited a moment for John Cole to say something, but of course he wasn't going to, so she said, "We don't *have* a relationship. Oh, we don't fight. We argue a little, but we do not have great big fights. We never have done that. The thing is, we don't *talk*. And we don't have sex. I know we have been married for a long time and are middle-aged, and I don't expect it all the time, but I do think somethin' sure is wrong when a couple can't talk or have sex. This has been goin' on for about ten years, too—it isn't like it happened yesterday. When it started, we were in our thirties. I've done everything I know to keep myself attractive and to try to talk with him. I've tried to talk about this with him. I've read books and tried everything I know, but nothin' has helped."

She abruptly shut her mouth, quite astonished at having said all that she had. What seemed to have happened to her was like what happened when

143

trying to get ketchup from a bottle: she had held everything back for so long, and now, with one shake, a whole lot was flowing out. She did not dare look at John Cole. She was too embarrassed.

Catherine said, "Can we say an accurate assessment of your complaint, Emma, is that you are not receiving the intimacy you want with John and are lonely in this union?"

Emma felt a little jolted by the term "lonely." She did not like the picture it made in her mind. "I don't know if I would call it lonely, but I do think that we should act like we're married, since we *are* married," she said. "I think a husband and wife ought to be able to have a conversation about more than what's on TV. And that we should have sex."

Good Lord, help her. She could not shut up. And it was all out there now. To a stranger. She felt horribly embarrassed, but she felt even more words trying to come out. She told herself she needed to calm down, and that she would not cry or in any way be a hysterical woman.

"What do you say to this, John? Would you say that what Emma says is an accurate picture of your relationship?"

John Cole slid a sideways glance at Emma. She mostly felt it, because she did not dare look directly at him.

"I guess." He coughed into his hand. "We don't talk all that much."

"Are you happy with how things are with you and Emma?"

"No, not really, I guess."

"And why do you think you and Emma don't talk or have sex more often?"

"I don't know. I work a lot, I guess."

"Are there things that Emma does that annoy you and make you feel you don't want to talk with her or have sex with her?"

"No. She's a great wife."

Emma could hardly believe how he said that. She looked at him then, to see his look as he was praising her. And acting as if she was making up all their problems.

Then he added, "We do have sex. We did just a week or so ago. It isn't like we *never* have sex."

"We did not." Emma said instantly. "A week ago, we had split up and you were gone. We have not had sex for two months."

"Okay, then a few weeks ago. We do have sex," he said to Catherine.

"I see there is a diff—" started Catherine.

"And before that, it was two or three months," Emma said, feeling the need to set things straight. "We just don't *relate.*"

"It was not three months," John Cole said, slipping in the contradiction. "It was the night I bought the new truck."

"Okay. Two months."

That sat there for a few seconds, and then

Catherine said, "I'd like to take just a few minutes to look back at the beginning, when you two were first dating. I don't want to spend a lot of time looking back, and it is important to remember that you were young and totally different people then. But sometimes a brief look at the past helps to put today in context and gives me more of a picture. Emma, I'll start with you. What attracted you to John?"

"Well . . ." She felt a little confused with the question, having to remember so long ago. "Somethin' just seemed to pull me to him. Right from the first time I saw him, I guess. I don't mean that it was like love at first sight, but I liked him right off. I thought he was really cute, for one thing. He had this way of lookin' right at a person and givin' a slow, sexy smile. He was really sort of with-it, compared to the boys in my small town. He had been around more, bein' older and in the Navy for a year when we met. He had a good sense of humor . . . and he liked animals. And we both liked the beach. He really liked it, bein' from inland, like he was. I'd always been to the beach, but it was more fun with him, since he got such a kick out of it."

She found a lot of memories coming out about their visits to the beach, until she realized she was talking on again, so she stopped.

"And does he still smile that way?" Catherine asked. "And have a good sense of humor and like animals?"

"He still has a sense of humor—when he wants to. And every once in a while he will smile at me like that, but really not much. It's like he doesn't have time and doesn't care to make the effort. We have just lost all passion."

Then she added, "He does still like animals, though. He all the time says that he does not want me to feed any stray cats, and then he goes and does it."

"Okay. Let's stop there a minute and give John a chance. John . . . what attracted you to Emma?"

"Lots of things, I guess," he said slowly. "She was real pretty. And she was always smilin' and happy. She seemed real intelligent. She knew more things than any girl I'd ever met. I just liked bein' with her."

Catherine asked him if any of that was still true, and he said, "Yes . . . all of it."

"If you still like bein' with me," said Emma, "then—"

She shut her mouth when—in a manner Emma thought was a little rude—Catherine held up a hand toward her and said, "I'll give you a chance in a minute, Emma." And then to John Cole, "John, would you say that your security and well-being are important to Emma?"

Emma, instantly interested, looked at him.

He blinked and said, "Well, yeah . . . yes, I would."

"Emma, do you feel that your security and well-being are important to John?"

Emma, who was already thinking about it, said, "In some ways. I mean, he makes sure that our house is nice and my car is safe. He's jumped up and gone out thinkin' we had a burglar, too. He's protective like that. It's just that he doesn't realize the importance of emotional and *spiritual* security and well-being. Of havin' someone in your corner, who shows it by believin' you when you say you need to be with him and that bein' together is important." She suddenly had to struggle not to cry.

Thankfully, Catherine began to talk, although Emma was so focused on not crying that she missed most of the first part of what the woman had to say. It was something about how their coming together for therapy displayed their respect and desire for each other and their obviously deep relationship.

Emma agreed with the respect part. She certainly still respected John Cole, although she wasn't so certain about respecting their relationship. They didn't seem to have a relationship, to her mind.

Catherine was saying, "For many years, you both have poured your energy into raising your child and building a secure business and home, so much so that you've lost sight of your relationship together. You are simply no longer connecting as man and woman. What is required is to learn to reconnect."

She gave them a reassuring smile and went on

talking in an equally reassuring manner about how different men and women were, and how compatibility was something of a myth. Even though Emma thought that Catherine's soothing manner was probably a requirement for being a therapist, she appreciated it.

Then Catherine said, "Now, I have some homework to get you started," and handed them each a thin sheaf of papers.

At a glance, Emma saw a lot of questions, with spaces for answers. She peered over to see if John Cole's papers looked the same. They did. She could not imagine him with a pencil in hand and working his way through the questions.

As if Catherine read John Cole's mind, she said they didn't have to answer every question, but she recommended taking time to read through them and to think about the answers.

Then she leaned forward. "I want you to understand that during these first weeks you will be doing some reconnecting to yourselves and your lives. You need to be aware that you will experience a lot of uncomfortable emotions."

She paused and seemed to be waiting for a reply, so Emma nodded and said, "Okay."

"For that reason, I strongly recommend that you do *not* discuss your marriage or pursue sex. In fact, I suggest that you do not even spend much time together over the next few weeks. You each need some time off."

Emma felt strongly disappointed and didn't offer another okay. She and John Cole were already not discussing their marriage or having any sort of time together. What good were these sessions, if they weren't going to start something going?

"The best thing you both can do right now is relax," continued Catherine. "Stop all the *trying*. You've done that, and it has not worked. It's time to lighten up and just go with the flow, until you come back here for another session. Okay?"

Emma didn't reply to that, either. She felt the woman's instructions were aimed directly at her. She didn't think this was called for. In fact, she felt a little left out, because Catherine chatted with John Cole all the way out to the receptionist's desk.

Then John Cole exhibited the most amazing behavior. He not only jumped in with Catherine to arrange the next appointment but readily agreed, without the slightest prompting from Emma, to the suggestion to schedule *two* more appointments. Emma was as astounded as ever in her life. She wondered if he were showing off for Catherine, who pretty well seemed to assume there was no question about them coming back.

Emma had the thought, although she did fight against it when she felt it coming up and knew that it was not very helpful, but then there it was full-blown: *Why couldn't he have been this willing ten years ago? So much wear and tear could have been avoided.*

Right away, on the drive back to the Stop, Emma experienced some of those strong emotions Catherine had spoken of, and she found out that it wasn't a good idea for her and John Cole to be confined in a car when that happened.

John Cole asked her if she was okay. Whenever he did that, it just made her so annoyed. She knew he wouldn't want to hear that she was so sad that their marriage had gotten to this point, so why did he ask?

"I'm fine. Why?"

"Well, you seem awfully quiet."

"I don't have anything to say." That she was the one who generally did all the talking was quite evident. She didn't expect him to talk, but he expected it of her. She felt her hair about to stand on end. "And Catherine said for us not to talk."

After a minute John Cole came out with, "I don't think she said not to have any conversation. She meant just not to talk about our marriage."

"And what do you want to talk about? You didn't do much talkin' in there."

"What do you mean?" He looked all innocent.

"You didn't hardly say anything, John Cole. You just mostly sat there. The only thing you volunteered was to about call me a liar when I said we don't have sex."

"I answered what she asked, and I was simply givin' my view. The point is for me to give my view. It doesn't have to match yours. We *do* have sex. You just apparently forget, and you haven't said anything about it to me."

"I have too said!" She could not believe it. She shut her mouth in exasperation, but then, "And answerin' what she asks is not takin' part. She can't ask you every little question about what she may need to know."

The next instant John Cole drew back and smacked the steering wheel, yelling, "So what do you want me to say? I just don't know what you want, Emma Lou!"

He was saying more, too, but Emma didn't hear him. She was screaming back at him, "I can't stand this . . . I can't stand it anymore. I hate you! Let me out!"

She had gone haywire-flooey, knew it full well, but was too caught up to stop. She grabbed at the door handle, which thankfully did not open because of the automatic lock.

John Cole took hold of her wrist. Even though she tried to shake him off, he gripped her, while they continued to say who-knew-what to each other in the worst fight of their entire married life.

Then all of a sudden, they were stopped in front of the Berry Truck Stop, and Emma saw Shelley Dilks standing there, right in front of them. She was looking right through the windshield at them. It was just awful.

Without a word, John Cole got out of the car and slammed the door behind him, leaving Emma there in the passenger seat. Just right there. He spoke to Shelley as he passed. The woman cast Emma a curious look and hurried into the building after John Cole, as if attached to him by a line.

Emma pulled herself together enough to drive home. She sat slumped over, like a woman defeated. She had tried her heart out to do all that she knew how to do with her marriage and herself. Heaven knew only a crazy woman would have behaved as she just had. And oh, Lord, John Cole had scared her when he exploded. Remembering, she began to shake.

She had to pull over twice on the way home, because she was crying so hard. In one day she had experienced a therapy session for the first time of her life, along with the biggest fight of her marriage and the most crying she had done in years.

That evening, they were as polite as strangers to each other.

Emma gave John Cole his supper in his chair, saw him look at her in surprise, then turned around and took her meal off to her workroom, where she ate and perused the questions on the papers Catherine had given them.

John Cole had left his copy in the car, of course.

Emma had given it to him when he came home, and he had promptly laid it atop his stack of magazines. Not to be negative, but she figured the papers would be buried there six months from now.

The first page of questions was a listing of beginning statements to be completed. Not a thing about marriage, either.

The first one read: My five best qualities are . . .

She grabbed a pencil from the jar and wrote: *My smile.* Then she tapped the pencil on her lip for a few seconds before writing *cooking.* She stopped abruptly, though, with the thought that possibly something like that wasn't the type of answer Catherine was looking for.

More tapping of the pencil, and frowning. How silly. Oh, well, she would think of more later.

Statement number two read: The five things that I think made my partner fall in love with me are . . .

She wrote: *my smile . . . and I was pretty.* Everyone had said she was pretty, even John Cole.

She gazed at the statement for long seconds. Nothing else came to mind, and the statement did seem something more for John Cole to answer.

The next few statements were equally as annoying, asking why her partner might fall out of love and five hateful things she might have done in recent weeks.

She wrote down about how she had yelled at him that afternoon. It came to her that she had yelled,

"I hate you." The memory made her feel so bad that she couldn't write anything else.

Finally she came to the statement that read: I wish . . .

She began to scribble rapidly. *I wish John Cole would talk. I wish the television would explode. I wish John Cole and I could be happy with each other again. I wish John Cole would pay attention. I wish I had lived the first part of my life differently. I wish I hadn't married so fast. I wish we had had more children. I wish John Cole loved me like he used to. I wish I could love John Cole like I used to.*

She drew back and gazed at that last sentence. Tears came to her eyes.

Jamming the pencil back into the jar, she snatched up the papers and put them away in a drawer. Then she swept her hands over her worktable, as if to clear away any residue of uncomfortable feelings.

She carefully chose fine card stock of various textures and hues. Meticulously, she arranged and drew and cut and pasted. She took refuge in her craft. She set about working on the cards with the engagement announcement for the families. One for the bride and groom, one for herself and John Cole, and one for Sylvia Kinney, whom she did not yet know. Night closed around the windows, where moths fluttered and June bugs buzzed. Emma didn't hear them. She did not notice the passage of time. She was totally focused on crafting each card into a mini scrapbook, each one an heirloom.

It would be for Johnny and Gracie an offering, a way to remember how they began, so that if ever the time came that they found themselves lost, perhaps this reminder of their beginning would help them find their way back to each other.

It was one more effort in all of those since his birth to give Johnny what she had missed.

At his workbench in his shop off the garage, John Cole was working over a lawn mower's carburetor when he looked over and noticed that he had tossed several greasy sockets atop the papers from the marriage counselor, which for some inexplicable reason he had carried out here with him.

He snatched up the sockets and saw oil splotches staining the white paper. Tossing the sockets aside, he went to clear the area around the papers, and in doing this, he succeeded in knocking over a Coke can that had just enough liquid left to splatter over half the top sheet. Snatching up the papers, he smeared them with dark greasy fingerprints.

"Ah . . . geez." If Emma saw this, she would not be pleased.

He intended to read the papers, he really did, only not tonight. That afternoon had been enough for him.

With a deep breath, he very carefully placed the now-soiled papers inside one of the toolbox drawers, atop the finest of his tools, and slammed the drawer closed.

Just then there came a loud meowing. A battle-scarred yellow cat—the one that until that afternoon he had thought Emma didn't know about—came through the opened door and ambled over to the plastic dish beneath the workbench. The cat sat down and regarded John Cole with expectation.

John Cole shook dried food into its bowl and watched the animal eat. He wondered if, now that Emma had revealed knowing about the cat, maybe he should take it in to meet her. She would really like it.

In two seconds of looking into the future, he saw Emma feeding it salmon and steak, and pretty soon it would be fat and in the house, curling up in John Cole's chair and sleeping in his bed.

"You're okay right where you are, buddy."

He went to the side door and looked toward the house, where he could see light shining from the windows of her office, and Emma inside, bending over her drawing table.

He thought, as he invariably did, that she was as pretty today as the first day he had seen her. It seemed to him that he got older, worn and tired and limping along, about like the old mower he was working on, but Emma was as lively now as then.

He stood there gazing at her for long minutes, then returned to the workbench and the carburetor, something he felt competent to take apart and put back together.

13

In the Beginning
1966

Emma and John Cole met on New Year's Eve, when Emma went out driving with three other girls from her senior high-school class. The girls were from a fast crowd, and had grown faster still with the thrill of being young women in their last year of school. Emma had taken up with them only a few weeks into this school year, when the headiness of being a senior had propelled her out of her shyness. This, coupled with providing a much-needed tampon to one of the girls in a particularly crucial moment, had put her into a new and quite nice *in* position of being *in* with the *in* group.

In a big Chrysler belonging to the head girl of the group, they all went on a lark up across the Virginia line to Norfolk, where they ended up meeting a party of sailors at a McDonald's drive-through.

Upon flirting with the group of sailors, Emma began to realize fully that she was attractive, something that had slowly begun to dawn on her. Until that time, she had immersed herself in books and silent dreams, and been influenced by her mother's efforts to keep her from being "too full of herself" with pretty clothes or makeup. Of course, by that year, Elvis movies and *Seventeen Magazine* were making it even to their little provincial part of the world. Emma had secretly begun to lighten her hair.

At the end of an evening of flirting, first in the McDonald's parking lot and then following the sailors to a party at a private house, Emma had paired off with John Cole, whom she considered by far the most attractive all around. There was something about the way he looked at her with his very blue eyes, something delightful that happened to her when he smiled at her. And he was exceedingly polite and didn't act as if he had a right to jump on her, as did a number of the other sailors. Emma might have been lacking experience, but she had a wisdom born of wide reading. She knew what was what.

When John Cole called her the following week, she could not believe that such a young man, from what sounded like a very good family, and who owned his own car—my heavens, a Galaxie 500 convertible!—and who was just so handsome and sweet and adorable, was actually interested in her.

Yet right then, had anyone asked her, she would have admitted to having decided that she had met her future husband and saw no reason to look further.

On Saturday, he drove south for a first date and to meet her mother—her father being out of town somewhere and totally forgotten—and had so impressed her mother with his manners, his sporty Ford and the fact that his family owned a hardware store, that her mother had said to Emma, "You'll be well cared for. Don't let him get away."

That had pretty much been the extent of her mother's advice in regard to marriage and a future. Not one word of consideration for higher education or a career. At that time, her mother did not have an education or a career herself. None of the Macomb women did. When they became of decent marriageable age—anything from seventeen upward was decent—they found their Prince Charming and married him, with the idea of living happily every after. Why it never occurred to any of them that life did not work in the way of Prince Charmings was a mystery. All but one of them had been married and divorced, and several more than once. They seemed to just keep going around the same pole made of men.

Emma's mother seemed to have somehow bumbled off the path when, after her husband had run off for the final time, she had enrolled in the local junior college. It had been pursuit of a college professor that had gotten her there. While nothing had come of the romance, Emma's mother had obtained enough education to get a teaching certificate. By that time, age had more or less been against her in securing a husband of a sort she could manage; however, with the good luck of Emma's father dying, she had taken on, even though divorced, the much preferred status of widowhood.

Emma and John Cole began dating steadily. A total of three times, John Cole made the trip south, but all the other times it was Emma taking the bus north, or catching a ride with someone. The bulk of their courtship took place through the mail. She wrote him every day, sometimes twice a day, long missives of five or more pages filled with flowing script, to which John Cole replied once or twice a week, very short letters in short printed words. He said he was not one to write much, and she had accepted this. Indeed, her own father had never approached conversation with her, nor really much with her mother that she had ever seen. She had for years known weeks when she did not even see her father, who was a traveling feed salesman during the week, and divided his weekends between watching baseball on television and passing out on the couch.

In the spring, she and John Cole decided to marry, setting the date for two days after Emma's high-school graduation. John Cole had not surprised her with a ring.

". . . I, uh, didn't want to take a chance on gettin' somethin' you might not like," he had said.

They had gone together to the jewelry store, where Emma made a selection according to the pleasure and displeasure that she read on his face as she tried on various rings.

"This one," she said at last.

"You sure?"

After a good study of his face, she said, "Yes," nodding at first tentatively, but upon seeing his smile widen, she said, "Oh, yes!"

He had stunned her by pulling out cash money that he had saved, surely since early in their relationship, paying in full for the entire wedding-ring set. She saw far into her future, and saw it looking good. The same could safely be said for John Cole. They left the store with their arms wrapped around each other.

Family Album

14

As the last note of John Conlee's voice singing "The Backside of Thirty" died in his earphones, Winston leaned into the microphone.

"You are listenin' to the *Home Folks Show,* where it's time for our new feature, *Around Town and Beyond,* with Belinda Blaine, brought to you by Blaine's Drugstore, where they still get up at night for you. Belinda's going to give us all the news and gossip going on in our community. Welcome, Belinda."

"Hello, Winston. **Hello, ever'body out there!**"

Winston moved her microphone. "You don't need to shout. The microphone picks up real easy."

"Oh. Okay." Belinda put a hand to her bosom and looked over to where Emma sat. Emma nodded encouragingly. Belinda looked back down at the sheet of paper in front of her. She was shaking so hard that she could hardly read. "Okay . . . first up . . ."

"You can speak a *little* louder," Winston whispered.

She wished he would make up his mind. "First we have the people news. The latest count on the pantyhose debate . . ."

165

Winston jumped in with, "We might like to tell the folks who may not have heard us the past few days that one of the hot topics around town concerns the wearing of panties with pantyhose. The latest statistic I've heard from my daughter Charlene is somethin' like twenty-eight who wear panties with pantyhose and five who go without."

"Yes . . ." Belinda was a little startled at him jumping in like that and had to get herself back on track. "You are right about that being the debate. And our count is now up to thirty-two who wear panties with pantyhose and still five who do not. There is one woman, who shall remain nameless, who reports that she never wears panties at all, period." She paused, looking at Winston, who thankfully remained quiet.

"It has been decided that thongs are to be counted as panties. We are continuing the count, so if any listeners out there want to take part, you can call or drop by the drugstore and leave a report. It is okay to tell about a relative or friend's preference, however, you are on the honor system not to make up numbers. We have had one woman, who shall remain nameless but who should know better, who tried to be counted more than once."

Thinking that maybe she was getting a little carried away, she glanced nervously over at Emma, who was smiling and gave her another encouraging nod.

"On to other news," she said more confidently. "Little Jenny Montgomery, whose horse took down several flags when it got away from her at the grand-entry to the Valentine Youth Round-Up Rodeo last Friday, did badly break her arm, but her mother reports Jenny is doing just fine. Her parents have good insurance, so no need for a collection, although her mother said she would sure appreciate visitors.

"I've been asked to say that there is no truth to the rumor that my mother Vella Blaine and local attorney Jaydee Mayhall are havin' an affair . . . and Connor Davis wants it known that he is back in town, and divorced from Tamara and available. Tamara said she is happy down in Dallas and is never comin' back. I won't say what I want to say about that."

Seeing Emma smiling widely, Belinda imagined lots of people smiling all across Valentine. Winston had sat back, so wasn't likely to jump in. Belinda straightened her shoulders.

"We have a new Valentine-ite this mornin'. Imperia Brown gave birth to a twelve-pound girl last night. You heard correctly—twelve pounds. Her daddy set a sign out front of their house that says Home of the Whopper, which is what he threatened to name her, but Imperia says her name is Jewel, and she is twelve full carats. As the long-awaited girl in the family, you know she is goin' to be spoiled rotten, which is her due.

"Now for activities around town. The Valentine Works Department will be cleanin' the fire hydrants this afternoon at one o'clock, and y'all know what that means. Don't go washin' your whites today.

"Miz Lillian Jennings reports that according to the U.S. Census Bureau, the state of Oklahoma is part of the Southern region of the U.S.A. Starting this week, she will be teaching a four-part series at the Valentine Library on how to trace your Southern roots. This will be on Wednesdays at 10:00 a.m. and is free of charge.

"Don't forget the Fire Department Ladies Auxiliary's third annual Christmas in July craft fair comin' up next month. That will be at the Auxiliary's house on Main Street.

"I want to emphasize that this is a fund-raiser, folks. To give you an idea of the delights available, there are twenty registered booths. We have wooden toys, decorative baskets, an artist all the way from New Mexico, glass etching and much more. I want to personally invite everyone to come by the Blaine's Drugstore booth and view the works of our own Emma Berry. We will be offering her line of greeting and note cards, as well as magnets and notepads, also, the finest in fragrances and nutrition supplements. These make great gifts all year long.

"Going beyond Valentine today—The Servants' Fellowship Church up in Lawton is holdin' the second annual Glorious Women's Day, Saturday, July eighteenth.

"Are you a woman? Are you a woman who feels like a lost sock in the dryer of the world? Are you ready to be revived and renewed and mended up into the woman that God meant you to be? Then, ladies, this full day of celebration, fellowship and encouragement is for you. The doors open at 8:00 a.m., with coffee and tea and scones—I think those are fancy biscuits—served in the lobby. The . . . program starts at nine and runs until five. There'll be a buffet luncheon. You can call Naomi Smith at the First Methodist Church right here in Valentine for more information. Naomi went last year and says this is a valuable seminar for every woman, and don't let not being a church-going Christian stop you from attending. We are all one in the Lord, and here's your chance to get a full day off, ladies. And yes, that is exactly what Naomi said. Any questions or comments, address them to her.

"Well, that's all I have. I will see you again next week, and until then, you can call me with your news. Back to you, Winston."

"Thank you, Miss Belinda. Everyone knows that you are in the know. And I think, since Miss Belinda brought it up right here on the air, a good topic for today's discussion is *do you wear panties under your pantyhose?*"

Belinda made her way around the back of

Winston's chair and gave him a smack on the arm. It was just like him to steal from her.

As she and Emma were leaving the little studio, Belinda leaned over and whispered to Willie Lee that he could have an extra scoop of ice cream, and for free, that afternoon. Behind them, Winston was saying, "We'll begin takin' your calls while we listen to 'Jolene' from that glorious woman, Dolly Parton."

Like schoolgirls, they burst out of the little block building into the hot summer sunshine, the both of them laughing. Emma was laughing mostly at Belinda laughing.

At last, Belinda felt she could breathe. "Ohmygosh, sugar, I about died at the beginnin'. I have never in my life been so terrified. The silliest thing, but I was."

To which Emma said how wonderfully she had done.

"Oh, my." Belinda fanned her face. "I did do good, didn't I?"

"Honey, you were delightful."

Belinda felt she had been just that, and she had loved it, after getting past the first fright. She had not known how much she would love it. She never, ever liked to be the center of attention, but on the radio, it was different. On the radio, she was hidden from view but got to say what she wanted.

At first Belinda had been pushing for Emma to be on Winston's show, and to publicize both her own line of card designs and the craft fair held by the Auxiliary, of which both were members. But Emma had refused, and in the way these sorts of things go, somehow it had ended up with Belinda starting a little sort of gossip column on Winston's show. When it came to the morning to do it, though, she had suddenly been terrified and had called Emma to come with her.

In the past months, since Belinda had been selling Emma's unique greeting cards at the drugstore, Emma had become Belinda's best friend, a fact that, in her high emotional state, she felt teary about. In fact, Emma was the first close female friendship Belinda had ever formed. She had always been easier with men. Her sister, Margaret, was the same way. They had gotten this trait from their mother and *because* of their mother.

She drove over to the drugstore, where Emma had parked her car. On the sidewalk, she impulsively took Emma's hand. Belinda almost never touched another woman, but suddenly here she was squeezing Emma's hand and saying, "Thank you. Thank you so much for comin' with me this mornin'."

"You are welcome. But, honey, I didn't do anything." Emma looked shy.

"Yes, you did."

Belinda entered the drugstore, where several

people congratulated her on the radio appearance. Even her mother said nice things. Belinda behaved as if it wasn't any big deal. She would never let on to anyone other than Emma, especially her mother, how very frightened she had been.

There were many sides to people, she thought, remembering Emma and watching her mother and taking note of people, many who she had known all her life but now saw in a different light as they came in and ordered drinks and lunch.

From being starkly aware of her own fear that morning, she had a fresh appreciation that everyone had their own fears, and that they each tried to hide them.

Today she had revealed herself to several thousand people on the radio. She pictured them out there, enamored of her, as she was sure they were.

Maybe she could talk with Lyle if she talked to him over the radio.

Miss Belinda was still in a good mood when Willie Lee arrived. She was in such a good mood that she not only made his ice cream as promised, but allowed him and Munro to take the ice cream over to Willie Lee's favorite spot on the wide windowsill on the other side of the magazine rack. Normally she did not allow him to have ice cream anywhere near the magazines.

Munro quickly licked his ice cream down, but

Willie Lee's sat melting beside him, while he lost himself in glossy magazine pictures of boys riding skateboards right up into the air.

It was an odor that brought him out of his fantasies.

It was a fart.

He looked up to see a boy standing looking at the magazine rack. The boy was a little taller than Willie Lee, with thick dark hair. His baggy jeans and T-shirt were torn and dirty. He looked like the tough boys at school, but Willie Lee did not remember ever seeing him before.

The boy tossed aside the magazine he'd been looking at, and it fell to the floor. He didn't pick it up but went to another magazine.

Willie Lee gazed at the boy's jeans and thought how a lot of the bigger boys wore such jeans with holes. But his mother wouldn't buy them for him.

The boy turned and saw Willie Lee looking at him. "What're you lookin' at?"

Willie Lee looked down, his heart beating fast. Sometimes boys spoke harshly to him. He didn't know why. But Munro rose to stand at his knee. No one could bother him with Munro around.

The boy slid himself down beside Willie Lee. "Hey . . . are you that boy that's sometimes on the radio?"

Willie Lee looked at him, hoping a little bit. "Yes."

The boy's eyes studied Willie Lee.

Willie Lee blinked, his nose burning. The boy was stinky.

"I seen you around . . . pushin' that ol' man that talks on the radio . . . you and that dog. What's his name?"

"Mun-ro."

"How come he gets to come in this store? Your folks own it?"

"No. Aunt Vel-la owns the store."

"Figures. Does he do tricks?" The boy nodded toward Munro.

Without Willie Lee saying anything, Munro sat and extended a paw to the boy, whose eyes widened.

"Cool . . ." The boy shook Munro's paw. "Does he do any other tricks?"

Munro dropped as if dead for several seconds, then rolled over twice, then picked up the magazine the boy had thrown on the floor and brought it to Willie Lee.

"Wow," said the boy, his eyes wide. "I wish I had a dog like that." Grinning, he petted Munro, who kindly allowed the touch.

Just then, a big boy came hurrying around the end of the magazine rack. "Come on, Nicky. We gotta go."

"Hold on a minute . . . watch this dog. . . ."

"I said come *on!*" The big boy grabbed the smaller one and dragged him up.

Willie Lee saw the boy, Nicky, stuff the magazine he had been holding under his shirt.

"Don't you tell nobody, or I'll get ya'," he said in a harsh whisper over his shoulder.

Willie Lee and Munro watched the two boys go out the door and pass by the wide window. For the space of a breath, Willie Lee saw a dark shadow that seemed to envelope the pair, and in a flash of knowing, he knew that the boys were desperate, in trouble somehow, and hungry. He felt all of these things inside of himself as he watched them. Then they were gone from sight.

A little while later, Miss Charlene's purse came up missing. "It's that little red one I ordered from you, Belinda."

She said she had hung it on the back of her chair when she had sat down with Mr. Winston and left it there when she went to the restroom. Mr. Winston said he had gotten up to make Miss Claire's strawberry milkshake when she came in, and an order of two barbeques to go for Larry Joe at the Texaco, because Aunt Vella was off with Jaydee Mayhall again.

Mr. Winston thought maybe Miss Charlene had made a mistake and put the purse somewhere or hadn't even brought it.

She got mad at him and said, "I know when I bring a purse, Daddy."

Willie Lee knew how she felt. Sometimes people did not believe him, either.

Everyone looked everywhere for the red purse, but no one found it.

"I saw some boy I've never seen before come in and go over to the pain relief and cold-remedy aisle," Miss Belinda said. "I try to keep an eye when I don't know somebody, but the UPS man arrived with my order from HSN and I got involved with that. I'm callin' Lyle."

Deputy Lyle Midgett came right away and talked to everyone who was left in the store. He wrote things down in his little notebook.

Then Mrs. Berry came in to get barbeque to go and told about a boy having stolen some candy a few weeks earlier in the Berry Quick Stop. That was where Willie Lee liked to sometimes get a Bama Pie after school. He had not gotten a Bama Pie since summer vacation had started, and he thought he would like to have one. If Paris was there, she always made it fun, like giving him a birthday present. Paris was his friend.

Just after Deputy Lyle left, Aunt Vella and Jaydee Mayhall came in, and pretty soon the both of them and Mr. Winston and Miss Charlene and even Miss Belinda, who generally didn't enter in, were mad and hollering at each other.

Mrs. Berry went right behind the counter and got the pitcher of cold tea and went around pouring glasses for everyone, calming everyone down. And then Mr. Winston told about Mrs. Stella Purvis, who ran the Merry Males Maid Service, telling him that she was the one who never wore panties under anything. After Miss Belinda's spot, he had brought this up on the radio but still not told her name over the air. Miss Vella said that he was telling Miz Stella's name now to everyone, so he might as well have said it over the air.

Throughout all of that, no one asked Willie Lee anything. He sat there, just as he often did, as if he was invisible, watching and listening.

15

Messy Business

They were going for it. Getting the pool. They chose a lovely, yet simple, design that the builder felt he could complete in six weeks, eight at the most. He was a confident sort of fellow, who said he could start immediately.

John Cole did not feel the builder's availability was a very good sign. He thought a really good builder would be booked up.

Emma said, "Why shouldn't we simply be fortunate?"

Immediately the bridal-shower barbeque was set for the fourth weekend in August. That would give plenty of time for the pool's projected completion and about a month before the wedding, the correct timing, according to the advice of two experts Emma read. Host a shower much earlier, and you ran a greater risk of having to face returning all the gifts, should something happen and the couple not get married after all. Later, it was too close to the wedding, causing havoc.

Early one morning, work crews with various equipment descended on them. From that time on, the yard was like an anthill swarming with muscular young men, with leathery tanned skin under ball caps, all in various stages of activity. The earth seemed to tremble in anticipation.

John Cole, in his work-worn Resistol, dark Ray-Bans and rolled-up sleeves, pored over plans and oversaw details, despite having argued with Emma up one side and down the other that a pool was a bad idea.

What still annoyed the fire out of Emma was that he had not wanted the pool when she was the one wanting it, but just as soon as Johnny and Gracie expressed a little bit of enthusiasm for the idea, he jumped in and said they would do it—*like it was his idea.*

Nearly before the ink had dried on the deposit check, Emma recognized that she had made a large error in coming up with the idea of building a pool.

She did not say it aloud, of course, but she had to admit to herself that John Cole had been right about there being a lot more to having a pool built than she had ever in her life supposed. It had seemed so simple. As she had thought of it, all she had to do was pick up the phone, call the pool company, and the next thing she would have a pool in her yard, complete with patio and landscaping and looking like the sample picture that she had clipped out of *Country Home.*

She had not imagined the many and confusing decisions about square footage and placement, soil estimation, and concrete, vinyl or fiberglass, not to mention what trees and bushes might need to come out. One of the big elms had to go, and there was more to getting rid of a tree than Emma had ever known. Tree trimmers came and cut down the towering elm limb by limb, which then, for an extra fee, had to be chopped up for firewood. There was also Johnny's old basketball court, which had to be broken up and hauled away.

Harder to dispatch were the memories. Each time one of the tree limbs had fallen, Emma would wince and remember things about the tree—how John Cole had tied a rope swing from it for Johnny, and then how she had used the swing herself at lonely times when Johnny and John Cole were both away. When the noise of the jackhammer had started on the basketball court, Emma had gone into the house and all the way into the bathroom to gaze at herself in the mirror, wondering where the years had gone.

Looking at her image in the glass so closely, she was forced to see not only a few more lines around her eyes, but also that she had the tremendous tendency to complicate matters. She could not understand her own actions. Why in the world had she entertained for one moment the idea of building a pool at this particularly stressful time in their lives? Was trying to recover her marriage and get another one started off on the right foot not enough of an effort? How could she not remember previous projects?

There had been the remodeling of the kitchen, when she decided that, since they were doing that, they might as well do the bathroom, too. There were days of not being able to cook and having to shower in five minutes, so that John Cole could keep the water turned off while he worked.

And the time they decided to tile the front entry and ended up ripping up every bit of carpet and laying tile all through the house, clear to the bedrooms.

And even the redwood swing-set for Johnny—by the time it was finished, they had added on a double-deck fort, and the project had taken a week and a half of hard work in the hot sun.

It always started out like such a wonderful idea, and she ended up hating it all, and once John Cole started, he would turn all his attention to the project and none to her and their marriage. Why had she not thought of any of this?

She made the mistake of voicing these questions to her mother, who said, "You *never* remember any of it. I've watched you. It is like you have no memory or idea of it. It's because you have never seen reality and always let your imagination run away with you."

"Thank you, Mother," Emma said. "But I can dig my own grave. In fact, they are starting the hole out back right now."

To deal with her sense that the matter had gotten out of control, each morning Emma took out refreshments and walked around like a Red Cross worker, serving plastic cups of cold tea and cookies to the crew. John Cole told her that the men brought their own drinks and took a good lunch break in town, but Emma did not feel she could have people spending all day in her yard and not serve something. At least it was something that she knew how to do to help with the progress.

Also, among the workers was one young man, surely not out of his teens, who was so skinny that Emma couldn't stand it. After the first time he wolfed down three cookies, she ended up bringing out peanut butter and jelly sandwiches and fruit, as well.

She was poring over pictures of patio furniture and trying to ignore the sound of a digging machine in the yard when the back door opened and John Cole came through, every stride announcing big trouble.

"Well, *your* pool just went up in cost by another six thousand dollars."

Her pool?

She watched him jerk open the refrigerator. "The

sewer line is not where it was supposed to be."

She wondered how a sewer line could migrate.

He brought out a Coke and slammed the door closed. "If you want your pool, we're gonna have to move the line. Dig it up and re-lay it. To make the completion date, that's gonna mean overtime."

He gazed at her, as if demanding some sort of answer.

Her mind cast around for salvation. "I thought they checked for the sewer line and said it was clear." Immediately, from his expression, she knew that had not been a helpful thing to say.

"Yes, they checked and found *a* sewer line. It is there, just like it shows on the old plans of the house. Unfortunately, that is an old line, and there is a new one, put in before we bought the house, and that's the one in use. It runs parallel to the old for only two feet, then it angles off and runs right across the yard." His tone was like the jackhammer the men had used to break up the basketball court.

Emma took this all in as fast as possible, and what came out of her was, "Do you want to call it all off?"

His eyes widened.

"We can do that and just go with a patio," she said. "Then we wouldn't have all this extra strain. I am perfectly agreeable to simply having a patio, right there where *our* pool would have been." She took special note that his eyes blinked when she said *our*.

"We can't do that! We've started on this now. We've taken out the tree and started diggin'. We're committed."

We ought to be committed, she thought, seeing him looking at her like she had lost her mind.

Her reply was, "Yes, we *can* change our minds." She put forth a calmness she had not known she could possess. "It is Goode Pool and *Patio.* We can just tell them to build us a patio with our down payment." Suddenly the urge to run away from home left her.

John Cole gazed at her for a moment in which she didn't blink.

Then his gaze slid sideways. He raked a hand through his hair. Something in the way he did it caused a softness to spring into her heart and sort of melt all over her.

"They're already diggin'," he said. "We're this far, we might as well finish," and he looked at her hopefully.

"I just want you to know that if you want to stop now, it's okay with me. The most important thing is for us to get along and be together for Johnny's wedding."

After a long moment, he said, "I don't want to stop. Not now."

"Okay." She tried not too appear too satisfied.

He left at a slower pace than he had entered, and she sat there gazing at the muddy footprints he had left behind.

As she got on her knees to wipe up the mud, all the while feeling the muddiness inside of herself, too, she thought that she was never going to see arguing in a favorable light, not ever, and she'd had about enough, too, of trying to understand herself and her marriage. No wonder people got divorced. It certainly was a lot easier and less messy to just give up.

But then, if one did not go through a mess, one would never get a pool, and probably the same for a good marriage, too.

Some thirty minutes later, the back door again opened. Emma looked toward it with hesitancy to see John Cole with face alight somewhere between sheepishness and elation.

"I just want to let you know that we don't have to move the pipes after all. We're turnin' the pool. Just thought I'd check—does that work for you?"

She told him that he was very clever to come up with a solution, because she had no doubt that the solution had come more from him than the pool builder, who was too busy worrying about three other jobs that he was doing and had pretty much laid this one in John Cole's hands.

"Whatever you think is necessary and best works for me," she replied, quite proud of *herself*, too.

"All right then, it's a go." With a happy expression, he shut the door.

As the days and work progressed, Emma repeatedly reminded herself that the important thing was that they were getting a pool that not only was going to serve wonderfully for the bridal-shower barbeque but would be a family gathering place for years to come.

Judging the importance of an issue was a saving grace that Emma had picked up in their marriage counseling sessions, of which they had now had three.

She had been a little surprised to see that, most of the time, the things that seemed upsetting really were not all that important in the long run. Yet she was a little disappointed that the marriage counseling seemed to be producing little in the way of positive results. It seemed like she and John Cole were getting worse, not better. It seemed that they got into an argument about every other day, although none so bad as the one that had happened after the first session.

Neither one of them mentioned *that* argument, not even to Catherine. Of course, it would have had to be Emma to bring it up, because John Cole still never brought anything up. He did, however, continue to go willingly to the sessions, and he would talk about a subject when Emma brought it up.

Contrary to how things seemed to Emma, however, Catherine said that the arguing showed their marriage had improved. She said that couples who bottled things up, as Emma and John Cole had been doing for years and years, were actually more in jeopardy than couples who argued constantly.

According to Catherine, Emma and John Cole had sat on a lot of words and emotions over many years, and now those words and emotions needed to come out. She used the illustration of a boil that has to be lanced so that the pus can drain away in order for healing to begin.

Emma did not appreciate her marriage and life being compared to a boil, and she was having trouble with the idea of arguing as actually being healing. She was doing her best, though, to keep an open mind about everything Catherine told them. The woman had special training, after all, and they were paying her.

To help them become more comfortable with the process of learning to face conflict, Catherine suggested that, between sessions, Emma and John Cole write down when they were having an "angry moment" as she called them, and then bring these concerns to be discussed in-session.

The previous week, Emma had brought a whole notebook page to the third session. That was when Catherine had brought up the idea of asking how important something was.

John Cole, of course, did not write anything down, or if he did, he did not show it. He appeared to be the calm one—a picture that was not all that accurate, Emma could have told Catherine.

Since the third session, Emma had continued to write down her concerns, which really did help to calm her. However, at future sessions, she did not intend to pull out her list unless John Cole brought out one of his own first.

The digital clock on her worktable read 1:35 a.m. when she finally laid aside her colored pencil and stretched her aching back. It would do.

She was pleased with her efforts, but her neck was stiff, her back hurt, and she thought she just might throw herself in front of a fast-moving truck if she had to think of one more card design.

When Belinda had begun selling her cards, Emma had been so excited. People liked them! She felt like a real artist! But now that she had to produce on a timetable, a contrary part of her was rebelling. It had been a hard struggle to finish even four new designs. Her mind simply balked, as stubborn as a recalcitrant child. Her muse wanted to think for hours about the situation with her marriage and the pool and the barbeque and wedding details, not to mention fantasies of being grandmother to the most wonderful grandchildren ever. With all of that to think about, she had great difficulty drumming up enthusiasm for the production of greeting cards.

After turning out the light over her worktable, she

went through the house lit by a bright moon. In the kitchen, she turned out the light over the sink and then paused at the back door to stare out at the yard.

Rather than heaps of dirt and wood frames for concrete, she saw the finished pool with water shimmering in the moonlight, and she and John Cole floating in chairs, a fragrant warm breeze gently stirring the leaves of the trees. Candles appeared all around the edge of the pool, and music came out of the darkness. It was George Strait singing a love song. John Cole had a bottle of champagne in a floating bucket. He poured a glass and gave it to Emma, then poured his own and led them in a toast.

Her mother was right: she did have quite an imagination. And it was a blessing. It was imagination and hope that kept people from throwing themselves in front of speeding trucks and propelled them to get up and try another day, even in the face of all they experienced.

In the family room, the television was tuned to the Speed Channel and John Cole was asleep in his big recliner. This scene was something of a jolt, coming right after her extensive imaginings.

She gazed down at John Cole for a long time. So often in his sleep he frowned deeply, and he was doing that now, as if he were working out some problem with the pool or with Berry Corp. *Or maybe with me,* she thought. Often he did look at her as if he could not fathom her.

Taking up the remote, she clicked off the television, and as she set the remote down, her gaze returned to John Cole. She thought: *This is the man to whom I have been married since I was a teenager. This is the man I have lain with and had a child with and pledged to God to share my life with.*

Hesitantly, wondering whatever she would say to him should he waken, she squeezed herself into the chair beside him. She had to move his arm, but he did no more than take a deep breath. She wiggled a bit and got her head onto his shoulder. His heart beat loudly in her ear. The position was not at all comfortable, but she continued to lie there, to listen to his heartbeat and his breathing next to her.

She would not have done it, of course, had he been awake, for a lot of reasons that she did not want to think about at that moment. She kept telling herself she was going to get back up, but she did not, and fell asleep.

John Cole awoke around four in the morning and found Emma wedged against him. He didn't know what to make of it. He scratched his head with his free hand and moved enough to ease his back and the arm upon which Emma lay.

She settled more deeply against him.

He smoothed her hair, then smoothed it again and gently laid his chin upon it, embracing her carefully with his other arm. Then he fell back to sleep.

He slept off and on for another few hours and was awake but pretending to sleep when Emma awakened and got out of the chair. He seriously doubted that he would be able to get up too easily.

On the morning of their fifth marriage counseling session, as she gathered John Cole's shirts for the laundry, a New Hope Counseling Center business card fluttered out of one of the pockets. No surprise. Each time after their session, the receptionist gave them a new card with the date and time of their next appointment. John Cole always stuck it in his pocket, because Emma noted the appointment on her pocket planner.

But her eyes fell on the card as she went to throw it in the wastebasket. The date penciled in was for the past Friday.

That was odd. She took a second look at the card.

She could not have made a mistake about their appointment being for today, which was Tuesday. She and John Cole had confirmed it with each other before he had left early that morning. They were meeting at the counseling office at two in the afternoon. John Cole was catching up on business while the pool building crew was occupied at another site. He would be visiting each of the Berry stores and a couple of suppliers, while Emma shopped for party items for the barbeque.

The time on this card was even wrong. It was for eleven in the morning.

And why was there a circle around Ted Owens' name? Catherine's name should . . .

A great light came on behind her eyes.

This was John Cole's personal appointment.

And he had not said a word to her.

She gazed at the card for long seconds. Then she grabbed up John Cole's shirts and headed for the laundry room. She put the shirts of the man who did not tell her important things in his life into the washer and switched the water to scalding hot.

Dropping the lid of the washer so that it banged, she went to the kitchen and drank stale coffee that she warmed-over in the microwave, the door of which she closed so hard it bounced open—twice. While she stood drinking the steaming coffee, she tapped the business card on the counter, thinking thoughts along the lines of: here she was again. How did she always end up in this confusing place? What had she done over thirty-two years to end up like this? How could she be so deficient that she could not talk to her husband and he to her? What other things had he not told her? Maybe she had just better ask him.

The telephone rang. By then, she had a lot to say to John Cole. She raced to answer, glancing at the caller ID and—seeing what she thought was John Cole's cell phone, ah-ha!—said, "I'm glad I caught you . . ." Then came her mother's voice.

191

Emma had a moment of disorientation. She had been so upset—and myopic—that she hadn't read the entire number, and the first digits of her mother's number were the same as John Cole's.

Her mother was saying, ". . . organization called League of the South, and they show Oklahoma on their map, big as lightnin'. And according to the *Congressional* . . ."

"Mama, I can't talk now, the toilet's runnin' over," she out-and-out lied, and her tone was rude.

"Well . . . okay, honey," her mother said. "Call me later, please? I want a box of pictures from your . . ."

Emma hung up and considered calling John Cole, then decided she would not speak of this on the phone. She would bring it out in their session with Catherine.

There was no trying on outfits. She went right for the smart summer-silk pantsuit. From the rear of the closet, she brought forth the little open-toed black patents Belinda had sold her. Two-and-a-half-inch heels. She had questioned being able to walk in them, but had not one difficulty. Checking her image in the mirror before leaving the house, she was satisfied to see that she looked like she knew a thing or two in many areas.

She drove over to Duncan and did the shopping that she wanted to do before the session. She had no trouble deciding between plastic or real glasses and dinnerware, or cheap or elaborate poolside furniture. She chose the real, the elaborate and the costly. She got it all done in a shockingly short time and arrived fifteen minutes early at the counseling offices, with plenty of time to visit the restroom, get the mascara smudges wiped from beneath her eyes and replenish her lipstick. Then she sat with crossed legs, one open-toed foot bouncing, and watched the door for John Cole, while she went over in her mind just how to greet him and what she wanted to say to him.

As it turned out, John Cole was late. She stopped thinking about what she wanted to say to him and worried that he might not come at all. Catherine had just greeted her when John Cole came rushing in the door.

By the time they'd got all settled on Catherine's sofa and Catherine had asked if either of them had anything particular to discuss, Emma had built up such a head of steam that she instantly said, "Yes, I do. I would like to know why my husband cannot discuss important matters in his life with me."

She then pulled the business card from her purse and handed it to John Cole. Watching his face carefully, seeing the damning evidence all over it, she explained in an explicit manner how she had found the card while taking care of his laundry.

"I guess I am fully trusted with washin' your dirty shirts and underwear, but not with the information that you have decided to have private counseling."

John Cole made no reply.

Across from them, Catherine said, "I see you are upset, Emma. Let's . . ."

"Yes, I am upset. I thought the purpose of comin' here was to bring us together. You knew he went to see your husband, didn't you?"

"Yes, I did, but . . ."

"See. I was the last to know." She had known the truth of it, but hearing it, a little bomb went off inside of her. "I live with him, I am his wife, and he did not tell me. He's just livin' this secret life, all apart. If he can't tell me this, I wonder what else he is doin' that he cannot tell me." She shut her mouth, because she was near tears and amazed at the line of her own thinking.

"What do you mean by that?" John Cole said then.

"Just anything you think it means."

"Do you think I'm runnin' around? Where would I have the time? Tell me that."

"I did not say that, but it is a thought. Not tellin' me things like this is the same as lyin'."

He shook his head, as if thinking she were crazy. "This is why I didn't tell you—I can't talk to you, because you get all upset about everything."

"I do *not* get all upset about everything! You don't think anything I think is important." She managed to say that with admirable calm, while more little bombs were going off in her all over the place. She actually looked to the side with the thought of getting a magazine to smack him.

By then they were each plastered to their end of the sofa, and Catherine was able to jump in and urge calm.

"Let's back up a little and take a look at what is going on here."

"What's goin' on is that I am good enough to clean his clothes, his dishes and his toilet, but not for him to discuss his life and our marriage."

"I'm here discussin' our marriage. I've been here for weeks."

"Huh. Your body may be here, but your mind is at work, or on the pool, or wherever. . . ."

Catherine held up a hand to both of them. "All right, let's slow down here and examine just what is going on. Now, Emma, are you saying that you feel angry at your situation in the marriage?"

"How I feel is *left out.* Oh, yes, he talks to me about bills or house repairs or that he might buy a new car, but not anything personal. Not anything that matters—anything like this—somethin' personal that's botherin' him—somethin' I have a *right* to know—he doesn't talk about."

"So you feel you have a right to know that John had a private counseling session?"

"Yes, I do. I am *married* to him. We are supposed to share together . . . he and I. That's the whole point of bein' married, as far as I'm concerned. I guess I may not be the sort of wife that a man can share with, but I have been comin' here to try to learn. I can say that."

"Do you think that a more accurate description of your feeling is hurt at your perception of being blocked out by John Cole?"

"There's no perception to it. It *is*."

"Is it also that you feel you are failing?"

In response, Emma's head came up. Catherine gazed at her, waiting.

Emma came out with, "What I feel is that when it comes to discussin' anything of a personal nature, I am the one who does all the talkin', and John Cole doesn't say a thing. He does not share anything about *himself*."

Catherine nodded and turned her attention to John. "I think it is important for Emma to know that you called me and asked if your consulting Ted would affect your sessions here, and I told you that talking with Ted might be quite helpful to you. Now I think it might be helpful for you to explain to Emma why you chose to see Ted."

Emma wanted to hear this. She watched John Cole, who shifted and coughed and swallowed about a dozen times and just generally looked so hopeless that she wanted to say she was terribly sorry for ever asking about any of it.

Finally he managed to say, "I thought I might ask him some things . . . things that I needed to talk about privately."

When he did not appear to be going to say anything else, Catherine said, "Did you think Emma would be angry about you seeing Ted on your own?"

At this question, Emma shifted and even leaned forward slightly.

He glanced at her, then at Catherine. "I didn't think she would have been angry . . . but she would have made a deal out of it. We had the pool goin', and the weddin', and I just really didn't think it was all that important that I tell her about one visit. I really just didn't think about it."

The last he said with the most thorough perplexity that Emma had ever encountered, and she knew in that instant that he really had not thought of it being important at all. It was as if a light from heaven shone down on him so that she could see him clearly for the first time.

She had no time to assimilate this knowledge, however, because Catherine had them stand and hug each other for a full minute. Then she had them sit holding hands and for two full minutes explain their feelings on the matter of talking to each other. What Emma noticed was that two minutes was not enough for her—and she did not care for Catherine sticking that hand up to cut her off— and that two minutes was at least a minute and a half too long for John Cole, who, bless his heart, had to be prodded along by Catherine saying, "Time's not up."

Catherine ended the session by saying that they had made real progress with honest communication, and then she suggested separate sessions for a while, with Emma seeing Catherine, while John Cole saw Ted.

Emma agreed, although she was not fully thinking of the matter. She was preoccupied with studying John Cole, searching his eyes, his expressions and his mannerisms in the way one sees something brand new and intriguing. When she caught sight of their image together in the mirror behind the receptionist's desk, she stared until jarred away by having to look at a calendar.

Her mind went over everything, and by that evening she went to John Cole and said, "We are so different," as if she had made a great discovery. He agreed with this, and then they sat going over their differences for nearly half an hour. Emma did most of the talking but was no longer overly concerned about it, nor about having to prod John Cole along with questions. He seemed perfectly willing to reply.

They each thought it quite possible that they knew the other better than they knew themselves. This provided ten more minutes of conversation, which Emma discovered was John Cole's limit. She felt very smart to pay attention to this observation.

That night, she sensed attraction between them of a sort she had not felt in a long time. She sensed it when John Cole came into the bedroom while she was at her dressing table, combing her hair.

In the mirror, she saw him look at her. She was wearing a brand-new negligee that she had had Belinda order for her. She had bought three such gowns in recent weeks, trying to boost herself and impress John Cole. It was the sort of gown that she imagined Liz would have worn in *Cat On A Hot Tin Roof*, and quite suddenly, she felt as bold and saucy as Maggie the Cat, too. Hadn't she been awfully bold and saucy that afternoon?

He surprised her by saying quite shyly, "You look nice in that gown."

"Thank you." In the mirror, she watched him remove his shirt, her gaze skittering across his bare muscular shoulders.

"John Cole."

He turned. "Yeah?"

What did she want to say? "I'm sorry about today . . . gettin' so angry."

He gazed at her. "I guess I should have told you."

"My gettin' angry wasn't helpful. . . ."

The phone rang. Instantly, and to her annoyance, John Cole reached for it. He always reached for the phone no matter what important discussion they might have going. Likely, he could not manage another important discussion and was glad for the phone distraction.

But then she heard, "Hey, bud," and knew it was Johnny calling, so she forgave him for answering.

While the two talked, apparently about some

matter with the stores, Emma went about spritzing on perfume, turning down the bed covers, opening the windows to the cooling night and generally being hopeful. They were making progress in relating, she was sure of it.

Then John Cole said, "He wants to talk to you," and handed over the receiver.

"Hi, sweetie."

"Hi, Mama."

With those two words and his tone, she knew something was wrong.

He said, "I got your message yesterday. I'm sorry I didn't get back to you until now. I've been real busy."

As does every attentive mother who has automatically stored possible future problems in the back of her mind, or perhaps has mental telepathy with her child, she knew instantly the trouble and marshaled her calm voice and good sense to deal with it.

"That's all right, honey. I would have called back if I'd needed to speak to you right away."

Annoyed at John Cole for the mundane and intrusive act of turning on the television, she started down the hallway for the family room, saying, "I didn't have Gracie's phone number, or I would have called her. Would you like me to do that? With not getting a reply to the engagement card I sent, I really think I need to speak to Gracie's mother. Maybe the card got lost in the mail, and we don't want Gracie's mother to think we aren't welcoming of her."

The line hummed with silence, and then Johnny said, "Well, we didn't want to say anything before. Gracie thought her mother would come around. But the thing is, her mother is against us gettin' married and probably won't be comin' to the weddin' or havin' anything to do with it."

"Ah." Well, there it was. She had suspected.

She listened to him explain, in the same brief manner his father always used—a fact that part of her mind took in even as she processed the knowledge that Sylvia Kinney had not been for the romance of her daughter with Johnny from the start.

"She doesn't like me, Mama." His voice broke her heart.

"Honey, it isn't you," she said quickly. "She doesn't know you enough not to like you. It is her own preconceived notions."

Johnny allowed as that could be true, but it did not change the fact that the mother of the woman he loved was against the marriage.

Emma's response was to advise patience and respect on his part. After all, it was not easy for mothers to face their children growing up. Not only was Gracie's mother facing her daughter getting married but also living so far from home. She told him that Sylvia Kinney would be his mother-in-law, so it was better not to give her any fuel to work with. After they were married, if not before, when the woman got to really know Johnny, she would change her mind.

The entire time Emma spoke these sound sentiments, she was thinking: *I knew this. I knew it the minute I looked at Gracie's face when she made up that story about her mother being unreachable. I knew it when I didn't hear anything about the engagement card—and it was a real nice card, too. Not like their Johnny Ray? What sort of woman was this? And should Gracie now be suspect?*

"What matters most, honey, is for you and Gracie to do what you want to do. It is your lives."

Johnny said, "Thanks, Mom," in a thoroughly grateful tone that brought tears to Emma's eyes.

When she hung up, she laid her head on the phone. She had calmed him, but she wanted to say a thing or two to Sylvia Kinney. Unable to do that, she hurried back to the bedroom to tell John Cole, walking so fast as to cause her gown to billow out behind her.

Unfortunately, and to her great annoyance, John Cole had fallen asleep. Just forgotten all about her and was snoring softly while a rerun of *The Twilight Zone* crackled on the television.

With a deep sigh, she clicked off the television and got into bed. She could tell him in the morning. After all, how important was it right that moment?

It was darn important. She sat up, switched on

the lamp and woke John Cole to tell him all about this rude, thoughtless and clearly misguided woman who was against their son.

"I knew it was somethin' like this. She probably considers us all a bunch of hicks and rubes."

His yawns and asking what was a rube and comments of, "Well, these things happen," and "I imagine it will blow over," were far from satisfactory.

"I think I'm goin' to fly out there," she said.

"You're gonna what?" That got him fully awake.

Ignoring his frown, she said, "I think I'm goin' to fly out there and talk to Sylvia Kinney face-to-face. Maybe if I meet her and talk with her, she'll feel differently. She's makin' a big mistake. She's goin' to alienate Gracie, her only daughter, and her whole attitude could end up ruinin' their marriage. Gracie might even decide not to marry Johnny."

"Emma, don't go blowin' it all—"

"Not talkin' about it is not the way to go, John Cole. Somebody needs to speak up and say somethin' to her."

He looked at her as if he had never seen her before.

She told him, "I just don't think we need to act as if her behavior doesn't matter. It needs to be confronted."

"I agree," he said, although she knew he was setting up to say how much he didn't agree. "I know things need to be talked about, but you can't go flyin' up there."

"Yes, I can. I've flown lots of times."

"That is not what I mean, and you know it." He raked his hand through his hair, and she could see him thinking very hard, an effort that softened her a little. "You need to stay out of it, and let Gracie and Johnny handle it. Isn't that what you're always tellin' me—that Johnny is old enough to run his own life? I know I don't know a lot about this sort of stuff, but I really think you need to listen to me this one time."

She sat there for long seconds, staring at him, until what suddenly came out was, "I do listen to you, John Cole. It's just that mostly you don't ever say anything."

His eyes widened with something of surprise, and she found she was quite surprised at the statement, too.

"Well, maybe I've learned a little, okay?" he said, with a slight grin as he reached for her, pulling her down onto his shoulder, another surprise.

She lay there against his warm and hard body, savoring a spark of elation about connecting with her husband. She offered to reconsider her plan.

"Good," was his muttered answer in an already half-asleep state. Indeed, another sixty seconds and he was again snoring gently.

Emma, while a little disappointed, was not surprised. She turned her attention to memories long-forgotten and things she was seeing for the first time. It was a lot of thinking to keep her occupied far into the night.

16

In-laws
1966

Emma had met her future mother-in-law, Nedda Berry, over a long-distance phone call, made at her own suggestion. She had John Cole place the call and make an introduction.

The conversation had lasted no more than five minutes, during which Emma had been forced to say, "I'm sorry, I didn't hear you," twice and then go to guessing at exactly what Mrs. Berry said, because she was too embarrassed to repeat again that she could not hear the woman, who sounded like she was afraid to speak above a whisper.

Admittedly, at that time, Emma's experience of speaking long distance on the telephone was limited. The farthest she had ever called was back home to her mother from a school trip to the mountains, but she had been able to hear her mother clear as day. Emma got up the nerve to ask John Cole if he had difficulty in hearing his mother. She wondered if maybe his mother had a voice problem, although she did not say this.

"Sometimes she's hard to hear," he admitted. "Sometimes she doesn't talk very loud . . . and Mom and Pop's phone is old. They've had it since they moved into the house over thirty years ago."

Emma remembered thinking, *Don't these people own a hardware store?* She was to find out that just like the last people to have cabinets live in a carpenter's home, the last people to have improved and helpful gadgets were the families of hardware store owners. Mrs. Berry's mops and brooms were all years old and frayed, and she didn't have a decent bucket, because her husband kept forgetting to bring any of those things home.

Two weeks before Emma and John Cole's marriage, Nedda Berry came down with shingles and was too ill to travel out to the wedding. Emma could not say why she had suspected from the beginning that the woman would not come, even had she been well. Perhaps it was because of the fact that at that time Nedda Berry had never been more than fifty miles from her home in Eastern Oklahoma. As it turned out, not only did Nedda Berry never come to visit Emma and John Cole in all their years away in the Navy, but when she died at the age of sixty-five, she still had not traveled more than those few miles from her hometown.

The only members of John Cole's family to come to the wedding were his daddy, Charles Berry, who was called Pop, and his eldest brother,

Charles Jr., who was called Charlie J. Strangely, the two men looked and acted more like brothers than father and son, the eighteen years between their ages seeming to be nothing. They drove out from Oklahoma in the elder Berry's big white Plymouth and brought wedding presents: a stainless flatware service for twelve, the pattern Emma had seen advertised in magazines for $14.99, and a pair of embroidered and hand-laced pillowcases made by Nedda. The embroidery and lace detail was such that either the woman was a very swift worker, or she'd had the cases stored in the cabinet and waiting for an occasion. It turned out to be the latter; Emma was to learn that Nedda kept embroidery going and had stacks of pillowcases, towels and doilies in the cabinet. She was extremely accomplished at the art. The pillowcases she gave Emma and John Cole were some of her nicest work, but not the bridal type that Nedda had some years later worked up for a niece. That niece had gotten *two* sets of pillowcases and a lavender sachet.

On first introduction, the men stood stiff as boards when Emma went to hug them. They wore cowboy hats and didn't take them off in the house. And they chewed tobacco, which was an enormous amazement to her. Almost all the men and women in her family, even Great Aunt Ida, slumped over in a wheelchair, smoked cigarettes, having started long before any medical advice to the contrary.

(But not on the street—the women in her family did not smoke on the street. Restaurants or cars were okay, but not on the street.) And here were these two, who looked just so nice in their crisp white shirts and dark ties and gleaming cowboy boots, which Emma found quite handsome, and who you would never tell had this disgusting black stuff in their cheeks, until they spat it into a little Coke bottle revoltingly half filled with putrid tobacco spit, or, worse yet, to the side in the lawn. Fifteen minutes after this sight, Emma got John Cole alone, gave him a big hug and told him he had better not ever for one instant consider chewing tobacco.

Whenever Emma recalled that time, she could only remember Pop and Charlie J. standing side by side, looking curiously at everyone and everything around them. She could not recall one instance of John Cole being with those two of his blood. It was as if he just passed by them and waved. And for her part, she could not recall any more conversation with them than a few awkward sentences of asking about their trip, directing the men where they were to stand for the wedding ceremony, and then thanking them for coming and bringing the presents. Right in the middle of the reception, the two men left. They wanted to get on down to Rockingham in order to be there for the NASCAR races the next day.

"They left already?" Emma's mother had said,

astounded. "They didn't even give me time to get them into my mind."

Weeks later, when looking over the wedding pictures, her mother said, "So that's John Cole's father . . . and that's the brother. Well, it's a good thing you picked the correct day for your weddin', or those men would not have come. They don't have races at Rockingham every weekend, you know."

Her mother never had occasion to meet Nedda Berry, and as far as Emma knew, her mother had never felt compelled to drop the woman a line of any sort, because despite all the writing that she did, her mother did not drop anyone a line.

17

Matters of Opinion

He was following her around, so she asked him to get the suitcase from the top shelf of the closet. He got it and put it on the bed, saying at the same time, "You are gettin' carried away."

Of course she had known he would say this, these exact words. She had a reply ready. "You may be right."

This surprised him so much that it was several minutes before he could speak. He looked at her, and she could practically read a ticker-tape running across his forehead that said, *This is the result of marriage counseling, and I am not happy about it.*

He said, "How do you even know she will be there? What if you fly all the way up there, and she isn't in her office?" Then a stricken look. "You are not gonna track her down at her house?"

"Well, I don't think so." She hadn't thought of that. "And if she isn't in her office, then I'll have a nice trip. But she'll be there. Remember that time when Johnny was fifteen and sneaked out in your truck? We only thought we knew where he was, and we drove all the way to Lawton on the faith that we would find him, because we just had to. And we did. It's like that."

He looked at her like she had lost her mind. She felt herself wonder about it, too. In fact, she was momentarily so shaken that she turned from the thought and went to the telephone.

John Cole followed, huffing and puffing in a threatening manner, and talking a great deal about all the money being spent on the pool and the wedding. He always brought up the subject of money when he was against her doing something. Even before he spoke about the expense of airline tickets, she knew he was going to do it, and again she was ready.

"Air miles," she said. "We get them with our credit card. We haven't used any this year. I have enough for two free tickets."

"Two?"

"Uh-huh. I'm askin' Belinda."

He said, "I'll go with you. If you have to go, I'll go with you."

"Oh, honey. Thank you." This she had not expected, and she was momentarily thrown, although she realized that she probably *should* have expected it. "But I think you are really needed here to see about the pool, and to tell Johnny that I've gone shopping, if he asks. We can't both go."

There was no way she could have him go along, telling her all the time that she was getting carried away and that she should not do what she was doing.

He looked quite relieved, and the next minute he left, saying he had to check on the pool and get to the office for a few hours. She thought that, for once, she was glad he was so occupied with business.

Belinda was at the bookstore in Lawton when Emma called. She was perusing the self-help shelf. It was loaded with books with titles like *Make Your Love Life Sizzle*, and *How to Get Your Man to Communicate* and *So You Are A Crock-Pot and He Is A Microwave*.

There simply was not anything for the woman who was a microwave and the man who was a talk-radio, which was what Lyle seemed to have become. It turned out that the new deputy, Giff Phelps, was the one responsible. Lyle was riding around with Giff on patrol, and Giff listened to talk radio and was putting all manner of ideas into Lyle's head about consciousness raising. The previous evening, Belinda had fallen asleep to Lyle talking about the problems of global warming.

Hearing the ringing of her cell phone, Belinda whipped it out with relief at an excuse to quit looking at books that she didn't want to read anyway.

Seeing Emma's number on the screen, she answered, "What is it, sugar?"

"Would you be able to fly up to Baltimore with me tonight and come back tomorrow evenin'? I need to see someone, and we'd have time to shop."

Belinda was capable of taking this in without saying *what?* After no more than two seconds, she replied, "Well . . . I think I could do that. Are you payin'?"

Emma said that she was. She had bonus mileage from her credit card. She wanted to leave mid-afternoon to drive to the Dallas airport, and added, "Just tell everyone that we are goin' to Dallas. That's not really a lie."

"You got it," Belinda said, and added, "I'll drive." She was so thoroughly her mother's daughter that she could not stand to be a passenger. She never even let Lyle drive her.

At three o'clock that afternoon, Belinda turned her champagne-pink Lexus down the Berrys' long, graveled driveway and stopped to the side of two battered construction-company pickup trucks. The backyard was mostly a big hole and piles of dirt, with men working in and around all of it.

Aware of the men looking at her, Belinda tiptoed her way in high-heels over the gravel and along boards laid toward the back door. Two of the closest men gave her appreciative smiles. She smiled back, making no pretense at innocence. Belinda radiated the charisma of a woman who took pride and pleasure in her hefty curves.

Emma came bursting out the back door. "I'm ready."

Wearing practical jeans and walking sandals, she strode directly for Belinda's car. John Cole came behind her, toting her suitcase. He did not look happy.

The trunk lid was already up. John Cole flopped the suitcase inside. He started to grab Emma's tote bag, but she held on to it, saying, "I need this," and got herself into the passenger seat.

Belinda, who had managed to pick her way back to the driver's side, slipped into the seat. John Cole leaned in through Emma's window and asked if she had the airline printout, her credit card, the confirmation of the hotel and dollars to tip the baggage handlers.

"Yes, I do . . . yes . . . yes," said Emma, dutifully showing each thing. "I've traveled before, John Cole."

Then he opened his wallet and gave her more money, despite Emma saying that she did not need it and would be fine. Belinda resisted putting out her hand to him; he seemed too agitated to get the joke.

He kissed Emma through the window, then ran his eyes back and forth between them and said, "You both be careful," as if they were going to war.

When Belinda turned the car and started away down the drive, she caught sight of him in the rearview mirror, standing there gazing after them. When she pulled out on the highway, Emma let out a long breath, sat back in the seat, and gave an explanation of the situation and her intention to go to Sylvia Kinney's office in the morning and convince her of the wrong-headedness of her opinion, or at least tell her a thing or two. These goals appeared somewhat at odds, but Belinda thought it wise not to point that out.

Besides, Emma was wound up and talking in a way that Belinda had never seen before. Belinda was fascinated.

Emma told of finding the address and phone numbers of the M. Connor store headquarters, and how easy that had been, and that she had even called and gotten as far as being put through to Sylvia Kinney's secretary.

"As soon as I heard the secretary, though, I realized that talking on the phone or sending a letter is just not going to work. I need to talk to her in person. So I gave your name, and of course the secretary put me on hold and then came back and said Sylvia Kinney was in a meeting, so I said I would call back. John Cole thinks I have lost my mind, but I am going on faith. I just have to see her in person."

All during the drive to the airport, Emma pretty well carried on a debate with herself about her actions, while Belinda offered nothing one way or the other, just saying a lot of, "Uh-huhs," and a few "I see your points."

Living with her mother, Belinda had learned how to be non-committal. Giving an opinion in these matters so often ended up badly. Mostly people did not want an opinion, anyway. People wanted agreement. And as far as Belinda could see, there was no reason why Emma should not go up there and tell Sylvia Kinney a thing or two. Johnny Berry was a really good guy. Belinda herself was a little annoyed at anyone who would not find him so.

Besides, Belinda was excited about making the trip and the prospect of six or seven hours of shopping in a big eastern city. And since she did not have to pay for her flight or hotel, she had plenty of room on her credit cards.

She had wondered if going through the airport security might undo Emma to the point of abandoning the trip. Instead, though, the posse of official-looking people who kept demanding to see identification and who ran them back and forth through the scanner caused Emma to be distracted from her doubts by having to pay attention to all the instructions.

Belinda got pulled aside. There was just something about her that she always got pulled aside and personally searched. The security woman said it was her underwire push-up bra. Belinda said that if that was the case, why weren't they pulling aside half the line of women?

"I think it is discrimination against all women over twenty-five and under eighty," Belinda said, and not happily.

At the security woman's frown, she shut up. Clearly she was not in Valentine anymore.

Then, as they waited at the boarding gate, Emma began to again get more and more worried and to repeat, "I have never in my life done such a thing. Oh, Lord, Mama would have a fit with me plannin' on makin' a scene. I am not goin' to make a scene. I'm just going to speak to her. I sure hope she is there. I don't know what I will say to John Cole if she isn't there."

Finally Belinda said, "You know, you can always change your mind right up to the time you enter Sylvia Kinney's office. And in the meantime, we are on a nice trip away from everything, and goin' to stay at a nice hotel and get to eat out."

Emma gazed at her a moment, then sat back. "It is good to be away." Then, "I am so tired of all that dirt with that pool."

Belinda got them cold drinks in paper cups and a sack lunch from the Subway. Then she sat and looked at all the men passing and thought things like how few men in the world had good physiques but they all wanted women to have them, and that she was glad to be away from the drugstore, and that she hoped to buy some really nice sheets in Baltimore. She wanted the 1000 thread-count ones of Egyptian cotton. She thought Egyptian cotton sounded exotic.

When she checked her telephone, she found Lyle had called three times already. She called him back and discovered that what he wanted was for her to pick up a copy of *U.S. News and World Report,* because those were delivered a day late to Valentine. She was so astonished to find out that Lyle was reading the news magazine that all she could say was, "Okay."

Afterward she sat there mentally telling God a thing or two, mainly: *I did not marry Lyle for him to be smart.*

Then they were on the plane and buckled into first-class seats. Belinda, pleased as could be, asked the stewardess for a glass of wine.

Emma asked for a glass of wine, too, and said again, "My word, I can hardly believe I am doin' this," but this time she chuckled.

217

Belinda repeated, "You can always change your mind right up until you get to her office. Here's to a lovely trip."

Gracie was working late again, so Johnny came to the store when he got off work at the Lawton Quick Stop. They had not seen each other since the past Sunday night, when he had left her at her apartment and driven out to work the night shift at the Valentine Quick Stop. They were both working really hard to save money to pay the expenses of the wedding and create a nest egg for setting up housekeeping. Johnny had said that his mom would have been happy to pay for a bunch more of the wedding, but Gracie would not let him say anything to his mother.

"Hey, babe," he said now when he approached her, his blue eyes all sweet and hot for her in a way that never ceased to amaze her.

Johnny always looked so out of place in the women's store. He would stand on the far right of the checkout counter, because on the left was the women's intimate lingerie. He would not even look in the direction of the women's intimates. His shyness in this was so cute. He was just cute, period, and lots of the other women who were in the store would try to flirt with him, so Gracie always took him into the rear office and storage area, which was what she did now, leading him by the hand.

Alone in the shadowy area, she immediately went into his arms and kissed him good. There had never been a boy who had ever made Gracie feel this way.

"Come on and quit early," he said, looking at her in that way as if to eat her up.

"You know I cannot do that," she said, all prim and proper. "I am a manager, Mr. Berry, just like you are. Sit there for a few minutes, but then you have to go."

He straddled the chair and talked about them possibly going water-skiing with a group of friends that coming weekend, and about some things going on at the Quick Stops.

Gracie listened and unpacked a new shipment of skirts and jackets, hanging them on the M. Connor black hangers lined on a rack. Her own mind was flitting around the final choice of a wedding dress, and how she looked forward to studying the pictures of wedding gowns again that night in the peace and quiet of her own apartment. She had never taken a roommate. She liked living alone. This was because she was an only child. Johnny was the same way, so they had not moved in together, and she worried a little bit about this in light of their getting married. They had joked that they might have to have separate houses, but deep down she wondered if this had been her mother's difficulty with marriage. She was thinking sadly that she did not want to end up like her mother, divorced and facing a lifetime alone, until she caught Johnny talking about *his* mother. It was like she came awake, wondering if she had heard him correctly.

"You told your mother about my mother not wanting us to get married?"

He gazed at her and blinked uncertainly. "Well, yeah . . ."

"I can't believe you told her! I *told* you not to tell her yet." A noise reminded her of the thin wall separating the storage room from the dressing rooms, and she dropped her voice. *"How could you do that?"*

She stared at him, the enormity of what had happened growing within her. Not only had he told his mother about her mother, but now he sat there casting her a dumbfounded expression about it all.

He said, "Look, she asked me. She's asked a couple of times if I knew if your mother had said anything about gettin' the card she sent with the engagement announcement. She hasn't heard a word from your mother in all these weeks. What else was I supposed to do?"

"I don't know—but you didn't have to tell her right out. You could have just said that my mother had told me that she liked it." Gracie had, in fact, been considering forging a reply from her mother to Emma. That such an idea was not only devious but a little crazy had made her hesitate a little too long, obviously, and now it was too late. "You could have told her to call me and let me handle it."

"She's my mother, and I was talkin' to her. And she was goin' to find out sooner or later that your mother doesn't like me or my family. I think she would notice when your mother didn't show up at the wedding."

She did not like his sarcastic tone.

Straightening to her full five-foot-three height, she said, "My mother has plenty of time to work this out in her mind and decide to come. That's her pattern. She wants her way, but when she can't have it, she'll come around rather than be left out. And it isn't that she doesn't like you and your family. She just doesn't want me living out here so far away. How would your mother like it if you were marrying me and moving off to Baltimore? She wouldn't like it, either."

She was happy that what she said sounded very plausible. She convinced herself, and could see him working up a retort, but she cut him off with, "What exactly did you tell your mother? I'll bet you made my mother look like some rich bitch."

"I . . . Mom didn't take it like that at all," said Johnny, looking completely guilty as charged. "She said that your mother loved you and was just havin' difficulty letting you go. She said we should be patient but go on with our plans, that it is our lives and not your mother's."

Gracie thought about that, torn between wondering if Johnny was slanting things in a more favorable light and the thought that Emma made her mother sound clingy and controlling.

"When did you tell her this?" she asked, turning her mind to count her options.

"Last night."

She considered that. "I talked to you this morning on the phone, and you didn't think to tell me this?" She knew instantly that he had come that evening specifically to tell her this particular instance of his betrayal and had tried to slip it in with all the other boring information without her noticing.

"I forgot, okay? It wasn't somethin' I was thinkin' about when I was talkin' to you at seven o'clock in the mornin'." He reached for her. "Look . . . it isn't that big a deal. My mom wasn't upset and didn't think anything at all. Really. It's okay."

She let him pull her to him, and hug her and kiss her. She felt herself turning to butter, but then she thought of what Emma must think about her mother. She felt guilty by association.

"You need to just go on and let me finish my work." She pushed him away. "I have to get this shipment hung up before I can leave tonight."

He suggested meeting her after work, and she made the excuse of being way too tired, which she really was. Then, thankfully, Nicole came and asked Gracie to come up front to clerk, so that she could go on her break. Gracie shooed Johnny away, steeling her heart against his little-boy beguiling expression.

Later, after closing the store and walking out to their cars, Gracie ended up telling Nicole all about the situation with her mother. She was just so upset that she broke into tears. Nicole was her closest friend of all the girls at the store, but Gracie had never told her such personal details of her life. Now they just came pouring out.

Nicole listened long without offering any advice. When Gracie remarked on this, Nicole said with her mother and four sisters, she hardly could get a word in, so she didn't talk much. This made Gracie laugh, as Nicole had intended.

Before getting into her car, Nicole put her hand on Gracie's arm and said, "Girl, what I do when I'm upset like this is go take a long, hot bubble bath, with candles all around the tub, and just cry as much as I want and pour my heart out to God. All of us girls and my mama do that. It sure does help. You just have a good heart to heart with God, and I think you'll get to feelin' better, sugar."

Instantly uncomfortable with the mention of God, as well as Nicole's warm hug, nevertheless Gracie nodded and thanked her friend for listening, then got into her own car and waved a friendly goodbye.

So many of the girls Gracie had met down in this part of the country just had to hug all the time and say the word "God." They said things like, "I'm trustin' God," or "I'm believin' in God," or "I'm prayin' for you." Or the one that really set her on edge: "Have you been saved?" The first time Gracie had been asked that, she had said, "From what?"

Gracie found all the hugging and talking about God and prayer embarrassing and maybe just a little insane. It wasn't that she had anything against hugging, but she did not care for people she barely knew to touch her. And she believed in God, but she felt too self-conscious to say His name all over the place, and she did not fully trust people who did. No one had behaved that way in her experience while growing up. People just didn't do that. They might say they prayed about something, but they didn't just say, "Talk to God." Those sorts of people were generally considered fanatical. Although Nicole didn't seem fanatical. She even wore low-cut camisoles and makeup. And when Gracie had confessed her experience with being asked if she were saved, Nicole had laughed and laughed, and said, "Oh, girl, you are the sweetest thing."

On the drive home, however, Gracie found herself praying for help to calm down and know what to do about this situation, because she had to do something. She just had to. She barely addressed God and didn't expect any answer, but by the time she arrived home, she had quit crying and an idea had come into her mind. Whether it was from God or her own anger, she didn't know, but at least she felt better and set on doing something.

She went to the phone, hesitated a few seconds, then picked up the receiver and dialed her mother, who was still awake, as Gracie had expected. She pictured her mother in her big bed with its all-white sheets and silk coverlet, reading glasses—which she never used at work—on her nose, and a stack of files in front of her.

Without preliminary, Gracie said, "Mama, if you do not send Emma Berry a polite note of acknowledgment of her card, and if you do not change your mind and come to my wedding and be nice to Johnny and his family, I am never again going to speak to you. And I mean it this time."

Immediately hanging up, she then switched off the ringer and went straight to run a hot tub with moisturizing bath beads and surrounded by fragrant, comforting candles.

As she sank back with relief into the soothing water and thought, *Oh, God,* her eyes popped wide open with the realization that she had both prayed fervently and called her mother *Mama*.

She was not exactly certain what her mother feared about her marrying Johnny, but maybe it was something like that.

Over a thousand miles away, Sylvia Kinney kept dialing Gracie's phone number and getting her daughter's voice mail. She tried Gracie's cell phone and got the same thing.

Frustrated beyond measure, she cursed voice mail as a horrible invention. Regular answering machines had at least afforded some satisfaction, because even if the party on the other end did not pick up, one could still scream across the line and imagine being heard.

Unable to reach out and snatch her daughter back where she belonged, Sylvia threw the receiver across the room at the padded headboard. Then she wandered down the hall to a closed door— Gracie's room, which was still as it had been when Gracie moved out.

She went inside and stood looking at the room lit only by moonlight. She sat on the bed and took up a stuffed bear and held it for some minutes. Then, throwing aside the stuffed bear, she strode to the kitchen, poured herself a large glass of wine, found a pack of cigarettes tucked in the back of a drawer, took out one and lit it with a shaking hand. She stood there drinking in gulps and smoking like a fiend.

The phone rang. She grabbed it up, expecting Gracie and jabbing the cigarette out in the sink, as if her daughter could see her.

But it was Wadley Johnson's voice that said, "Hi, beautiful woman." He was down below in his car and wanted to come up.

She wanted to let him, but would not. She

could not bear for him to see her. While making all sorts of excuses, she walked to the corner beside the large refrigerator, away from her image in the dark window. She finally had to say straight out, "No, Wadley. I don't want to see you or anyone."

He took that well, so well that when she hung up, she was angry all over again. Why did Wadley have to be so accommodating?

She downed two sleeping pills, turned up the air-conditioning and went to bed, pulling the covers over her head.

18

The Nucleus of the Universe

In the cab on the way to the M. Connor offices, while Belinda made a running commentary on the sights, Emma took out her compact mirror and checked her teeth to make certain none of her breakfast had stuck there. She checked her hair and makeup, and kept reminding herself to keep her chin up. Lifting the chin always encouraged confidence.

Catching her reflection in the glass on the way into the building, she decided she would leave on her dark sunglasses. Unfortunately, with the dark glasses and her chin up, she didn't see the unexpected steps and stumbled. A hand came out to catch her. It was attached to a handsome and stylish-looking man.

"Thank you," she said, and he said, "My pleasure," in the way of a man appreciating a woman. That returned her confidence.

She cast him a nod, then proceeded onward to locate the office directory on a wall across the wide lobby.

Turning to call to Belinda, she saw that her friend had entered into a conversation with the man who had helped her. They apparently found the subject of steps just inside the door quite interesting.

"Belinda, I'm goin' over to the directory."

Belinda waved that she had heard and continued talking to the man.

Discarding her sunglasses in favor of seeing, Emma found *M. Connor, Incorporated. Fifth floor.*

Belinda appeared beside her, and accompanying her was that same man, who said, "Can I help you? I have offices in this building."

Emma said she had found the floor, thank you, but Belinda put in, "We're lookin' for Sylvia Kinney's office. Would you know where that is?"

"Well, yes . . . actually, I was just going that way. I'll be glad to show you." He stepped over and pushed the elevator button. Immediately the doors of one parted, and he gestured gallantly for them to enter.

Belinda went right ahead, while Emma hesitated.

The man regarded her expectantly, so she stepped into the elevator and turned to look at her reflection in the shiny doors. While the elevator went up, Belinda and the man flirted with each other, exchanging the information that Belinda and Emma were visiting from Oklahoma and that the man was from North Carolina but also lived in Baltimore part-time because of business.

To this Belinda said, "Emma's from North Carolina, aren't you, Emma?"

Manners forced Emma to say, "Yes, I am," and to give the man a nod, because one simply could not *not* acknowledge someone from one's home state. His accent was so faint, though, as to make him suspect.

So then he said, "Are you two friends of Sylvia's?"

"Acquaintances," Belinda answered. "Actually, we know her daughter, Gracie."

"Ah."

Emma wondered why Belinda didn't just tell him their names and phone numbers, and that Emma had come to address Sylvia Kinney's animosity toward her son.

The elevator doors opened onto a lobby. Emma turned to give the man a cordial thank you and bid him goodbye, but he strode ahead to a pair of large doors, saying, "It's through here."

Belinda went right on after him, and Emma trailed behind, thinking that she did not need an audience for her confrontation. It crossed her mind to turn around and head right back down the elevator, but then the man was greeting the tall receptionist, who seemed straight out of *Vogue* magazine.

"Good morning, Angel—we're just going down to see Sylvia."

"Okay, Mr. Wadley," the woman said with a flirtatious smile.

Emma did not think he looked like he could be connected to a name like Wadley. She took note of him smiling and greeting women who passed, as if he were a kindly visiting prince. She peered into offices and cubicles. There was more modern design—glass, stainless steel and black lacquer—surrounding her than she saw in six months, without going to Las Vegas. The young professionals who passed looked every inch attractive executive types out of a television drama. She felt thoroughly an alien in an alien land.

Their escort came to a stop at a desk manned by the first no-nonsense matronly looking woman Emma had seen in the entire place. The woman greeted him by the name of Mr. Johnson, and he called her Miss Lenore. Seeing the door with Sylvia Kinney's name on it, Emma quickly concluded that either Sylvia Kinney was smart to employ a very capable sort of woman, or she wanted no competition in the area of youth and style.

"These ladies are old friends of Sylvia's," the man said, moving to the office door. "I'll just take us on in."

The secretary protested, but the man paid her no mind, simply rapped and entered breezily. "Sylvia . . . sweetheart, how are you this beautiful morning?"

"Wadley, I have neither time nor inclination . . ." The woman behind the elegant desk—upswept dark hair and sophisticated suit—came swivelling around from a computer screen.

Then she saw them. Instantly her countenance changed to impassive. Removing her glasses, she slowly stood. The man with the unlikely name of Wadley Johnson went to her and kissed her cheek, then presented Emma and Belinda, saying, "I ran into these lovely ladies downstairs—they've come to see you from Oklahoma. They're friends of Gracie's."

Emma saw the woman's surprise, and saw the color leave her face as she met Emma's gaze.

Emma extended her hand, saying, "I'm Emma Berry. I know this is bargin' in, but I had the opportunity to stop into Baltimore today and thought it would just be too rude not to introduce myself to the mother of the woman my son is marryin'." It was as if all that she had been taught forever about politeness and graciousness just took hold of her.

Sylvia Kinney stared at her and her outstretched hand for a noticeable moment, before taking it in a reluctant shake and saying, "Yes . . . this is a surprise."

Emma then introduced Belinda and made up a story about having come to Baltimore for Belinda's business. "Belinda owns our drugstore in Valentine. It's on the national register of historic places." She went on about coming along on the spur of the moment, not even remembering Sylvia lived in Baltimore until that very morning. Belinda fell into the spirit, saying how Emma had been just "the kindest thing alive to get herself together and come with me." There was something about the moment that caused both Emma and Belinda to fall into a thick drawl.

Sylvia Kinney's reply to all of this was, "How nice." She stood there gazing at them as if counting the very hairs on their heads.

Mr. Wadley Johnson, who seemed to now be pondering the situation, apparently decided on retreat. He promised to return a little later and left.

Directly after his departure, Belinda said, "I'll just wait outside and give you two mothers time alone." As she softly closed the door, Emma had the image of her planting herself firmly on the other side of the office door, like a sentry.

Emma and Sylvia Kinney gazed at each other. Emma thought clearly that John Cole was correct. She had gotten carried away again.

She said, "Well, I am glad to meet you," and,

without invitation, sat herself in the chair facing the desk.

"You'll have to excuse me if I seem surprised," said Sylvia Kinney, who slowly lowered herself into her high-backed chair behind the desk. She sat back, appearing to measure Emma for hat size. "Does Gracie know you are here?"

"No," said Emma in a pleasant tone. "I haven't spoken to Gracie since last Sunday. She and Johnny were out to the house for supper, and we were discussin' the wedding and shower plans."

The woman made no reply, but looked at Emma as if to say: *Get on with what you have to say and be gone.*

"We find your Gracie a lovely young woman, and we are thrilled to have her joinin' our family."

"I can imagine."

"Can you? I'm so glad. I thought that it must be nerve-wracking to have your daughter halfway across the country and marryin' a young man you barely know, and can't be certain will love and value your daughter as she deserves. I thought you might need reassuring that Johnny loves your daughter with all his heart. His father and I welcome her, and you, as well."

This was received with a cool nod and murmur of, "That's very kind of you, I'm sure."

Emma leaned forward slightly and continued on with the theme, which was that Gracie was marrying not only a solid young man, but one with a solid family and business behind him. Certainly Berry Enterprises was not anything on a grand scale—minuscule, actually, compared to M. Connor Corporation, quite obviously.

"Obviously," Sylvia Kinney murmured.

"Just the same," Emma said, "our family business is a prosperous concern, and will support Johnny and Gracie and their family quite well. And Valentine is a good place to live. Oh, it is country and not at all sophisticated by your standards, I'm sure. But there are compensations. You know, it has a slower pace, and people take time to talk when they pass on the street . . . and they watch out for each other. Kids can play all over town, and old people can take walks in the middle of the night, if they want.

"I just want you to know that in our community and in her marriage, Gracie has as much promise of a happy future as could be found on earth."

At all of this, Sylvia Kinney appeared unmoved. Her expression remained cool and impassive, and she commented only that she was sure Emma's son had a lot to recommend him.

Emma, however, had thoroughly succeeded in moving herself. In presenting the picture of what they had to offer Gracie, she experienced a rush of gratitude for her own life and even an eagerness to get back to it.

"Well, that's all I have for you," she said. "Take it for what you will. You know, I don't think there's anything a parent can say, once an adult child has decided to get married. I know there was nothing that could be said to me, and when Johnny brought Gracie home, I knew there was nothing I could say to either one of them. Those two are goin' to get married, with or without us, and if we don't go along, we'll be the ones to miss out. I don't intend to do that."

That last brought Sylvia Kinney's eyes wide. Although perhaps it was because Emma, who had said what she needed to say, had gotten to her feet.

She reached across the desk and shook Sylvia Kinney's hand firmly, saying, "I'm glad we got this chance to chat. I do hope to be seein' you at the wedding. Come on down anytime. We'd love to have you visit . . . oh, the bridal-shower barbeque is in August. I'll send you an invitation. No need to see us out—we can find our way."

Out the door, she found Belinda again talking to Wadley Johnson. Emma paused long enough to shake his hand, too, and to decline the offer of lunch, clearly to Belinda's disappointment. Then Emma was leading the way to the elevators. As they rode down, she thought of heading to the airport to go home, until Belinda, with a little bit of emphasis, reminded her that they did not leave until evening and, until then, were scheduled to shop.

Belinda also informed her that the man's name

was Wadley R. Johnson, and his family was the Johnsons of apparent fortune and fame made in tobacco. He was also Sylvia Kinney's significant other.

"You found all that out in that short a time?"

"Sugar, people just talk to me. I can't help it."

When Wadley went into Sylvia's office, she was looking out the window. She told him to go away, but he heard something strange in her voice. Being braver than he had ever felt—maybe after talking to Belinda Blaine, he vaguely thought—he asked, "What is it, Syl?"

She turned as if to yell at him, but then her face crumpled, and she threw herself onto him. "Oh, Wadley. Gracie's all I have. I can't lose her. What am I going to *do?*"

His reaction of astonishment was followed quickly by something near delight. At last this self-contained woman needed him. He held her, and stroked her hair and murmured to her, as he had long desired to do. Wadley was a man who cried, who had never expected himself to stay strong, and he always felt that his knowledge of emotion was something he could give to Sylvia, if she would ever let him.

He got her tissues, he sat her down, he told Miss Lenore they were not to be disturbed, and he told Sylvia to tell him all about it. She was so broken that she did.

• • •

Emma laid her head back against the airplane seat. "Well, for better or worse, I'm glad I made this trip." The experience had given her something that she could not quite define.

"Do you think you changed her mind?" Belinda asked. She laid her head back on the seat, too.

"I don't know. She didn't seem like it. But have you ever had a strong feeling that you needed to do and say something? I just felt like I should come, and I'm glad I followed that feeling. I feel satisfied now."

"I often have that feeling," Belinda agreed, deciding not to mention that very often it got her into trouble. She kept an eye on the stewardess so as not to miss her opportunity to order wine.

Emma felt nervousness creeping up on her. Her mind had begun to whisper all manner of recriminations about how she had butted into her son's affairs, and how there was definitely something not right when one felt the need to keep it secret. Her high emotion, which had carried her along, had begun bobbing, like a balloon when it began to lose helium.

That was the difficulty when caught up in high emotion. One rose up high, where there seemed no obstacles, but what went up had to come down, and then one could see many things that had not appeared before.

Beside her, Belinda had gotten her glass of wine

and was sipping it happily. "I think we should take a trip like this at least once a year. Next time to New York, and I'll pay."

They arrived home in Valentine just before one in the morning.

Emma sat up in the car, taking in the streetlights, the old Blaine's Drugstore sign on one side of Main Street and the brand new one shining forth from the Main Street Café's window on the other, a woman in curlers and nightgown watering her bushes, a man walking his dog and two joggers taking advantage of the cooler night temperatures.

When Belinda turned into Emma's driveway, Emma saw that the lights were on inside the house. Even before Belinda came to a stop, Emma was gathering her shopping bags. Then, my goodness, there was John Cole coming over to the car.

He said, "You're home."

Of course he would say something like that, and she was actually glad to hear the silly statement.

He veered away to the trunk Belinda had opened, calling a welcome to Belinda, then getting Emma's suitcases—two now—and carrying them back to the house.

Emma waved Belinda away, then took up her shopping bags and walked toward the back door that John Cole held open. She heard the chirping of cicadas and nightbirds, ran her gaze over the dark shadows of the construction in the yard, the darker trees, the majesty of stars above, the yellow cat who sat near the back door.

Inside, the precious familiar scents and sights engulfed her. She stopped in the kitchen, while John Cole carried her cases on to the bedroom. She dropped her two bulging shopping bags to the floor and looked around, as one does, very glad to be home in this one place, in her life.

John Cole reappeared. She went to him and put her arms around his neck. "I am so glad to be home."

"Well, I'm glad you're home, too," he said in a manner that touched her deeply.

They kissed then, long and passionately. When they broke apart, they looked into each other's eyes. Then Emma, suddenly overwhelmed, dropped her forehead on his chest, while he rubbed her back. Slowly he turned her, and, with his arm supporting her, they walked down the hall to the bedroom, leaving the lights burning behind them.

She began undressing, and he went to get her robe from the closet. As she got ready for bed, she gave him a brief overview of her encounter of Sylvia Kinney. She told him that Sylvia Kinney was a beautiful woman, and cordial, but that she gave no indication that she would change her mind and approve of the marriage. "She's a diplomat. She speaks but doesn't really say anything."

John Cole turned out the lights, and they crawled into bed. Curling into his shoulder, Emma said, "It doesn't matter that she didn't say anything. I was the one who had something to say. I extended a hand. That's what I wanted to do."

And then, with a great gratitude at being back where she belonged, she fell asleep.

This time it was John Cole who lay there staring up at the patterns in the ceiling, quite bewildered by the woman lying against him and by his own feelings of relief that she was once more with him and that she apparently had the family matters all straightened out and was happy again. He was finally accepting that he, a mere man, was never going to understand her, and certainly, he could not control her. He could give up that effort.

Emma, he thought, in a profound moment, was the nucleus of his entire universe. When she was happy, he and Johnny and everyone around her were happy. But most assuredly, when she began to shake, so went the ripples all around.

This provocative thought was something of a revelation. It came to him that a very smart thing for his own self-preservation might be to do what he could to keep Emma happy.

The following morning, Emma awoke to the startling fact that not only had she slept until well after nine o'clock, but John Cole was still in bed beside her.

She sat up abruptly to see him looking at her.

"What are you still doin' in bed?" Then, anxious, "Do you feel all right?"

"I think so." He scratched his head. "Do you?" He amazed her by snaking a hand around her waist and up onto her breast, and giving her the most amorous look that she had seen in quite some time.

After a moment of feeling shy, she responded by melting into his arms and throwing a leg over his in rising enthusiasm. Things proceeded in this improved and delightful manner until Johnny's voice rang out through the house.

"Mama? Are you back here?"

Instantly, Emma jerked away, and literally vaulted over John Cole and out of the bed, racing into the bathroom, where, through the door, she heard, "Hi, Dad. I saw your truck. What are you doin' here?"

To which John Cole replied, "I happen to live here."

Johnny, as they discovered once they joined him in the kitchen, had come to tell them that Sylvia Kinney was flying down the following day. It took him a few minutes to get to this news. He clearly was distracted by the surprise at finding the parental unit, as he called them, having just gotten out of bed at such a late hour, most especially his father. Apparently realizing what he might have interrupted, he apologized with shy embarrassment, and, as if perplexed, he said, "But, Dad, you're never here at this time in the mornin'."

"I've been here for weeks, workin' on the pool," John Cole responded. He seemed to want to make a point of his presence by not leaving the kitchen to get dressed but remaining in his pajama pants and waiting impatiently for coffee from the maker.

Quite eager to enjoy both of her men for breakfast, a phrase that caused her to smile, Emma got them set down at the table. While she popped frozen sausages and cinnamon rolls into the microwave oven, and poured cups of coffee, Johnny gave them the news of Gracie's mother's upcoming visit.

"Oh?" Emma met John Cole's eyes and pulled tight the belt of her robe.

"Yeah. She's flyin' down in her boyfriend's private jet. He's some big rich guy, I guess. Gracie says he's a pretty good guy. Anyway, Gracie and her mom had a pretty good talk last night, and her mom said she would fly out tomorrow."

"Well, that is good news."

Holding her mug in both hands, Emma gazed with all attentiveness at her son, as he related that it appeared Gracie's mother was willing to give her approval of the marriage. He was excited to say this. He looked like a boy all filled with hope.

"Mom, would you mind havin' them out for Sunday dinner?" he asked with eagerness.

"Of course, sweetheart," was her instant reply,

and she got a tablet straight away in order to plan the menu.

She was about to ask John Cole if he would want to barbeque steaks when she looked around and saw him walking out of the room. Without a word.

A few hours later, Emma was just hanging up the kitchen phone when John Cole came in the back door. She told him, "One of Stella's Merry Males is comin' in half an hour. I said for him to use the front door, so don't get all excited when you see a strange man in the house. Where's my list?"

She was moving at great speed, keeping just one step ahead of the worrisome thought of coming face-to-face again with Sylvia Kinney. It was true about subterfuge—it grew all by itself. There had been a time for total disclosure, but that had passed when she did not tell Johnny about visiting Sylvia, and apparently Sylvia had not told Gracie. Perhaps the woman was waiting to make a scene in front of everyone.

Emma was vibrating at so high a pitch with all of these thoughts that she was only vaguely aware that John Cole had not gone to the refrigerator, as she had expected, but lingered near the end of the counter.

He said, "There's somethin' I forgot to tell you."

Hands in her purse, she paused.

"Pop and Charlie J. and Joella are comin' tonight."

She stared at him. "They are?"

They were, John Cole confirmed. "They're staying through till Monday. Pop wants to meet Gracie, and Lloyd's not travelin' with the rodeo this summer, so they felt they could leave the store in his hands. They called last night, before you got home."

"Didn't you tell them about the bridal-shower barbeque? We're havin' it for everyone to meet Gracie." She thought maybe she could catch them before they left and could explain.

"It's my dad, Emma. He wants to come now."

"Oh, of course." She knew Pop Berry, and she regretted her tone. They were family, she thought, seeing John Cole regarding her helplessly. She picked up her pen to jot notes on her list. "I'd better make it ham for Sunday for your daddy and Charlie J. . . . and some beans, too."

She started to mention hoping Joella was still on the wagon, but held her tongue. John Cole looked a little forlorn. She smiled and gave him a hug. "It will be real nice," she said, and he looked a little better.

Two hours later, when she returned from shopping, her father-in-law's Suburban was in the driveway. Pop and Charlie J., in their starched white shirts and straw cowboy hats, were standing in the yard with John Cole, telling him everything the builder was doing wrong with the pool. Joella sat in the shade, fanning herself with a magazine and drinking a Coke. When Emma went over to give her sister-in-law a hug and smelled her breath, she knew it was a beer in an insulator sleeve with a Coca-Cola emblem.

When John Cole asked what was for supper, Emma said they were all going to the Main Street Café, and she called her mother and Johnny and told them to join them. It was not a request. They came, and Johnny charmed his Grandpop and Uncle Charlie J., who both adored him, and Emma's mother chatted happily away with Joella, who fanned herself with a menu and nodded a lot. Emma and John Cole sat close together, holding hands and wondering at themselves for coming from these, their very own people.

Emma, standing in the dark yard amid the pool construction, looked back at the house, where lights glowed. Through the wide window into the family room, she saw Pop and Charlie J. firmly planted and staring at the television, which she could faintly hear. Through the screen porch and glass door into the kitchen, she saw Joella, glass in hand, come dancing past with an imaginary partner, no doubt to music from the radio on the counter.

A light came on in their bedroom, behind the layers of sheers. Likely that was John Cole.

Emma looked around for a tree to hug, but those of good size were farther out in the pitch-black yard. She did not want to chance stepping on a snake. She looked upward at the beautiful moon and stars. It was wonderful where they lived, with no lights to crowd out the stars.

If only one could have such a view of one's life, she thought.

Just then something touched her ankle. She jumped and let out a gasp.

It was the yellow cat.

"Oh, you." She bent to pet it.

There came a sound from the house—the sliding door of their bedroom opened. "Emma?"

"Over here."

She watched his shadowy figure come agilely around the dirt and construction. "What are you doin' out here?" he asked.

"Oh . . . I came out here to hug the old elm, but now it's gone."

"Ah."

"I wish I would have thought of that before the pool."

He said nothing. What was there to be said?

Then he commented on the bright stars, and how Valentine threw off a lot more light than when they had moved there, and did she remember what it used to look like? She agreed with it all.

Finally she said, "I don't know what I'm going to do when Sylvia Kinney shows up. I hope it goes okay."

"It probably will."

"I guess I've made a mess of things by goin' up to see her and not sayin' anything about it. I just hope I haven't ruined everything for Johnny."

John Cole's arm came around her. "You haven't ruined anything. It doesn't look like she's said anything, either."

"She might wait until she gets here to tell Gracie in person."

"If she does, you'll handle it. At least you got her out here. You can look at it like that. It's goin' to be okay."

He squeezed her close, and she laid her head on his shoulder. They stood there for some minutes, until mosquitoes drove them inside. Mosquitoes always bit John Cole. He was a magnet for them. As long as he was there, mosquitoes would not bite Emma.

19

The Out-of-Towners

Sylvia gazed out the window of Wadley's private jet. It banked for a turn, and for an instant the sunlight reflected off the wing. She squinted, even behind her dark glasses. She felt as if her entire body was one big squint.

"Phil says that's Valentine down there. He's making a curve, so we can see it," said Wadley, who slipped down beside her.

Far below, the earth looked like a patchwork quilt, as if someone had drawn and colored it in shades of green and brown.

"There . . . where that blue water tower is sticking up." Wadley pointed.

Sylvia peered hard, not really knowing what she was looking for. The town was a cluster of trees and buildings. One main street, it appeared. Vehicles, like little toys, were moving on the roads. Everything looked perfectly tidy and clean. From a distance things always looked so perfect. One could not see the grime and potholes and crumbling.

Thinking of seeing Gracie, she felt frightened and sat back from the window so fast that she bumped Wadley. He took her hand and told her it was all going to be fine.

"You're going to tell her, and you'll see that it all turns out just fine."

She said, "You sound like a broken record. I wish I had never told you."

He gave her an encouraging look and squeezed her hand, and she felt worse because of how she'd spoken to him. She wanted to tell him that she was sorry, but what came out was, "When she finds out that I have not told her all these years, she will never forgive me."

"Yes, she will. She's your daughter. She doesn't have a choice. Have you had a choice with your parents? Children have to put up with parents who keep coming around. It's the law."

She sighed. After a minute, with eyes closed she said, "Wadley."

"Yes?"

"I cannot imagine how you put up with me . . . but I thank you for . . . everything."

He kissed her.

Some fifteen minutes later, they had landed and were taxiing toward a private hangar. Sylvia peered again through the window and thought everything seemed so flat, and empty.

The plane stopped, the steward lowered the door, and the stairs were put in place. Sylvia stepped outside and said, "Good God." It was like stepping into a convection oven with glaring thousand-watt bulbs. Even behind her sunglasses, she squinted again as she went down the stairs. Upon reaching the ground, she looked up to see Gracie hurrying toward her.

"Mother!"

"Gracie?" She had not expected this. Johnny was beside her daughter. Why did he have to be here? She touched her cheek to that of her daughter and blinked back surprising tears.

"I know Wadley has a car waiting, but we came to welcome you," said Gracie.

Oh, she looked beautiful.

Standing a few yards away, Johnny looked from the two women to the plane. He had never seen a private plane up close. He eyed Wadley Johnson and thought that the man looked as everyday as any of them. Johnny had seen a few pretty-rich men. Shorty Lightfoot had millions made in oil but still came into the Valentine Stop in his twenty-year-old beat-up Chevy truck.

Wadley Johnson came forward, smiling in a friendly manner, and introduced himself. He shook Johnny's hand and congratulated him. Johnny thought this showed that maybe Gracie's mother wasn't going to try to bust them up, which was what he half suspected.

Then Johnny was shaking Sylvia Kinney's hand and greeting her, and suddenly the image of the shaving kit that he kept in Gracie's bathroom cabinet popped into his mind. He was struck with the panic to get in there and hide it before her mother saw it.

As he drove to Gracie's apartment, he reminded her about the shaving kit.

"Oh, sweetheart, my mother isn't even stayin' with me . . . and we *are* getting married, after all," Gracie said, laughing at him.

"I know, but she might look in there, and I don't want to give her any cause to back up," he replied. He also had a worry that her mother might get very angry and say something to his mother. This idea had taken such a hold on him that when they reached Gracie's apartment, he went straight to the bathroom, grabbed his shaving kit and stuck it three places before finally settling on behind the cleansers in the rear of the sink cabinet. He didn't think Mrs. Kinney looked like someone who would be cleaning a bathroom. As he quietly closed the cabinet door, he wondered when a guy began to feel grown up. Maybe not until his parents died.

Johnny visited politely with everyone for over an hour, then made his escape. He drove down to his parents' house, where he told everyone about the arrival of Sylvia Kinney and Wadley Johnson, and the private plane. His mother made him a peanut butter and banana sandwich, and he watched the NASCAR race with his father, Grandpop and uncle, just as he had been doing ever since he could recall. For dinner, his mother made cheeseburgers, and his Aunt Joella made fried potatoes just for him, so he stayed for that.

In the end, he slept on the living-room couch. His Uncle Charlie J. used his old room, because his Aunt Joella, who snored, was in the guest room, and his grandfather was in the family room watching the television. When Johnny was half asleep, his mother, who was wearing herself out getting everything ready for Gracie's mother, came into the living room and stood there staring at him. He felt her love fall all over him like a warm winter blanket, nice but heavy.

The next morning his mother fixed him sausage and eggs and pancakes, everything exactly as he liked it without him having to say a word. When he left, he hugged her tight and even stopped to hug his dad, and then he walked slowly to his car and drove away, thinking that when he married Gracie, he could never be the boy come home again. He would be a guest, just as his Grandpop, uncle and aunt.

He couldn't explain it to anyone and would have been too embarrassed to try, but he worried what his parents would do without him as their boy.

By the time their very special out-of-town guests arrived for Sunday dinner, Emma was a nervous wreck. She was trying to prepare a dinner for a woman whom she was pretending never to have met, and whom she wanted to please and impress beyond all reason.

On Saturday, she had received the delivery of a dozen roses with a card that read: *Looking forward to meeting you.—Sylvia Kinney*. After that, Emma put the gelatin salad in the cabinet, and it would have stayed there all night if her sister-in-law hadn't found it when she was looking for a bowl for chip dip. She let the potatoes for the potato salad boil over and was cleaning the stove at ten o'clock at night.

John Cole came in and found her, and asked what she was doing, and she told him, "I don't want Sylvia Kinney to think that Johnny comes from trashy people." She even got paint and touched up a couple of nicks in the dining-room walls.

Sunday afternoon at one o'clock, the special guests arrived. Emma was removing the cream pies from the oven and heard her sister-in-law call from the living room, "They're here!" followed by her mother's lower tone, "Get your hat and girdle!"

Emma set one hot glass pie plate on the butcher block and went back for the other, and while passing the family room entry, waved a hot pad to get John Cole's attention. She could have just as well yelled at him, though, because Pop Berry and Charlie J. had been glued to their seats and the television all day, and didn't even look around. It crossed her mind that they could have been dead with their eyes open.

Swinging to check her appearance in the mirror, she then went for her purse to get a lipstick.

Joella came running into the kitchen. "Well, they're in a Mercedes, la-de-da. I didn't know people could rent Mercedeses. Do you think he bought it?"

There came a crash of breaking glass, and Emma looked around to see that Joella had dropped her glass.

"Oh . . . oh, I'm sorry!" In something of a frenzy, Joella went down on her knees and began grabbing broken pieces.

"Oh, honey . . . be careful. You'll cut yourself." Emma came quickly with a cloth. She caught the faint scent of bourbon.

Then John Cole was there, shooing Emma out. "I'll get this . . . go on."

Hurrying through the living room, she glanced out the wide window and saw the cars stopping out front.

At the door, she paused. *Help me, Lord,* she asked, and she lifted her chin.

Sylvia Kinney gazed through the windshield and grudgingly admitted that the house was lovely. Long and low, it was rock with a wide front porch graced by large pots and plants.

"Mother, those are the pool-construction trucks," Gracie said, just as Sylvia's eyes went beyond Johnny's car stopped ahead of them to see a group of battered pickup trucks at the end of the driveway. There were also a cement mixer, wheelbarrows and mounds of dirt. At least there was no grass growing up around any of it, she thought as she unbuckled her seatbelt.

Wadley was at her door. As she got out, she saw a figure coming from the front porch. Emma Berry. Blond hair glimmering in the bright light, earrings swaying at her ears, she came toward them with the joyful laugh of a girl.

"Welcome! We're so glad y'all could come!"

Emma Berry threw her arms around Gracie, who responded in the same manner, the two of them hugging, while Sylvia stood there watching. Then Gracie, still arm-in-arm with the woman, made the introductions. Emma Berry looked right at Sylvia and said, "Of course I know who this is. You and Gracie strongly favor . . . just beautiful women."

For a distressing moment Sylvia thought the woman was headed to embrace her. Sylvia stuck out her hand, saying, "I'm very glad to meet you. Gracie's told me so much about you."

Then it was Wadley's turn, and he went so far as to lean over and kiss the woman's cheek, saying, of all things, "I believe we could be kin. Your son tells me that you are a Macomb-Jennings from North Carolina."

At that Emma Berry laughed even more gaily, if that were possible. "I *am* . . . and *you* must be a Car'lina boy, if you would say somethin' like that."

Sylvia imagined spraying them both with a hose.

They all went inside, where there was more family to meet. John Cole, not just John but clearly John Cole Berry, was something of a surprise—the surprise being that immediately upon looking into his sparkling blue eyes, Sylvia judged him an intelligent sort and liked him immediately.

As for the rest, well, they were all about what she had expected, as was the situation, both being a little boring and awkward. The grandfather appeared to be of the same opinion. After being introduced, he left, never again to appear. Sylvia gathered by the sound of a television coming from the family room, and later seeing Emma Berry carry a plate that direction, that he was in there. In a moment of fantasy, Sylvia imagined what might have happened should she have joined him.

Emma Berry proved to be the perfect hostess, serving up refreshments along with smiles and welcoming words. Sylvia set herself to equal the woman at every turn. Their conversation was like a tennis match, each batting compliments back and forth, until it got embarrassing and they both quit. A minute later, Emma Berry excused herself to put dinner on the table.

"I'll just go help Emma," Gracie said, and Sylvia watched her daughter trail off after the woman. Responding to fashion questions posed by the aunt, who seemed to be regarding her with a schoolgirl crush, Sylvia heard the sound of her daughter's and Emma Berry's happy voices floating from the kitchen.

The grandmother, Emma Berry's mother, brought out a scrapbook that she was building about the family tree as a wedding gift for Gracie and Johnny. She showed the pages of old photographs of her relatives, even a tintype, and went on at great length about ancestors who—apparently single-handedly—settled America and carried out the Revolution.

Sylvia saw it coming and prepared to answer questions about Gracie's family tree; however, as it turned out, Wadley, being thoroughly swept up in the conversation, jumped in to say that his great-grandfather had owned farms in and around a place with the unlikely name of Pittsboro. This information appeared to have a great effect on the older woman, who peered at him and said intensely, "Are you any relation to Harold Johnson?" as if there were not a million of them. Wadley, however, eagerly answered that he was. Then and there the two seemed enamored with each other. Wadley all but abandoned Sylvia and spent the entire time so deep in conversation with the older woman that at times their foreheads practically touched. It was amazing.

The dinner was enormous. It was the sort Sylvia had attended a couple of times during her short marriage to Paul Mercier. John Cole served wine and offered a toast to the young couple. Sylvia drank her wine and later Wadley's glass; he was still enamored with the old lady and didn't notice. By then, she had observed that the aunt was definitely drinking something stronger than iced tea. The idea of stealing it from her played across Sylvia's mind. When the grandmother tore herself away from Wadley for a few minutes and returned smelling of cigarette smoke, Sylvia almost asked her to share, or at least breathe in her direction.

After dinner, Emma Berry went to the kitchen to make mocha. Gracie got caught up in serving more pie to the men, who had all joined the grandfather in the family room, watching NASCAR or something. Except Wadley, who remained at the dining table with the grandmother, talking as intently as if planning a robbery.

Sylvia was left sitting across the table from the aunt, who commented about Gracie and Sylvia being Catholic. Sylvia said yes, they were.

The woman then said, "John Cole and Emma have a mixed marriage, too. We're all Baptists. All the Berrys are. John Cole was until he married Emma. It broke Mother Berry's heart, Emma bein' Methodist. And now Johnny is marryin' a Catholic. Y'all'll be the first Catholics in our Berry family. I was wonderin' if Gracie's daddy was maybe Mexican. She sure is a dark-eyed beauty, like so many of those Mexican girls."

Sylvia had a moment of wondering if she had heard correctly. Then she replied, "No, she isn't. Excuse me. I need to go to the rest room."

"Oh, the guest powder room is just right through there, honey," said the woman, pointing.

When she came out, Emma Berry called her to have coffee on the rear porch, where all the shades were rolled down over the screens and the door had been left open for the air-conditioning. Passing the dining room, Sylvia saw the aunt lying facedown on the table, asleep with her mouth open.

Sylvia went on to the porch and drank coffee for another half hour, and offered to buy Gracie's wedding gown, as well as to buy and do all manner of things in order to overcome all that Emma Berry was doing. The woman was hand-making decorations for the church pews, forgodsake. Sylvia thought that she could not compete with handmade items, but she sure could buy her way into her daughter's good graces.

She was satisfied that she equaled the woman in the pretense of never before having met. Actually, by then, they had both performed so thoroughly that Sylvia had an odd feeling their exchange in her office was but a figment of her imagination.

"That seemed to go very well," said Wadley, behind the wheel of their rental car, heading it down the highway in a thoroughly happy manner. "You charmed their socks off. They're all in love with you, darlin'." He caressed her leg.

Sylvia, who had her head laid back on the seat, cut her eyes to him. He had called her *darlin'*.

He said a few more words of praise about the dinner and went on for a bit about how Lillian Jennings had reminded him of his grandmother. Sylvia had never heard him speak of his grandmother or much of any part of his life in North Carolina. He had actually begun to drawl, and he used the phrase *might could be*. Within hours of being with these people, he was losing years of education.

After he had fallen quiet for some minutes, and as she watched the countryside through the passenger window, she said, "The damn woman is a cross between Martha Stewart and Dolly Parton."

Wadley didn't need to ask to whom she was referring.

Emma watched her son hug his aunt goodbye, and shake hands with his grandfather and uncle and receive a few pats on the back, then get into his car with his bride-to-be. She watched her husband tuck his family into their Suburban, take several steps back and slide his gaze over the vehicle, as if doing a safety check. She stood in the circle of his arm, waving them all away with calls of sweet goodbyes back and forth, then watched as both vehicles disappeared from sight.

"Well," she said.

"Yep," he said.

Another moment and John Cole turned in the direction of his shop. "I need to check something out here," he said as he was already walking away.

Emma went in the opposite direction, into the house and kitchen, where she looked at the mess remaining, then put the kettle on for a good cup of comforting tea, and got out the fine china teapot and cup and saucer that had belonged to her grand-mother. The tea made, she sat at the table, propped her feet on a chair and considered the events of the afternoon.

All in all, she was quite satisfied. Her obligation as the mother of the groom had been fulfilled.

What she had wanted was for the families to meet and be cordial. This was crucial support for the beginning couple. Becoming great friends was not a requirement—although it did seem that her mother and Wadley Johnson had become bosom buddies, which was quite a humorous turn.

The back door opened, and John Cole came inside. He went to the refrigerator, got a can of Coke, saying, "Well, it all seemed to go pretty good."

"Yes, it did."

"Sylvia Kinney seems pretty nice." He popped the top on the can.

"Yes." She sipped her tea and murmured, "She liked you."

He looked at her with confusion and took refuge in drinking deeply from his Coke.

She said, "What matters most is that Johnny and Gracie have the blessing of both sets of parents. We will likely see Sylvia again for the barbeque—and the wedding, of course—but our social obligations have been met and are over."

He nodded in that way that a man nods when he feels it necessary but likely he doesn't understand any of it.

Then, after a minute, he asked with a little hesitation, "Why do you think she didn't say anything about your goin' up to see her in Baltimore?"

To which Emma replied, "Oh, honey, for the same reason that I didn't—because any way it comes out, we are both goin' to look real bad."

He blinked at that, then gave the same perplexed nod.

He stood there sipping his Coke, while she sat there drinking her tea, the both of them thinking their own thoughts.

Then she put her feet on the floor. "I guess I'd better get some of this cleaned up." Dishes remained in the dining room, and filled the sink and counter, along with food not yet put away and pans on the stove.

"Is there anything I can do to help?" he asked, standing next to a bag of garbage, one he had stepped around on his way to the refrigerator.

She looked at him. "Well, I don't know. What did you have in mind?"

He blinked. "I don't know . . . anything you need me to do."

"No," she replied, "not a thing."

He then said something about needing to check the oil in his truck and headed again out the back door.

She took her cup to the sink and washed it by itself, drying it carefully, marveling at how an intelligent man could stand in the midst of a mess and not figure out anything to do.

20

Private Session

Monday morning, Emma sat at the kitchen table with her planner, a tablet and a sense of accomplishment at the fulfillment of her social obligation toward Sylvia Kinney. Now it was full steam ahead with the production of the bridal-shower barbeque and her part for the wedding. She saw the events rolling out ahead of her like a bolt of white satin: the bridal-shower barbeque, all lovely and happy around the new pool, then the wedding-party dinner, the wedding, the reception, waving Gracie and Johnny away on their honeymoon. Her heart filled with anticipation, joy—and sadness, too. So many emotions.

There was a lot to do, she thought, bringing herself back to the moment. Picking up her pencil in a purposeful manner, she then sat looking at the blank tablet. She made a couple of notations, then stopped again. She had never been very good at getting organized with goals.

Likely Sylvia Kinney was very good with goals, she thought. A person didn't get to be in a management position without knowing all about setting goals. She remembered the woman from the previous afternoon. Sylvia had whipped out some sort of electronic gadget and gone to making notes. She had immediately given out first, second and third places to look for a wedding dress, as well as dates for making decisions about them. For the wedding invitations, she had said, "Preston will handle it." There had been no discussion of styles, no perusing a catalog or samples, which was how Emma would have had to do it, then think on it all and look again before finally choosing.

Emma had been playing with designs for the wedding invitation. Something very personal. She had once volunteered to take care of the invitations, and Gracie had seemed quite taken with the idea. But since Gracie hadn't mentioned it yesterday, Emma had kept silent. From all that she had read, the wedding invitations were the domain of the bride and her mother.

There remained the invitations for the barbeque. She put that on her list. Then she drifted off in thought about various designs and other things, until all of a sudden she was gazing at her daily calendar and read the notation: *Catherine, 11:30.*

Oh, my word. She had totally forgotten her private session!

Gazing at the notation, as if doing so would erase it, she tried to recall making the appointment and for what purpose. It seemed all of it had happened months ago, rather than less than a week. She thought of canceling, but only for a split second, because, of course, she couldn't do that at this late time. Not only did canceling at the last minute mean that she would still be charged the fee, but it would be irresponsible and rude.

Then, "Emma . . . yoo-hoo!"

It was her mother's voice calling out from the front of the house, followed by heavy footsteps approaching. This was a surprise, since it was only eight-thirty in the morning. Her mother was not an early riser; in fact, she rarely rose before ten, then usually sat reading until noon.

"You're up so early. What's wrong?" Emma said, having a small panic and inspecting her mother for signs of possible heart attack or something of that nature. Her mother looked a little disheveled. Perhaps she had *been* attacked.

But her mother replied, "Why, nothin', honey. I'm not up early. I haven't been to bed." Pushing a curl from her forehead, her mother plopped heavily into a chair and went on to say that she had gotten pumped up from something Wadley Smith had said, and had been up all night researching and writing an article about General Linus Gregory, a family ancestor and hero of the Revolution in North Carolina.

"Wadley's family and ours are related—I'm sure of it—through the General Gregory connection." Her mother was still so jazzed—likely from the pots of coffee that she always drank during these marathon writing sessions—that she leaned forward with intensity and continued with all the names of who had married whom and produced

265

whom. This sort of subject was born in her mother's blood. It was like hearing a reading from the Bible. Emma had grown up with it. She had listened to her grandmother do the same thing to her mother, and it occurred to her that she was likely to do this to Johnny. It was a disconcerting thought.

"I'm goin' to send it to *American Heritage Magazine,*" her mother said of her article. "Or possibly each of the Southern state magazines. I get an article in any of 'em and that will put cotton in Pamela Markham's mouth, by cracky."

"That will be wonderful," Emma said, instantly feeling a little torn. Wishing cotton into someone's mouth did not seem quite appropriate. Still, one's loyalty lay with one's mother.

"Might I have a cup of coffee, honey?" her mother asked.

"Oh . . . I just poured it out."

Her mother regarded her expectantly.

"I'll make a fresh pot," Emma said.

While Emma made the coffee, her mother went into the living room to retrieve the family album that she was compiling for Gracie and Johnny, which she had forgotten the previous evening. Returning, she pointed out a photograph of a large rural house and identified it as her great-grandparents' home—the "home place," she called it—saying they had been descendants of General Gregory.

"Mother . . . what is this?" Emma pointed to a

black-and-white photograph of her mother and herself. Another figure had, apparently, been standing behind her but had been neatly snipped out of the picture.

"Oh, that was your father, but he left our lives," said her mother. "That's how I illustrated it . . . but that tree . . ." She pointed. ". . . It stayed for as long as we lived there."

Emma could think of nothing to say to that. She gazed at the picture until her mother turned the page to a wedding photograph of her and John Cole.

"You do remember those photographs of you and John Cole that you said you would find?" her mother said.

"Yes. I will look this evenin'."

"Oh, good. Sylvia said she would send me the info and photographs for Gracie's pages. She said there weren't many. That her family didn't keep pictures. Can you imagine?"

Emma said she couldn't imagine it, and she really couldn't. Her family saved everything. Even pictures where her mother had cut out her father. Her mother had once had a stack of bills saved by her grandmother for over forty years. Emma herself had some drawers of colorful wrapping paper that she saved just in case she found a creative use for it.

"I can make whatever she gives us look larger," her mother said with confidence. "But would you remind Sylvia about the pictures when you talk to her?"

"I doubt I'll be speakin' with Sylvia, Mama."

"Oh?" Her mother regarded her.

"There's no reason for me to. I just had her to dinner because it was the polite thing. We aren't close friends or anything. We won't be related," she added, rising to tidy up around the sink. She was going to have to get ready for her appointment, but she rather hoped her mother would leave first. She did not want to tell her mother that she was going to see a therapist.

"Well, honey, maybe if you call Johnny now, you can catch them before Sylvia and Wadley fly back. I really can't give the kids a half-empty book."

Emma turned and met her mother's gaze. Then she stepped to the phone on the wall and called Johnny. He didn't answer, so she left a message.

"Well," said her mother, clearly disappointed.

"We can tell Gracie at the first possible moment. She will get what you need."

Her mother brightened somewhat. "Yes, that will have to do—and Gracie is a *lovely* person."

"Yes, she is," Emma agreed.

"And Sylvia is lovely, too. Don't you think?"

"Yes." Emma took up her mother's now-empty coffee mug to put in the dishwasher. "I have to get goin', Mama. I have an appointment late this morning."

Halfway expecting her mother to ask where she

268

was going, she was ready with an explanation about visiting the printer to order invitations to the barbeque. She even had her mouth open.

But instead, as if not hearing her, her mother said, "I do hope Sylvia marries Wadley. That will help a little."

"In what way?" asked Emma, puzzled.

"Well . . . it'll bring her and Gracie a little farther south."

"Oh, Mama! Now you sound like Pamela Markham."

"I do not. North Carolina and Oklahoma *are* Southern. But Baltimore is stretchin' it—I don't care what the Census Bureau says."

Emma drove over to New Hope Counseling Center with both hands on the wheel, air conditioner blowing hard, eyes shielded by dark glasses and foot firmly pushing the accelerator. Several times she blinked and realized that she had been so lost in thought as to have gone through intersections without any memory of them. Since she was on the road and between the lines, she held to hope that she had done the required stopping at the signs.

Her thoughts were bouncing from one thing to another in that rapid and annoying manner that sometimes took hold of a person—especially, it seemed, women—when they had a whole lot to do, and when they were puzzling out situations.

Emma kept returning to the memory of Sylvia

Kinney coming into her home, and how they both pretended so well to be meeting for the first time. They could have been awarded an Oscar. She imagined standing at the microphone with the woman, both holding on to their Oscar. And then both starting to tug and ending up in a physical fight.

That she had lied by omission began to torture her mind and made her promise never to do such a thing again. *God, if it can all just turn out all right . . .* By "all right" she basically meant "stay hidden."

She also remembered Sylvia with Gracie, and how she had felt jealous. Yes, she had, and she didn't like it, so she moved on from that thought.

Then she was thinking of her mother's comment about Baltimore, which illustrated using a fact for her purpose when it suited her and discounting it when it did not.

Everything in life was a matter of opinion. Having an opinion did not make it absolute truth.

For example, John Cole and her mother said Sylvia Kinney was nice and a lovely person. Emma could agree—somewhat—with that opinion, but not wholeheartedly. She did not agree that marrying Wadley Smith was going to greatly improve the woman. She rather believed it quite possibly might end up detracting from Wadley. Sylvia was a forceful sort. She was likely to wear him down.

To describe Sylvia Kinney, Emma would more use words like elegant . . . sophisticated . . . *chic,* although Emma was never certain if the pronunciation was *shick* or *chick* or *sheek.* She could look the word up in the dictionary. Or ask Belinda, although Belinda might be just as country as Emma was and not know, either.

Educated, Emma thought, was a word to describe Sylvia. But surely that could apply to herself, as well. She did know the meaning and spelling of the word "chic," even if she couldn't say it. Likely Sylvia would not know how to pronounce coyote. She would probably say, as many did, *kie-oh-tee,* but the original pronunciation was *kie-ote.*

"Highfalutin." That was a word to describe Sylvia Kinney. Although the woman was not the type to use such a word.

Just then, glancing down and seeing her speedometer, she instantly lifted her foot. She was like Belinda. She tended to press the accelerator harder when she was thinking harder.

"How do you say the word, C-H-I-C?" Emma asked, as she followed Catherine into her office.

"Ah . . . I believe it is *sheek.* But I could be wrong."

Emma was a little surprised that Catherine wouldn't know. She had thought the woman very educated, certainly more along the sophisticated lines of Sylvia Kinney. She was also a little surprised that Catherine sat in the upholstered chair, rather than in her desk chair. Not that it mattered, but Emma noticed it. Things were obviously different in a private session.

Emma sat in the same place on the couch where she sat when she and John Cole came together for their sessions. She looked over to the empty place where he normally sat and felt funny.

"So why don't you tell me what's been going on?" Catherine said.

"Oh. Well, there's been a lot, actually."

In the manner of diving off a pier, she launched into the telling. She started with the Sunday dinner and her impressions of Sylvia—which, she explained, was why she had wanted to know how to say the word "chic." She also put in that she did know how to say and spell "highfalutin." Because of starting with the dinner, she then had to back up and tell about everything else. It seemed as if she repeatedly used the word "because."

As she had done in the marriage counseling sessions, she found herself just talking and talking. A number of times she had a sense of standing off and observing herself rattling on. She could not seem to stop. Perhaps it was the way Catherine seemed to listen with attentiveness. And that Catherine was not family or a friend, so Emma could tell her how angry she had really been about Sylvia Kinney not liking Johnny, but how she had pretended to be all calm to Johnny and Gracie. And

272

then she confided about Joella's drinking, observing how Charlie J. ignored her, hardly noticing that she was in the room, his own wife.

Once, when Emma was speaking about finding Sylvia annoying, Catherine managed to get in, "Let's look at that. What do you suppose is happening?"

"I suppose that she is looking down on us."

"Uh-huh. Suppose we take a look at your feelings . . ."

"Well, my feeling is that she is on my last nerve," Emma responded. "She's standoffish. I'm as friendly as I can be—I extended a hand of friendliness, but it's like all of it bounces right off her. She just looks at me and all the family like we aren't up to her level. She doesn't hardly talk. She'll answer if you ask her something, and she smiles, but she doesn't really carry on a conversation. It is like talkin' to a brick wall."

"Why do you think that is?"

Emma was a little surprised. She would have thought Catherine, being a therapist, could tell her the reason.

"Well," she said, thinking about it, "you know, maybe she just doesn't know what to say." This thought came suddenly and intrigued her. "We really are quite different from each other. Our whole family is as different from her as night and day, and there she was, thrust into our environment. What is funny is that Wadley Smith isn't—

so different from us, I mean. He talks, and he's just like home folks. Maybe that makes it harder for Sylvia. Maybe it's hard to be so chic."

She still had trouble with the word, but she was beginning to feel a little sorry for the woman.

"You know, I think maybe she annoys me because I try so hard but feel like she is set not to accept any of it." This seemed quite a revelation. "My tryin' isn't helpin' at all, is it? You can't make someone like you. And I don't know why her being uppity should bother me. My own mother can be uppity. She likes to criticize me for being too emotional. And my Lord, my grandmother could take the cake for uppity . . . . Well, we all have things about others that bother us. I'm sorry . . . you were about to say something?"

"Just that it helps to try to see from another's point of view, which you are doing. Go ahead."

"I guess I'm still annoyed at Sylvia's point of view of not liking Johnny. I don't care that she came out and gave her okay to the marriage. I could tell she still is not happy with it. But that's just how it is, and I've tried and can't change it."

She felt a lot better with the insight. It was a little amazing how much better she felt. She had not fully understood how her feelings toward Sylvia Kinney had been weighing upon her.

Her eyes slid to the clock on Catherine's desk, and she saw that the session was almost over. It had gone by fast.

"I can see why John Cole wanted a private appointment," she said. "This has sure been helpful. I was able to talk about some things I wouldn't, if he was here. Like about his brother and sister-in-law. John Cole would not have wanted to talk about any of that. He is not goin' to talk about anything that might sound like his family is not perfect. I really would like to get your feedback on them, on what I might do to help them, the next time I come."

She had gathered her purse and was halfway up when she noticed that Catherine had not moved but remained relaxed in the chair.

"I have a few minutes," Catherine said. "Before we end today's session, I'd like to touch on a few points."

"Oh." Emma slid back down on the sofa. She hadn't known a session could be extended. She hoped no one was waiting, especially if they might be crying.

"One thing I'd like to touch on is how you feel about hiding your confrontation with Sylvia from Johnny and Gracie."

"Well . . ." Emma gazed at Catherine, who was gazing at her; then she slid her eyes to the books on the shelf just beyond Catherine's chair, saying, "It wasn't so much of a confrontation. We did not speak a cross word. I extended a cordial introduction and invitation. And I don't know how it got to be hidden." The memory of not wanting to tell

Johnny from the outset pricked at her mind. "I guess I didn't think it through at the beginning, and then everything happened so fast. It's just ended up this way, and everything has turned out. Speakin' about it now would not help."

Catherine nodded. "And what do you think might have happened if you had not interfered? Do you think that Johnny and Gracie are not capable of handling their own problems?"

The use of the word "interfered" echoed in Emma's mind, falling right over the word "confrontation." She thought Catherine might have a slightly wrong idea about the situation.

"They were not handling the matter very well," Emma said. "Gracie had been hiding the problem from the beginning. It was Johnny who told me, and not until he didn't know what to do. And sometimes when we are young and startin' out, we do need help. I think Johnny and Gracie would probably have gone ahead and gotten married, but there would have been hard feelings. It just isn't a good way to start, with one of them feeling unwanted. That affects us all. And Sylvia could have ended up losing out, and she was smart enough to see that. Someone needed to speak up, and I did."

When she ended with this, she felt quite certain, although she watched carefully for Catherine's reaction, which was to nod in a manner that allowed Emma to relax a little, and to say, "All right, you seem satisfied. That's good."

Then Catherine slid forward in the chair, giving the indication of winding up the session. Emma prepared to rise, too.

But then Catherine stopped at the edge of her chair, so Emma stopped, too.

"I just have one more thought for you," said Catherine. "In all you told me today, you haven't talked about yours and John Cole's relationship. You've barely mentioned John Cole at all. Where is he in all of this?"

"Oh, he was there. He hasn't gone anywhere. He's still home."

"Yes, I gathered that. But you haven't mentioned him in connection with you. How's the sex?"

Emma was surprised at the sudden question. "Well . . . we've been awfully busy what with the pool and everyone droppin' in to visit. We haven't hardly had a minute alone."

Then she remembered the morning after her return from Baltimore. "We are connecting, though. John Cole was very interested the morning after I came back from Baltimore. But . . . then Johnny stopped by. It was mid-morning. He naturally expected us to be up and about," she explained.

"Uh-huh." Catherine nodded. "There are a few things I think you might want to think about. It was your son's wedding that brought you and John Cole back together, but then, for a variety of reasons, you both made the decision to seek a permanent reconnection. You've been working well on that for some weeks, and then along comes a problem in your son's life, and from everything you've said today, yours and John Cole's relationship has for the past week pretty much been pushed to the side."

Emma nodded slightly, to indicate she heard.

"I think you might want to ask yourself where your relationship with John Cole fits into your life. Where do you *want* your marriage to fit in?"

With a short smile, Catherine then rose and moved to her desk, saying, "Just something you might want to think about for the next few weeks. I'm going to be out of town and won't be back until the middle of next month."

Emma followed her with her eyes, but was still sitting on the edge of the couch when Catherine turned to ask if she might want a morning or afternoon the next time.

When she came out of the counseling clinic, a woman was going in. Coincidentally, she was the woman who had sat crying so hard in the waiting room the first time Emma and John Cole had come to the offices. Emma felt a little shocked sensation to see her. The woman's eyes carefully avoided Emma, who experienced the silly urge to say to her, "You'd better get in there quick. She's going out of town."

Holding tight to her keys, Emma walked swiftly

to her car, got in and sat there for a moment, reading the date on the appointment card Catherine had given her. Then, dropping the card into her purse, she started the car and drove to the Berry Truck Stop and offices.

Shelley Dilks wasn't at her desk, and the door to John Cole's office was closed. Emma went to it and, hand on the knob, heard the murmur of voices inside. Giving a light knock, she entered.

John Cole looked up from behind his desk. Shelley Dilks sat beside him and looked up, too, as did two other men sitting near the desk.

"No one was out here," Emma said. She stopped in the doorway.

John Cole rose, and made quick introductions to the two men, who didn't get up but did shift to face her and replied politely. She felt as unwelcome as if she had intruded into the careful planning of a robbery or something.

"We're in a meeting," John Cole said. "Is it important?"

"Oh, no. I was just passin' and stopped in. I'll see you later." She smiled cordially to everyone and retreated.

Shelley Dilks had risen and came out of the office with her, closing the door behind them. "It's a meetin' with the bankers," she said in a low voice. "They're makin' the final arrangements for the new store." She remained at the closed door, with her hand behind her on the knob.

"Oh. That's right. I forgot," Emma said, not wanting to give the impression that she knew nothing about it. Had John Cole said anything about a new store? She didn't think so.

Shelley Dilks asked if Emma wanted to leave a message. Emma said no, repeating that she had stopped on the spur of the moment. "I was just goin' to talk to John Cole about the pool," she added, feeling the need to come up with a bona fide reason.

As she left, she saw Shelley Dilks slip back into John Cole's office to rejoin the important meeting, about which Emma had not known, and in which she had no part.

Returning through the store area toward the front doors, she passed by the aisle of toiletries and over-the-counter medications. This section was one of the most profitable in the store, providing necessary items to many truckers on a long haul. For some reason this information crossed Emma's mind quite prominently, as giving testament to her knowledge about the business.

She ran her eyes over the items arranged on the shelving. The packaging of many things was quite different from what she remembered. She straightened toothbrushes and tubes of hemorrhoid cream, then took a package of aspirin from a hook. Going to the refrigerated section for a bottle of water, she found the water had been moved to the far end. Or maybe she just didn't remember correctly, she thought, as she went to the checkout, where she stood in line behind an enormous man in a black leather vest—how could he stand it in the heat?—and a tiny woman with bright red hair.

When it came her turn, Emma stepped up to the counter, where a clerk she did not know rang up her bill. "Any fuel?" the girl asked with a perfunctory smile.

"No." Emma looked at the girl's face, trying to remember knowing her. She could not recall when she had last bought anything from the store. She had not been around any of the employees since the New Year's Eve party they always held at their home.

Just then a voice rang out. "Hi, Miz Berry! How're you doin' today?"

"Hello, Cherry," Emma said with warmth, foolishly happy at seeing someone she knew and at being recognized. "I'm fine . . . and you?" She had been the one to hire Cherry and help to train her. Her mind calculated the years. *Fifteen?* She couldn't look at it.

She asked about the woman's children and talked so long that she was embarrassed to see the woman finally edge herself away.

"I've got to check on the diesel that was just delivered, Miz Berry. Good seein' you."

Emma went out to her car, downed two aspirin and drove home. Halfway there she realized that she had forgotten to stop at the print shop to order the shower invitations. A mile from her house, she realized that she could not recall making two necessary turns. She really needed to get home and stay off the road.

Yet she passed her driveway, and went into Valentine and to the drugstore, where she was grateful to find Belinda sitting on her mother's tall stool behind the counter. The lunch crowd had pretty much cleared out. Emma sat on a stool and ordered a barbeque sandwich and glass of cold tea. A few people she knew from the fire department auxiliary and chamber of commerce came and went. Emma finished her sandwich and had two refills on her tea, and kept on sitting there. She wanted to discuss with Belinda the subjects that Catherine had brought up, namely her behavior in regard to Johnny and smoothing over the difficulty with Sylvia, and the implication that she was slipshod or something of that nature in her marriage. She was now not at all certain what Catherine had been saying and thought her friend might be able to help her sort this out.

Yet for some reason, she could not bring up the subject but chatted on instead about her greeting cards, and the town news that Belinda intended for her new radio spot, and shopping and the weather.

Finally she did come out with, "Do you think I interfered in Johnny's life when I went up to see Sylvia?"

Belinda barely blinked. "Oh, yes, of course it was buttin' in, but it worked, didn't it?"

"It seems to have come out all right." Emma went on to tell about her therapy session, and Catherine's questions about Emma's motives and handling of the matter.

Belinda, by then having come around and sat herself down on the stool beside Emma, since they were alone, gave her opinion, which was that there were times when interfering was necessary. "These days, people make a religion out of stayin' out of everyone's business. But there are times when we can do a small thing that helps. When we're older and a little wiser, it is our responsibility to speak up."

"That's how I see it. I don't intend to run their lives, but they needed a little help. It was all of our lives that would have eventually been affected," she said, suddenly thinking of it. "All because of a misconception on Sylvia's part, and I was the best one to address it."

"The point was a larger truth, and that of Johnny and Gracie's welfare," said Belinda.

"Well, that's how I saw it. I suppose it is a case-by-case basis, though."

Belinda agreed with this, and then they had to stop the intimate conversation because Naomi Smith, the pastor's wife, came in to get three milkshakes to go and to sell raffle tickets for a chance to win VIP tickets to the Glorious

Women's seminar. "These are not chances to win," Naomi said. "We don't call them that. We call them tickets for a drawing to raise money for a good cause."

Emma and Belinda each said they would buy four tickets for the good cause. Then Emma was embarrassed to discover she had only two dollars in her purse, so Belinda paid for hers, too.

When she drove home, she made an effort to keep her mind on her driving and to go slowly. She was very glad that she did, because as she drove down Church Street, Willie Lee and his dog and another little dark-haired boy ran across the street in front of her. She likely would have had plenty of time to stop—Willie Lee got to the curb and turned to wave at her before she was fully past—but still, she was reminded of what could happen when she wasn't paying attention.

It occurred to her that sometimes a person's attention was drawn in many directions at once. It was simply the way of life and could no more be stopped than the shadows at evening.

When John Cole arrived home, she was in the kitchen, with photographs from a box spread out across the table. She chose half a dozen snapshots of her and John Cole in their early years together. She lined them up and put her face close. She studied them, trying to recall the circumstances under which each one had been taken.

The phone rang. It was Johnny, who said he had gotten her message and reported that he had already requested that Gracie remind Sylvia about the information his grandmother needed.

Emma said, "Your grandma says to be sure and tell Sylvia that she will get the photographs copied and will return them."

"Okay . . . I'll have Gracie tell her," Johnny replied.

Emma imagined their future, with Gracie running herself ragged back and forth between Johnny and Sylvia.

As if in response to this thought, he then added, "But Gracie's mom won't be able to send the pictures right away, because she's decided to stay out here at least another week."

"Oh, really?" Of course, there was no reason why Emma should care about this. None at all.

"Yeah. You know Gracie's girlfriends are givin' her that weddin' shower, so her mom is stayin' for that, and to go shoppin' and stuff. She moved over to Gracie's apartment from the hotel this afternoon." There was a small note of resignation in his voice at this part of it.

Emma said in an upbeat tone that this was wonderful for both women, and Johnny said, "Yeah, it is."

Unable to help herself—and it was the polite thing, after all—Emma inquired about Wadley. Just what Wadley's actions would say about him

285

and Sylvia she could not say, but she was interested.

Johnny explained that Wadley had already flown back to Baltimore, because of some business, but that maybe he would return to get Sylvia. "He said he sure liked Grama," Johnny added with laughter in his voice.

"I'll have to tell her. She'll be thrilled."

They exchanged a few more bits of conversation and then said goodbye.

Directly after hanging up, Emma called her mother to tell her what Johnny had said about Wadley liking her. Her mother was, as she had expected, thrilled. While Emma was enjoying being the bearer of good news, she went on to say that she had succeeded in getting a reminder to Sylvia about the promised photographs and information for her mother's album project. Then she had to dampen this pleasure somewhat, when she explained about Sylvia extending her visit, which obviously meant a delay in producing the photographs.

Her mother took this news with some irritation, as if Emma should or even *could* do something about it. Having expected this, Emma deflected the irritation by saying that she had found young photographs of herself and John Cole, as her mother had requested. They spoke for some minutes about the propensity of her mother's people for picture-taking. Emma had found a number of snapshots of her mother and herself as a baby, and a number of her mother's aunts and uncles, taken by her Grandmother Maisie.

"I found two of Daddy," she told her mother. "You really need to put one in the kids' album. It won't be complete if you don't include him."

"Oh, all right—the smallest one," said her mother.

After saying goodbye, Emma gathered a number of the pictures and carried them into her workroom. There she turned on her drawing-table light and stuck the photographs up on the slanted table for ease of viewing. Pulling out a round magnifying glass, she peered over them like Miss Marple looking for clues.

21

Pictures of the Early Years
1966—1970

Within the first weeks of their marriage, they excitedly bought a fancy, expensive camera. John Cole had raved over a camera that a buddy of his aboard ship had bought, and four times he dragged Emma down to the Navy Exchange to gaze at one just like it in the showcase, while extolling the camera's virtues and asking Emma if she wanted it and thought they should buy it.

This was to be a pattern that repeated itself. John

Cole often wanted Emma to make decisions about matters in which he felt uncertain. That way, if the choice turned out to be a poor one, he did not have to feel responsible. He could blame Emma. It took Emma years to see that this was happening, and even when she did realize the pattern, she did not pay it any attention. Making decisions was her natural inclination. She was simply doing what she had learned in her family, which was that the women were supposed to run the show. Even the men in her family had believed this, and had not appreciated it when their women didn't keep things going along.

Later, when she came to live in the midst of the Berry family, she was amazed at the autocratic manner of the men. It was simply the reverse of what she had known, John Cole once said, but she argued that it was not true. None of the women of her family were convinced of their rightness simply because of their sex. They relied on their intellect and experience.

In the Berry family, Pop Berry was king. His sons were his princes, although kings in their own households. The women of the family were the servants, although Mother Berry was queen of her daughter, daughters-in-law and granddaughters.

John Cole was somewhat the exception. That he did not run Emma ragged made him instantly suspicious. John Cole had several strikes against him. He was the youngest in a family where age determined placement, and the only one to have one go at high-school football and not like it. He turned out to be the only one to go into the Navy and spend six years away from home, and to end up married to a woman from a totally different state and different background, and a Methodist, which might as well been a different religion entirely. His family rather treated him as if they did not know what to do with him. They did not trust him. His every decision came under constant scrutiny.

The Berrys generally found things lacking everywhere, in people, in circumstances and in money. They worried so much about the latter that Pop Berry at one time kept an enormous amount of cash hidden in a coffee can buried underneath the garage. Emma had been shocked when she learned this. She asked what would happen if the garage burned. This produced a lot of discussion about how much the ground would protect the money from heat. A few nights later, when she got up to go to the bathroom in their apartment over said garage, she looked out the window and saw Pop Berry below, approaching with a shovel. She watched and could see little, but could hear scraping. Sometime later, she saw him walk back to the house. She had always wondered where he moved the money. She also always suspected that the Berry family sometimes regretted that they more or less drove John Cole away. It was plainly evident now that he was by far the most financially astute of the lot. In the past few years, and always late at night, his father called him asking for advice about the hardware store. Likely the older man never told his other two sons of the phone calls.

In the case of the camera—and many other purchases—Emma instantly read John Cole's face and manner, and knew having it would make him happy. "Yes, get it," she said each time he asked, and on the fourth time, he did. He enjoyed it immensely for several days; however, it was not one of those point-and-shoot jobs, but had many dials and complications that required reading the instruction booklet. John Cole had no patience for that, so he handed it over to Emma to figure out. He seemed to equally enjoy seeing her work the camera and be in no great hurry to grab it back.

From that time, there were many photographs of John Cole, who was very photogenic, of the little dog they'd had at the time, and of places they went, a number of Emma—who more often than not was captured with an awkward expression, probably because she was instructing John Cole as he attempted to use the camera—but only a few of Emma and John Cole together. This seemed a curiously telling fact of their existence in those years.

To begin with, asking someone to take their picture with the fancy camera proved daunting because of the detailed instruction required. One had to turn a dial to focus and press a button to measure the light, and then finally press the button to take a picture. Emma would set the camera up, hand it over to the person to take the picture and then run over to join John Cole. She usually came out looking harried in their pictures together, because of the rush.

Then, during the years when John Cole was in the Navy, they lived away from both of their families. There were no automatically available people with them on their excursions, or living next door, to take their picture. During the first months following their wedding, Emma's mother and Grandmother Maisie had several times made the trip to Norfolk to visit them, and there were a few snapshots of the newly married couple from that time. Grandmother Maisie used her own little Brownie. These shots all had a flowering bush or tree included in the background; Grandmother Maisie did not feel a photograph complete without a bush or tree.

Their faces were shockingly young. In the few pictures where John Cole wore his Navy uniform, he appeared a little older, but in all of them, Emma looked about twelve. Looking at them in later years, the thought always crossed her mind: What in the world had her mother been thinking to allow her to marry while still a child?

After Emma and John Cole had moved to Florida, however, they were completely on their own. No family came to visit them, and, as inconceivable as it seemed from this distance in time, they had no couple friends. John Cole spent much of the time at sea, where he formed friendships with fellows on the ship. Left alone and at home, Emma made a life of her own, with friendships with neighbors and people at the insurance office where she worked. The two of them formed more or less separate lives, and yet it was this separateness away from family and the places where they had grown up that gave them a strong bond. It was during that abundant time on her own that Emma halfway realized that what she and John Cole shared the most was the desire to be away from their individual families. They were very much like children in a free and happy world for the first time.

That first summer, John Cole's ship spent many weekends in a row in port. Nearly every Saturday and Sunday, they would get up early, get doughnuts at a bakery and head for the beach, where they would then stretch out on canvas cots. Emma would turn her head to face John Cole and gaze at him for long minutes, imprinting the sight into her mind, to carry her through when he would be gone. When their bodies were made hot and sweaty by the strong sun, they would jump up and run into the water. Many evenings they would walk the beach hand in hand. They padded on bare feet through the lapping waves, and gathered seashells and kissed and watched the water glow with the coral setting sun.

One evening, when the light was especially wonderful, Emma had embarrassed John Cole to death by going up to a woman whom she saw taking pictures with a complicated camera and asking her to take their picture. Emma had suspected that the woman would be able to handle their fancy camera with ease, and this proved the case. The woman was a travel photographer, she told them. She was particular about positioning Emma and John Cole in relation to the golden rays of the setting sun. She took half a dozen shots. It was as if Emma and John Cole were there for the woman's pleasure.

Surprisingly, John Cole, once he had felt reassured by the woman's friendliness, had liked the attention. It had been Emma who began to get impatient with it. She worried at the cost of the film and developing. However, when she had seen the results, she had been thrilled. She had framed her favorite, and had sent copies to both her mother and grandmother, and to John Cole's parents.

Two years later, when they had moved back to John Cole's hometown, she had found the beach photograph that she had sent the elder Berrys in the possession of Joella. "Mother Berry didn't like you in the bikini," Joella told her in a low and furtive voice.

During those early years, Emma and John Cole hardly ever had a cross word. Neither of them liked to argue. It reminded them too much of their own families. Very probably those years were where the habit of swallowing their words had become entrenched.

An only child, Emma had been used to being alone and was not overly upset with John Cole's absences when he had to go to sea. There had been two long cruises, however, that had stretched her capacity for alone time. After the first of these, when he had sailed for nearly two months down toward Cuba, she had welcomed him with the eager anticipation seen in all the movies, flying into her conquering sailor's arms when he disembarked from his mighty ship. She could not get enough of him, kissing and holding him. She eagerly expected him to spend every moment with her. This was the way of a woman and surely not too unreasonable a request, except it likely overwhelmed him, a man.

The following day, he announced that he was going off to a football game with several single buddies from the ship. Emma told him that she wanted to be with him and reminded him that he didn't even like football. He insisted he was going anyway, and off he went. Emma could not believe that he would choose football that he did not like and male companionship over being with her when she asked him to be.

After he had stalked out the door of their apartment, she flew into a major hissy fit and threw their eight-by-ten wedding portrait at the door. The glass shattered and ripped tiny holes in the photograph. Seeing this, she then sobbed all afternoon. She cleaned up the mess before John Cole returned home. The following day, she sought out a professional photographer who advertised repairs of damaged photographs.

"It looks like you broke the picture in the frame," he said, examining it closely.

"I did," she said in a small voice. "Can you fix it?"

He smiled gently and said that he could. He did a wonderful job, and Emma had bought a stately new frame. John Cole had never even noticed. For years she would pick up the photograph and remember, and vow not to get into a fight with him ever again.

There was a distinct difference between the photographs of their first year and one taken on the day of his release from the Navy. In that picture, they were standing together, John Cole's arm draped around Emma in a nonchalant stance, in front of a brand-new sporty Dodge Charger. John Cole had by then made an extended cruise to the Mediterranean Sea and managed to grow a mustache. Emma, having spent those eight months on her own and praying daily fervent prayers that her husband would not be sent to Vietnam, had her hair up and wore a Lady Winston pale blue linen sheath dress and little white boots. She had prevailed on their mailman to take the picture. He had cut off the very end of the car, and John Cole had been disappointed about that.

They had become proud owners of the sporty maroon sedan four months earlier, upon John Cole's return from extended sea duty. He had, as always, saved up quite a bit of money. Emma had surprised him with savings of her own. With their nest egg—and the confidence of youth that they were only going to progress to greater things—they decided to buy their first new car. John Cole knew exactly what vehicle he wanted. He had always wanted a convertible, but they could not afford one. They could, however, afford one of the new sunroof types. "It's practical," he told Emma during one of their trips to look the car over. "Easy to close, won't lose heat or air."

Emma told him they should buy it. They went over their finances and knew exactly the limit of what they could afford. They visited a car dealer and found just the color they wanted.

"Are you sure you want this car?" John Cole asked Emma.

"Yes," she answered.

It was very likely that the dealer took one look at the young couple with their innocent and eager faces, and thought, *I'm in the money.* He took the details of their trade-in and finances. Emma told him the limit of what she and John Cole could afford each month and was pleased at how easily the salesman agreed to it. Everything seemed set.

They were taken back to the business manager's office where about a hundred papers were put before them for their signatures. The business manager went through each page in two seconds, pointing at the figures. Emma followed as best she could. All of a sudden, a figure jumped out at her.

"That's not what we said we could afford for a monthly payment," she said, drawing back her signing hand.

The business manager met her gaze. "Oh." He flipped through the papers. "This is what you agreed to pay." He showed her.

"No. There's been a mistake."

The salesman was called. She and John Cole were told they must have misunderstood. While John Cole looked at her, Emma said very politely that perhaps they had misunderstood and she was sorry, but they were not going to pay any more for the new car. She and John Cole were asked to wait for the dealership manager to be consulted. They spent the time taking turns getting in and out of the car, John Cole opening and closing the sunroof, as he said, "Do you think we ought to go ahead and pay the extra? It's not so much."

"If you want to, we can," Emma said. She was stuck between making him happy and stubborn annoyance at the salesman.

Frowning, John Cole went off to get a Coke out of the cold-drink machine.

Emma wandered around. The plate-glass windows reflected her image and the vehicles in the showroom. It had gotten dark while they had done all the talking and waiting. Quite suddenly, she saw John Cole behind her, his image reflected in the glass. He was standing gazing at the car of his dreams. She did the wildest thing, something she would only do on two more occasions in her life. She said, "God, if You can get us the car, please do. If they meet our price, I'll know that we should agree and have the car. If they do not meet our price, then I accept that we are not to have this car."

When the salesman returned, he said, "I'm sorry, but we just can't lower the price of the car any more."

Emma and John Cole thanked him and left. Emma watched John Cole and was relieved to see he was not crushed. In fact, he said, "Our car is paid for," as if he was seeing this for the first time. And he was so happy with this thought that he grabbed Emma to him and kissed her.

"Hey!" A shout came from the showroom, where, in a rather startling manner, their salesman burst out the door. "O-kay! You win. It's yours!" he yelled, so worked up that he seemed to jump into the air.

Emma and John Cole stared at the man, who actually said exactly, "The damn car is yours!"

John Cole shook his head. "Nah . . . I don't want it now."

But Emma put a hand on his arm. "Oh, but . . ."

He gazed at her, then sighed deeply and said, "Okay, if you want it."

He was to call it her car for as long as they owned it, which was ten years, but the only time she got to drive it was when he was not around.

When John Cole was released from the Navy and they drove back to his hometown and showed the car to his mother and father, Pop Berry said, "I think you'd get more use out of a pickup," and Mother Berry said, "White seats? You'll never keep those clean."

One thing Emma never forgot about the night they bought the car. It was the memory of driving home in it. John Cole cranked open the sunroof and told her to turn on the radio. It was a wonderful, top-of-the-line stereo, with speakers in the back and the doors. They felt rich. The night air and stars came in the sunroof, and the Supremes singing "Someday We'll Be Together" came out of the radio. When they arrived in their driveway, they opened the doors, then danced to the music there in the moonlight.

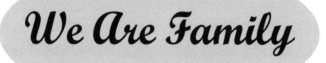

We Are Family

22

1550 AM on the Radio Dial
The Home Folks Show

A chorus of melodious bells rang in Winston's earphones, and Jim Rainwater grinned at him from over at the controls.

"How do ya' like those bells?" Winston asked his audience. "We thought we'd liven up the *Home Folks Show* with some new sound effects. Those big-city stations don't have anythin' on us down here at 1550 AM on the radio dial, comin' at you from Valentine, America, which is as close to heaven as you can get on earth."

A choir pealed out, *"Hal-le-luyah!"* followed by bells and cymbals.

"We've got a pretty busy show for you today. We are going to be playin' music from Oklahoma artists and have a few contests to see if you out there can guess the identity of some of the talented people our state has produced. In the second hour, Miz Lillian Jennings, a retired history professor, is goin' to visit with us about the history of our state. You might just learn somethin', so stay tuned.

"In just a minute we'll have Belinda Blaine with her *Around Town and Beyond* report. She's doin' the show by phone today from over at the drugstore. But first, here's a message from one of our sponsors . . . ."

He heard the advertising jingle come on for the *Valentine Voice,* and then a click of the phone. "Hey, Belinda. How're you makin' out today?"

"Hello, Winston. Hello, ever'body."

Winston jumped and grabbed his earphones, at the same time seeing Jim Rainwater rapidly adjusting buttons. "You're not on the air yet, honey . . . and you don't have to shout. We can hear you fine. And I think you need to turn your radio down."

"Oh . . . I forgot. I'm sorry. There. Is that better?"

"Great." Winston liked how Belinda got contrite on the radio. It was the only place she ever got contrite about anything, as far as he could tell.

Down at the drugstore, standing tensely behind the counter, Belinda held the phone receiver to her ear with one hand and flagged her other hand at Lyle and the new deputy, Giff Phelps, who sat on the other side of the counter talking their fool heads off. She was already aggravated because her mother was off somewhere with Jaydee again, apparently completely forgetting that today was Belinda's day on the radio, and Cousin Arlo had called in sick with measles, of all things, a story that his mother, if she could be believed, backed up.

Belinda had not been able to find one person to help her out, so she was stuck at the drugstore. She had counted on the mid-morning lull, but then Lyle and his new best buddy Giff had come in for coffee. Giff had even had the audacity to go and tune the radio to the all-talk station. She could not believe his high-handed rudeness.

She had gone to the radio and jerked the dial right back where it belonged, informing both men that it was time for her show and for them to be quiet. They did not see her waving at them right then, though. To get their attention, she threatened to shove Giff Phelps's coffee into his lap. He cast her a startled looked, and she mouthed, *Shut up.* It was not so much Lyle and Giff talking as it was Giff expounding and Lyle listening with the devotion of a puppy dog. The sight made Belinda nuts.

Just then she realized that Winston had cued her with, "What's the news about town today, Miss Belinda?"

"Oh . . . we've got some exciting happenings to tell you folks." She found her notes. "As many of you may know, there has been a rash of petty thefts in Valentine in the past couple of months. Two of the latest were reported just yesterday evenin' by Mrs. George Julian, who had a cotton flannel blanket stolen off her clothesline, and Naomi Smith, who lost two brand-new pairs of jeans and a blue T-shirt that belonged to her son, Fisk, off her line."

"Don't forget . . . Berry Stop . . ." Lyle said, holding up a finger.

Shooting him a glare and waving an impatient hand, Belinda said into the phone, "I didn't even know that people used clotheslines anymore. It obviously is not safe. If you want that fresh-breeze smell, you can just throw a Downy sheet in your dryer."

"That might be a good subject for a poll," stuck in Winston. "How many of our ladies still use a clothesline?"

"Uh, yes, it would be." She wished people would quit interrupting her. "Then, only two hours ago this very morning, there was a theft from the Quick Stop that turned into a pretty good mess. Some little girl came in there grabbing things. Paris Miller was clerking. She was back in the cooler, stocking the racks. She recognized the girl—only she thought it was a boy who had previously shoplifted and gotten away. She hollered at him, uh, her, and the girl grabbed candy and a bag of diapers, and ran out. Paris ran after her, which she thought was a him, until she saw a ponytail hanging out from beneath the little girl's hat.

"Paris tackled the girl around back of the Stop, but the girl got away and ran into the ladies room and locked the door. There she jammed up the toilet with a diaper and flooded the room. Paris didn't know at the time that this was what had happened, of course, since she was still outside and hollerin', tryin' to get someone's attention. When she saw the water runnin' out from under the door, she worried that the girl might have been trying to drown herself, a situation that did happen sometime back at the sheriff's office. Paris then ran for help, which left the bathroom door unguarded, and the girl was able to get away.

"The sheriff's department believes that all these thefts are related and are being committed by a gang of youths. They are asking everyone to keep a lookout and for anyone who knows anything to come forward. If you even think you have a clue, please call the sheriff's office.

"Please don't call me. I repeat—call the sheriff's office, not me." She halfway expected Winston to break in, but he didn't.

"Now, on to excitement of a good kind—our own Charlotte Conroy from down at the *Valentine Voice* has been selected as a contestant on the *Wheel of Fortune*. The show's production company recently held an audition in Oklahoma City. Charlotte practiced being exuberant for two weeks to prepare. Exuberance is a requirement for the show. It wasn't too easy for her, but obviously she did that okay, and obviously the show's producers are not prejudiced against tall people. Those other contestants aren't gonna have a chance, because Charlotte has been watchin' *Wheel of Fortune* since it began. Charlotte and her husband, Sandy, will leave here on Thursday and be gone to California for two weeks, one of those spent at a romantic, seaside resort of unknown name and destination. That was all Sandy's idea, too.

"And saving the best for last, I'm goin' to right now on the air do the drawing for the free tickets to the Glorious Women's Day. In case you haven't heard, this is a one-day event of revival and celebration for women, being held at the Servants' Fellowship Church up in Lawton . . . but all of you who bought the chances know this, so . . ."

"You're gonna do the drawin' right now?" Winston asked.

"Yes." She had forgotten to be prepared for his interrupting. It was like he waited for her to forget him. "It won't take but a minute. I only have to draw two winners."

"Then we're gonna do a drum-roll for you."

"Oh, really?"

"Yes . . . here we go. Can we have a drumroll, please, sir?"

The drumroll sounded in her ears.

"Are you drawin'?" Winston asked.

"Yes . . . I'm reachin' my hand into the Lance cookie jar. It doesn't have cookies in it. Naomi was goin' to do this, but she had to take her mother to the doctor. If I pull out my own ticket, it will be disqualified, of course. And the first winner is . . . Marilee Holloway!"

There came the sound of a crowd clapping, then Belinda said, "I'll bet Marilee needs this day away. Does everyone know that she is havin' *another* baby? And she is well into her forties. Marilee, sugar, you got a whole day away from dishes and diapers, and I'll bet they get a stool for you to put your feet up."

Then she said she was drawing again, and there came the sound of the drumroll. She pulled out a ticket and waited through several more seconds of drumroll before she read it out.

"Okay, the second winner is . . . well, for heavensake. It is Emma Berry!"

Belinda was so excited that all she said into the phone and over the air was, "That's it for today. Bye."

Then she pressed the receiver button, cutting off the clapping, and dialed Emma's number. As she did this, she looked up to see Lyle leaving with Giff. She covered the speaker with her hand to call to him, but then heard Emma's voice over the line. She told her friend the good news and went on to say, "I'll buy a ticket and go with you. I don't mind at all. In fact, I'd really like to go. I'll drive, too."

She was quite satisfied. She was getting a complete day away. She would get to dress up and look nice all day, and maybe she could get her consciousness raised and figure out a way to lure her husband back where he belonged.

• • •

Over at the radio station, Winston said into the microphone, "Let me see what we have in the prize vault."

Jim Rainwater set off a squeaking door. He and Winston looked at each other with the glee of two boys with a new toy.

Holding out the paper to read, Winston said, "Here's one . . . a gift certificate for a half-hour therapeutic body massage by Oralee Beaumont down at the newly opened Body Beautiful Salon and Day Spa. This gift certificate goes to the first caller to give me the name of Hoyt Axton's mother and the famous song she wrote. While we take your calls, here's Hoyt singin' 'In a Young Girl's Mind.' "

Vella Blaine's Land Rover sat in an old drive a quarter of a mile up the hill from the radio station, with its four doors open wide and Hoyt Axton's voice singing out of the radio in the dash. Vella, on a blanket with Jaydee in the shade of an elm tree, brought out her cell phone and dialed the radio station.

"Hello, Jim," she said, when the young man's voice came over the line. "The answer is Mae Axton, who was co-author of 'Heartbreak Hotel.' "

Jim Rainwater replied that he didn't know if he could take her call, since it wasn't on the radio station line. "And anyway, I don't know if you're right. I'll have to ask Winston, and he's in the bathroom."

"I know I am right," Vella told the young man. "Hoyt was born right over there in Duncan, and my family knew Mae's. I'll come by and get my gift certificate this afternoon. Thanks." She clicked off.

Chuckling, Jaydee shook his head as he passed her a glass of wine. "You are a woman mighty certain of herself."

"At my age, I cannot waste time being uncertain." She touched her glass to his in a salute. Wine and it wasn't even noon. Mercy!

They kissed, and Vella felt Jaydee's hand slip beneath the hem of her skirt and run upward on her thigh. She asked him what he thought he was doing. He said he thought he would find out if she was wearing panties. She told him that he was acting like a schoolboy. He said he had never felt more of a man in his life.

"Vella, darlin', I think I may have finally grown up enough to enjoy myself . . . and I'll tell you somethin'—for the first time in my life, I think I know what love is."

Hearing the words "darlin'" and "love" mentioned close together, Vella lost some of her good sense.

Vince Gill's voice floated out from the Land Rover's radio, and they laughed and kissed, and in between talked about a business deal to use

Jaydee's money to build a housing development on the eighty acres of land spreading out from where they lay and which Vella owned. They enjoyed themselves as only two people can who are in the twilight of their lives and have learned how to live in the moment, and how to give unconditionally.

They were also two people who did not particularly hear too well any longer. They did not hear the faint noise from the old abandoned and dilapidated house some distance up the hill, nor the whisper of the tall grass as something moved through it.

Then, quite suddenly, Vella looked over Jaydee's shoulder and saw that her Land Rover appeared to be moving. It was actually rolling backward!

Letting out a scream, she thrust aside a startled Jaydee, hopped to her feet and began chasing her beloved vehicle, which picked up speed down the incline, while Garth Brooks' voice sang out from the radio.

"Stop! Stop!" Vella yelled in her panic.

The vehicle did not obey. It did stay in the ruts of the old drive all the way to the bottom, where it rolled within two feet of the radio-station building and stopped. It was as if an angel had put out a hand and stayed disaster. Had the vehicle continued on, it would have ploughed into the studio's concrete block wall and picture window, where Winston sat on the other side.

As it was, Winston, upon seeing Jim Rainwater

glance around and go wide-eyed and Willie Lee get to his feet, turned and looked out to see the back end of the car in front of his eyes, and Vella standing there with her hand on her chest, her blouse partially displaying her black bra.

His first thought was of Vella having a heart attack, and he just about gave himself one as he got to his feet without even thinking that he had any joint problems, and hurried out and around the building. He found not only Vella but Jaydee there, too, his hand on the hood of the vehicle and trying to catch his breath. The man's shirt was hanging out of his trousers. Winston surmised there was no heart attack involved.

"I suggest you both get yourselves put back to rights," he told them sharply, annoyed as all get-out at the sight, and pointing to the people hurrying over from MacCoy's Feed and Grain.

Then, with Willie Lee bringing his cane, he went back into the radio station to give a report of the near-accident. After that, he told Jim Rainwater to put on a couple of gospel tunes.

Fifteen minutes later, after a lot of discussion as to how the Land Rover had managed to roll down the hill, and innuendo as to what Vella had done or failed to do, Vella and Jaydee drove back up to collect their blanket, wine and picnic basket.

Underneath the tree, they found their blanket, wine and glasses, but the picnic basket was missing. Jaydee thought Vella must have put the basket back into the Land Rover before the incident. She knew she had not done so and was not surprised that Jaydee didn't find it there. He then made the suggestion that it might have fallen out of the vehicle during the wild ride down the hill. Firmly convinced this had not happened, she did agree to search the hillside.

The basket was not found. The circumstances appeared plain to Vella. She had not forgotten to put the Land Rover into park, nor had the transmission somehow failed.

"It was a calculated diversion so as to get the picnic basket of food," she said.

"Well, maybe," said Jaydee, far from the full conviction that Vella required.

"It was. And I don't think I like it that you made the immediate assumption that I had been forgetful and caused the whole thing." It fell all over her that her knight in shining armor had turned out to be a frog.

She started the Land Rover, and Jaydee had to be quick to get into the passenger side. He knew he had made a grave error, and all the way to the sheriff's office, he employed every bit of his attorney's persuasion skills to get himself back into her good graces.

In the small radio studio, Winston was crammed into the corner in his chair, making room for his guest.

"We are here at 1550 AM on the radio dial, chattin' with Miz Lillian Jennings, a retired history professor. Welcome again, Miz Jennings. Glad to have you with us this mornin'. Now, for the benefit of the people who may have just joined us, tell us again why Oklahoma is a Southern State."

"Thank you, Winston. I'm delighted to be here. As I was sayin', the South as defined politically by the *Congressional Quarterly* is the eleven original Confederate States, plus Kentucky and Oklahoma. While Oklahoma *is* very Western, the heritage of this state is distinctly Southern in history, linguistics and tradition. This is a natural result of the westward expansion process that made this entire nation. Quite early in the process we see that the Cherokee, Chickasaw and Choctaw Indian tribes were pushed off their lands in North and South Carolina and Georgia, because the whites stole their property when gold was found on it. Now . . ."

Winston loved to hear Miz Lillian talk. It was not so much what she said, because he tended to get bored with all the details the woman insisted on putting forth, but he was enamored with her smooth tone and cultured drawl. The sound of her voice rolled over him like a lazy river on a hot day.

However—he frowned as he gazed at her mouth near the microphone—that arresting, melodious voice came out of the ugliest pair of lips upon which he had ever laid eyes. Thin and wrinkled like an accordion, they had black hairs sticking out over them. It was a revolting sight. He could not imagine why the woman didn't shave.

But as her seductive voice flowed on, Winston began to be mesmerized. Right before his eyes, her lips changed to those of a young and beautiful woman, all soft and full and red.

Winston became so spellbound that he rested his chin in his hand, and when it was time to take a break and play an advertisement, Jim Rainwater had to practically pull out a red flag to get his attention. This happened several times, and each time that Winston saw the real Miz Lillian, he got disappointed all over again.

Then he recalled Belinda's telephoned radio spot. That was the answer. In the future, he would interview Miz Lillian by telephone.

Winston moved the microphone as far out and low as it would go, and Willie Lee did the sign-off for that day's show.

"Mis-ter Hoyt Ax-ton said 'Jer-e-mi-ah Wass a Bull-frog,' and to clo-ose out to-day's show we will pla-ay his so-ong. This is fro-om Wil-lie Lee to Gab-by. Mis-ter Win-ston says remem-ber Is-ai-ah for-ty-one ten."

Winston helped Willie Lee by holding up fingers for the numbers. By the time Willie Lee got it all said, a lot of listeners were sort of leaning toward their radios and having the urge to help him. Those who followed the show every day smiled and thought Willie Lee was improving.

Willie Lee thought he was, too. He felt very proud of himself. When they left the radio station, he stood up tall and pushed Mr. Winston in his wheelchair down the short-but-bumpy gravel drive to the paved road, and then to the IGA Grocery. He was certain that he was growing, because he could see over Mr. Winston's head pretty good.

While Mr. Winston went inside the grocery store to talk to Mr. Juice Tinsley, who owned the IGA, and see if he could get some more advertising money out of him, Willie Lee chose to sit out front on a bench, and watch people come and go from the store and on the road.

While he was there, the boy, Nicky, who he had now met twice, once in the drugstore and once when walking home one day, came along. With Nicky was another boy who looked just like him, and who was pushing a crying baby in a stroller.

"Hey, Willie Lee," Nicky said when the two got close.

"Hel-lo." He tried not to stare, but he puzzled over the other boy looking so much like Nicky, and that the baby was having what Willie Lee's mother would have called a hissy-fit. He knew quickly that something was wrong with it. The next instant, Munro went right to the baby, standing right in front of the stroller, bringing it to a halt.

The baby stopped crying and gazed at Munro,

who cocked his head. The stroller was real old and beat up, not at all like the pretty one Willie Lee's mother had for his little sister, Victoria. And the baby's shirt was stained. And the baby did not smell sweet like his little sister, either.

"This is Willie Lee and his dog I told you about," Nicky told the boy who looked just like him. "This is my sister Nina."

"Nicky! What are you . . . ?" The girl, who looked like a tough boy, yelled and startled Willie Lee.

"Willie Lee's okay . . . aren't you, Willie Lee?" Nicky went to petting Munro.

"I gu-ess I am. Hel-lo," he said to Nina, wondering at her being a girl. But then the baby started fussing again. Willie Lee knelt beside Munro and regarded the baby. "The baby is sick."

"She's got a fever," said Nicky. "She's gettin' some new teeth, is all. We come to get her some cold juice."

Willie Lee reached out to take her hand.

"Hey . . . get your paws off my sister!" said the girl.

Willie Lee, focused on the baby, kept hold of her hand and looked into her teary baby eyes. She quit crying and blinked. "Hel-lo," Willie Lee said softly.

The next instant the stroller and baby were jerked backward. "You don't need to go touchin' my sister. You might give her whatever's wrong with you." The girl pushed the stroller on toward the store doorway, and Willie Lee saw a long braid hanging down her back. He thought of Miz Belinda's story on the radio.

Nicky said, "Sorry," and hurried after his sisters.

Willie Lee scooted himself up onto the bench again. He had sat there about two minutes when there came Nicky out the doors, pushing the crying baby on the run. He came straight to Willie Lee and said, "Do what you did before."

Willie Lee and Munro got in front of the baby, and Willie Lee took her hand. The baby stopped crying. Willie Lee held her hand for some minutes, and gradually he began to grin and so did the baby. She showed five teeth.

"She is bet-ter now," Willie Lee said.

Nicky looked at him, tilted his head and squinted his eyes. "What do you got—you and yor dog? Some magic powers?"

Willie Lee looked downward and shrugged. He was not supposed to let strangers see what he could do. His mother told him not to.

Just then, he was relieved to see Mrs. Berry come walking past out of the store. She was toting three heavy bags. He hopped up and asked if he could carry one for her. He wished he could talk faster, but Mrs. Berry was handing him a bag before he finished and thanking him for his help. She smiled at him like she always did. A lot of people would pretend not to see him, but Mrs.

Berry always smiled and said, "Hello, Willie Lee."

Then she looked at the baby and Nicky. "That's sure a fine baby you two boys have got there. What is her name?"

Nicky mumbled, "Lucy."

"Did you say Lucy?" Mrs. Berry said.

"Yeah," Nicky mumbled, glancing up at her. He was red in the face.

"Ah . . . that means light." As if knowing Mrs. Berry had said something nice, the baby smiled big at her, and Mrs. Berry talked to her silly, like people were always talking to Willie Lee's little sister.

Behind her, Willie Lee saw the girl, Nina, come out of the store, see them, and turn and go back inside.

Mrs. Berry said to Nicky, "I think we've met before. Maybe I know your parents."

"No." Nicky shook his head. "We just come this week to visit our uncle. He lives down there a ways." He pointed in a general direction. "I just took Lucy for a walk, while our mom made lunch. I come last year, too, though, and met Willie Lee . . . ain't that right, Willie Lee?"

Willie Lee was startled. "Ye-s." He nodded slowly, feeling his face warm. He had lied.

Nicky said, "I guess I'd better get along now. My mom probably has lunch finished," and walked rapidly away pushing the stroller.

Willie Lee noticed Mrs. Berry looking after Nicky. He could feel a great dial in her head going around. But then Mrs. Berry headed for her car, and he went along, carrying the groceries. She thanked him for his help and gave him a dollar. He couldn't take it, though. He felt so badly about lying. He shook his head and walked back to the grocery store, where Mr. Winston was now waiting for him. He looked around but did not see the girl, Nina.

23

Cold Feet, Now and Then

Johnny was able to cut out of work a half an hour early. He drove over to Gracie's apartment and went up the stairs two at a time. To his good fortune and delight, it was Gracie, not her mother, who answered the door.

He grabbed her and pulled her outside. She started to speak, but he kissed her, with the wonderful result that she put her arms around his neck and returned his kiss in a manner that made him dizzy. When he finally came up for air, he could hardly see.

"Man," he said, rubbing his hands up and down her arms. "I sure wish this wedding was over and done with."

"Johnny Berry, this is the single most important

time of our lives, and you are wishing it away," she said, scolding, but ending with a smile and stroking her fingernail along his temple. "We won't ever get married again. This is for once and always, and we need to celebrate."

"That's what I would like to do—celebrate," he teased, and kissed her neck.

Just then the door opened, and there was Gracie's mother.

Johnny instantly dropped his hands from Gracie and even took a step backward.

Her mother frowned at Johnny, then said to Gracie, "I couldn't figure out where you went. Nicole is on the phone for you."

Johnny would have left, but before he knew it, Gracie had dragged him inside, then left him standing there while she went into the bedroom to answer the phone. He didn't know what to do. The apartment seemed like a completely strange place with Gracie's mother there. He couldn't seem to make himself cross the room to sit on the couch. He got as far as the breakfast bar that separated the kitchen and propped his arm on it.

Gracie's mother was over at the dining table, where she had set herself up with a notebook computer, printer and fax machine. Gracie had said that her mother was working from the apartment in the same manner that she worked from anywhere that she traveled.

All of a sudden Sylvia Kinney spoke to him. "I

understand that you are going to have a bachelor party tomorrow night."

He started to answer, and his voice squeaked. He cleared his throat and said, "Not really a party. Just some of the guys are gettin' together to play pool and stuff. Kim's husband and some others, while the girls are havin' the bridal shower." His foot started itching.

"I see. Well, have a good time."

"Yeah . . . we will, I imagine. Thanks."

She looked him up and down, and he realized he was rubbing the toe of his left boot on the back of his right pants leg. He lowered his foot to the floor, slowly, trying to act nonchalant.

He could handle the most difficult customer at the stores. He didn't know why he couldn't do the same with this woman.

"It's great that you could stay for a-while," he said. "Gracie's real happy."

She looked at him. "Yes. I'm glad for the opportunity, too."

He didn't know what it was about the woman, but when he was around her, he felt like a balloon pricked by a needle, and all of his self-confidence whooshed out.

After what seemed an eternity, Gracie finally came back. He wasted no time saying that he had to leave. He bade Gracie's mother a polite goodbye, and she gave him a nod and a look that clearly said she thought him an idiot.

Gracie walked down to his car with him, her hand in his. He kept glancing at her and wondering about the differences between them. The doubt about him and Gracie that seemed always to shadow him grew into a big dark cloud. This time even the sexy parting kiss she gave him did not seem to help.

As he got into his car, something made him glance upward. He saw Gracie's mother looking down from the apartment window. Driving away, he felt like darts were shooting through the air at his head.

Before he fully realized his decision, he had turned his car for Valentine and home. He drove at top speed over the blacktop, with the hot air blowing around the car and the air conditioner going full blast on him. When he passed the Welcome to Valentine sign, he relaxed a little. On his way through town, several people called hello and waved. He felt himself filling up.

He drove on to his parents' house, where his mother came out to greet him with her usual enthusiasm, and he filled up a little more. The idle thought occurred that maybe after each encounter with his future mother-in-law, he would need to return to his mother to get put to rights. He saw the idea in pictures in his mind like a long glimpse of a disconcerting future.

"Do you want supper?" his mother asked with eagerness. "I have made tamale pie."

But he could not eat, and declined. That would not do, of course, and she went away to get him at least a snack, while he stayed out back, looking at the progress of the pool and talking with the foreman of the construction crew. He felt a strange reluctance to go into the house. He was already beginning to feel he did not belong. He was having the dismal feeling of not belonging anywhere, as if he had left behind one part of his life but had not yet fully entered another.

The crew knocked off for the day, and his mother came with a cold can of Coke and three of her homemade chocolate-chip cookies, the type that had greeted him on his return from school each day as a boy. They sat together, too, as they had then, on the back steps. His mother had always liked to sit on the back steps in the early evening. The concrete was warm through their jeans. She laughed about it, as she laughed about so much. He saw her shiny hair blow in the breeze and her bright smile that was only for him. He was suddenly very grateful for her, so much so that he had to look away, not wanting her to see his face.

He asked where his father was, and she told him that he was working late with the accountant on the new store opening. Johnny felt a little guilty that he had not been paying much attention to those matters and being more of a help to his father. He had been preoccupied with Gracie and getting married.

His mother pointed out at the yard and began talking about how the pool area was going to look for the family bridal-shower barbeque. She painted him such a thorough picture that instead of seeing the mounds of dirt and construction debris, he saw a manicured lawn, sweep of tile veranda and sparkling water. He saw the tables and the strings of Chinese lanterns his mother said she had just purchased, and the big new barbeque grill his dad had ordered.

"It's goin' to be lovely," she told him, excited as all get-out. His mother could get excited about such stuff.

He agreed, but he felt a little nervous, too. "Who all is comin' to the barbeque?" he asked.

His mother recited the invitation list from memory. He began to see the pool area milling with family and friends that he had known since birth. He tilted his can of Coke and drank deeply.

After a few minutes of silence, the both of them staring at the yard, his mother asked, "So what's up with you?" as deep down he had hoped she would.

Without looking at her, he told her that he had been seeing Gracie when he could. "With her mom there, we don't get much time together." Hearing jealousy in his voice, he added, "It's nice for Gracie, though, that her mom could be here for a while. She's really happy about it, and it won't be for too long."

"Of course it's nice her mother could come out and spend some time. But it's natural for you to be a little lonesome for her, too."

"Yeah," he said, feeling a little better at getting out some of the nagging feelings, and because his mom was on his side.

He felt enough better, in fact, that he turned to her and was able to speak about the worries that had been piling up. "Her mother may have come out and quit bein' against the marriage, but she sure isn't for it, either, and she lets it be known, too."

After a moment, he added, "I guess it is true—Gracie and I are really different, Mom. Even some of the guys have noticed it. I mean, look at where Gracie comes from and look at where I come from. Gracie's been all over to places like New York and Paris. She just knows all sorts of stuff that I don't. She can speak French and knows about wines . . . and knows right where all these little foreign countries are."

"I imagine you know things she doesn't know. You know all about cars and the convenience-store business and how to guide yourself by the stars."

He was more irritated than comforted by his mother trying, as she always did, to put a good face on things. "Gracie and I are like night and day. She's from all the way back east, and I'm from out here. Those are two different worlds. You know, sometimes I can't even understand what she's said. Maybe Gracie's mom is right and this whole thing is a mistake."

"I came from the East Coast, too, and your dad was from out here," she said.

"Well, yeah . . . but you both more or less talked the same and lived the same."

"Oh, no . . . no, we didn't. And right before we got married—and I mean only two days before the wedding—I went to your grandmother and just cried that I couldn't get married."

"You did?" He peered at her. He had never heard this story.

"Oh, yes." She told him that she did not have any examples of a good marriage in her family. She could not name anyone in her family who had not either been widowed or divorced, usually divorced.

"With a family history like that, all I could think of was that I was crazy to get married. When I came face-to-face with marryin' your father, I pan-icked. I saw that he was a pure stranger, and one from halfway across the country. Sometimes he said things a little different, used different words—and he ate different food than I did. He ate a lot of beans and cornbread, pork ribs, and everything smothered in gravy. My family didn't eat like that. We ate roast beef and glazed chicken, gelatine salads and white rolls. It was just like steppin' off a cliff into mid-air. I was so scared that I told your mamaw that I didn't think I could go through with it."

He watched her, fascinated. And suddenly he caught a glimpse of his mother as a young woman, remembering that she had still been in her teens when she had married his father. That glimpse of her as a girl, rather than as his mother, caused him to have to look away.

"Oh, honey, chin up. Everyone has doubts when they are gettin' married. Its a big, scary step." Giving a little laugh like she always did, she put an arm around his shoulders and hugged him.

Then, more seriously, "Don't go thinkin' that if you just find the perfect person, you will know it and not be afraid or not have doubts. For one thing, there is no such thing as the perfect person. No married couple is completely compatible. You have to learn to be compatible. There'll be things about Gracie that make you want to run away. Your dad and I have almost divorced, more than once."

He couldn't imagine his parents divorced, and he wished she would not have said that. The idea was not helpful.

"Honey, what you have to do is what we all do, and that is the best we can at the time. You love Gracie. She loves you. You've talked all this out together. You can't let people from the outside determine this for you. You have to listen to what you hear from inside yourself. Ask yourself what you really, really want. What you feel is right for you. Follow that, because that's God leading you."

Johnny thought his mother's words all sounded wise, but he had hoped for more. When he drove off, he took with him a dozen of his mother's sumptuous chocolate chip cookies, but what he had really wanted was for his mother to tell him if he should or shouldn't marry Gracie.

He realized he was long past his mother telling him what to do, even though he was annoyed at her for not doing it.

Then, while driving a long stretch of straight road, it came to him: *Marry Gracie.* It was like hearing a voice in his head, which seemed to indicate the level of his emotional stress. He sort of asked himself if he had heard right. The answer came again: *Yep, marry Gracie.*

He supposed hearing a voice could not be stranger than the idea of marriage.

The more he drove along, the more certain he became that, dadgummit, he was going to marry Gracie.

A few miles farther, and the full memory of something he had heard a guy do with his fiancée came to him, and he imagined carrying it out with Gracie. It would impress her, and maybe even knock her mother's socks off.

Since he was getting married, he decided that he could go whole-hog with being foolish.

After Johnny left, Emma remained on the back steps thinking of all the things that she wished she had said to him. A whole heart and world of things. She also considered, briefly, the wild idea of getting on the telephone to Sylvia and telling her a few things.

She restrained herself.

Then she recalled the morning all those years ago, when she had gotten her own cold feet and almost called off her own wedding.

She had awakened with first light, tiptoed out of her room and across the hall to peek at John Cole asleep in the guest room. He had come three days early to attend the various wedding functions. She gazed at him for a long time, realizing that she had never before seen him sleep. She was a little amazed, even mildly irritated, that he could sleep so soundly with her staring at him hard enough to bore a hole into his head.

Turning from the doorway, she went downstairs and found her father sprawled stomach-down on the couch like a dead man. He had not appeared for the wedding rehearsal the night before. Her mother had been furious over that, and for a crazy moment Emma had wondered if maybe her father was actually dead, that her mother had killed him in his sleep. She bent over to see if he was breathing. He was, and he smelled of beer.

In the kitchen, she found coffee left in the percolator that her mother had likely made an hour earlier. Her mother swung wildly between sleeping until noon, or waking in the early hours of the morning and going out to the small room at the back of the old house that had once been a grand plantation home but was now rapidly deteriorating, where she read or wrote things for hours. Her mother had for years been writing a passionate historical novel in which, so she said, she killed the people she would like to kill in real life.

Emma poured out the coffee and made fresh. Her mother made awful coffee. She also did not bother to keep a clean kitchen. It really was as if, had not Emma been in the house, neither her mother nor father would have been there, either. Emma knew that when she married and went off with John Cole, her parents would probably leave, as well.

Emma began automatically to tidy up the kitchen as the aroma of coffee filled the air. She anticipated one or both of her parents smelling it and coming quite quickly. They did not come quite so quickly, though, so Emma got to have a good half a cup before her father showed up. He thanked her for the coffee, apologized for not being at the rehearsal and gave some story about his car breaking down. He had it fixed now, though.

Looking down the rear hallway and likely seeing her mother coming, he said, "I'll be at the weddin' and give my girl away," kissed her forehead, and hurried from the room as if on the run, which he was, because a second later, Emma's mother appeared through the back door.

She called after him, "You can run but you

cannot hide." She poured herself a cup of coffee and said "good morning" to Emma in an absent manner, having stuck her nose into a book.

Emma went to gaze into the dining room at the table set up in the corner that was holding an array of wedding gifts from her mother's side of the family. There were things from people she had never met: great-aunts and uncles, and third and fourth cousins. It was a rule, and likely written somewhere, too, that in their family, when anyone married, a gift was sent whether you knew the person or not.

Then Emma turned around and told her mother, "I don't think I can go through with it."

Her mother, without looking up from her book, said, "Hmmm?"

"I don't want to get married. I can't."

Her mother must have heard something in her tone, because she looked up then and set the book aside. Emma burst into tears and began saying hysterically that she wasn't ready to get married.

Her mother took her to the kitchen table and sat her down. "You don't want to get married?"

"I'm not ready . . . I just can't." She repeated this a number of times.

"You don't have to get married, then," her mother said.

"But we have everything ready . . . the dresses, the church . . ." she said.

"We'll cancel it," her mother said.

"But we have all those presents." Emma waved toward the dining room and cried harder.

"We'll send them back."

"But John Cole is here, and his dad and brother are comin'."

To which her mother said, "We'll send them back, too."

With that, Emma quit crying as she imagined telling John Cole and his family to go away, followed by the image of returning the gifts to her grandmother and aunts and cousins. The entire prospect of all that would be involved scared her into straightening up. There was no way she could face such embarrassment. There might have been a lot of divorces in her family, but there never had been a wedding that had been called off at this late date, after everyone had gone to so much trouble.

What she also vaguely realized was that she didn't want to run away. She wanted her mother to tell her that it was all going to be all right. But that was not going to happen. For one thing, her mother likely did not believe it was going to be all right, and also, her mother was incapable of giving her guidance. Emma had to do what she had done ever since she could recall, which was determine things for herself and tell herself that she could do it.

She did, and when John Cole got up a half an hour later and came down to breakfast, she sat at the table with him and ate the burnt bacon and crispy-edged fried eggs that her mother cooked for them. She was greatly impressed that he never once complained about her mother's poor cooking.

When John Cole came in that evening, Emma told him of her conversation with Johnny. She then asked him, "Did you get scared before our wedding?"

"Yeah, a little."

She looked at him, trying to judge the comment. Then something struck her. "My mother adored you."

"That's true."

A few more minutes, and she asked, "Why did you marry me? What made you go through with it?"

He shrugged. "I don't know." She had expected that and decided that likely was the best he could do.

After a minute she said, "I'm glad we got married. I've never been sorry. I've been angry, but deep down, I've never been sorry."

They looked at each other for a long moment and sort of smiled, then looked away, both falling silent for minutes, thinking about the ins and outs of all of it. And for a moment she remembered gazing at his head in the bed that morning so long ago.

Later, she heard John Cole on the phone with Johnny. She caught mention of roses for both

Gracie and Sylvia. She thought that her husband could be very wise at times and wondered why he rarely used that wisdom in his own marriage. This was likely the question of women throughout the ages.

24

Woman to Woman

The bridal shower was a gathering of Gracie's friends—young, modern and fashionable.

All but two of the guests were women employed by the M. Connor store, and they quite naturally viewed Gracie's mother, a person from corporate headquarters, as their boss. The other two girls were from the misses department in JCPenney, so with all of them in fashion sales, Sylvia Kinney was an object of study and admiration. Their attention went to her like straight pins to a magnet.

Gracie, having anticipated that this was likely to happen, patiently waited it out. While her mother more or less held court on the couch, Gracie sat in a high-backed chair across the room and took note of the lovely home of her friend Kim, who was hosting the party. The house was brand new, as was everything in it. Gracie looked around and absorbed decorating ideas with the happy anticipation of having her own home in the near future.

Then, two old friends with whom Gracie had worked in Dallas arrived. Gracie was amazed and delighted. They squealed at the sight of her, and she squealed in the same manner upon seeing them, and the three shared a group hug. After this, everyone seemed to get back to the point of the party, which was the celebration of Gracie's upcoming marriage. All the attention swung back to her, and she was urged to start opening the gifts.

Among the normal things—blender, toaster, table and bed linens—she also received two sexy peignoirs, fragrant candles and, quite surprisingly, a book, *Intimate Matters: Woman to Woman,* which Nicole saved for last and passed to her with a wide grin. As Gracie slowly peeled back the silver wrapping paper, she noticed the other women sort of leaning forward. There was, of all things, a feather taped to the cover of the book. Gracie about died. No matter that her mother laughed, she was still her mother. Gracie was highly surprised that such a gift had come from Nicole, and that in fact Nicole's mother had also signed the accompanying card, which contained a quote: "My beloved is mine and I am his." Song of Solomon 2:16.

That quote and the picture that popped into Gracie's mind caused her to blush even more. She found it hard to imagine something like that being in the Bible.

"Look." Nicole opened the cover, and tucked

inside were two tickets. Nicole explained that the tickets were to a seminar for women at her church, where her mother was a deacon. She said that she and her mother and sisters and Kim were all going. "We thought you and your mother would like to go, too."

"Oh, yes. Thank you," Gracie said, thinking there would be no way in this life that her mother would go to such a thing. A glance at her mother confirmed this.

Just then Kim stood and announced, "And now, one last gift." Producing a child's plastic horn, she blew on it, and music started. *I'm gonna love you . . .*

A man appeared from the hallway. It was Kim's husband, with his hair slicked back and wearing a shiny silk shirt and tight jeans. He danced into the room and right behind him came Nicole's boyfriend, wearing the same sort of outfit, both of them looking like something out of an old disco movie. It was hilarious. The two men danced in between chairs and into the center of the living room in a manner that brought hoots and laughter. They went around to the back of Gracie's chair, and then here came a third man dancing into the room—*Johnny!*

Gracie could not believe it. He wore a cowboy hat, black silk shirt unbuttoned halfway down and black skin-tight pants. She did not think he had ever worn a silk shirt in his life, and she had never seen him in any pants but blue jeans, and she certainly had never seen him dance in such a manner. Her eyes got wider and wider as she watched him come across the room with an enormous bouquet of roses.

He paused in front of her mother, and in a very courtly manner in which he removed his cowboy hat and gave a little bow, he presented her with a single rose from the bouquet.

Then he turned toward Gracie. She pressed her hands to her burning cheeks as he came gyrating his hips toward her with the big bouquet of red roses. His face was the same color as the roses, too, but he came on, and when he got to her, he went down on one knee and laid the bouquet in her arms. Then he took her hand and kissed it, and when his blue eyes came up and looked at her, she felt like her heart burst inside her chest. Through tear-blurred vision, she watched him and the other two men retreat out of the room.

In a stunned state, Gracie looked around at her friends, then burst out crying.

Nicole started to go over and put her arms around her, but remembered Gracie's mother was there. Stuck halfway between sitting and standing, Nicole looked uncertainly at the other woman.

Finally, hesitantly, Gracie's mother rose and went to sit on the arm of Gracie's chair. She patted Gracie's back, saying, "Come on now . . . it's not anything to cry about."

Nicole found a box of tissues and passed it around, because everyone seemed to be tearing up.

After that, everyone sat around in a relaxed and lively atmosphere, having more cake and punch and perusing the gifts, and going on about how fortunate Gracie, Nicole and Kim were to have such men in their lives. There was a great deal of talk about Gracie's promising future. Gracie was in a frame of mind—helped on by the large bouquet of roses—to believe all the wonderful predictions.

When the party broke up, Gracie hugged each of her friends in a manner that she had never before hugged people. She was hugging everyone right and left. She found herself hugging her mother several times when they got home, too. While the bridal shower had not been anything on a grand scale, it was about the best thing that had ever happened to her. She would remember it for all of her life. She was amazed to find that she, a painfully shy girl, had somehow blossomed into a full woman who not only had friends but also a man so fully and passionately in love with her that he would make a fool of himself and display it for everyone to see.

Now, Gracie thought, her mother had been shown what a special man Johnny was. There was no way her mother could continue to object to him. There was simply nothing she could say, so now her mother would surely go home.

Gracie was fully ready for her mother to leave.

With Johnny's concrete display of love, Gracie, who had been suffering some small doubts of her own, was eager to get on with her wonderful life with him. She wanted to be with him every minute, and to talk over and over about their wedding and honeymoon and all of their grand plans for the future. She could hardly wait for her life with Johnny to come roaring at her.

But she could not do any of that as long as her mother was ensconced in her apartment and demanding her attention.

As it turned out, however, her mother continued to linger. She changed her air-flight reservation after a phone call from Emma Berry, who told Gracie that the florist in Valentine had a new catalog of wedding decorations and asked if Gracie might want to come down and look through it sometime that week. Gracie said that she would, and also that she would like to view the church, to get an idea of arrangements. They had quite a long conversation, in which Gracie told her of Johnny's most wonderful display of love at the bridal shower. Emma was delighted, as Gracie had known she would be.

The entire length of this conversation, her mother came in and out of the room. Once she stopped as if surprised and said, "Oh, you're still talking." When Gracie hung up and relayed the plans she had made to meet with Emma on Wednesday morning, her mother said, "You know, there's nothing that won't wait a few more days. I think I'll change my flight and go with you."

Gracie did her best to appear pleased and tried not to be nervous about being around the two women. She really had no idea why she was nervous. Her mother and Emma had been polite and cordial to each other during the Sunday dinner at the Berrys' home. She told herself that she was being silly.

Wednesday morning, Gracie and her mother met Emma at the Valentine First Methodist church. Within five minutes, Gracie began to wear her neck out from turning her head back and forth between the two older women, as she attempted to make decisions about decorations, and using the hall and lawn for the reception. She could not quite figure out why she felt so nervous. Her mother smiled a lot, and so did Emma. Gracie did carry a lot of guilt about having the wedding so far away from her mother's home territory, but she was a practical girl and knew that her future lay in Valentine.

Emma, who was much more sensitive than Gracie and knew the lay of the land immediately, quickly realized that Sylvia was not happy when she hugged Gracie, nor when she put in any suggestions for the wedding plans. She stepped back and said several times, "This is your wedding, Gracie, and up to you and your mother." She tried not to jump up and down and clap when Gracie was delighted with the church lawn, and decided that the church hall and lawn would be perfect for the reception.

There was some relief for each of them when they took separate cars to the florist on Main Street, where the owners made a fuss over Gracie and praised Johnny at length. Gracie checked her mother's face to see the effect of this. She had to admire how her mother's smile never slipped as she gave every evidence of praising Johnny herself, while not really saying anything.

After reserving decorative items and ordering the flowers, they crossed the street to the Main Street Café for lunch. Gracie and Emma both got the hamburger special, and Gracie's mother, after some deliberation, got the chicken salad plate. This turned out to be mayonnaise-y chicken salad on a bed of iceberg lettuce, very pale and certainly nothing like the fresh leaf-lettuce salads with exotic fresh herbs served in the restaurants where she normally ate. Gracie saw her mother look down at the salad for a full minute, as if trying to identify it, then slowly begin to eat.

"How's your salad, Sylvia?" Emma inquired.

"Fine . . . just fine, thank you," said Gracie's mother, with the smile she had been giving all morning.

A few minutes later, two of Emma's friends stopped by their table—Belinda Blaine, who wore a blouse that displayed deep cleavage and the most impossible crystal high-heels, and Naomi Smith, who turned out to be the wife of the pastor who would marry Gracie and Johnny. In the course of the conversation, when Belinda slid into the booth beside Emma and stole some of her fries, the subject of the Glorious Women's seminar came up. The pastor's wife told of something called the Ladies Circle filling two vans to drive up to the church where the seminar was to take place, and Belinda said that she and Emma would be driving themselves.

Belinda said, "I couldn't possibly stand that many women for a forty-minute drive. Could you?" she said directly to Gracie's mother.

Taken by surprise, Gracie's mother at first stared, then replied, "No, I don't believe I would appreciate it, either."

"I have tickets to that," Gracie told Emma, forgetting her mother's presence and getting excited. "I got two tickets as a wedding gift."

With this, Emma enthusiastically asked Gracie if she might want to go with her and Belinda.

Right then Gracie's mother said, "I plan to go with Gracie."

Emma looked at her. "Well, that's nice. We can all meet up there."

Gracie didn't say anything until she was driving home with her mother. "I thought you didn't want to go to the seminar, Mom. You really don't have to."

"Oh, I want to. It sounds interesting, and I've already stayed this long, I might as well stay until next week."

Her mother changed her flight reservations again, and Gracie wondered if there was a limit for that sort of thing.

By this time, Gracie was getting very tired of so much togetherness with her mother as well as her future mother-in-law. She thought her neck might just twist off if she had to be with both of them for an entire day. She also began to have a little fear that should she and Johnny take up residence anywhere near Emma Berry, her mother would straight away move down from Baltimore.

That night, with the excuse of having to go down to the store and handle some piled-up work, she slipped over to Johnny's apartment for two hours. She felt silly having to make up some story. After all, she was a grown woman and Johnny was her fiancé. She told herself when she drove home that she was going to have a frank talk with her mother. They were going to have to reach an understanding, seeing as her mother had decided to take up temporary residence in her apartment. There was not only the problem of Gracie having private time with Johnny, but she also did not like the way her mother threw towels on the floor and tea bags in the sink.

But when she came in, she could not say anything to her mother. She did not know why she had thought she could.

25

Amen, Sister!

Belinda called twice that week to remind Emma not only of the women's seminar but to press her to finish the new set of greeting cards. The sets they had placed at the gift store had sold out. Emma was amazed.

"Sugar, I do not know why you would be amazed," Belinda told her. "Your cards are delightful. And we need to ride the momentum."

Emma agreed to do two more designs. But when she hung up the phone, she was highly annoyed.

She had done the same thing she had done when she had learned that she had won two tickets to the Glorious Women's seminar. She had gotten all excited about winning something and told Belinda that they could go together. About an hour later, when she really thought about it and realized she did not want to go, she wished she could learn to say no first. If you could say no first, you could always back up and say yes. But if you said yes first, people got very disappointed if you backed up and said no.

The idea of being in a mass of religious women was a little disconcerting. Emma had never considered herself especially religious, although she was spiritual. She found her communing with God best done alone and in quiet. There were too many distractions in a church setting. And who knew what all way-out stuff might go on at this Glorious Women's thing. Her mother had said the Servants' Whatever Church was a fundamentalist congregation. Now that Emma thought about it, she did not know what that meant, and she didn't especially want to learn at this point in time. Not only that, but she did not care to again come face-to-face with Sylvia Kinney. That had not been working out well. It put her under a lot of strain.

She had enough strain in her life at the moment. What Catherine had said about Emma's tendency to get preoccupied with Johnny and other things and forget about her marriage to John Cole was very clear to her now.

After finding those few early photographs of her and John Cole for her mother's album project, she had gotten curious and gone digging through all their old photographs. She found a small cigar box full of snapshots of herself throughout her childhood, up until she married John Cole. She concluded that it was evidence of her grandmother Maisie's picture-taking passion, as well of her father's absence. He showed up in only a few of those childhood pictures, and always a little off to the side.

The fancy camera had been put to good use after Johnny's birth. There were many shots of him and the three of them—her and John Cole with Johnny standing in between them. There were many of Emma and Johnny together. But there were very few pictures of her and John Cole. Even more telling, she found only two of herself alone.

For years Emma had held out hope that marriage counseling would prove the answer. It had not worked as she had expected. She and John Cole were little changed, except they were a lot more agreeable to one another. They rarely had so much as a cross word now. Neither of them seemed to have much to say at all. The only time they were together enough to talk was during supper, which was when John Cole came home, and afterward he would fall asleep in his recliner. When he did come in to bed, Emma had given up wearing her sexy nightgown.

Things appeared to be about as good as they were going to get. Emma pretty much felt she had failed, and it was a lot easier to turn her attention to where she could succeed and knew she did well.

She threw herself into planning and executing the family bridal-shower barbeque, and designing things for the wedding reception. She was making up hand-lettered cards with uplifting quotes on marriage, a different one for each table, to be displayed as part of each table centerpiece. And she had drawn up the prettiest thank-you cards for Gracie. There were also the invitations to the barbeque, which required printing the announcement with the computer on parchment, then putting that on wonderful cover-weight linen, and adorning each with a ribbon and concho.

Saturday morning, while she was putting on her face for the seminar, another thank-you card idea—this one for the bridal-shower barbeque—came to her. She often had her best ideas while showering or putting on makeup. She dashed to her worktable to sketch out the idea, and that was where she was when Belinda arrived.

"What do you think of this?" Emma showed Belinda the invitation and the thank-you card mock-up. "I'm so excited."

Belinda was suitably impressed. "I like it." Then, still studying the cards, "I would like some for a Christmas party I'm plannin', and I know two other women right now who would snatch these up. We could take orders."

Emma felt a rush of heady delight. Then she caught herself. "All right, but not any time soon. Here are the new designs, and that is *it* until after the wedding."

Whew, she had said *no* first—and cleverly, without actually using the word "no."

Belinda took that well, then peered at Emma. "Do you intend to go to the seminar with eye-shadow only on the right eye?"

"Ohmygosh."

While Emma ran to finish getting herself

together, Belinda lingered in the workroom, looking around. She took note of the curious sight of family photographs stuck around the edges of the drawing table and haphazardly scattered out on a table, atop some books, and even a couple taped to the wall. It seemed the work of a distracted woman—which fit with Emma.

Wandering into the kitchen, Belinda poured a cup of coffee, then rinsed the coffee pot and wiped up so that Emma wouldn't be tempted to do any of that and get further behind. Belinda had known that Emma would be running late. She didn't think the two of them had gone anywhere that Emma had not been running late. It was her highly creative nature to get distracted, and Belinda, being of a practical nature, always came early to keep her friend on track.

It was sort of like Mary and Martha in the Bible, she reflected as she leaned back against the counter, sipped her coffee and perused the brochure for the seminar, where a title of one of the talks was given: *Like Mary in a Martha World.*

Mary, the spiritual one, and Martha, the busy one. Mary was supposedly the better one, but Belinda had always felt that Martha had been maligned. How would those men, who hogged the writing back then, have liked it if Martha had not been concerned with making their dinner? Maybe Jesus could make his own bread, but those other men would have been ordering Martha right and left. And Belinda would be willing to bet that Martha had been good in the bedroom. Women who got things done generally were women of action.

In that moment, she imagined Mary at the feet of Jesus. Something dawned on her. She thought about Lyle's attraction for Giff Phelps. Just as Lyle had been attracted to Belinda for her intelligence, so was he to Giff. Although to Belinda's mind, Giff simply played the part of being smart and was not so much so in fact. This was clearly illustrated in that he had allowed his wife, Penny Lane, to drag him down to Valentine from Seattle, just because she was lonesome for her sisters. Any man who would leave a place like Seattle just to come down and live among the passel of Lane sisters could not be all that intelligent.

Glancing at her watch, she put away the brochure and went to Emma's bedroom. "Time check. You have ten minutes."

"I'm almost ready," Emma called from inside the closet.

Belinda sat on the bed, then leaned back on the large pillows and put her feet up. A few minutes later John Cole came through the door and saw her there.

She said, "Surprise."

"Uh . . . is my wife around anywhere?" He looked as if he thought he might be in the wrong house.

351

"No, I just came to put my feet up," Belinda said, then chuckled at his confused expression. "She's in the closet, but don't go bothering her. We have five minutes to get her out of here. We're goin' to the Glorious Women's Day."

"The what?"

"The Glorious Women's Day. It's an all-day seminar where we learn to be more glorious, if you know what I mean." She winked and enjoyed watching John Cole turn red.

"O-kay."

"I told you about it," said Emma, coming out of the closet carrying shoes and a matching purse. "There's ham and cheese, if you come home later for lunch. I'm not certain when I'll be home this evenin', but I made you a little chicken pot pie. It's there in the refrigerator. All you have to do is put it in the microwave."

Belinda could not believe that John Cole had to be cared for like a little boy. She swung her head to see his reaction.

He said, "Oh, okay. I just wanted to tell you that the water is runnin' in the pool."

Belinda thought he did look like a boy.

Emma said, "Oh—wonderful!" Putting on her shoes as she went, she did a little hop-skip over to the glass doors to the yard.

Standing just behind her shoulder, John Cole pointed at a big tanker truck, explaining that it was filling the pool, rather than have water dribble for days through a hose. He went on about additives to the water, and pressure, and things of that nature, while Emma admired everything.

Belinda thought it was like watching a little boy do handstands in front of a wide-eyed applauding girl.

When this had gone on for upwards of three full minutes and John Cole opened the door to take Emma out for a close-up look, Belinda grabbed her arm. "I'm afraid we don't have time for that. I'll bring her back this evenin', John Cole, and you can show her some more."

As they got into the car, Emma said, "All I care about is that the pool gets in, looks pretty and works. But John Cole likes to show me *how* it all works and everything that went into it, and to have me ooh and aah. It's important to him."

"I can see that," said Belinda, hitting the accelerator and sending the car down the driveway and out onto the highway heading north, driving easily with one hand on the steering wheel.

Emma glanced over at her friend, from the toe of her coral high-heel shoe pressed on the accelerator to her hair, held in place with firm spray. While Emma was more relaxed in her own appearance, she felt a little disheveled, likely because she had not had her heart in going. She flipped down the visor and checked her appearance, saying, "I'm glad I went back in and put on this skirt. I had been goin' to wear pants, but Mama said she thought this was a Pentecostal or Charismatic Church, or something like that. I didn't want to offend anybody."

Belinda, who could not imagine that Emma could ever do anything to offend, said, "You look real nice. You always do. And I think it's non-denominational."

"Non-denominational . . . I've seen that a lot. With so many of them, they are rather makin' a denomination of it, aren't they?"

Belinda could not find a comment to that. She did say, "They have lively services. Mama and I have attended up there a few times."

"You have?"

"Uh-huh." Noting her speedometer, she let up a little on the gas. "Back last January, Naomi went up to speak one Sunday, and we went along to give her support. We had such a good time that we've gone back every now and again. Don't tell anyone about Naomi havin' such a good time. Everybody knows she goes to speak at other churches, but no one knows sometimes she just goes to enjoy herself."

Belinda shut her mouth on any further information about Naomi's life and endeavors, but she felt free to give her own view. "I sure wouldn't want to say anything to Pastor Smith, and I know our Valentine First Methodist services are supposed to be stately and reverent, but sometimes I think another word for them is dead. Heaven knows that

Pastor Smith has tried with his guitar, but every time he brings in new music, he gets jumped on for it. And since old Mr. Emerson died, not one person hollers out 'amen.' I've done it a couple of times, but it just doesn't seem the same. I've tried to get Lyle to do it, but he won't. He was raised Episcopalian."

"Oh, John Cole wouldn't do it, either, and he was raised Baptist. The quiet sort of Baptist," she added to distinguish.

They drove along in silence for some minutes. Belinda thought of snatches of their conversation, and saw in memory Emma and John Cole standing together and looking out at the pool, and Emma doing what she called her "oohing and aahing."

Quite suddenly she said, "You know, Emma, no matter how frustrated you are with your marriage to John Cole, there is no denyin' that you two have held it together for thirty-two years, and you both still get on with each other. He's still showing you things, and you're still oohing and aahing. I think churches are sort of like that."

"You do?" Emma couldn't quite figure out what in the world Belinda meant.

"Yes." Belinda said.

And then the steeply pitched roof and spire of the Servants' Fellowship Church came into view, and Belinda pointed it out, going on to explain how the church building was patterned after those mega-churches you could see on television. "Only about a fourth the size, of course, but it has a basketball court and a cafeteria."

"Well, my word."

The church came into full view. Very modern, with a lot of sharp angles and glass. There were also young people, with Follow Me to Servants' Fellowship Church printed on the backs of their yellow T-shirts, directing the stream of cars, vans and church buses into the parking lot.

Pulling into a parking place and noting the number of women heading toward the front of the church, Belinda commented, "I think a lot of women wanted a day off."

At the entry doors, a very nicely dressed woman, who smelled unmistakably of Interlude—Belinda carried it at the drugstore—handed them a program and said with a bright smile, "Welcome, sisters. We're glad you're here."

"Thank you. We're glad to be here." Emma shook the woman's hand with delight. She always appreciated polite friendliness, and she especially liked being called sister. It made her remember going as a child on a number of occasions to visit the family of a distant cousin. It was her chance to play with about a hundred children, and the whole family said "sister this" and "brother that." She seemed to recall that the father had been a minister. The mother had played the piano and would round up the children for group singing. Being an only child, and lonely, Emma had loved it.

While Emma went off to find the restroom, Belinda looked around the lobby and quite happily took note of the many nicely dressed women.

She saw with high approval a number of black women dressed to the hilt. They wore feminine suits of vivid colors, with purses and shoes to match. Belinda, in brilliant coral-colored silk, also with a purse and heels to match, fit right in. And there were a lot of hats. Studying the hats, Belinda toyed with the idea of getting herself one.

If anyone asked her—and no one did, but she generally spoke up anyway—this was the way all women should dress. Especially women of the size and shape that Belinda was, which was what she thought of as buxom and which half the women in the world were. Dressing up lifted a person up. This had been her own experience. Back when she had been sloppy, she had been depressed and going nowhere in her life, but when she began to dress well, she began to feel well and make something of herself. Weren't all these women smiling?

Maybe that was the reason for the liveliness of the church, she thought, the idea coming to her in a rush. Back at Valentine Methodist, there were only a handful of women who dressed as elaborately as Belinda did, generally in a suit and with full accessories.

Just then she saw a woman come through the doors wearing a sloppy T-shirt, knit pants and sandals. Looked like she was going to a picnic. If it had been up to Belinda, she would have told the woman to go home and take ten minutes to put on some decent clothes. But of course it wasn't up to her, and she saw a greeter smiling and giving the sloppy woman a program.

The next instant she felt contrite. It was not for her to judge, yet what could be better than for the sloppy woman to be surrounded by good examples of how to dress? The wheels of her fertile mind began to turn, and an idea for a commentary for her radio spot came to her. She would start giving easy fashion tips to raise women's consciousness. This was obviously a ministry to which she was well-suited. Maybe she could start a revival of dressing up and liveliness in her church. And she could come out with a line of clothing, too—Glorious Woman by Belinda Blaine.

Although Lyle got upset that she did not use his last name of Midgett. Why she didn't was pretty evident. You just could not have the name of Midgett planted on a woman who wore a DD cup bra.

Just then Emma returned and said in a hushed voice, "I didn't wear pantyhose and I feel like maybe I should have."

"Uh-huh." Belinda gazed at her.

"I didn't figure I needed to under a long skirt. But I did wear panties."

"That's good news."

"Well, it might be if a wind comes up." Emma

smiled sweetly. She had gotten pretty lively being around all the women smiling and greeting each other. There had been several women "sister-ing" each other in the restroom.

They went to the refreshment table and had both gotten tea when Gracie, Sylvia and a number of Gracie's friends showed up. Introductions were made all around, and since the mother of one of Gracie's friends was a deacon in the church, introductions just kept going on as people went past. With so many people, it was easy for Emma and Sylvia to more or less ignore each other.

Emma was surprised to encounter two women whom she had known during Johnny's school days, and further surprised that the women remembered her after so many years. They each reported proudly on their now-grown children and how each of their lives was now going. One woman was a financial advisor and the other a yoga instructor. Emma was glad to be able to report on Johnny, as well as have something to say in answer to the question: "So what are you doing now?" When telling of her artistic endeavors, she had the odd but profound sense of having stepped across a threshold and back into life.

The Ladies Circle from the Valentine First Methodist showed up—Belinda approved of how each one was very nicely dressed, if rather sedately—and more introductions had to be made. Everyone was very excited to meet "our little

Gracie," as Naomi Smith introduced her to the church ladies. Inez Cooper, President of the Ladies Circle, brought up the subject of the group holding a shower for Gracie. She put it off as neglect on Emma's part that a date had not been set. This was discussed for some minutes. Inez was impressed with Sylvia Kinney and anxious to set a date when she could join them. She cornered Sylvia, who kept edging backward, until she bumped into the refreshment table.

"Emma!" a voice called out.

Emma looked around to see, of all people, her sister-in-law Joella rushing toward her with outstretched arms. With a squeal, Joella gave her an enthusiastic embrace.

"I was visitin' my cousin Marylou over in Purcell. That's her, the one with the heart earrings and the hearts around the bottom of her skirt." Joella turned to point toward another group of women halfway across the lobby. "Her husband's sister down in Elmore City had the tickets, so we thought we'd all just drive over. It wasn't so far at all." Then she turned her head and looked just beyond Emma's shoulder. "My good Lord— Sylvia! What in the world are you doin' here, girl? I am glad to see *you!*"

Sylvia, who had been released by Inez and was attempting to be invisible next to the wall, was hauled out and hugged by Joella. Emma thought Sylvia held up well.

Then Joella took both Sylvia and Emma by the hands and leaned in close. "I just had no idea there would be *blacks* here. My cousin and her mama didn't know, either."

Emma stared at her sister-in-law. She could not face Sylvia. Before she could get out a response, Joella, who did not require any response, rattled on about being thrilled to see them, until her cousin hollered her name.

"Oh, I got to go. Marylou won't go to the toilet without me. I'll see y'all later, though." She blew them kisses as she hurried away.

Emma tried to get her eyes to come around to look Sylvia in the face but was given the excuse to avoid it, as Gracie drew her mother away at the same time that Belinda motioned to Emma from across the lobby. She went over, and Belinda introduced her to a woman who was the manager of the church bookstore. The church had its own little bookstore. What an amazement. And right then and there Belinda went to hawking Emma's stationery.

For godsake, Sylvia thought at both Joella and everything going on around her. Women were chatting and laughing and saying things like, "Praise God, I'm so glad to see you, sister," and "Bless God, I am glad to be here."

Sylvia had not been inside a church since Gracie's confirmation at the age of twelve. For all of her life, anyway, her experiences had been confined to the old moss-grown Catholic churches, or Presbyterian and Episcopal ones for the occasional wedding or funeral. She had gone through a phase for about six weeks of tuning in on Sundays to one of those popular television preachers. When she realized that she was trying to scoot Wadley out of the house in order to watch the preacher, because she could not bear for anyone to know, she had broken off watching altogether.

As she went with Gracie through the doors to the sanctuary, Sylvia had the sudden absurd but very real anxiety that she, a fallen-away Catholic, might be struck dead. She furtively crossed herself.

Nicole and her mother, Evelyn, took on the duties of playing hostess for their church, and led the group to the first and second rows on the right side. Sylvia managed to get the end of the pew, so as not to be sandwiched in. She thought she could not breathe if she was sandwiched in. Emma and her friend Belinda sat right behind them, chatting happily all around. Emma leaned forward to say something to Gracie. With Emma's face on the other side of Gracie, Sylvia could not hear what was said, but she saw Emma's hand lying on Gracie's shoulder. The woman always seemed to be touching everyone.

When Emma had sat back, Sylvia put a hand over and patted Gracie's leg. Gracie smiled at her.

Sylvia was so glad she had pleased Gracie by coming that tears sprang into her eyes, and she quickly averted her face. She just hoped the day went by fast.

26

Glorious Women Come Out

The Glorious Women's Day seminar had been organized primarily by Reverend Mae Stamp, the assistant pastor of the Servants' Fellowship Church, and Naomi Smith, wife of the pastor of Valentine First Methodist.

Sister Mae, as she was generally called, was as large, dark and dynamic as Naomi was petite, pale and reserved. However, the women were fast friends, sharing an abiding faith in God and the firm belief that the chief need for women was joy to carry them through the whirlwinds of modern life. Having greatly enjoyed a number of massive women's spiritual renewal weekends, both women were dedicated to bringing something similar to their small neck of the woods. Also, both had reached the daring and amazing age of fifty and knew the ins and outs of pleasing the sensitivities and prejudices of differing denominations.

In the audience were upwards of three hundred women from a cross section of Christian denominations, as well as many who didn't know what they believed, if anything in particular. There were those who had been to the seminar the year before and had a good time, those who felt compelled to go to church any time the doors opened, and those who had been dragged there and couldn't find a way out of it. Some came out of desperation for some time off, or because of sad lives and the small hope of finding something, even if they didn't know what it was.

A young stylish woman at the electronic keyboard began playing what some recognized as "Michael Row the Boat Ashore." This sent stragglers hurrying to their seats. A few minutes later, a tall, handsomely dressed man came striding out and introduced himself as Reverend Ambrose Perkins, head pastor of the Servants' Fellowship Church. He made a couple of jokes about his wife having told him to say what he had to say and get out. Everyone in the audience knew that he was the respectful offering to those in attendance who did not believe in women ministers. As the male head pastor of the church, he led the opening prayer and then officially turned the proceedings over to Sister Mae.

Sister Mae was a lively woman who moved fast. She said, "We are glad you are here and want everyone to enjoy today, so let's get goin' with this celebration."

She brought out the Servants' Fellowship women's gospel choir, six women in deep purple robes, accompanied by three lead singers, who turned out to be Gracie's friend Nicole Davies, with her mother Evelyn and older sister Cherise.

The three were tall and elegant. They lit into a popular eighties-style rendition of "Come Out the Wilderness," followed by the old tunes "Sweet Baby Jesus" and "Amazing Grace."

The gospel beat and rousing voices filled the high-ceilinged room, and got hands to clapping and toes to tapping. The more enthusiastic in the audience stood and danced in place. Even those of more reserved inclinations could not help tapping their fingers. This went on for quite a while. They sang all six verses of "Amazing Grace," then went back and sang the first verse a second time.

Emma and a few of the other women from Valentine First Methodist could not ever recall singing the fourth and fifth verses. Pastor Smith always skipped over them in order to keep the service on schedule. A few of the women from Valentine Episcopal and First Presbyterian only knew the first verse, because that was as far as they ever got.

After this, a beautiful young woman in a stunning white suit and very high heels walked out. She looked like a recording artist, because she was, and apparently well-known by the younger women of the audience, many of whom listened to modern Christian rock music on the radio. A round of enthusiastic applause went up. The young woman gave a Miss America wave, then brought her hands together. A hush fell over the crowd.

". . . Here we are all gathered to sing praise to God . . . Halle-lu-yah, hal-le-lu-yah!" she sang out with a strong voice and perfect pitch, as she strode up and down with energy. There were a drummer and electric guitar player behind the woman at the electronic keyboard, who was now standing and playing those keys with all her might.

There were a lot of wide eyes watching.

Emma noticed Belinda and others singing along, and wondered how they knew the words. Then Belinda elbowed her and pointed out a screen in the corner with the lyrics projected on it. Emma began to sing and then to clap along with everyone else.

". . . sing, sing, hal-le-lu-yah! Hal-le-lu-yah!" The young singer ended with a deep bow from the waist, and another, louder round of applause went up. After this, the young woman led them all in singing "Redeemed" and "She's Somebody's Hero," with a definite country sound. She got a standing ovation.

Following the singer were two speakers. One was a comedienne who told a lot of funny stories about her life as a wife and mother. She was a big hit. Then, after a break and while they were all still in high spirits from laughing, the second speaker came on to give the Mary-and-Martha talk about the special and varied gifts of women. Belinda was not the only one pleased to hear Martha praised. The speaker said that women were the healers and keepers of the family, and that they more or less held up the sky. Both speakers were given many an "Amen, Sister!" and "Halleluyah!"

When Belinda hollered out an "Amen!" Emma jumped. She thought Belinda did it very well and could be on the amening committee.

A buffet luncheon was served in a lovely fellowship hall. It was the sort of catered affair that many of the women seldom, if ever, got to experience. A lavish buffet, and tables covered with linen and set with gleaming china and crystal, was spread out before them. Wait staff supplied cold tea and hot coffee.

Belinda was quite pleased with the civility of it all, as was Inez Cooper, who had been in charge of stocking the Valentine First Methodist's remodeled kitchen. Inez had pushed through china and silverware over paper plates and plastic forks and knives in a heated meeting.

Belinda recalled the incident for Emma. "It was one of the rare times I found myself on Inez's side. After I did it, she thought I was her friend. She was invitin' me to all kinds of women's retreats and Tupperware parties. I was pretty relieved when it came to carpeting the sanctuary and she wanted white, and I vetoed that insane idea. She hasn't invited me to a single thing since . . . amen to that."

The luncheon was an extended one, where women lingered over glasses of cold tea and cups of hot coffee, giving everyone ample time to relax, chat and get to the restrooms, and visit the tape table to purchase cassettes and CDs of the singer and speakers.

Very quietly the information was passed that smoking was not allowed on the church grounds. This was quite different for a few of the women, who attended churches where all they had to do was step out on the front lawn. A number of the attendees piled into cars and drove down to the nearby Seven-Eleven parking lot, where they had a quick smoke. Each carload thought they were the only ones, and then they looked up and recognized others parked around the edge of the lot. They rolled down their windows and chatted. It led to a lot of camaraderie.

One unfortunate incident happened at the tape table, when two women got into a fight over a CD by the singer in the white suit.

Inez Cooper witnessed the display and went over to give the two women a lecture on proper Christian behavior. This approach—plus Inez snatching the CD out of one of the women's hands and threatening to break it in half, as King Solomon would have done—ended up with one of the women pushing Inez into the table, and tapes and CDs going everywhere, while the other woman grabbed the CD and took off.

As the story got retold around, Inez was the one named as inciting the fight. She was in hysterics at being accused of such behavior.

"I was only trying to help," she said, sobbing, to Emma.

"Of course you were," Emma said, digging an aspirin and fresh Kleenex from her purse, and handing them to the woman. "Anyone who knows you will know that you didn't start a fight."

At that, Inez quit sobbing and looked straight at Belinda. "You've got to say on your radio show that I did not start this fight." She would not leave the table until Belinda promised to set things right on the radio.

The afternoon consisted of more singing and an uplifting personal testimony by the young woman in the white suit.

After that there were few dry eyes in the house. Belinda leaned over to Emma and said, "Do you see how she's dressed?"

Emma did not quite understand the relevance, but left off asking as Sister Mae took the stage to say, "The *joy* of the Lord is your *strength!*" in a most surprising and commanding voice.

Sister Mae was blessed with fire and faith. She proceeded with brief but vivifying preaching. "You were not given a spirit of timidity. *No, ma'am!* You were given a spirit of *power* and *love* and *sound mind.* God loves *you* . . . and there are no exceptions, honey. God doesn't play favorites, no, ma'am!"

"Amen!"

"Yes, Sister!"

"You do not have to worry, sisters . . . Yes, you can forgive yourself. Yes, you can forgive your neighbor. *Shout it out! Sing praise!*"

"Amen!"

"Halleluyah!"

"Love yourself and your neighbor."

"Step out in *faith!*"

Many in the audience had at one time or another seen men preach the way Sister Mae did, but few had ever seen a woman do it. The few Catholics and a couple of Southern Baptists were not certain what to think. A number of the Presbyterians and Methodists, and the two Unitarians visiting from up north, sat stunned.

Nevertheless, no one could walk out, because Sister Mae had a manner that tended to make believers out of the most ardent doubter. She spoke as a woman who knew a happy secret about life.

"You are *women,*" she told them. "Made so by the hand of God, and for a *good* purpose. Don't let there be any question about that whatsoever, honey. You are made by love and for love and to spread love. And you can do all things through Christ, who gives you the *strength,* honey."

Her joy and faith, combined with the voices of

the gospel singers who began humming in the background, swept the room like a strong breeze down the street, lifting hearts like leaves and sending them soaring.

When Sister Mae ended with the call to be saved, women began popping up in the rows like buttercups and going down to the front to receive hands-on prayer.

Emma looked up and saw Joella hurrying down. She watched as Sister Mae laid her black hand on Joella's pale, bent head.

As the last person received prayer, the gospel singers raised their voices. Then the Valentine First Methodist Ladies Circle received something near as momentous as the Spirit when their pastor's wife lit into singing "I Will Trust in the Lord."

Naomi Smith was a plain woman, with her graying brown hair pulled back to the nape of her neck and weighing in at no more than one hundred and fifteen pounds. But she proved to have an inner passion that no one would have guessed— except her husband, who had given her six children. With one hand tightly holding the microphone close to her mouth, she waved the other hand to the beat of the music. Her feet in her very sensible SAS shoes began to dance. Turning into a presence of power and projection, she belted out, *"Sister, will you trust . . ."*

From all over came the answer, *"Yes, sister!"*

"And I say again . . . Sis-ter, will you trust?"

"Yes, I will . . ."

The lyrics were repetitive but heart-stirring. When Naomi finally let go of it, the ten women from the Valentine Methodist, as well as Naomi's sister, were reeling with amazement.

Sister Mae ended the day by praying a blessing that each heart would be uplifted and held by the Power of Loving Joy as they left and went out into the world. "Remember . . . you are *Glorr-ious* Women of God. Go and *light* the world."

A lot of the women did not know what to make of all the exuberant talk about God and singing of religious songs; however, every one of them shared one thing: they had been away from their normal world of work and troubles for an entire day, and had sat still with themselves and their thoughts.

For many, this was the first time they had sat down for more than fifteen minutes all week, or had time to do anything more than think about how to pay the next bill or pacify whomever in their family needed pacifying. After being surrounded by hundreds of other women singing gospel songs, and laughing and hearing the uplifting words of faith and love and hope, and having all the sweet tea and ambrosia cake that they could hold, they could not help but feel a little hopeful. And as they had sat there, solutions to problems had popped into their minds and heartaches had seemed to ease. A number of women shed ten years off their faces.

Those from reserved families, or non-believers altogether, thought that they could not possibly go home and tell their friends and relatives of what they had seen and done. It was just too amazing. A number of closet gospel listeners were born. Many a mother asked her daughter to find the Christian rock station on the car radio.

There was a lot of evidence of miracles. Mended relationships occurred all over the place. The two women who had earlier gotten into a fight at the tape table were seen walking arm-in-arm back to the table, where they bought each other recordings of the talks.

Joella located Emma and told her with tears in her eyes, "I know I'm never gonna drink again . . . I know I've been cured this time."

"I'm so glad for you," Emma said, giving her a heartfelt hug.

Several other women confessed to being cured of gambling and shopping addictions, and one woman got so carried away as to ask another's forgiveness for an affair with her husband. That went okay in the moment, although there was consternation about the possibility of honesty being carried too far.

The Valentine First Methodist Ladies Circle went en masse up to Naomi and praised her for her talent. Inez Cooper began to talk about Naomi being song leader at church.

Sylvia had to step outside and call Wadley on her cell phone. She could not wait another moment. Being surrounded by all those women and such a foreign atmosphere overwhelmed her. She was dying to hear a male voice. Wadley's voice was so very precious when he said, "Hi, sweetheart. How'd it go today?"

She said, "Oh, God, I don't know . . . I think I might have been saved without knowing it."

Belinda and Emma hardly talked at all. They strolled out to the car and got in, and Belinda waited with uncommon patience in the traffic. They drove home with the air-conditioner at full blast and the windows down. They rode along with their hair blowing in the wind and looking out from dark glasses at the passing scenery, each one in her own thoughts. Occasionally they would look at each other and smile. Emma kicked off her shoes and waved her skirt, enjoying the cooling air up between her legs. At this, Belinda threw her head back and laughed.

Belinda suggested going to the Main Street Café for take-out dinners, and Emma agreed that this was a fine idea. Belinda pulled into a space at the curb, the two of them dashed inside, and shortly came out carrying bulging red-checked paper bags with handles. Belinda had gotten two Saturday steak specials, with dried-apricot pie slices for dessert, and a quart jar of cold sweet tea, because she never made her own. Emma had gotten two deluxe cheeseburger plates—John Cole's favorite thing to order at the café—one with double fries and a slice of apple pie.

When Belinda dropped Emma at her house, they kissed each others' cheeks and hugged, then Belinda drove away with a happy wave.

She headed quickly home, where she found Lyle sitting in front of the television news with Giff Phelps. She more or less swept Giff up and out the door, telling him, lying without one bit of compunction despite having spent the day hearing of God, that she had seen Penny downtown and that she had said to tell him to come home. He was getting into his car before he realized that if Penny had wanted him, she would have called him on his cell phone.

Belinda told Lyle not to get up. "I'll bring our dinners in here."

Lyle wondered if he had heard right. Usually it was him getting their meals. He liked to cook and Belinda did not. He sat nervously thinking that maybe he should go ask her and afraid to do so, because she sometimes got testy if he didn't do what she said.

Experiencing a willingness to please that she had never before experienced, Belinda dressed the part to serve by digging out an apron from the rear of a kitchen drawer. She had to figure out how to put it on. She did not have television trays, never having eaten a meal in front of a television in her life; however, she did have two teak trays for eating in bed that served nicely.

She arranged their food on their best china and carried it all in to Lyle, who was surprised, of course, and a little nervous that he might spill something on the carpet and get yelled at, but she assured him that the carpet could be shampooed.

As they ate, she prodded him with questions for his opinion about the news on television, and from there she went on to ask about his day driving around on patrol. She responded to everything he said with great interest, looking at him and oohing and aahing wherever possible.

A few times while she looked at him she drifted off into thoughts of her plans for Emma's stationery or changes at the drugstore, and she would blink and find herself staring at him and him waiting for some response on her part. A couple of times it came to the tip of her tongue to tell him that his idea was the stupidest idea she had ever heard, but she bit back the criticism. She was a *glorious* woman of love, after all.

Lyle proved to get talked out very quickly, and by their normal time of eight-thirty, they were in bed and in each other's arms. Lyle was the most ardent lover he had been in months. It was stupendous.

Belinda could not believe how simple it had been, once she had given Lyle what he needed.

• • •

John Cole was not home. Emma had seen this immediately upon arrival, since his car was not in the drive. She was just as glad. She was not ready to see him, although she eagerly anticipated his arrival.

Emma stuck the hamburger dinners in the warming oven, shook off her shoes and padded barefoot into her workroom.

She flipped on the light just above the drawing table, illuminating all the early photographs of her and John Cole tacked around it.

Reaching into a drawer, she pulled out the papers that Catherine had given them at their first marriage counseling session. She took up a pencil, read the questions again and quickly jotted a few things, noting her good qualities as an ability to comfort others, and having an eye for comfortable beauty and humor, and listening. She noted that these things were what had caused John Cole to fall in love with her.

Then she skipped to the statement of "I wish" and read what she had written: *I wish I could love John Cole like I used to.*

With teary vision, she wrote: *I wish John Cole was home so that I could tell him that I love him very much.*

Sometime in those hours of sitting still at the Glorious Women gathering, away from hiding in her artwork and obsessing over the details of the wedding celebrations, the pieces of the puzzle had come to her. It was not that John Cole did not love her or she him, but that they had somehow gotten blind to it. They had been, as Belinda had pointed out, loving all along.

She put down the pencil, gathered up the photographs of her and John Cole together and took them into the kitchen. Pulling her hamburger dinner out of the oven, she ate it in snatches as she went around the house, taping certain photographs in certain places. She even went outside and taped one on the door of the garage.

When John Cole finally drove up, the sun was going down. His headlights hit the garage door. He sat there looking at what he thought, but could not believe really was, a photograph.

Leaving his headlights on, he got out of the truck and went closer. It *was* a photograph, an eight-by-ten of him and Emma at their wedding.

He looked at the house and saw light from the windows.

Wondering what Emma was up to now and trying to figure out any lapse that he might have committed, he walked toward the back door, where he found another picture of them when they had been young taped to the glass.

He entered. The kitchen was empty.

Pretty much by habit, he went to the refrigerator. There was another picture taped on the door.

Inside, there was even a picture taped to a can of Coke. He took the picture off the can, popped the lid and drank deeply, then gazed at the picture for a long moment. It was of the first car they'd bought together.

Hanging on a string in the entry to the family room was a snapshot of them at the beach.

There was another on the remote control.

It dawned on him that Emma knew exactly what path he would take upon coming into the house.

It was a little eerie being given this visual history of their relationship. He stood there thinking a whole lot conflicting thoughts, wanting to find Emma and discover what all of this was about, and at the same time worrying that maybe he would not want to know.

Then he saw a shoe and a skirt lying on the floor near the hallway. He went over and picked them up. He looked at them and had a moment's panic as he thought about some bizarre murder.

He hurried into the hallway, where he found another shoe and a blouse, and another picture, and then a bra. The door to the bedroom was closed, and taped on it was a picture. On the doorknob hung a pair of lace panties. He lifted them with his fingers.

By now he no longer thought of a murder. But he wasn't certain he wanted to go inside the bedroom. He wasn't certain he could face Emma and be overwhelmed with emotion. He wanted to run away.

He thought about driving out to the highway and calling her. He had actually done that on many occasions in their married years, and if he found Emma too emotional, he would find an excuse not to come home.

But he knew this time that he needed to face her. He did not want to run away anymore.

With a deep breath, he opened the door and stepped inside. The room flickered with candle-light, and the air was heavy with a sweet scent. Emma was in bed, wearing something skimpy. In the candlelight, she seemed to shine, too. There was this sort of halo behind her as she smiled and raised a glass of wine. "Welcome home."

Emma watched John Cole stand there and stare at her. She got amused at the stunned look on his face.

And then he turned around and left.

"John Cole?" Rising up on her knees, she looked down the hall and saw him turn into the family room, practically at a run.

A moment later, she heard the back door open and close.

Thunderstruck, she sat there. Realizing she still had the wine glass lifted, she lowered it.

She slumped back against the pillows. He had left. What had she done wrong?

Knocking back the wine, she looked around the room at the candles and the scarves she had sprayed with perfume, then tossed over the lamps. The comedienne that day had given her the idea, and it did work to give a nice light and lovely fragrance.

Maybe it had been a bit too much to spring on John Cole after all her years of being inhibited.

She began to cry quietly and sank into misery of the sort that did not care if she fell asleep and the candles burned down and caught the house on fire. In fact, she wished they would.

Suddenly she heard something—John Cole's footsteps. He appeared through the door and came straight to the bed. He had a quite happy smile on his face and something wrapped in a greasy rag in his hands.

"Know what this is?" he said, jutting the item toward her and unwrapping the cloth to reveal some sort of engine part.

"A carburetor?" she guessed, wiping away her tears.

"Yes . . . it's the one from that first Dodge we bought together," he said, offering her the snapshot that had been taped to his Coke can. "I saved it all these years."

Uncertain as to the significance, but knowing there was some, she looked from him to the greasy car part and then back at him again. The expression on his face went clear through her. He was trying so hard.

"Oh, John Cole."

She threw herself at him. The carburetor went somewhere, and John Cole's arms came around her. He kissed her and laid her back on the bed.

The phone rang, and neither of them paid any attention.

Sometime later, they located the carburetor at the foot of the bed. It was also at this time that they discovered that the scarf on one of the bedside lamps had begun to smolder. All of that seemed of little consequence, however.

"I love you," she said into his ear.

27

I'm Your Mother

Gracie was awakened by Johnny's phone call. She lay in bed talking to him for a long time. It was lovely. She so missed seeing him alone.

"The three of us could go out to lunch," she suggested, thinking of something that would not be too confining, despite involving her mother.

But Johnny gave the excuse of having promised to take a shift at the Berry convenience store in order that a manager could have the day off.

More and more Johnny was refusing to be around her mother. He had totally stopped coming to the apartment. Gracie could not blame him. She knew her mother had an attitude toward him. Gracie kept hoping that this would change in time, but for the present, the matter was a strain that could only be alleviated by her mother going back home.

"She is leaving on Tuesday morning," Gracie told him. "For certain this time."

After hanging up, she got leisurely out of bed and puttered around the room for some minutes, savoring the time alone. She could hear her mother moving around in the living room and kitchen, could smell the aroma of coffee. She was tired of smelling coffee and felt a little sick with it. She had to curb the urge to fly into the guest room, pack her mother's things and shoo her out the door along with the coffeepot her mother had bought.

The thought made her a little nervous about marrying Johnny. What if she wanted to do the same thing to him after a couple of weeks?

She was just having marriage jitters, she thought. Kim and Nicole had both talked to her about that. It would have been nice to speak to her mother about it, but she knew that her mother would tell her not to marry Johnny. Any time she had attempted to speak to her mother about any difficulty had generally ended up a disaster.

When she emerged from her bedroom she had a smile on her face and gave her mother, who was on the sofa with the Sunday paper, a kiss on the cheek. She continued into the kitchen to make a pot of tea, which was her preference. Returning with tea and toast, she curled up in the armchair.

"Did I hear the phone ring early this morning?" her mother asked.

"It wasn't so early. Eight-thirty."

"Uhmm . . . Johnny?"

"Yes."

"Were you talking to him all this time?"

"A good deal of it."

"I can't imagine what you find to talk about for so long. I can't imagine that he talks that much."

Gracie waited for more in the way of explanation. When none came, she asked why her mother imagined that Johnny did not converse much.

"Oh . . . most men don't . . . and he certainly doesn't seem the type."

Gracie was annoyed, which was probably what prompted her to say, "One thing we talked about was the album his grandmother is making for us. Please don't forget to send the childhood pictures of me when you go home on Tuesday."

"You can call and remind me," her mother said without looking up from the newspaper folded in front of her face. Her black-rimmed reading glasses were far down her nose.

"It's important to Miss Lillian, doing this project. She would like the names of my grandparents, too. She's doing a family tree, you know. She's going to a lot of trouble." She couldn't seem to hold back from pressing the point.

Her mother looked over the rim of her glasses. "I'll get the pictures. I just might need a reminder, that's all. You call her Miss Lillian?"

"Everyone does . . . didn't you hear them when we were at the Berrys'? Even Wadley called her Miss Lillian."

"Oh, yes, that's right."

Gracie watched her mother straighten out sections of the newspaper and refold them. She could feel the energy being sucked right out of her by her mother.

Hopping up, she said, "I'm going to wash some delicates, if you have anything," and departed.

Five minutes later her mother joined her at the washing machine. She had brought a handful of panties and bras. Gracie put the machine on the delicate cycle. Realizing her mother was lingering, she looked around. "Do you have something else?"

"Yes . . . oh, not clothes. I have something I need to discuss with you. Let's go sit at the table."

Her mother took a chair, and Gracie, a little curious, followed. She noticed that her mother was clutching her hands. She wondered if her mother was about to launch into another criticism of Johnny, or if maybe she was going to say she was going to marry Wadley, which likely would not produce hand-wringing, so it had to be something else. Perhaps about Gracie's grandparents. Maybe her grandfather or grandmother was ill, and her mother thought it might upset her. Perhaps they required her mother's attention, in which case her mother might be leaving sooner.

Her mother cleared her throat, then said, "I think I need to tell you that your father was part black. *Is*, I suppose. I don't know if he is still alive . . . but—"

"What?" Gracie broke in.

Her mother's eyes met hers. "I said *your father is part black*. He is black-Creole, which is French, too, of course, as much as he is black. Actually there's some sort of way they follow it, but I've forgotten. I do know that his—"

"Oh, Mom . . . I don't believe you."

Her mother put a hand to her hair. "I'm not making it up. I know that I—"

Gracie jumped to her feet. "I cannot believe you would go to such lengths to break me and Johnny up that you would come to me with some wild story. . . ."

"I am not making it up, Gracie. I guess I should have told you a long time ago, and I'm sorry."

"You guess?" No one, absolutely no one, had as much gall as her mother.

"Okay. I *should* have told you. I meant to, but time went by, and it just all sort of faded." She might as well have added: *you know how it is.* "It didn't seem important. Your father never had a part in our lives. But now, when you're going to marry Johnny . . . well, it could be important to his family. That's why I am telling you now."

"What else can you throw in here that you might have left out, just to make sure Johnny and I break up?" Gracie yelled.

"That is not what I am doing, Gracie," her mother said with patent patience. "I'm simply trying to rectify a . . ."

At that Gracie raced from the room. Gathering clothes, she went to the bathroom to dress.

Her mother was sitting on the bed when she came out. "I knew how you would take this. That you would think I'm trying to break you and Johnny up. That's why it has been so hard for me to tell you. Try looking at it from my point of view. It's not easy being a mother, Gracie. You'll find out someday. I have done the best by you that I could. Maybe I wouldn't even have told you—I mean, it really doesn't matter—but your Miss Lillian is making such a point of all this stuff."

"Why don't you try blaming everything on the postman, too?" Gracie commented as she went into her closet, got a duffel bag from the shelf and began packing, while her mother followed her around saying that she was reacting badly, and that Gracie's father had been from a small town in Louisiana, the name of which she had forgotten, which she'd visited with him for some months in the heat of July, which no one should do, but they could look it up.

When Gracie zipped her bag, her mother said, "Perhaps I should have told you more about your father, but you could have asked, too, Gracie. You never have asked."

Gracie almost slapped her.

"Mom . . . just go home," she said, and headed out the door.

Her mother ran out after her and called down over the stair railing, "I'm your mother. You have to put up with me in your life."

"Yes, but not in my apartment," Gracie called back, and continued racing down the stairs and out to her car.

She drove around for half an hour, in which she passed by the large Berry convenience store where Johnny was on duty, but ended up continuing on and heading to Valentine with the faint idea of talking to Emma. After a couple of miles, she made a U-turn on the highway.

Finally she went to the M. Connor store, where Nicole was working. As it was yet only noon, Nicole was alone on duty. She had to listen to Gracie's story in increments between popping out to wait on customers. Growing up and living in a household of so many women, she was able to do this and pick up with Gracie exactly where she left off and not get one bit confused.

Gracie said, "I just can't believe she would do this. She says I never asked, but how could I ask, when every time I brought up anything about my father, she would get this weird look on her face? I just learned not to ever mention him. I mean, I lived so long without him . . . and obviously she's the one who is so bothered by the whole thing. It's all just so complicated.

"And I don't even know if she's telling the truth, and if she is, I just can't believe she would come out with it now. It is so hard to believe that she would go to this length to ruin my relationship with Johnny."

"Do you think it will?" Nicole asked.

"Oh, no, of course not. It's just that my mother believes it will." ·

Now the question sat in her mind, though, and it was not helped by Nicole telling her, "Well, my dad and granddaddy and uncles sure went ballistic when my sister Sydney started goin' with a white guy. Honey, my Uncle Arthur arrested Justin a whole bunch of times and tried to run him out of the county."

Gracie took that in and thought about the Berrys.

"It should be real easy to look up about your daddy," Nicole said. "I can call Sydney and get her to do it. She knows how to do these things now that she works for the police force. That's the good thing that came from it. Uncle Arthur kept harassing Justin and hauling him down to the police station, and it ended up that both Sydney and Justin got jobs there after they got married." The bell went off, indicating a customer, and Nicole hurried away to the front counter.

Gracie's phone rang in her purse; it was Johnny. She turned her phone off.

After that, Nicole suggested that Gracie leave her to run the store and go over to her family's house, where there would be so many people on a Sunday afternoon that one more would not be noticed. This proved the case, and Gracie was able to sit back and listen to all the talk and not think about any of her own perplexities. Nicole's mother, Evelyn, was very kind and didn't ask a thing. Gracie met Uncle Arthur who was the policeman and thought that he resembled Johnny's Uncle Charlie J.

"Gracie . . . are you all right? I've called you three times this afternoon."

"I know. I had my phone off. My mother and I got into an argument today, and I just had to get away." Right then she stood alone on the Davies' terrace, surrounded by the scent of honeysuckle and watching the sun go down.

"I guessed that. She called me lookin' for you. I was about to call the police, but I called the store and Nicole said you were at her house and okay. You want me to come get you? You could come stay at my place."

He sounded hopeful, and she hated to disappoint him, but she had to tell him *no*. She could not see him, although she didn't tell him that.

She said, "I'm getting ready to go to bed, and I

have all my stuff here at Nicole's. I really just need some time alone. That's all."

He said he understood.

"Please call my mom for me. Tell her I am okay, but I just want her to go home. I'm not going back to my apartment until she is gone."

"You want *me* to call her?"

"Yes, *you.*" It displayed her state of mind that she pulled the phone from her ear and looked at it with an angry glare.

"Okay," Johnny said, not wanting to risk her getting more testy with him.

After hanging up from Gracie, Johnny put away his phone and walked around a few minutes, getting a soft drink and chips and as much courage as he could for speaking to Sylvia Kinney.

The woman answered after the first ring, and so abruptly that Johnny felt jarred.

"Hello, Mrs. Kinney." He felt five years old. "I talked to Gracie. She's okay. She's stayin' over at Nicole's."

He immediately regretted having given that information. He didn't know if Gracie wanted her mother to know where she was. If her mother went racing over to Nicole's, Gracie could end up really mad at him.

Sylvia Kinney's response was, "I guess expecting any more from you is asking too much," and she hung up.

He wondered what she had meant, like he always wondered what she meant. Then he realized that he was safe on the score of her driving over to Nicole's, as she would not know the address. However, he had neglected to give her the further message that Gracie had said for her to go home. He was not about to call her again.

Five minutes later and without a lot of thought, Johnny was in his car and heading to his parents' house. Lights shone from the windows, and both of his parents' cars were in the driveway, but his mother did not come running out to meet him. He imagined her when he popped in, all surprised and happy to see him, and maybe even with some sort of dessert to feed him.

Just as he put his hand on the backdoor knob, he looked through the glass and saw his parents inside. Seeing them together gave him pause. They were bent over the kitchen table, their heads almost touching. They were looking at pictures. His mother lifted her head and laughed. He could hear the sound through the window glass. He caught snatches of, "And remember when he . . . you thought . . ."

His father grinned that slow grin. "I did not . . . I thought . . ."

And then his father did the most surprising thing. He reached over and took his mother by the back of the neck and drew her to him, and kissed her in a manner that caused Johnny to instantly turn from the sight.

Once it had been the three of them, but now it was just those two.

He went back to his car and drove away in a sneaking manner, feeling a little homeless. Without Gracie or his mother, he really wasn't certain what to do with himself.

Emma was sitting on the side of the bed, rubbing lotion into her hands, when the phone rang. For an instant she didn't know what to do. She didn't want to get lotion all over the receiver, but then she saw it was Johnny calling. She got all excited and snatched up the phone.

"Hello, sweetheart."

"Hi, Mom. Hope I didn't call you too late."

"Oh, no . . . we were just gettin' ready for bed. It's good to hear your voice. What's going on?" She looked over to see John Cole come to the bathroom doorway, gaze at her a moment, then disappear back into the bathroom.

"Oh, I just thought I'd call," Johnny said. "Gracie's over at Nicole's. Her and her mother got into an argument. She's left her apartment until her mother goes home."

"That happens a lot with mothers and daughters, honey. They'll make up. When is her mother goin' home?"

"I think on Tuesday. I sure hope so. Gracie isn't really even talkin' to me, either. I don't know what's goin' on. I'm sort of afraid Gracie may be gettin' the marriage jitters, and her mother won't help that."

Johnny's dispirited voice sounded in her ear, and John Cole came out of the bathroom and gazed at her again.

She said into the phone, "Don't go jumpin' to conclusions, honey. It's probably just too much togetherness for both of them."

As Johnny agreed with this in a half-hearted manner, she missed all of what he said, because John Cole flipped on the television. She got out of the bed to leave the room, then stopped, saying, "Here's your dad. Say goodnight to him," and handed the phone over to a somewhat startled John Cole.

Father and son spoke briefly—two sentences about work, one about the NASCAR race—and when John Cole had hung up, Emma explained what Johnny had told her.

"What do you think is goin' on?" John Cole asked.

"I have no way of knowin'."

"You want to call him back? Maybe you need to talk to him."

"No . . . I'm sure that Johnny and Gracie can work it out. That's what you and I have had to do all along."

28

1550 AM on the Radio Dial
The Home Folks Show

Winston was in an especially good mood. "Great day in the mornin', friends! You're listenin' to the *Home Folks Show*, and if you are hearin' my voice, you're alive and so am I. That makes it a good day.

"A special welcome to our new sponsor, the folks at Ol' Blue Dog Food. This is the best sellin' brand in a three-state area. Ol' Blue is the only brand eaten by my best dog friend, Munro. Give us a word on this, Munro."

He swung the microphone downward, and Munro, who had his paws up on the desk, gave two good barks.

"So there's your testimonial, folks. We want to thank the bosses over at Ol' Blue Dog Food for pickin' our *Home Folks Show* to sponsor on all of *eight* stations in Southern Oklahoma. Yes—you heard right. We are now on a total of *eight* stations, one of them heard all the way down into Texas. We are a hit, folks!"

A loud *wha-hoo* sounded over the airwaves, followed by applause and a bit of happy banjo. Jim and Winston loved their sound effects.

"Okay, to keep things perky here, what do you call a cow with no legs?

"Stumped on that one, are ya? No, that's not the answer. Y'all think on it, while Alabama sings that it feels so right. This one goes out to Miss Vella." Jaydee had called in the dedication, but Winston conveniently forgot to say that part.

Belinda came hurrying into the studio. "I'm here. Am I late?"

The men and Willie Lee regarded her, wide-eyed. Winston had a moment of wondering about his faculties. He raised an eyebrow at Jim and was relieved to see the boy shrug, indicating he was equally surprised.

"I don't think so," Winston told her. "I think you're a day early."

"Isn't it Wednesday?"

"Tuesday."

"You're kiddin' me." She looked at Jim, who nodded. "Well, darn it, I've been thinkin' it was Wednesday all mornin'."

"I guess you might as well come on and do your show," said Winston. "Willie Lee, slide that chair over here."

"I can do two shows," Belinda said as she pulled papers from her purse. "Today and tomorrow."

"This is called the *Home Folks Show* with Brother Winston. You can go on today *or* tomorrow, then wait until next week."

"Then I'll wait." She started out of the room and came back. "Since I thought it was Wednesday, I made an appointment for tomorrow, which I thought was Thursday, but it isn't, so I'd better go on today."

There was no way Winston could follow that, and anyway, the boy was pointing at him. Winston said into the microphone, "Did you think of what they call a cow with no legs?"

What? came a recorded chorus.

"Grumpy," supplied Winston, and recorded laughter followed him. He and Jim Rainwater laughed together.

Belinda had herself sat down, and she gathered her breath as Winston got mileage out of telling how she had come to do her *Around Town and Beyond* program a day early. He was having a grand time, and she glared at him.

"But first it is time for our birthdays today," he said.

With a large sigh, Belinda sat back in the chair.

There came the sound of a trumpet. "We wish a happy birthday to our pastor over at the First Methodist, Reverend Stanley Smith, who reaches the ripe age of fifty-five today."

In his study, updating his words for a funeral he would have to preach that afternoon, the pastor heard the announcement from the small stereo on his shelf. He paused, knowing his family had called it in and feeling especially grateful, as he had survived triple-bypass surgery six months

397

earlier. Naomi came through the door and set herself on his lap and told him there were more birthdays to come.

"Fred and JoBeth Grace's little girl Christy turns sweet seventeen today."

In her bedroom, Christy stood in front of the mirror in a new Wonderbra her mother had bought her against her father's wishes.

"And it was Iris MacCoy's birthday yesterday, but she has refused to give her age for the past five years. Let's just say we all agree that Iris is one full woman and we're all glad."

Down at the Main Street Café, where Iris was having coffee with her husband, she heard this come over the radio. She stood and gave a bow, and her husband was both proud and annoyed at how the men all looked at her. She did not need a Wonderbra and was the happiest woman alive.

A recorded chorus sang "Happy Birthday."

Belinda sat up and got herself all ready again, only to have to sit through songs by Garth Brooks and Vince Gill, and Winston giving the weather and touting the IGA's sales.

Finally, when she was sitting there wondering if she should get up and go to the restroom, she suddenly realized Winston was saying, "It's time now on *The Home Folks Show* for *Around Town and Beyond* with Belinda Blaine."

He was ready and quickly moved the microphone back several inches.

"Hello, everybody . . ." Belinda grabbed the microphone and brought it closer, speaking carefully. "I would like to say that I read in the *Valentine Voice* that today is Be Late for Somethin' Day. I guess for me it is Be Early for Somethin' Day."

She was pleased with how all of that had fit together. She wished Jim Rainwater would do some thinking on his own and play the laugh track.

"Also according to the *Voice,* this week is National Singles Week, and the month is National Spinach Lovers Month. I don't know who makes this stuff up, but I imagine there's money involved somewhere."

There came the sound of a *ta-dum,* and Belinda jumped. She saw Jim Rainwater grin at her. The sound effect was nice, but now she had to find her place again. She wished she had gone to the bathroom while she had the chance.

"Comin' up this Saturday, the Red Cross is holding a first aid and CPR course for babies, children and adults. I don't think they mean babies and children can take the course—it's for adults to learn how to *do* CPR, includin' on babies and children, too. It's at the high school. Call 555-1010 to get registered.

"Delta Blankenship has started giving piano and dulcimer lessons. You can look her number up in the telephone book, because she didn't give it to me.

"Larkin Ford called to say that if you've found two black steers west of town, they are his. They obviously had legs, since they walked off." She looked at Jim to see if he took note to put on the laugh sound, but he was cleaning his fingernails.

"Under make-ups this week are Cory Makescry and Vicki Dinwiddie, and Amber and Glen Dixon. You can get in on a pool for how long things will last with Amber and Glen over at the domino club. Under divorces are Emmett and Laura Starter, and firmly under break-ups are Vella Blaine and Jaydee Mayhall.

"Last of all, Inez Cooper says she did not start the fight at the tape table up at the Glorious Women's Day. This has been backed up by several witnesses.

"That's it for today, friends. Call me with your news. Back to you, Winston."

Winston had been reading the paper and came up with a start. Grabbing the microphone, he launched in with, "We got a beautiful day . . . just a minute and I'll find the forecast. . . ."

Belinda passed Willie Lee without offering him extra ice cream. She hurried into the restroom.

A half an hour later Willie Lee was outside bidding good-bye to Winston, who was a little torn about leaving the boy behind.

"Sure you don't want to change your mind and accompany me?" he asked.

Willie Lee shook his head. "I will some-time." All he knew was that today he was to do something else.

"Okay. See you tonight, and we'll tell each other our adventures."

Winston got into the black limousine that was to drive him to personal appearances at a grand opening for a Wal-Mart Super Center store and the dedication for a new senior community center. Thinking of the excitement ahead, he quickly forgot to miss Willie Lee. Life was just carrying him onward in new directions.

When Jim Rainwater came jumping out the door behind Willie Lee, all that was left of the limousine was a rooster tail of dust.

"Dang, I missed him." Jim looked down at Willie Lee. "The *Today Show* in New York is on the phone for Winston," he announced. "I guess I'll go tell them he's gone."

Then, "He has a cell phone!" and he raced back inside, leaving Willie Lee looking from the door to the now-empty road.

Willie Lee walked along with Munro down the gravel lane to the highway, where they turned toward the Berry Stop. Nicky appeared from behind the big elm tree.

"Hey,"

"Hel-lo."

"I watched ya' comin' from way down there. You didn't see me comin' along, did ya'?"

"Yes."

"Aw, you did not."

"Mun-ro saw you. He told me."

"Aw, yeah, right." Nicky petted Munro, wishing, not for the first time, the dog was his own. "I saw that old man yous always with drive off in a limo."

"Yes."

"He's pretty big around here, ain't he? Is he your grampa?"

Willie Lee had difficulty with the two questions being asked together. "Mr. Winston is not too big. No. He is . . . Mr. Winston. We live in his hou-ouse."

Nicky looked at him with a puzzled frown. Willie Lee wished he could speak better.

Just then a van coming along the opposite lane stopped. Willie Lee recognized it as the Smith van at the same time that he heard Gabby call his name. "Willie Lee!" Mrs. Smith was waving from the driver's window. Then there came Gabby, running around the front of the van and across the street.

"Gab-by!" he said quite fast.

She stopped to wave at her mother, who drove on

down Main Street, and then, laughing, she threw her arms around Willie Lee. He hugged her in return.

"I'm so glad to see you. I can hang out all afternoon," she said, and petted Munro, who licked her face. "Hi," she said to Nicky.

"Hey. Who are you?"

"I'm Gabby, Willie Lee's best friend."

"Aw, you ain't. He don't have no girl for a best friend. I ain't never seen you with him."

"I am too." Gabby said quietly and taking a step closer to Willie Lee.

Willie Lee felt the discord and wondered what to say. He came out with, "I have to call to tell my mo-ther I am o-kay . . . or I ha-ave to go home. Paris will call. We can get Bama Pies," he said, thinking quite happily of the treat and that it would please his friends.

"Yeah, and we can get Cokes there, too," said Gabby.

"Where?" asked Nicky.

"The Berry Quick Stop."

"Uh . . . you got money?" Nicky asked her after a minute.

"Yes." She pulled the folded bills out of her pocket. When she opened her hand, Nicky went to snatch the money but she was quick and pulled her hand back. She had two brothers. She looked straight at him, and he turned his head.

"I wasn't gonna take yer ol' money."

As they walked along, Gabby alternately held Willie Lee's hand, then danced ahead like a fairy and came back again. Her honey curls caught the sunlight, and her smile was all for Willie Lee, and his for her.

Nicky watched the two and considered pushing Gabby in the ditch.

After a few minutes, Gabby asked Nicky his name and he told her. She danced off with Munro dancing with her, then came back and asked Nicky where he was from.

"We just moved here. To a ranch 'bout a mile out. My dad's a cowboy. He's at the feed store. He comes every day, and I been comin' to play with Willie Lee."

She pirouetted away and came back, saying, "I know you are lyin', but I will buy you a Coke anyway." Her father had always taught her to share, especially with those who were "the least of these." She strongly suspected that Nicky was one of "the least of these."

They reached the Berry Stop parking lot. Willie Lee and Gabby headed toward the door, but Nicky held back at the corner of the automatic carwash. "I'll wait here. Will you guys get me somethin', too?" he asked, dropping his voice.

"Yes, we will," Willie Lee said.

"Why don't . . . ?" Gabby started to ask, but Willie Lee pulled her by the hand, and they entered the store.

Today Paris was on the outside of the counter and Tiffany was behind at the cash register. Willie Lee asked Paris to call his mother to report on him. As she had often made the call and was an old friend of the family, he did not have to explain further.

Paris explained to Tiffany, though, while Gabby and Willie Lee got their cold drinks and snacks. "Willie Lee's mom likes to be told from time to time where he is. Here's her number written on the list beside the cash register." She dialed and spoke quickly to Marilee Holloway.

"Your mom wants to know what you're gonna do this afternoon."

"We are go-ing to hang out." Willie Lee told her, then added, "We will be care-ful."

Paris grinned at him and repeated this into the phone, then hung up.

Gabby and Willie Lee put their purchases on the counter for Tiffany to ring up. Tiffany was brand new at the Stop and had to look at the prices.

"You got your Bama Pie," Paris said. "Don't charge Willie Lee for that. He always gets his Bama Pies free from me." She smiled and winked at him. "Gabby's, too, today. Who's the third one for?"

Willie Lee gazed at her. "A friend."

Gabby looked from Willie Lee to Paris's eyes, which were heavily outlined in black and quite a curiosity to her.

"Oh, yeah?" Paris said.

"Yes. We are tak-ing it to him. He is . . . wait-ing." Then he added, "We are shar-ring, ar-en't we, Gab-by?"

"Uh-huh. With the least of these." She gave what she knew was an innocent smile.

"Well, you guys have fun," Paris told them as they left.

When Willie Lee and Gabby came around the corner of the automatic carwash, Nicky eagerly took his drink and snack.

"Come on." He ran ahead, all the way past the empty lot where people parked cars for sale to the shade of the crepe myrtle trees on the other side. There the three sat and ate their snacks. Nicky swallowed his Bama Pie in three big bites; then, as the other two leisurely ate theirs, he told them all about his fascinating life on the ranch with his father. Gabby kept interrupting him with pesky questions about details that seemed to have little to do with his story: "Where is the ranch? What is your last name? Do you have a mother? Why don't you wear cowboy boots?"

The most Willie Lee said was, "Whe-ere are your sis-ters?"

"You have sisters?" Gabby asked instantly.

"Yeah. They're there at the ranch, but they don't do nothin'."

A few minutes later Willie Lee saw Munro get up in an alert manner. Willie Lee began to push to his feet, too, and as he did so, he saw the girl who looked just like Nicky running toward them across the IGA parking lot. She was hollering for Nicky. Munro took off running toward her, and Willie Lee went after him. Willie Lee was not very fast, though, and Nicky passed him and reached his sister, who was all upset.

"You got to come. I can't get her to quit cryin'. Somethin' is wrong. . . ."

Munro had continued on running past the girl. He turned to see if Willie Lee was following, which he was. Nicky and his sister passed him, but Gabby matched her pace to his.

They went down the block of the older, poorer neighborhood behind the IGA. Munro, still out front, went across the brown yard and up on the porch of a very run-down clapboard house. He sniffed impatiently at the screen door. When Nicky reached the door and opened it, Munro disappeared inside.

Willie Lee heard the baby crying before he reached the yard, louder when he got to the door. The inside was very dim after the brightness of the summer day. And hot. Stifling hot, even though a fan blew from the corner. There were a playpen, a couch and a chair in the room, all old and broken down. Nothing else.

Nicky's sister started walking around with the baby. "I gave her the baby aspirin. I fed her, but she spit it all up. I don't know what to do."

"If she has a fever, you have to get those clothes off of her," Gabby said in a very knowledgeable voice that belied her tiny stature. All eyes swung to her. She set about ordering everyone around, telling Willie Lee to sit on the couch to take the baby, and telling the girl that after Willie Lee quieted the baby, she could take the baby's clothes off.

Willie Lee sat on the couch, Munro jumped up right beside him, and they waited, but the girl held on to the still-squalling baby. She and Nicky began to argue.

"I'm not givin' him Lucy."

"Sissy, he can help her."

"No . . . he's retarded."

"*You're* retarded," put in Gabby.

Just then the screen door squeaked, and Paris strode in and across the room, took the baby from the girl, who was too stunned to protest, and plopped her into Willie Lee's arms.

"Y'all are busted," Paris said to the girl, who was about to fly at Willie Lee. "Get back and shut up."

Willie Lee, experienced with his own little sister, held the baby quite confidently. Tears were squeezing out of her tightly shut eyes. Munro licked her toes, and she jumped and opened her eyes.

Rubbing her back, Willie Lee began to talk to her. "You are going to be all right . . . there now . . . sweet baby."

She gazed at him, and he kept on talking to her,

while those watching and listening experienced not only the miracle of the fever leaving the baby's face, but Willie Lee's words coming out amazingly smooth.

Emma was out in the backyard serving afternoon refreshments to the work crew when Sheriff Neville Oakes drove up.

She knew most of the young workmen by name now, and they always greeted her with a smile and an easy, "Hi, Miz Berry."

"You're spoilin' my crew," said the pool construction foreman Ralph Goode. As he said this, he helped himself to three large oatmeal cookies and a banana out of the basket. "They get in fights to be on the crew to come here."

"That's the idea," replied Emma, continuing on around the backyard, handing out cold bottles of lemonade and generous helpings of fruit and homemade cookies, and stepping over trenches and around holes and concrete forms to do so.

The work was all going to be completed in plenty of time for the bridal-shower barbeque. John Cole had told Emma with a little bit of admiration that her serving refreshments was the secret of getting a good job done.

She had not meant it as any bribe. "I just wanted to make sure we didn't have anyone with heat stroke . . . and to fatten up some of those skinny ones."

It turned out that the young man that she had especially wanted to plump up just a bit—to put a smile on his face—was the person the sheriff came looking for.

The sheriff got out of his car, and heads all over the yard turned to look at him. Not only was he in a sheriff's car and uniform, but he was an enormous man and people quite naturally had to look at him.

"Hello, Sheriff Oakes," Emma called, and started hurrying his way with the instant and horrible fear that something awful had happened to John Cole or Johnny. She stumbled in stepping over a trench, and the young man she had been serving dropped his drink to reach up and catch her by the hand.

The sheriff called back, "Everything's fine, Miz Berry. No emergency. I'm not here to arrest anybody." He waved both hands and seemed very anxious that no one get upset. It was well-known that Neville Oakes was an enormous pussycat; he could not stand people to get upset.

"I'm just here lookin' to see a Sammy Varela. I understand he is on this crew."

It was Sammy who had hold of Emma's hand to help her over the trench. She looked at him, and he looked as if he wanted to run. Then, without a word, he picked up his drink from the dirt and, still carrying his cookies, he went just behind Emma toward the sheriff. He walked stoically but with his head down, as if going to a firing squad.

The sheriff called him Mr. and said, "We got your brother and sisters at the station. I think you might want to come down and help us get the situation straightened out." He held open the patrol-car door for Sammy, who slipped into the seat.

Then, to Emma, the sheriff said, "You can come, too, Miss Emma. Paris who works for you at the Stop is involved. You'll have to drive yourself, though."

With the image of the young man staring forlornly out the window burning in her mind, Emma raced inside for her purse, returned to her car and took off so fast that she caught up to the sheriff on the highway. Seeing him, she slowed down, afraid he would give her a ticket for speeding. She called John Cole, taking the chance that the sheriff wouldn't look in his rearview mirror and see her using her cell phone while driving.

Then she looked in *her* rearview mirror and saw that Ralph Goode was following her in the pool-company truck.

It turned out that the Varela children had arrived in town from Dallas several months before with their mother, who had come with a man who got a job as mechanic at the Ford dealership and worked only three weeks before being fired for stealing tools. When he left town, their mother left with him. The children's parents were divorced, and

411

they did not know for sure where their father was. Mr. Varela was an Air Force sergeant based down in San Antonio, but he had been deployed overseas at the first of the year.

Fearing separation if taken by the authorities, the children had not told anyone about being abandoned but had struggled along on their own. Sammy admitted to stealing a number of things around town—aspirin from the drugstore for the baby, the cash from the yard sale, clothes off people's lines, anything to feed and clothe his brother and sisters—until he got the job on the pool-construction crew, as well as washing dishes in the evenings at the Main Street Café.

He had been getting up before dawn every morning to walk to the house of one of his fellow workers, where he picked up a ride to the construction site, and in the evening he was dropped off in town, so he could go over to his job at the café, where he would get supper as part of his pay. In this manner he had managed to keep the electricity and water on and keep them from starving. He didn't say, but everyone knew that the children, all but the baby Lucy, who was quite round, had often gone hungry, and virtually existed on hotdogs and peanut butter and jelly sandwiches. And there had been nothing Sammy could do but leave the younger ones on their own and caring for the baby while he worked.

"I'll pay back everything we owe soon as I can,"

he said earnestly. "I already gave that yard-sale lady back twenty dollars. I left it in her mailbox. I don't want them to go to juvy or Children's Services."

Sheriff Oakes, seeing that the boy was near tears, passed him a soft drink and said, "It's all gonna get straightened out. Nobody's goin' anywhere."

"He doesn't owe the Stop anything," John Cole said, having shown up when Paris called.

"I'll settle with anyone else," said Ralph Goode. "He's been a good worker on my crew."

Fayrene Gardner had come over from the Main Street Café when she heard of the hoopla and said she would chip in, too. "Sammy does all sorts of extra things over at my place."

In the outer office, the younger children were being kept quiet with hot-fudge sundaes that Belinda and Vella brought over. After a few bites, the girl, Nina, sat hers aside as a show of defiance. "I'm not goin' away from Lucy and my brothers. If they send me somewhere by myself, I'll run away."

"Oh, eat your ice cream. It won't help you not to," said Paris, who was also enjoying a sundae on the house. When both Paris and Nicky stuck spoons into her sundae, Nina grabbed it and began to eat.

Until permanent arrangements could be made, Sammy and Nicky were invited by Tate Holloway to stay with them at Winston Valentine's home.

Willie Lee was excited, because his father said that he would put a cot in his room for Nicky. It would be like having a brother.

Naomi and Pastor Smith took the girls to stay at their house. Naomi said her three-year-old would entertain the baby, and she had Gabby and two older daughters to help. "When you have six children, a couple more don't really matter."

Sammy looked at his brother and sisters. "We'll only be a few blocks apart," he said, hugging them. He didn't want to say it, but when he found out he would get the guest room, with a whole double bed and tiny bath all to himself, he was relieved to be on his own.

Nina had been the main protector of her baby sister and was reluctant to let go of her. After a few minutes of Naomi holding Lucy, though, Nina began to act like a little girl again. Within twenty minutes, she was playing with Gabby on the tire swing in the Smith backyard.

When once more Sheriff Oakes had his office to himself, he sat in his high-backed chair with relief. "Those are really nice kids," he said. "Not one of them cried. Not even that baby."

"That little girl took my compact," said secretary and dispatcher Lori Wright. "I'm pretty sure she did. I'd laid it right there beside the telephone."

"Have you seen my *Muscle and Fitness* magazine?" said Deputy Lyle Midgett, looking around. "I was readin' it when they got here. I bet that boy took it. He was lookin' at it . . . and I still wanted to read the article about buildin' mass."

"Those kids are born criminals," said Giff Phelps. "They'll always be that way now. It all starts in the first six years of life, and obviously they've had the criminal influence for many more years than that, and—"

"Giff?" the sheriff hollered.

"Yes, sir?"

"Go patrol or somethin'. Lyle, go buy another magazine."

That taken care of, the sheriff settled back to watch his afternoon soap opera, which he had taped. He was halfway through it when Lori came to his doorway.

"I just got this from San Antonio. Those kids have been reported as being kidnapped by their mother. Their daddy has been lookin' all over the country for them since he got back from overseas."

"Well, let 'im know he can come get 'em."

"I already did," she said, and went back to her desk to do her nails.

The sheriff put his feet up on his desk and thought that he could not have a better life than the one he had in the town where he had been born and where everyone pitched in to settle matters.

The next morning, Winston had a grand time with all the news.

"The mystery of the recent rash of petty thefts

has been solved and some young lives rescued, thanks to our own Paris Miller down at the Berry Stop."

There came the sound of applause.

"By now most everyone knows of the young children who have joined our small town, and if you haven't, just go down and ask Belinda at Blaine's Drugstore.

"We want to wish a big congratulations to Miss Lillian Jennings." More applause, along with a trumpet. "Miss Lillian called me not five minutes ago to say that she has sold an article to *American History* magazine.

"And last, but certainly not least . . ." A loud trumpet fanfare sounded for some seconds. ". . . your own Brother Winston has been asked to appear on *The Today Show*. Yes, sir. I am a curiosity— the only ninety-something-year-old radio personality in the nation, and very likely the world.

"There is no doubt about it, we home folks here in Valentine are a special breed."

Two minutes later, when he had cut to music, Belinda called to berate him for telling all the town news, leaving her nothing to report next week.

29

Holding On

Emma was on the phone with her mother when she heard the beep of a second caller.

She always got rattled when she heard the call-waiting beep, and seeing that it was John Cole calling, she got further rattled. Here she had her mother talking and now her husband wanted to talk. It wasn't like the call-waiting gave her long to make the decision, either. Worse, she would have to interrupt her mother in the middle of telling her all about not only having sold her article to *American History* magazine, but also the reaction from her online writing group. It would be rather awful to break off her own mother from talking about the biggest event of her writing life only to hear John Cole ask if she had washed his under-wear or something like that.

Still, reminding herself that she was married and living with John Cole, not her mother, she man-aged to say in the midst of her mother's happy dis-course, "Mama, I'm gettin' a beep, and it's John Cole. I'll call you back, okay? Bye."

It just seemed such a rude thing to do, especially to one's own mother, who of course, was jarred as all get-out.

Answering John Cole turned out to be a very

good choice, because he also had some exciting news. He had called to ask if she wanted to join him for a public relations meeting with the banker and builder on the land for the new Berry Truck Stop. He was apologetic for not asking her sooner.

"This just came up. Today's the only day for a couple of weeks that we can get everyone together to put on a ground-breaking ceremony and get pictures for the newspaper. I need to get a sport coat, so I thought I could swing by the house and pick you up . . . and we could go out to dinner afterward. I understand, though, if you've got things goin' there."

"Oh, I'd love to go with you." She had already left her worktable and was removing her apron. "I'll be ready."

This was the first time that John Cole had asked her to do anything related to the business in a very long time, and the first time he had suggested dinner out in ages.

Racing around, she did a full makeup job, with lipstick by the name of Luscious Red. She dressed in a summery sleeveless dress that swirled around her ankles, and, with a thought of the sun, she pulled out the wispy, horribly expensive wide-brimmed hat that she had ordered from Nordstrom's and never had a chance to wear. She tried it on and delighted in the way the brim dipped over her left eye.

She was ready just as John Cole arrived. Peering

out the back door, she saw him stop and speak to the workmen, who were laying sod around the freshly cured concrete area of the pool. He even got down on one knee, pointing out something. Emma smiled to think of what he was likely saying: "Make sure you get it in firmly, now . . . and you are plannin' to water it thoroughly before you leave, aren't you?"

Then he was coming to the door, so she stepped back to the counter, busying herself with pouring him a glass of cold tea, no ice, just as he liked it. When he came in, she turned quickly to face him, causing her skirt to swirl.

He said, "Your pool is just about finished," speaking with satisfaction.

"*Our* pool," she said, and handed him the glass of cold tea.

He gave no indication that he heard the correction, simply thanked her for the glass and drank deeply. Then he seemed to see her for the first time. "You look nice."

"Thank you. I tried."

Then he cast a worried glance at the hat. "You might better be careful about that hat. It'll probably blow off if a good Oklahoma wind comes up."

She took that in and smiled. "You don't like the hat?"

"Oh, no . . . I mean it looks nice," he said, as if he recognized his mistake, which may or may not have prompted his quick kiss before heading away. "I'll get my sport coat and we can leave." Then he called over his shoulder, "You don't look like the mother of a grown son."

Thrilled, she called back, "Good. I did not intend to."

He could so often surprise her. He always had, she realized.

Rather than grab his sport coat, John Cole decided to shower and don fresh clothes. He said she looked too good for him to go all sweaty and wrinkled. He even put on some "good-smelling stuff," as he called it. It took him barely fifteen minutes and they were getting into the car, where Emma knocked the wide brim of the hat on the roof of the car. She found that once inside the car with the hat, she could not sit there with it on. It hit the seat back or the window just every way she turned her head. Finally she took it off and flung it into the backseat.

"How do women wear those things anywhere?"

"What women have you ever seen wear them?"

"Well, in the movies. They show them wearing hats like that."

"That is in the movies, Emma," he pointed out. "Ready?" His hand on the key in the ignition, he raised an eyebrow at her.

"Yes . . . and I imagine women with hats like that ride in larger cars, or convertibles."

This idea was not pursued, however, because as

John Cole backed around, here came a car up the drive. "Who's that?"

"It . . . it's Gracie," Emma said.

"What's she doin' here?"

"Well, I don't know. I'm sitting here with you."

"We don't really have time for talkin'." He looked at his watch.

"You wait here. I'll speak to her for just a minute. It has to be somethin', or she wouldn't have come by."

John Cole watched her get out of the car, and walk across to greet Gracie and hug her. He shoved the gear shift into park, looked at his watch and then gazed out the windshield at the women. Gracie was a small woman, even just a bit shorter than Emma, although Emma was wearing heels. Emma still had a youthful shape. Emma's profile was toward him. The breeze fluttered her hair. He saw her glance quickly in his direction.

Then he saw Gracie look in his direction, and he averted his gaze to the rearview mirror, reaching up to adjust it. He didn't want to appear to be just sitting there staring at them. Although he didn't know what else he was supposed to be doing, because he *was* sitting there and couldn't help but be looking at them.

He shifted his gaze to the air-conditioning vents in the dash and held his hand over one to check the coolness of the air. He needed to get maintenance done on the system.

Again his gaze drifted to the women. They had moved a couple of feet away, into the shade of the big old crepe myrtle. He thought, she's going to come over and say that Gracie needs something—needs to talk to her or do something with her—so she isn't going. He knew this so thoroughly that he waited for Emma to turn his way and walk to his window, and he could hear her words in his mind. *You go on. I need to help Gracie out with something or other.* The idea caused him to look over at the pool and tap his fingers on the steering wheel.

He would not let her see him waiting so hard for her. He would tell her it didn't matter. Which it really didn't. Gracie was more important than a silly, trumped-up ground-breaking ceremony.

He kept telling himself this for another five minutes, and had the reluctant thought that he was going to have to get out and address the situation. More time ticked away. He checked his watch a hundred times, while his annoyance increased to near fury level.

Just when he reached for the door handle, he saw Emma hug Gracie, and the next moment she walked Gracie to her car and saw her into it. Then she came toward their car, and John Cole could hardly believe that she got in and settled herself into the passenger seat beside him, saying, "I'm sorry that took so long, but we can go now."

"You sure?" What he had really wanted had happened. He had trouble bringing himself around to it.

"Yes . . . go on, and I'll tell you all about it as we drive. We don't want to be late."

She dug into her purse for her sunglasses, which required pulling out half the things to find them at the bottom. Then she checked her image in her compact mirror. Being out in the breeze had caused her eyes to water, plus she felt suddenly a little teary about Gracie coming to see her.

That Gracie would confide in her caused her heart to swell and run over. She really was gaining a daughter. Her mind went ahead imagining it— shopping with Gracie, discussing home decoration, tending the children that would come, and long, quiet times over tea and coffee.

John Cole brought her out of this by asking, "So what did Gracie want?"

"Well . . ." She dropped the compact back into her purse. ". . . it seems that Sylvia has kept secret all these years that Gracie's father is part black, and now she has told her."

John Cole looked at her with both eyebrows raised high.

She said, "I know. It sounds strange. I really can't imagine how Sylvia thinks. And of course Gracie is thrown every which way. She thinks her mother is still trying to break her and Johnny up. She didn't even quite believe it at first, but she questioned her mother a little bit and found her father on the Internet—he's an artist over in Memphis.

"You know, I think we might have been right past his studio when we were over there for that convenience-store convention two years ago. I seem to recall his name and this gallery of paintings that I really liked. Just wonderful bright colors . . . very folky kind of stuff. It was a little too expensive for us, though.

"Well, anyway, I think one thing that really worried Gracie was our reaction to all of it."

"What did you tell her?" said John Cole, wondering what his own reaction was.

"I told her about my daddy."

John Cole looked a little perplexed. "What about your father?"

"You know, how my daddy went off all the time until he finally never came back, and how Mama cut him right out of the pictures and never spoke of him again."

"Ah."

"Then I just told Gracie that Johnny loves her and we do, too. And she has seen our side of the family."

She paused, and John Cole glanced over at her, wondering where this statement was going.

"I told her that if she is willin' to come into our family, we are thrilled. Although I did point out, since she has seen the Berrys, she should know that there are some in the family who might have somethin' to say about her daddy. You know that is true," she added, to ward off his protests, although he didn't say anything.

"But they are goin' to talk no matter what. They'll have a great deal to say about Gracie being from up north, and bein' Catholic and from a well-to-do family and who knows what all. The thing is, they will never say it to her face. No one ever said to my face, 'Mama Berry didn't like you, because you are not good enough for her son and come from back east.' They'll just talk behind her back and among themselves, and she won't ever have to be around them much, anyway."

She saw his eyes slide over to her, but he wisely remained quiet.

"I told her that besides all that, she is not marryin' any of them, or us, either. She is marryin' Johnny. She hasn't told him anything. She says she doesn't think it will matter to Johnny, but she has not shared with him this really big upset in her life. That right there shows her attitude, and a lot about need in their relationship.

"I told her not to start out this way. I told her to get in the habit of talking honestly about every worry, and joy, too. Not to get started in the way you and I have done—not talking about important things. I wish someone would have said that to me, when we were first married. But there wasn't anyone to tell me about havin' a good relationship, because no one in my family ever had one . . . just like poor Gracie. If you don't have anyone who can show you how to have a good marriage, then you just have to learn everything the hard way."

She went on, then, about how no one in John Cole's family ever knew how to relate, either.

John Cole sat there nodding in appropriate places. When it seemed that she was done, he said, "You told her a lot in a short time."

"Well, I talked fast. I didn't want to make us late for such an important event as breakin' ground for your new store . . . but I think we are."

She was looking ahead out the windshield and saw a number of cars parked at the edge of the future site of the Berry Truck Stop No, 2, and people milling around.

"*Our* new store," John Cole said.

Emma was brought up short by his correction. She was about to comment on it when she saw Johnny striding toward them. "You didn't tell me Johnny was goin' to be here."

"I didn't think of it," John Cole said, bringing the car to a stop. Then, in answer to her look, "I really didn't know. I couldn't reach him, so I just left a message."

Johnny hugged each of them, then said, "If it's okay, I've got to cut out. Gracie called a few minutes ago, and I told her I'd meet her. She said it's important." He looked at Emma. "Her mom didn't leave yesterday. She's still at Gracie's apartment and won't leave until Gracie comes to talk to her." Then to his father, "But I can stay, if you need me here."

Instantly, Emma said, "Gracie is more important, isn't she, John Cole?"

John Cole agreed. "Go on . . . and thanks for holdin' the fort until we got here."

"Oh, honey, wait." Emma gave him a firm hug. "I love you."

"Love you, too," he tossed back as he strode away.

Emma stood there watching after him, her boy now grown into a man.

"Emma."

"Yes . . . I'm coming. Oh, my hat!"

She ran back to the car, got the hat and put it on her head, and held it there as she ran back to John Cole, who had waited for her. He reached out and took her hand, giving it a squeeze.

Determined, Emma held her hat on throughout the entire time that she was introduced and shaking hands, and while the brief and informal ceremony of ground-breaking took place. She was able to let go of it for several minutes when the photographer took her and John Cole's picture with their hands on the shovel. She requested that the photographer take several shots. To her delight, the young man had a computer and printer set up in the back of his little minivan and gave them prints before he left.

Emma looked at their image captured together on the glossy paper. She was struck deep in her heart. She saw fresh in memory the early snapshots of them and the contrast to this one. She was at once amazed at how old they looked, proud of how good they still looked, and misty-eyed at the fact of how it had come round again to just the two of them.

And she didn't know how it had happened, but they had somehow found their way back to each other. It was as if they had each been about to blow away but had reached out and caught each other just in time. And had held on.

"We are a good-looking couple," she told John Cole.

"Pretty good," he agreed, giving the photographs a quick glance before asking, "Where do you want to eat?"

She named an expensive steak restaurant, and he made a face.

She asked him why had he asked her, if he didn't really want to know what she wanted. He said he didn't know what she wanted before he asked her. She asked him where he wanted to eat. He said he didn't really care, except for the steak restaurant. She named a hamburger place. He said he thought he wanted more than just hamburgers, since they were dressed up. To this she pointed out that he was being totally illogical and highly annoying, and she was making no more suggestions.

They threw this discussion back and forth, as John Cole drove directly to the steak restaurant Emma had specified, where he appeared to thoroughly enjoy an enormous steak dinner and acted like he had been the one to choose the restaurant all along.

The next morning at dawn, trying to beat the August heat, the work crew arrived in the backyard. Emma and John Cole both happened to be in the kitchen. Emma was already at work on final preparations for the barbeque, as well as listing a couple more people to receive wedding invitations. John Cole was pouring his coffee and preparing to oversee the work crew before heading off to the Berry Corp. offices.

"It's all worth it," Emma said, gazing out the window and running her eyes over their new backyard, all bathed in the first golden glow of a new day. It did look very much like a magazine picture. Maybe she could get it into *Southern Living*. Maybe that would put cotton in Sylvia's mouth. *Oh, dear, sorry.*

"It's pretty nice," John Cole admitted, standing just behind her shoulder. "And we're gonna make it with a bit of time to spare."

Then, from Emma, "We should add a water feature."

John Cole looked at her in horror. "A water feature?"

She nodded and explained just where she would like it. "We have time before the barbeque."

"There is already a water feature," John Cole pointed out. "It's big, and everything is built around it."

She had known he would not go for the idea, but if she gave him time to think about it . . .

The phone rang. Emma sprinted for it, her mind instantly going to Johnny.

It was him. "Hello, sweetheart. You're up early." She bit back asking what was wrong. There was no need to anticipate trouble. But she did. And John Cole stood there looking at her. "Your father and I were just watchin' the crew out back. They're finishing up today. It is goin' to be so lovely for the bridal-shower barbeque."

"Well, Mom, that's why I called."

She closed her eyes. "Oh, it is?" *Please don't let him say the wedding is off.*

"Gracie and I have decided to go ahead and get married today."

"Oh?" Her eyes opened wide. She looked at John Cole, who stepped closer.

"I know how much you wanted the weddin', Mama, but we don't want to wait. We just want to get on with it before Gracie's mother . . . well, we just want to go ahead and get married. I'm sorry."

It took her several seconds, but then she lifted her chin and said, "There is no need for an apology, honey. I understand . . . and I'm so happy for you both. For all of us."

Then, "Could your father and I still come and be there? We'd just like to see, and we won't make a big production. I can bring—"

"Mom . . ."

"Yes, honey?"

"We're on our way to Dallas right now."

"Oh." She felt suddenly quite old.

She stared at John Cole, at the bit of gray at his temples, while Johnny's voice in her ear was saying, "We've got a suite for tonight at the Ritz in Dallas. I don't know exactly what we're goin' to do after that, but we won't be back until Sunday. Is Dad still there? Can I talk to him?"

"Oh, yes. Here he is."

She handed the phone to John Cole and moved to look out the window at the magazine picture of a backyard and the men working there. The water in the pool sparkled in the now-bright sunlight. She noted that the young man, Sammy, was out there, and thought she had better get together a basket of cookies and drinks. She heard John Cole telling Johnny that he would handle everything for him for the next few days.

Then John Cole said, "Congratulations, son. Yes, she's still here . . . Emma . . ." He passed the phone back to her.

"Emma . . ." It was Gracie on the line. ". . . I'm awfully sorry. I know you've gone to a lot of trouble with all the plans for the wedding, and spent so much money. I thought we could still have the barbeque, if you want to. Only now it would just be a celebration for us being married."

"That is a lovely idea. And don't you worry at all about any of it. You and Johnny just go on . . . and have someone take pictures. Okay? Maybe you could get one of those throwaway cameras. Just ask someone to take your picture. People don't mind."

"Oh, yes—we didn't bring a camera. We'll try."

Emma thought Gracie might be crying. "I'm so very happy for both of you. I love you."

Johnny got on the phone again and very quickly said, "I love you, Mama."

"Me, too, you sweetheart."

She could not breathe. She ended the call but held on to the phone for several seconds before turning to John Cole.

"Well, they called before they got married. I think they just needed our encouragement." She grabbed a rag and went to wiping the kitchen counter.

"They'll always need you, Emma." He was regarding her as if ready to reach over and hold her head on.

She gave him a smile and took up the pot to pour him more coffee. The next second, she reached for the phone again and called information for the number of the Ritz in Dallas. She had a large bouquet sent to the room of Mr. and Mrs. John Ray Berry.

John Cole was still hovering in a worried manner. She told him, "Shoo . . ."

She waited until the door closed behind him before she let herself cry.

It was really silly, but she felt the great need to call her mother. She waited until mid-morning, to make sure her mother would be up and around.

"Johnny and Gracie are drivin' down to Texas to elope," she said, and went on to tell everything that had happened, about Gracie's father and the argument with Sylvia that led up to it all.

Her mother amazed her by saying, "I knew that about Gracie's father."

"You did?"

"Oh, yes. Sylvia acted strange about it from the beginnin'. I did some investigating on my genealogy site online, and I found Paul Mercier."

"And you didn't say anything?"

"Well, a writer does not tell everything she knows," her mother said. "We all have secrets . . . although it seems with the Internet they are not nearly as easy to keep anymore. Remember your Aunt Clemmy who ran off with the neighbor next door and never talked to anyone in the family again? Well, I found her in Sarasota. She can stay there, too.

"Besides, I've been busy . . . ." She turned the conversation to her own news, which was having sold yet another article to the North Carolina state magazine. Word had gotten around her circle of writing friends about her sales to such prestigious publications, and she had received a call from her arch rival Pamela Markham, who wanted to confirm the news.

"She didn't believe it, and I got to tell her it was true," said Emma's mother with great delight. "Her writers group had appointed her to call and ask me to come speak at their conference in the spring. She can hardly stand it!"

She was so gleeful that she went on to tell the news twice.

Finally, when Emma managed to get a word in to excuse herself from the conversation, she surprised herself by asking, "Mama . . . what did Daddy die of?"

"Don't ask. You don't want to know, and I don't care."

Emma hung up the phone and thought that she knew exactly how Gracie felt.

John Cole spent only an hour at the office, then came home for the rest of the day and supervised the finishing of the backyard. He wanted to be around in case Emma might need him. He didn't know what he would do, but he just wanted to be there. She did not appear to be much herself. She hardly said anything, except after each of Johnny's phone calls.

Johnny called again right after he and Gracie had gotten married, and then after they had gotten to their hotel and seen the flowers Emma had sent.

Emma reported these calls to John Cole and said, "I think they wish we had been with them."

John Cole said, "I'm sure they do. They'll be home before long."

She just looked at him and went back into the house. When he went to check on her an hour later, she was working on a card to send out to everyone, announcing the elopement and canceling the wedding. It was a really cute card, and he raved over it. She didn't say much to that either, though.

At sunset, when he came out of the shower, he couldn't find her in the house. He had a moment of feeling abandoned—his son had taken off, and now he couldn't find his wife. He realized that he had held for a long time in the back of his mind the fear that when Johnny left them, Emma would go, too.

He found Emma sitting on the back steps, watching the sun go down and gazing out at the backyard. He joined her.

"It really is beautiful, John Cole. Thank you. It'll make a lovely place for a celebration party."

John Cole said, "I've been thinkin' about that water feature. I figured out a way to—"

"Oh, no. We don't need it."

"Maybe not *need* it, but it would be really pretty over there. And I can get it in without too much digging. We can connect the line right over there."

"No . . . this is enough."

He fell silent. He watched her face. He felt inadequate to know what to do.

They sat there some minutes, and then Emma said, "You know, I can't remember our wedding."

Her eyes came round to his. They were wet with tears.

"I guess I was just so nervous that I went right through it in some sort of shocked state. We've got pictures to show me what happened, but I don't remember it, John Cole. Not any part. I've tried over the years to remember, and today I tried all day long, but I can't. I just so wanted Johnny's wedding to remember."

He reached around her and brought her into his shoulder, where she cried.

"Well then," he said, a great idea stealing over him as he saw the lights coming on in the pool, "we'll just have to get married all over again."

She looked up at him.

"You mean renew our vows?"

"Sure. We've got everything for a weddin'. We're having the big barbeque. You and me will just get married again, and you'll have that to remember."

A look came over her face, and he wondered what he had done wrong. She said, "John Cole . . . how many times did I ask you to renew our vows with me, and you said you were not goin' to do it?"

"Okay . . . so I'm sayin' now let's do it."

"Oh, John Cole, I swear to heaven. If you would have gone to marriage counseling when I wanted to and renewed our vows when I suggested it, we could have avoided so much. . . ."

John Cole, who had now gone to marriage counseling and come around to thinking of renewing marriage vows, knew just what to do.

He took her face in his hands and kissed her—a surefire way to shut her up. It worked well—for both of them.

30

Keeping It Together

You are cordially invited
to join the Berry Family in celebration.
Just married:
John Ray Berry and Gracie Kinney-Berry
Still married:
John Cole Berry and Emma Lou Jennings Berry
August 22nd 1998
Renewal of vows ceremony at 6:00
Barbeque dinner at 8:00

John Cole feared what he might have opened up with suggesting they get married again at the barbeque. Already Emma and Gracie had decided that Johnny and Gracie were going to repeat their vows, so that their parents could see it.

Wanting to edge out of it, he suggested that he and Emma slip off and have Pastor Smith give them a small private ceremony.

"Honey, we can't do that," said Emma. "It will be wonderful to have Johnny and Gracie see us renew our vows. It will give them something to remember and something to inspire them for the future. God knows they're gonna need it," she added.

He thought about that remark for a moment, then asked, "Will I have to wear a suit?"

"No . . . but you could put on a sport coat, John Cole. That's not so much. And I bought you a new summer-weight one."

There was no way around it. He set himself to get through. And Emma was happy. This made him feel pretty satisfied. And grateful. He had not lost her, as he had feared those few months ago. He had his home, with a darn nice backyard, and his family and his wife. He was a fortunate man.

They kept themselves from building a water feature but Emma did rent a deluxe-model canopy for the occasion.

"It's goin' to be mostly in the evenin'," John Cole protested. "The sun will be on the way down behind the trees."

"Yes, but this canopy has three ceiling fans." She saw his expression and spoke quick to head off discussion of cost. "It is August, John Cole. The breeze stops in the evening, and we're goin' to swelter."

"It's a barbeque. You're supposed to swelter." He realized that he would get nowhere with protesting, but he did add, "Do you know what a job it is goin' to be to get a thing like that set up?"

"The company will set it up Saturday mornin'. You don't have to do it."

Of course, he could not let the workman do the job in his yard, and with his electricity, without his supervision.

John Cole fully appreciated Emma's point about the ceiling fans when, an hour before the guests arrived, they suddenly shut off, and he and Johnny went to work trying to locate the problem. With the caterer's buffet table and a three-piece band, there were electric cords everywhere.

Out of two hundred invitations, fifteen had been sent to members of the extended Berry family in Eastern Oklahoma. Out of those, the only ones to come were the same two who came to the first wedding thirty-two years earlier—Papa Berry and Charlie J., plus Joella. They arrived early in the day so the men could watch the televised NASCAR race that started at eleven-thirty. They came and sat in front of the television in the family room, while people ran in and out behind them.

Emma told Gracie, "All these years I felt badly for having the weddin' so far away that all of John Cole's family couldn't come. It appears we could have been married in their backyard, and they still wouldn't have attended. I wasted a lot of energy worryin' about what they thought. Let that be a lesson to you. They *don't* think."

Also in attendance were many of the parishioners from the Valentine First United Methodist Church. With Pastor Smith, who was officiating at the ceremony, came his entire family, and this, at the moment, included the two Varela girls, Nina and baby Lucy, for whom Emma had purchased a playpen. She said, causing Gracie to be a little nervous, that she was getting ready for grandbabies.

The Holloways, with Winston, brought the Varela boys, Sammy and Nicky, and their father. The Varela children were still living with their Valentine families, because they were not yet certain of trusting their father not to leave them somewhere, as their mother had done. The Smiths and the Holloways also wanted proof of Mr. Varela's good intentions. Mr. Varela was working to prove himself; he had applied to be transferred to the Army base in Lawton and was considering buying a house in Valentine.

Having spent so many weeks working in the Berrys' backyard, Sammy Varela felt quite proprietary about it. He went around picking up every scrap of paper that anyone threw down, and repeatedly cautioned the younger children when they got into the pool. He didn't want water splashed too much and harming the fresh landscaping. Nicky and Willie Lee followed after him.

Nina Varela had decided to adopt Paris Miller and followed after her. As a proud Berry Corporation young employee of the year, who had been given a future college scholarship, Paris took it upon herself to make certain the chairs under the canopy were in order and to assist in seating guests, and to simply keep an eye on things.

She took note of a prissy woman who went up and kissed John Cole on the cheek and then sat where Paris thought only the family should sit. Paris went over and asked the woman who she was.

"I'm John Cole's office manager," Shelley Dilks said.

"That's not family. You need to move back."

"I'm his *private* secretary."

To that, Paris said, "So?" and beside her Nina said, "Yeah, so?"

Shelley Dilks looked from Paris—who sported dyed-black spiked hair, black eye-makeup and black clothes—to the smaller Nina, with a tough expression under a ball cap.

Shelley Dilks moved.

Sylvia and Wadley flew down for the weekend, bringing Sylvia's father and stepmother, Albert and Giselle, who mostly sat together and kept smiles on their faces as they stared at everyone. They had a little bit of trouble understanding exactly what was being said around them. With all of their traveling, the only Southern state they had ever been to was Florida, where they spoke almost exclusively with either other elderly people from the northeast or Cubans, with whom they easily spoke Spanish.

Then, when Joella asked if she could get them something to drink, Albert said he would like some bourbon. "Neat will be fine."

Joella stared at him a moment, then said, "We use clean glasses, if that is what you mean. But we do not serve alcoholic beverages in this house."

A few minutes later, when John Cole was pouring wine for the guests, much to Joella's disapproval, Sylvia looked up and said, "Oh, my God."

Everyone followed her gaze to see a tall, thin and handsome man with graying hair come around the corner of the house. On his arm was an equally tall and stately black woman in flowing clothes. There was about the man a manner that caused every female eye to return to him. Those women with good sense thought: *There's a heartbreak waiting to happen.* And they were eager to watch it.

Gracie hurried forward to greet her father, Paul Mercier, and his wife, Simone. While away on their honeymoon, Johnny and Gracie had driven up to Memphis to find and meet him. Johnny had later called to issue a personal invitation to the man to join them at the barbeque, but Paul Mercier was not one to give firm commitments. He had said, "Oh, perhaps . . . we will see." Mostly he liked to surprise people and to make an entrance.

He came in now like the free spirit that he was, kissing his daughter and Emma and even Sylvia, who he said was as beautiful as ever. Then he introduced his wife, Simone, who smiled in an elegant manner and greeted everyone with a faint accent. She was from Haiti, had been a model and now managed Paul Mercier's art career.

With their closest friends and family standing behind them, in the comfort of ceiling fans, Emma and John Cole, and Gracie and Johnny, took their places in front of Pastor Smith.

Both Gracie and Emma wore simple sun dresses, although Gracie's had been a gift from her mother and bought at a New York Fifth Avenue shop, and Emma's had come from a sale at the Dress Barn. Emma wore her wide-brimmed hat, which Belinda had managed to fasten onto her head so that she didn't have to hold it on. Gracie wore gardenias in her hair. John Cole's and Johnny's coats matched; Emma and Gracie had chosen them together. All of that pretty well illustrated their future.

The simple ceremony was over so quickly that Emma thought it was no wonder she had not remembered it the first time. She listened to Gracie and Johnny say their vows. She watched their faces and imprinted the moment on her heart.

Then she smiled at John Cole. He squeezed her hand on his arm as she looked deep into his eyes and repeated the vows that she had helped to compose.

"I promise to love and cherish you, John Cole. For better or for worse, I will meet life beside you and with you, for the rest of our lives."

"I promise to love and cherish you, Emma Lou. For better or for worse, I will meet life beside you and with you . . ." he smiled so tenderly it took her breath ". . . for the rest of our lives."

They kissed, and everyone applauded.

"Throw the bouquets!" came the shouts.

Gracie threw hers high up in the air, and it came down right to Vella, who stared at it with amazement.

Emma stood poised for several seconds, then drew back and pitched her bouquet right at Sylvia's head, giving the woman no choice but to catch it or risk having her eye put out.

Sylvia looked at Emma, then at the bouquet as if to throw it down. But then her gaze went to Wadley. With trembling lips she nodded, and the next instant he kissed her.

Belinda said, "Good Lord, this is gettin' out of hand. Mama, don't you dare say yes to Jaydee."

Vella didn't listen. She was so taken up with the atmosphere that she agreed to begin seeing him again.

Papa Berry and Charlie J. slipped away to the family room to catch the end of the race, which had started two hours late because of a rain delay. Unfortunately, it had already finished, and they had missed Darrel Waltrip winning. No one had thought to record it. Charlie J. was inconsolable.

"Your mama told me that Gracie's father's black," Joella said.

"Yes," said Emma.

"Oh . . ." Joella digested that. "Well, I guess it doesn't matter now that Mama Nedda is dead. It would have just killed her."

"Probably."

"Pop will never know. He does not pay attention to anything but that television anymore . . . and maybe Johnny. He just loves Johnny to death. I won't tell him about Gracie's dad."

Emma had no reply.

A little later, Emma stood with John Cole, looking at the people enjoying themselves. Children—and Vella Blaine, who was a champion swimmer—were splashing in the pool. Others were eating and chatting beneath the canopy, and still others were dancing—Johnny and Gracie, and Sylvia and Wadley, Winston Valentine and Simone. Simone was laughing at something he said.

Miss Lillian had cornered Gracie's father, and

had a pencil and note pad, taking down the Mercier family tree.

"All of the work was worthwhile," Emma said.

"Yep, you're right," John Cole said.

Just at dusk, when the Chinese lanterns were turned on, Emma was surprised to hear John Cole call for everyone's attention.

"I have a special present for my wife," he said.

The next instant, Johnny and two of his friends came pushing a car into the backyard. It was covered in a green tarp.

Pulling Emma by the hand, John Cole went over and whipped off the tarp, revealing a long, gleaming white vintage 1957 Cadillac convertible.

Emma was shocked. She could not believe that John Cole would bring himself to buy something so impractical and expensive.

He grinned at her.

There was more. John Cole had made plans for a romantic road trip to California.

Belinda and Gracie had packed Emma's bags, and they were already in the trunk. Johnny and Gracie would stay and clean up from the party, and take care of the house. Everything that Emma could think of had been considered and taken care of.

Almost before she knew it, John Cole had shoved her into the front seat and slipped in beside her. To shouts and waves, John Cole started the car and headed down the driveway.

Quickly Emma went up on her knees and leaned over the seat to wave goodbye at everyone.

She gazed at them, Johnny and Gracie, and Belinda waving like mad, and even Sylvia waved, for heaven's sake—all of the precious people in her life—until they were out of sight. Then she sat down and squeezed up beside John Cole, who put his arm around her.

They drove away, side by side, still together after all these years.

31

1550 AM on the Radio Dial
The Home Folks Show

"Good mornnnin' out there, Valentine-ites! It's ten-O-five in southern Oklahoma, and this is Brother Winston comin' at you once again and glad to do it. Seein' the Big Apple and bein' on *The Today Show* was quite a trip, but, as little Miss Dorothy said, there is no place like home.

"Mr. Willie Lee, you and Munro get up here and say hello to the folks."

"Hel-lo, ev-er-y-bod-y. Hi, Gab-by and Nick-y."

"Rufff."

"Our weather for today calls for sunny skies—what else at the end of summer?—and a high of ninety. That's good news for Mr. Paul Mercier, who's doin' the mural on the side of the *Valentine*

Voice building. He is depicting our town's history and its present. The name of the painting is 'Colors of Oklahoma.'

"And now let's hear from the Silver Fox himself, Mr. Charlie Rich, singin' my personal anthem, 'Rollin' With the Flow.' . . ."

All over Valentine, people turned up their radios. One of these was a man driving out on the turnpike. He caught what Winston said about *The Today Show.* He was a producer for NPR. He saw an exit sign for Valentine and took it, intrigued by hearing a radio show similar to what he had grown up with in West Texas. It was like coming home.

Center Point Publishing
600 Brooks Road • PO Box 1
Thorndike ME 04986-0001 USA

(207) 568-3717

US & Canada:
1 800 929-9108
www.centerpointlargeprint.com

448

BOOK "MARKS"

If you wish to keep a record that you have read this book,
you may use this space to mark a private code.
Please do not mark the book in any other way.